DAUGHTER
of
AUSTRALIA

D1057575

DAUGHTER *of* AUSTRALIA

HARMONY VERNA

BAY COUNTY LIBRARY SYSTEM
ALICE & JACK WIRT PUBLIC LIBRARY
500 CENTER AVENUE
BAY CITY MI 48708
989-893-9566

To the extent that the image or images on the cover of this book depict a person or persons, such person or persons are merely models, and are not intended to portray any character or characters featured in the book.

This book is a work of fiction. Names, characters, places, and incidents either are products of the author's imagination or are used fictitiously. Any resemblance to actual persons, living or dead, events, or locales is entirely coincidental.

KENSINGTON BOOKS are published by

Kensington Publishing Corp.
119 West 40th Street
New York, NY 10018

Copyright © 2016 by Harmony Verna

All rights reserved. No part of this book may be reproduced in any form or by any means without the prior written consent of the Publisher, excepting brief quotes used in reviews.

All Kensington titles, imprints, and distributed lines are available at special quantity discounts for bulk purchases for sales promotion, premiums, fund-raising, educational, or institutional use.

Special book excerpts or customized printings can also be created to fit specific needs. For details, write or phone the office of the Kensington Sales Manager: Kensington Publishing Corp., 119 West 40th Street, New York, NY 10018. Attn. Sales Department. Phone: 1-800-221-2647.

Kensington and the K logo Reg. U.S. Pat. & TM Off.

eISBN-13: 978-1-61773-942-2
eISBN-10: 1-61773-942-1
First Kensington Electronic Edition: April 2016

ISBN-13: 978-1-61773-941-5
ISBN-10: 1-61773-941-3
First Kensington Trade Paperback Printing: April 2016

10 9 8 7 6 5 4 3 2 1

Printed in the United States of America

To Leonora,
From your earth, I'm born anew.

ACKNOWLEDGMENTS

As a writer, I am deeply aware and humbled to be a small part of the creative process. The real honor goes to those who have helped guide and support me along the way. Thank you to my beautiful agent, Marie Lamba, of the Jennifer De Chiara Literary Agency, for slaving through a nine-hundred-page manuscript and deciding to represent me anyway. Thank you to my brilliant editor, John Scognamiglio, and the whole Kensington team for bringing this book to life. Thank you to my family and friends, my early readers and allies—without you, this novel would still be a dream.

And finally, thank you to my husband, Jay, and my three boys . . . my champions, my peace, my life.

PART I

CHAPTER I

Western Australia, 1898

They walked into the sun.

Her small legs moved without thought; fingers rubbed eyes full of sleep. No need to dress; the clothes she wore day and night. Hunger as normal as breathing.

The fiery ball inched up the horizon leaving waves of heat in its wake, rippling across the landscape as a black shallow lake. Nocturnal beings scurried and slithered and hid with the light, sought shade for slumber. The animals of day woke fresh and loud from nests and mounds and burrows. Flocks of birds settled heavily on the few branches sturdy enough to bear their weight. Brightly colored feathers and noisy chatter quickly brought life to an otherwise dead plain.

The earth was cooked, the red ground baked and brittle. Morning air rested still and hot. The black flies flocked, landed on faces, inched into clothing—a normal nuisance. Only the most intrusive, the ones seeking a nostril or an eardrum, were worth the swat.

Her shoes bulged with stuffed rags, each step kicking a miniature sandstorm. Rust-colored earth stained her stockings to the knees. Over and over she tripped upon the floppy shoes, the soft impact of heel to dirt echoing singularly through the swelter.

She clutched his hand, though his fingers remained limp within her palm. She looked up. He was so tall that his hair seemed to scrape the sky. The sun moved higher and his head appeared as one blinding orb. As he stretched out his neck muscles, his features sharpened—

thin cheeks, dark skin tanned as leather, gray and black stubbly chin. He stared at his feet, his eyes vacant, glazed, almost wild, like a sick dingo. Her stomach sank. In the next moment, the sun eclipsed his face and she turned away from the painful glare.

Step. Step. Step. The hole in her shoe chased the shadow of her hat brim, a shadow shortening under the ascending sun. They walked for minutes or hours or days. Hunger and thirst gnawed. Burning heat. Each breath a poker to the lungs. Her feet broiled inside the ragged shoes; her hat melted on her head. Dripping sweat blurred vision.

A lone gum tree rose in the emptiness, its sparse leaves faded gray with a powdered finish. He pulled her weakly to the trunk and made her sit, slipped his fingers from her hand. His arms quivered and his eyes watered as he took the dented billy can from his belt and laid it next to her feet. He turned and began walking. She watched him rub his hands through his thinning hair and rest them on the back of his neck. She watched as his shoulders shook and his legs wobbled, as if he might fall to his knees. She watched as his figure got smaller and smaller in the distance until he was a tiny black dot on the horizon. In another moment, the dot evaporated into the wavy air.

Sinking. Sinking. Sinking. Her stomach lurched, her mouth too dry to vomit. She picked up the can. The water sloshed inside with dull, constrained waves. She tried to turn the top just as she had seen him do, but her tiny fingers slipped from sweat. She tried again and again, her throat tightening. Finally, she cradled it upon her stomach. He would open it. She leaned her head against the smooth bark. He would open it. Patience and sun mingled with throbs of thirst and lulled her to sleep.

Flies flitted across her eyes, tickled her lashes and buzzed in satisfaction upon moist skin. She woke startled, smacking her face and clothes. She looked for him. Panic swelled her throat and she tried to swallow, the reflex painful and chafing. Pushing against the panic, she focused on her feet, clicked them several times and watched the dust fall in puffy clouds. Tree limbs, emaciated lines of shade, pointed inertly—no wind, no breeze, would offer relief.

The sky changed from blue to pink, clouds trimmed lilac. The hues darkened. She wanted it to stop. Dread crept across her flesh and tingled sharply. Her eyes strained to see his emerging figure across the plain. Her pupils searched for a spot moving, one that would grow and lengthen. Blood throbbed as drums. Water pooled in her eyes, dropped down her cheeks and landed salty on her lips, precious water draining. Blackness inched and played tricks, distorting mulga scrub into dogs, tree limbs into extended arms. Shadows magnified, took over the landscape and drowned out the light.

She grabbed her knees and buried her head between them, held her ears against the pulse of terror. "Papa?" she whispered, the fear in her voice breaking any ties of control. She scrambled to her feet, searched the darkness. "Papa? Papa!" She choked in raspy spats, morphed the word into a howl. "Papa!"

The moon climbed.

She bent into her screams and tears, shook with the chilled air. The animals began their night shift, replacing the singers with the chirpers. Her cries echoed over the plain, carried away and diffused by the sounds of insects—a child's pleading call lost amid the vacuum of night.

CHAPTER 2

༄༅

The sun beat through Ghan's shirt, not a patch of fabric dry of sweat. He took a swig of water from the duck skin bag and pulled the hat farther down his forehead. Eternal landscape—red dirt; blue, cloudless sky; low, scraggly saltbush; a spotting of salmon gum and gimlet wood. The rattling caravan, the doughy camel steps, the only noise, the only indication of movement, a small animation in a sea of stillness.

Neely stretched his legs until his feet pressed against the front boards. "Hellova lot hotter than yesterday."

"Gonna be a scorcher."

"Should've left earlier," Neely decided.

"No shit." Ghan glared at him.

A fly chewed Ghan's arm. His hand holding the reins smacked it absently, then brushed off the flattened blob. White scars dotted his arm, all the more obvious against his coppered skin. They were the markings of his mining history, his own collage of abuse underground—along with a missing ear from a carbide lamp explosion, a crippled, twisted leg crushed at the knee. His cheek poached from burns, the nose bulbous and hopelessly slanted from fists—an ugly face to match an ugly life.

Neely ground his cigarette stub into the old wagon wood. Suddenly, his shoulders rolled and convulsed. He gripped his shirt at the neck, his body shaking in choking spasms.

"Not again," Ghan mumbled, but his eyes flitted with worry. "Breathe into it, mate."

Neely's head reared, his mouth silent and begging for air, his eyes wide and desperate before the violent hacking erupted again. Ghan turned his face away. The wagon rocked under the man's barking body for minutes on end. Then the relief, the wheezing inhale. Neely raised his bottom off the bench, leaned over the wagon and spit out a bloody mouthful. He pulled out a new cigarette, lit it with trembling hand and sucked in slowly, evenly, with sallow cheeks.

"Need water?" Ghan asked softly. Neely closed his eyes and shook his head. The man would be dead within six months. Ghan had seen it before. That cough, the one carried by so many of the men underground with dust on their lungs—the "miner's complaint."

Neely reached under the seat and dug through a brown sack.

"Yeh just ate!" Ghan snapped.

"I'm hungry." Neely rummaged through a second bag. "Whot's it to yeh?"

"Don't complain when yeh got nothin' t'eat later on."

Neely found the wrapped sandwiches, opened one and threw the waxed paper into the dirt. "Like t'eat when the meat's still cool." He chewed slowly, sideways like the camels. "Don't like mine crawlin' wiv maggots like yeh do."

A crowd of emus skipped off in the distance on silent prehistoric legs. The dust quickly sprayed around the creatures' haunches before settling back as if never stirred. Ghan abruptly pulled the camels to a stop, sending Neely's body halfway off the bench.

"Jesus, give a man a little warnin'!" Neely barked. "Why yeh stoppin'?"

Ghan pointed into the sun's glare. "See that?" His eyes narrowed on the object—a rock, maybe an old pack, a dead dingo. His vision blurred, then spotted black.

Neely squinted. "Naw, it's nothin'."

"Gonna check it out." Ghan climbed from the wagon, his boots landing with a puff. The dead leg instantly cramped and for a moment he struggled to keep upright, the sensation of wagon movement still throbbing under his rear.

"Don't waste yer time." Neely clicked his teeth, settled back into the seat. "If it was anything good, someone would 'ave picked it up by now."

Ghan walked slowly, both legs stiff from sitting. He left footprints of one boot heel and one swerving rut trailing like a snake. The sun poked his eyes. Sweat fell from his nose one lazy drip at a time.

He inched closer to the lone gum tree in the distance, its branches at one moment shielding the sun and the next conceding, blinding him again. It was not a dead dingo, no stink. Somewhere between the blotches, the object began to take shape—clothing, old rags maybe, left in a small heap, innocuous enough that he could have turned back. Instead, he quickened his pace and galloped, felt like ants were crawling atop his flesh.

A few more dragged steps and the tree eclipsed the stabbing glare. Despite the heat, each bead of sweat chilled and his thick breathing grew loud and unsettling in the stillness. Details no longer blurred as he made out the lines of a dress, of tiny shoes. He froze. Sharp light reflected off a metal canteen. Ghan's stomach pitched at the tiny fingers clutching it.

His knees dropped and crunched the earth beside the small, lifeless child. *A child.* The innocence cuttingly detailed in the oversized socks that hung at her ankles and the tiny brimmed hat crushed under her matted hair. His fingernails bit into his palms.

Ghan rubbed his hand over his dry mouth, his chest hollow—he couldn't breathe. He reached out slowly, but his hands quivered so severely that he pulled them back, afraid his clumsy touch would break the child's bones into a million pieces. He set his jaw and reached out again, putting one arm under her knees and the other under her neck. Her body moved with the motion, had not hardened.

A light moan escaped her lips. Ghan's nerves iced from feet to hair. *She's alive.* Fear, whole and total, pushed the horror away. She was barely alive, closer to death than life, a delicate, ebbing balance that he now held in his incapable hands. With one swift swing, he lifted the child and held her tight against his chest. Air labored through his nose. Sweat dripped onto the girl. He ran toward the distant wagon, cursing his slow dead leg, trying to propel it with panicked pulls. "Neely!"

With one hand, Neely shaded an eye; then his body stiffened tight as a rod. He jumped off the wagon, raced to Ghan, stopping short in a flurry of raised dust. Ghan did not stop, did not hand her over. She was alive now—alive in his arms.

Ghan sputtered through panting breath, "Get my water."

Neely dug for the water bag. Small cries squeaked from his throat as he fumbled through the supplies.

"Put it to 'er lips. See if she'll drink," Ghan commanded, holding the girl's arched body under the opening.

Neely's hand shook as he put the spout to her dried, cracked lips. The water splashed and ran down her chin. She made no movement. Her head, deadly still, hung as if her neck held no bones. Ghan shuffled her to the back of the wagon. "Move the crates so I can put 'er down."

Neely pulled out the padding and Ghan laid the child down in the shade of the canvas. He dribbled the water onto her lips, only to have it roll down the sides of her cheeks. He tried again, this time holding her mouth open with his fingers. "Come on, girl; drink it."

His nerves cringed at the sunburned face and hands, the half of her that had faced the sun completely covered in blisters and scabs. The weight of helplessness hit with suffocating force. He tried to read Neely's face for an answer that wouldn't come. He rubbed his hand hard across his lips and looked at the wide expanse of desert, a pit in his gut. "She needs a doctor."

"Christ, Ghan." Neely clawed his scalp, pulled his face back tight. "Whot we gonna do?"

"Think there's a hospital in Leonora." Ghan pinched the bridge of his nose as he tried to remember the route. "We could veer west toward Gwalia. Not too far off, I think."

Neely wasn't paying attention, his mouth drawn. "How yeh think she got 'ere?"

"Don't know. Can't think of that now."

"We'll miss the delivery to the train," said Neely, his tone neutral, resigned to the new course of action.

"Fuck the train," Ghan said with equal tone. He stared at the little girl and his voice croaked, "I need yeh t'drive, Neely. Think yeh know the way?"

Neely nodded, his eyes alert. "I know it."

CHAPTER 3

❧

Ghan, Neely and the burnt child inched across miles, ticked through hours too drowsy to quicken. Ghan chewed a hard sliver of cuticle along his thumbnail. Through the canvas flaps, the dust pillowed around the back wheels, every turn impossibly slow. Each minute that passed in the desert brought her closer to death. He chewed the cuticle farther until a drop of blood squeezed in response.

Tucked between boxes of explosives, the child's body swayed with the wagon's rocking. Desperation tightened Ghan's muscles to sinew. Emotions—weak, stingy pulls that choked his throat and sat on his chest—threatened to take over. He slapped them away like blowflies and only glanced at the girl long enough to trickle water into her chapped mouth.

With a sudden fury, Ghan hated this place, this country. Madmen lived here. Men who left jobs and cities to live in the bush, sick and dry with drought. Not a handful of men, but men by the trainload. Spurred by rumors of alluvial treasures, the men flocked, dragging their families in tow or leaving them behind to fend for themselves. But wealth wouldn't fall for these men, just as the rain wouldn't fall for the burnt shoots of wheat. Only the churning beasts, the large mining companies, found the gold.

Ghan turned to the child, lightly pushed a strand of hair away from her face. His large fingers, stubby and filthy, were monstrous near her tiny features. She was covered in rags and the fury shot hot again. *Madmen.* The hardships of life under the sun, without money or hope, a brutal existence that could turn sane men to madmen. Ghan scanned the scars along his arm. This was a place where a madman leaves a girl to die and a crippled madman is left to save her.

As the wagon rolled, intermittent signs of civilization appeared. The road widened, dirt settled solid and compact. The ruts deepened. The occasional broken bottle signaled the familiarity of human litter. Ghan leaned out of the wagon. "How much longer?"

"Comin' on Gwalia now. Mount Leonora's up ahead." Neely whacked the camels and the wheels lurched.

The white canvas overhead dimmed to beige as the sun descended, each inch toward the horizon a small reprieve from the day's swelter. Ghan put the water bag back to the girl's lips. This time they parted slightly. For a moment her eyes opened, and he stopped dead, the canteen suspended half-tipped in the air. Her listless pupils locked with Ghan's, a fleeting moment of communion before rolling into unconsciousness. His throat constricted. If she died, that look would haunt him until his last days.

Outside, signs of life burst forth. Prospector tents of the transients dotted the landscape. Through an open tent flap, a bent man cooked over a blue flame. At another, a sleeping man's feet stuck out from under the canvas. Then came the more permanent homes, the humpies, constructed by the prospectors who decided to stay. Humpies, exaggerated tents reinforced with flattened cyanide drums and corrugated metal, miserable structures that held in the heat during the summer and the cold in the winter. If a fire caught, the canvas would burn on the inside while the iron held in the inferno like a covered pot. Life in the diggings. Here a man builds his palace from scraps of steel and canvas, holds it together with green hide and stringy bark.

People. Ghan exhaled for the first time in hours. *People. Help.* The road was smoother now. The humpies transitioned to shacks surrounded with rudimentary wire fences or old rusty bed frames, only strong enough to keep the chooks from wandering off. Feral goats roamed the streets, the animals looking more at home than the human inhabitants. At first glance, it was hard to tell if the town was up and coming or one that was on the brink of desertion.

The wagon pulled into Leonora under a blinding ball of orange setting over the plain, silhouetting the few trees in the distance. Neely stopped the camels and came around, glanced at the girl. "She still alive?" The question came out too easy, too quick, and Neely lowered his eyes. "There's a pub up ahead," he offered. "Want me t'go?"

"I'll go." Ghan got out, his legs so tight he gasped. He stretched his neck, fully aware that Neely watched him. He took a crippled step and bit his lip. Damn it, he hated this leg.

A few steps more and he found his stride, made his way to the pub. Two metal doors, pulled back and tied with wire hangers, flanked the opening. Lamps flickered across the bar, but the recesses of the room were black as night. Two dusty men sat on stools. The barkeeper greeted him with a bored nod. "Look like yeh need a good drink, mate. Whot can I get yeh?"

Ghan worked to control his sizzling nerves. "Lookin' for the hospital."

"No hospital, mate." The man wiped out a glass with an old cloth. "Sorry."

Ghan's mouth went dry and he fumbled on his words. "I heard . . . thought there was a hospital . . . drove all this way."

The barman chewed a wad of tobacco in his cheek but slowed his jaw at the rising pitch. "Yeh sick?"

"S'not me." The day raced through his head, but talking took time. "There a doctor somewhere?"

The man tucked the rag into his belt and addressed a slumped figure at the bar: "Andrew, ain't that young Swede a doc?"

"Believe so. Stayin' at Mirabelle's."

The barman slid around the counter. "Come on; I'll walk yeh over to the boardinghouse. Drew, watch the bar for me, eh?" Andrew gave a listless nod and went back to his pint.

The man noticed the wagon parked out front. "Up from Menzies?" he asked.

"Yeah."

"Work in the Bailen Mine then?"

"Used to," Ghan answered numbly. "Run transport up t'Laverton now."

The man brightened and spit out a rust-colored wad of phlegm. "Carryin' any cases of whiskey wiv yeh? Give yeh a good price."

Ghan shook his head, balled his hands into fists. *Yabber. Everybody always talking.* His heart throbbed in his ears.

"Figured as much." The man shrugged, then pointed at a yellow brick house on the corner. "Orright, that's Mirabelle's." He turned away with sudden urgency. "Gotta get back 'fore Drew finishes all the grog in the pub."

Ghan climbed the short stair to the verandah, his dead leg thumping. A woman appeared behind the screen. "All filled for the night," she said with hands at her hips. The hard woman scanned his features, didn't try to hide her distrust.

"Not lookin' for a room." He skipped the manners. "Need a doctor."

"Yeh don't look sick," she said gruffly.

"S'not for me. It's a child." His voice cracked helplessly. "A little girl."

The face softened behind the gray screen and the woman opened the door, her features now clear without the shadow of wire mesh. "Doc's in the back havin' dinner wiv his wife."

Ghan followed the woman down the hall, her heavy footsteps echoing on the smooth floor planks. She brought him through the sitting room to the rear verandah, where a well-dressed blond couple watched the sunset. "Dr. Carlton," she said with the same short tone. "Man's 'ere t'see yeh. His girl's sick."

"She ain't mine!" Ghan snapped. The words rattled him. "Found 'er on my route, lyin' in the dirt, fryin' under the sun." Just saying the words, remembering her out there, flamed panic up and down his chest. *Don't lose it. Not here.*

The blond man dabbed at his lips with a napkin before dropping it on his plate. "Where is she now?"

"In my wagon. Got 'er under the canopy."

"I'll help bring her in," the doctor said calmly. "Mirabelle, do you have an extra bed?"

"Top of the stairs. Just need a minute t'put the sheets on." Mirabelle lumbered up the carpeted stairs, holding her skirt above her toes.

Ghan retraced the steps down the hall and left the house, the Swede following silently behind his heels. "Where did you find her?" asked the doctor, his voice as soft as a woman's.

"Middle of the bush. Maybe fifteen miles east." Ghan pointed to the wagon. "She's in there. Tried t'make her drink but can't get in more than a few drops."

Neely heard the voices and came out from the wagon, dropped his cigarette on the ground and crushed it with his boot. The doctor pulled back the canvas flap, his eyes drooping at the first glimpse of the child. "Let's move her quickly."

Ghan cradled the limp body, as light as a jute sack, against his chest and carried her back to the boardinghouse. Mirabelle peered over the upstairs banister at the floppy form, her throat muscles tightening and her chin set hard as she rang like a general, "Bring 'er up. Bed's ready!" It was the first voice that gave him any comfort.

Ghan placed the child on the bed with the fluffed pillow and starched white sheets. The room was plain but clean, cleaner than any hospital. Within minutes Mirabelle had the dirty stockings and dress removed and gently wiped the grime off the girl's face and neck. She placed a cold cloth on the child's forehead, all the while making *tsk-tsk* sounds and shaking her head.

The doctor felt the girl's pulse. He pried apart her eyelids, checked the pupils and then let go, the lids snapping shut. Ghan slid his hat off the pressed, sweated hairs of his head and squeezed it in his hands. The tiny girl, hopelessly burnt, appeared lifeless.

Dr. Carlton soaked a sheet in water, then wrapped the girl loosely in its folds. "We have to get her temperature down," he said to no one in particular. He opened a small vial of smelling salts and put it under her nose. The little girl moved her head uncomfortably. Her eyes opened, then flitted across the faces before landing on Ghan. His back flattened against the wall. A wave of gratitude fluttered his chest. Then her eyes closed and she winced from pain, her moan raspy and sore.

Mirabelle gently pushed her head back. "Try not t'cry, love."

"I'm going to apply a salve to the burns," stated the doctor blandly. "It would be better if you all wait downstairs."

"Whot's yer name?" Mirabelle asked as they entered the kitchen.

"Claudio Petroni. But everyone calls me Ghan."

She scrunched her forehead and looked at him oddly. He shrugged his shoulders. "I got a way wiv camels, like the Afghans."

Camels. Neely. Transport. The world hovered distantly. Ghan sat at the small, round table, conscious of his dirt-covered clothes and boots in the spotless house. The panic that had held his shoulders tight under his ears for hours dissipated, leaving every cell exhausted. He sank into the hardwood chair. The girl would live. He could breathe again.

Mirabelle heated the teapot and crossed her arms. She was a strong woman, not a pretty one. Ghan stretched his elbow onto the oilcloth. "Thank Gawd the doc was 'ere. Don't know whot I would've done," he said. "Heard Leonora had a hospital. Reason I came all this way."

"Hospital? Oh no!" she huffed. "Good two years away. Been all tied up in Perth. Men just sittin' around talkin' 'bout it. Like t'see some doin' for a change." A strand of hair dropped down her face and she blew it upward with a gust more powerful than necessary.

A whistle hollered from the teapot. Mirabelle pulled out a mug and the sugar and turned off the flame. "Doc works for the Plymouth Mine. Another year an' they're movin' out near the camp. Feel for his wife. Gets lonely out there all day, especially for a woman. That pale skin of hers is gonna cook faster than a slab of bacon." She pushed the mug at him and poured the tea, the steam rising between their faces. "Yeh want cake wiv that?"

His stomach rumbled. "If it's no trouble."

Mirabelle slid a piece of flat yellow cake onto a chipped plate. The Carltons returned and took seats at the table. Mirabelle brought more mugs and plates and cake.

The doctor's face was tired, sallow. "Her temperature is level. She's sleeping now."

"She's gonna be orright, then?" Ghan asked, his eyes wrinkling in relief.

"Her burns are severe. She'll be in a lot of pain as she heals."

Mirabelle snorted. "Where she came from is whot I want t'know. Like to 'ave a go at whoever did this to her, I would!" She turned to Ghan. "Where'd yeh find her?"

"In the bush. 'Bout four hours east."

"Just lyin' there?" The disgust in her voice echoed the sharp pounding in his chest.

"Maybe she wandered away from home, got lost?" asked the doctor.

"Dead land. Ain't no homes out that way," said Ghan. "Just salt-bush an' dust."

"Girl comes from a bad lot. No denyin' that! Her clothes ain't more than rags." Mirabelle wrung a towel in her thick hands like it was a neck. "Those damn prospectors don't care a lick 'bout nothin'."

"Well, in any case, we'll need to alert the authorities," said the doctor. "How long will you be staying in Leonora?"

"I'm not." Ghan finished his tea with a gulp, suddenly aware of the time. "I'm late as is."

Dr. Carlton's eyes widened. "You can't move her; she's too weak."

Ghan looked at Mirabelle, then at the doctor, his nerves frayed. "Course she's too weak! I'm not takin' her wiv me, for Gawd's sake."

Silence hung in the room, surrounded the four people set around the table. Mrs. Carlton squeezed her husband's arm, her whole expression begging. Dr. Carlton sighed in defeat and addressed Mirabelle: "May we keep the girl here?"

The muscles in Mirabelle's neck stretched and tightened like a celery stalk. "I feel for the girl, but I got an inn t'run. I can't take care of a child."

"My wife would care for her. *Temporarily.*" He stressed the last word, looked at his wife's hopeful face, and his eyes grew weaker. "We would pay for the room. Would that be all right? Just for a while."

"Of course." Mirabelle's neck softened. "Long as yer payin' for it."

Mrs. Carlton smiled, clapped her fingertips.

"I'll wire the constable in the morning." The doctor fished for a piece of paper and handed it to Ghan. "We'll need your information in case the police want to speak with you."

Ghan stared at the pen and paper, as useless to his illiterate mind as it would be to a goat. He handed it back. "It's the Bailen Mine in Menzies. John Matthews is the manager. He can track me down." The room fell silent again.

Ghan didn't want to stay, the ticking clock of the transport already nagging. He'd be fired if the supplies were late. Wouldn't be able to find another job—no one hires a cripple. Yet he couldn't stir his body to rise, didn't know how to leave this place, how to leave the girl. He rubbed the stubble at his jaw. All eyes rested on him. The girl would live; shouldn't that be enough? After all, he did all a man could be expected to do. These people would care for her. His part was done.

Ghan swallowed the unfamiliar lump lodged in his throat. "Be goin' then."

"Whot about yer cake?" Mirabelle asked.

"Not as hungry as I thought."

The doctor rose. "We'll contact you if the police have questions."

From the kitchen, Ghan stared at the dark hallway leading to the stairs, his stomach hollowing. "Orright if I say g'bye to her?"

"Of course," allowed the doctor. "Just don't wake her."

Ghan climbed the stairs to the bedroom and opened the door, the hinges creaking. The child was sleeping, her light brown hair strewn about the pillow, her tiny fist curled under her chin. Her skin glowed hot with the terrible burns, all the redder from the salve. Sadness lumped his throat while gratitude that she was alive swelled it. His prayer for her, if there was even a God to hear it, was razor sharp. He hoped that the rest of her days would not be as harsh—that she would not have a life steeped in the unthinkable—that the burns would not leave scars.

Ghan left the room as silently as he had entered and stepped heavily down the worn and bowed stairs. He gave a short nod to the doctor on the way out, feeling more a stranger now than when he had arrived.

Ghan entered the cool dark of Leonora's main street. He was halfway across the road when Mirabelle called out, "Hold up a minute!" She shuffled after him, her big hips swaying like the haunches of a packhorse. "Brought yeh some meat pies an' the rest of the cake." Mirabelle handed him a basket covered with cheesecloth. "Thought yeh might get hungry."

"Kind of yeh, Mirabelle. Real kind."

She touched his arm then and looked hard into his eyes. "That girl would 'ave died if yeh hadn't found her." She squeezed his fingers. "Yeh saved that little girl's life."

Ghan nodded briefly, stared down at the food. The strange lump rose in his throat again. "Thanks for the tucker, Mirabelle." She seemed to know that lump and patted his arm before turning around without a word.

Despite the thick black sky, the moon lit the sleepy street and energized the constellations until they popped. He wouldn't sleep tonight. He would ride through the night to Kookynie, hope the supplies still waited and then rest in the heat tomorrow.

At the wagon, Neely's snoring wheezed under a blanket heap. The shift from unyielding heat to brittle cold was clear as the transition from light to dark. Ghan had numbed to both.

Neely woke to the footsteps, rubbed his eyes. "How's the girl?"

"Good." The lump itched his throat again. Ghan handed the basket of food over.

"Thank Gawd!" Neely snatched the food. "Bloody starvin'." Then he paused and raised an eye. "Want me t'drive?"

"Naw, I'm awake. Get some rest an' yeh can drive some tomorrow."

Neely and his bundle of blankets hobbled under the canopy. Ghan gave a whistle and a whack to the camels. As they moved, Mirabelle's words trickled. *Yeh saved that little girl's life.* He let the words rest in his thoughts, reverberate in his mind. Something inside awakened from the shadows. *Yeh saved that little girl's life.* A grin formed on his lips and his hunched shoulders straightened; a live wire pulsed through his body. The wagon rolled in front of the boardinghouse. A lamp burned in the child's window. *Yeh saved that little girl's life.* Something in his chest, something that had been crushed and buried deep, peeked through the blackness and blinked at a glimmer of light.

CHAPTER 4

The heat woke her; the sun seared her face. But this burn was different. It flowed with her, hid under covers and bit at the tiniest movement. The place was different, too. Her body did not lie on rocks and roots but instead rested on cushioned softness, until she moved, and then it all sharpened to broken glass.

She slowly unpinched her eyes from the glare of sun, only to find no reason to squint. There was no sun, only a room not quite light and not quite dark. She touched her cheek, the stinging pain immediate. She did not touch it again.

Her fingers rounded against the smooth white covers, the outline of her feet stuck out in front. There was a small window with pulled curtains. Furniture, large and dark, pressed against the walls. In currents too subtle to notice, the room shed its gray. She lay there awake and burning and tried not to move.

The door creaked, drew a triangle of light across the bedcovers. A blond woman stepped noiselessly across the rug and sat on the edge of the bed, sinking the mattress. "Your name?"

The woman waited, then thumped her chest. "Elsa. My name Elsa." She cocked her head to one side. "Can you say? El-sa."

No response. Elsa patted the white sheet. "It all right. Will come. Time. Time." The words sounded like the ticks of the clock that sat next to the bed.

Elsa reached a hand toward her, cautiously, and she could tell her burns would not be touched. The woman stroked her hair with her fingertips, tucking it behind her ear, the sensation more breeze than touch.

"You stand?" Elsa asked. "All right for you?"

She pushed the covers off. The nightgown she wore was new and reached all the way to her bare feet. She turned onto her belly and slid to the edge of the bed through the fire and let her feet drop to the wooden floor. It hurt but could not compete with the flames of her face.

Elsa crouched until their eyes were level. The woman's were wet but not sad; she was smiling. "Goot. Very goot." She stood and extended a hand. "Come. We eat."

The little girl took the hand offered. No matter that another hand drew her to a place of suffering only a few days ago. No matter that the pale, outstretched hand calling to her now was unfamiliar. She took the hand because a child does not have a choice.

CHAPTER 5

Ghan was becoming a sentimental old fool. Six months had passed since he found the little girl in the desert. Six months of seeing her face every time he closed his eyes; six months of catching his breath every time he passed a lonely gum tree. Her image did not haunt him like the other memories; it fluttered like soft wings, brought the warmth of an afternoon breeze across his skin. But her fate weighed on him like his dead leg, pulling him back whenever he tried to move forward. He couldn't put off the trip any longer.

The sun was a core of orange with petals of pink stretching east and west when Ghan returned to Leonora. The wagon stopped. Ghan slid from his spot and handed the driver a few bills. His stomach was uneasy, the acid pricking in waves. He pushed his canvas bag into his gut, scrunching the new shirts he had bought from the supply store. Better to get it over with now; better to get his head back to rocks and camels, not bloody butterflies.

The air was dry and pleasant, infused with the scent of roses climbing along Mirabelle's fence post. Stiff broom bristles grated on the verandah and then stopped abruptly. "I don't believe it!" Mirabelle called out from the shade of the porch. "Look whot the willy-willy blew in!" She shook her head and put the broom against the post. "Yeh didn't pluck another child outta the bush, I hope?"

Ghan grinned at the woman, sturdy and hard as the banister. "G'day, Mirabelle."

She nodded at the driver pulling away. "See yeh traded in yer camels. Yeh struck gold or somepin?"

He'd never been able to converse naturally with any woman, but Mirabelle was more bloke than lady. She made talking easy, like six minutes had passed instead of six months.

"I wish. Takin' a few days' leave from the mine is all. Guess yeh could say I'm on vacation." Even the word sounded strange.

"An' yeh chose Leonora as yer slice of paradise? Yer dumber than yeh look!" Her words were joking, warm to his ears. Her heavy bosom reached from her chest to her waist and the mounds chuckled. "Come on up, Ghan. How long yeh stayin'?"

"Couple days. If yeh got the room."

"Same as last time. Only the Carltons an' the girl."

Ghan paused mid-step. "She's still 'ere?"

"Guess that'd come as a surprise. Never did find who she belonged to."

"Who's been carin' for her?"

"The doc's wife, Elsa. I'll fill yeh in on the whole story." She swatted at an invisible mosquito. "Let's get yeh settled first, 'fore the mozzies eat us alive."

Lines of sweat filled the creases in his forehead. The girl wasn't supposed to be here. He thought of turning back, cursed himself. He was a damn fool for sure, a grown man with nerves of noodles over a kid.

Ghan followed Mirabelle through the hall past yellowed rosebud wallpaper and over faded foot carpets, worn in the middle but intact at the edges. Seemed like he was seeing everything for the first time. Six months ago he couldn't see anything past that poor child.

"Girl's in the kitchen," Mirabelle said briskly. "I'll get a cold drink while yeh say hello."

Once Mirabelle's bulk veered toward the cupboards, the girl came into view, her back turned. He remembered the burns on her face and his stomach soured. If she was deformed, he wasn't sure if he could hide the pity from his eyes.

Mirabelle tapped the girl on the shoulder. "We got a guest."

The head of golden hair turned. He blinked for a moment before turning away. There were no burns, no scars, only the smooth face of an angel, too bright for his eyes.

Mirabelle handed him a glass of cool tea, didn't notice the way his hand quaked and made the brown liquid spider down the sides. "Elsa's just restin'," she said, and then pulled out a loaf of bread and began slicing thick ovals. "Doc's at the mine." Mirabelle placed the bread on a plate and slid it on the table, smacked a jam jar on the counter and nodded at the child. "Don't take it personal if she don't talk t'yeh. Don't talk to no one."

"At all?"

"Not a word. Not a single one in all the time she's been 'ere." Mirabelle spoke about the girl like she was deaf as well as mute. "Doesn't bother me none. I like it quiet."

Ghan slept sporadically in the small room with blue-papered walls and waxed wooden floors. He tried to remember the last time he had slept in a bed, not a cot or on the ground. His body didn't know how to relax into the softness and he lay stiff. The room sat still and quiet, but it was lost on him. Even after all these years aboveground, his mind still replayed the sound of pick against rock, an endless *ding* between the ears.

The smell of eggs and bacon hit halfway down the stairs. In the kitchen, Mirabelle worked a spatula over two sizzling iron pans. "Breakfast be out in a minute."

Ghan poured tea from the waiting kettle. It was nice here, warm and homey. A yellowed calendar from the local co-op hung in the kitchen, an advertisement for Borax starch glaze dedicated to June. It was September, but it was easy to see why no one changed the page. In the Outback, one month was hardly worth noting from the next.

"Hope yeh didn't get up at this hour just for me."

Mirabelle grunted. "Had the laundry finished 'fore yeh put a foot outta bed." She set down a plate of steaming eggs. "Most mornin's, I'm the one wakin' up the chooks."

The grease from the bacon pooled around the eggs as he shoveled them in. "Noticed yer front door's hangin' off the hinge. Can fix that for yeh, if yeh like."

She gave a short laugh. "Thought yeh was on vacation."

"Yeah." He grinned and scratched his head. "Frankly, not sure whot t'do wiv myself. Never had time off before."

"That's the problem wiv buggers like us. We've been workin' so long we don't know how to stop."

A step whispered from the hall. And there was the girl in a neat blue dress standing in the edge of the doorway.

"Come 'ave yer biscuit, child." Mirabelle grabbed a plate from the cupboard. "Don't eat more than a bird, this one."

The girl wafted through the kitchen like a ghost. A great sadness poked Ghan as he watched her peripherally, as if all she wanted was to slink into the shadows of the room. Then shame barged through the sadness. Maybe she was scared of him. Wouldn't be the first. *Better leave the poor child in peace.* "I'll get t'work on that hinge now."

"Appreciate it," Mirabelle said from the sink without turning. "Tools are in the closet."

Ghan pulled out the screwdriver and sat on his hams in front of the warped door. He hardly had a chance to shimmy out the first hinge when the wisp of the girl settled into the room, perched herself at the dusty window and rested her chin on her arm. Ghan glanced at her as he picked at the nail. *Has that puppy dog look,* he thought. *Like she's waiting for someone who's never going to show.* In the quiet of the room, a bloated blowfly beat against the pane, the buzz of wings futilely trying to get past the dirt-speckled glass into the open air. The girl tapped dully against the window at a spot next to the fly, the sound of affinity.

Warmth flowed into Ghan's muscles, had nothing to do with exertion. *Be nice to have a child waiting for you,* he thought. *Be nice having eggs and bacon every morning, having your own door to fix.* With his wrist, he wiped the sweat from his crooked nose, saw the speckled scars across his arms. He gritted his teeth, pounded the nail with the screwdriver. *Bloody fool.*

Footsteps echoed between the stair spindles. "Goot morning," Elsa greeted Ghan.

Then the door banged loudly and Ghan stepped back. Elsa hurried to her husband's side and hugged him, taking off his dusty hat and coat in a nervous flurry. Dr. Carlton looked over at the girl, a scowl clear on his face.

Elsa fawned over the doctor, holding his face in her hands, subtly trying to turn his gaze from the child. Her native speech spilled out

animatedly to the only ears that could understand. Even in her bubbled chatter, the edge was there, a highness to her voice that made every
statement sound like an apology. She grabbed his arm and pointed to
Ghan in the corner.

Dr. Carlton lowered his eyes as his manners haunted him. "I apologize. I didn't see you there." He recovered quickly and straightened.
"It's Ghan, correct?"

Ghan studied him. "That's right." Something was off in the man.

"Are you in town long?"

"Few days. Passin' through."

"I didn't see a wagon out front. Did the other man come with you?"
The doctor searched the ceiling. "What was his name?"

"Neely," Ghan answered. "Passed on."

"I'm sorry." There was no emotion behind the sentiment, just a
blend of sounds from the man's mouth. His eyes lifted heavily to the
ceiling. "I need to clean up. It was a long night." He stepped past
Ghan and climbed the moaning steps.

Ghan busied his hands with as much work as he could find. By afternoon, doors and windows slid easily on dust-free hinges, the woodpile was restacked in a grid of even, crossed lines and the tear in the
verandah screen was knit secure with wire. Sweat darkened his tan
shirt to brown, but he didn't want to stop. Every idle moment led to
shaking fingers.

Mirabelle tapped on the glass window. "Get outta the heat an'
come 'ave a bite."

Ghan fingered the fixed screen and entered through the door
Mirabelle held open. "No more work outta yeh! Swear yer makin' me
feel lazy!" she scolded. "Vacation my arse."

Dr. Carlton sat at the formal table, his frame tight and postured
against the back of the chair as he read the paper. He was clean now,
his blond hair slightly damp and slick at the crown but his eyes still
wrinkled at the edges with fatigue.

Elsa entered, her hands on the shoulders of the little girl. Dr. Carlton's eyes narrowly followed the child, his top lip curling as Elsa
kissed her silky gold hair. "Sit next to our guest," he ordered.

The child's eyes met Ghan's face briefly before he turned away. He swallowed hard and wiped his forehead with a soiled handkerchief. A warm, silent breeze passed behind him as the girl took the neighboring seat.

The room thickened with silence until Mirabelle grunted over an iron pot held tight in oven mitts. She loaded the plates with stew, the steam glistening faces already warm.

Ghan tugged at his hat, painfully aware that the open eardrum was right in the girl's sight line. He picked up his fork and nervously rubbed the silver, all appetite gone. The little girl watched him, her gaze boring into his skin. He never blushed in his life, but the heat rose quickly from his neck. He wished she would turn away. No child should see a man so grotesque.

Eyes were everywhere, burning into him, and his ear grew hotter and hotter and his heart pounded in his chest. He shuffled one foot under the table, rubbed it back and forth over the carpet. *Goddammit, stop staring at me!* Ghan focused on the cells and webbing of the lace tablecloth, yet he felt the eyes. Watching. Judging. Elsa watched with inward thoughts, her eyes deep and sad. Mirabelle watched forks and plates and food that sat untouched. And the doctor watched, too. The doctor watched him, observed Ghan's discomfort with analytical eyes, watched with a new half smile that made Ghan chew his bottom lip.

He shouldn't have come. The adrenaline pumped for him to run. He was just a reminder to this poor girl of the day she almost died— her ugliest of days. *Ugly. Ugly.* All he brought was ugliness to this world.

Ghan's hand trembled. He put the fork down. And then the girl placed her hand upon his. It was a touch that stopped air to his lungs and numbed his chest—five tiny fingers, as light as feathers, curled on top of his thick knuckles.

He looked at her now—fully—and she did not turn away. Her cherub face was not twisted in disgust or horror. Instead, she smiled and the sunbeam eclipsed every shadow since the beginning of time. The child looked at him as if she thought him beautiful.

Mirabelle's voice whispered above a suspended ladle, "She likes yeh."

Words and sounds blurred. The stitches that held his hard parts together, sutured over a lifetime, disintegrated with the touch. He fumbled for each strand, trying to quickly sew them back into place, but the look was too soft. The simple purity hurt. Just as when the workhorses were brought up from the mines, months after living in the underground shafts, they emerged blind, their skin and fur revolting against the fresh air, peeling off in shreds. The light, the freshness, was too much to bear.

Ghan snapped his hand away and stumbled off the seat before his bones crumbled. "I n-n-need some air," he stammered. He held on to the back of the chair to keep it from falling over and blindly limped through the dining room, limped through the sitting room, through the front door into the blinding sunlight that could not compare to the child's. He did not stop for a moment, dragged the dead leg over the furrows of the road, cringed at the wrinkling of his chin and the crumbling of his very cells.

Ghan found the pub and barreled into its shadows, hid from the filtered dusty light. Tobacco and sweat and stale grog embedded the woodwork and flooded his nostrils, made the pub more man than timber and steel. No flowers here; no rinsed floors or talc. He could breathe. And with the darkness, his heartbeat slowed and he felt his feet in his shoes again and his chin stopped quivering. He found a seat at the bar and ordered a whiskey. He didn't drink, but he needed to drink, needed it more than he needed air in his lungs. Ghan brought the short glass to his lips before the alcohol had a chance to level in the glass, the liquid trailing fire across his tongue, down his throat into the empty pit of his belly where it warmed instantly. The bartender did not move and refilled the glass. Ghan held this one tight between his stubby fingers, did not plunge it into his mouth. The bartender took the cue and moved down the line.

With warm insides Ghan could think, and he exhaled weakly, rubbed his hand over his eyebrows. He could see again, his pupils widening in the dim light. He was all right. Ghan glanced at the bar, couldn't remember coming in here or leaving Mirabelle's. Didn't want to think about it anymore; didn't want to think, period.

The pub didn't appear the same place he had visited six months ago. Nothing did. Everything about that day seemed half dream, half nightmare. It all blended in dizzy waves of hot and cold, nausea and euphoria. He gulped down the alcohol and closed his eyes to the burn, then opened them quickly to wipe away the haze. He flagged the bartender for another fill.

Brutes lined the bar; brutes hung in the corners; brutes drank hard liquor and smashed butterflies between their fists. *Damn butterflies.* He had chased them, let them tickle his skin with their delicate wings. *Bloody fool.*

Silent footsteps gave no warning to the hand that landed on his shoulder. Ghan jumped and sent half the whiskey sloshing over his fingers. "Whot the hell!" Ghan flicked his hand dry.

"Sorry." Dr. Carlton laughed and squeezed his shoulder. "Didn't mean to sneak up on you." He sat down on a bar stool, unbuttoned his coat jacket with one hand. "Figured you'd be here. Not many places to go." He smiled at the bottles lining the shelves. "Mind if I join you?"

The doctor's tone rippled between amusement and hard intent like he was dissecting some oddity of science. Ghan took what was left of the drink and swallowed it hard, the burn mild now. He missed the fire. He stood to go.

"Stay." The doctor checked his tone this time. "Please." Dr. Carlton flagged down the bartender. "Two whiskeys. We're celebrating."

Ghan slumped into the stool and turned the empty glass in half circles between his fingers. "Yeah?" he asked with disinterest. "Whot's the occasion?"

"A reunion, of course," Dr. Carlton said keenly.

The bartender brought the new bottle and poured it carefully. Dr. Carlton raised his glass and clinked it against Ghan's stationary one, his smile goading. "Cheers." Ghan pinched his lips together while the anger grew in his stomach and veined through his limbs.

Dr. Carlton leaned casually against the bar with one elbow and intertwined his fingers, shook his head and laughed at some conversation dancing in his head.

Ghan shifted in his seat, rolled his eyes. The doctor was pissing him off and the whiskey fueled it. "Yeh drunk, Doc?"

"No." Dr. Carlton laughed again. "No, not yet." He examined the ceiling. "I can't believe I didn't see it the first time we met. But when I saw your face, I understood." He finished the whiskey in one drawn gulp, his eyes stretching to ovals. "Guess some prayers can still be answered, eh? I'm curious, though . . . what changed your mind?"

Ghan rubbed his tongue against the inside of his cheek. "Changed my mind 'bout whot?"

"Coming back." Tiny hiccups of laughter rocked the doctor's shoulders. "Taking the girl, of course."

Ghan felt tangled in cobwebs, his thoughts sticking. The anger was collecting, pulling together from all areas, past and present. His fingers squeezed his glass as he stared down acidly.

The smile froze on the doctor's face. Then he leaned over, shot a glance at the men at the bar and lowered his voice. "Don't worry. No one needs to know. They've stopped looking months ago. You have my word, no one will be the wiser, like it never happened."

Ghan rubbed his hand against his stubbly cheek, hot tickles of rage plucking his nerves. He tried to control his voice and spoke evenly. "Like whot never happened?"

The doctor leaned in closer and whispered, "That you left her in the desert. That you are her father."

The anger, blue and fierce, snapped and barreled through his veins to his temples. Ghan grabbed him quick as a hawk, his talons wrapping around the doctor's white neck and squeezing into the flesh. The force lifted the doctor and pressed him against the bar, knocking their glasses to the floor, shattering them to pieces. Every face turned to the violence, stunned and briefly immobile, but Ghan only saw one face, one man—the one he was strangling.

The doctor's eyes protruded out of their sockets as Ghan's hard fingers tightened against the thin bones. "Yeh fuckin' bastard!" he growled into the bulbous eyes, his spit wetting the man's purpling face. "Yeh think I would do that to a child? Yeh think I would do that t'*my own fuckin' child?*"

Something hard and straight hit Ghan in the back of the knees, his hand slipping from the doctor's throat as he buckled. In another instant, the piece of wood was shoved under his chin, blocking his airway. Strong hands held his elbows backwards.

Dr. Carlton's face blotched as he rubbed his throat, put a hand up. "Stop." His voice was hardly audible through gasps. He pulled himself up and tugged at the wood. "Stop! Let him go."

No one loosened a grip on Ghan, his windpipe smashing in his throat. "We'll take care of this cripple for yeh, Doc!" panted the man closest to his ear. Ghan's eyes rolled into his head, the dizziness leaving his limbs numb, the black parts growing with the pain.

"No!" Dr. Carlton's voice was hard and stern now as he pulled sharply at the man's arm. "It was my fault. I insulted him. Let him go!"

Instantly, the wood disappeared and Ghan crumpled to the ground. The air rushed to his starving lungs and he grabbed the edge of the table, the thrust of returning air torture as much as relief. He closed his mouth and sucked through flared nostrils. The smells returned, rose up from the floor where his bent knee rested—old beer that made his stomach pinch; layers of packed, rotten earth—sharper now than before. Worn boots shuffled away. Conversations and the clink of glasses started up again from the bar.

A pale hand extended. Ghan slapped it away and sucked in hard, grabbed the edge of a table and hoisted himself back onto his feet.

Ghan scanned the room, his vision crisp with fresh oxygen. Not a man looked his way. His lungs labored while his body stood limp and numb down to the bones. The whiskey in his veins was gone now, the fire from anger and drink extinguished.

The doctor pointed to a chair, his face gray and aged. "I apologize. Please sit. Please."

Ghan sat. He was worn. Violence tempered his anger like a choke collar on an attack dog.

Silence swirled amid the cigarette smoke that clouded above their heads as neither man spoke or made a movement. Two new whiskeys showed up at the table. "No hard feelin's, eh, mate?" chirped the bartender. The fight was already filed away into the grains of the worn wood.

The doctor took one glass, his hand shaking, sloshing the drink against the rim. Instead of putting it to his lips, he put it back on the table, lowered his head and reached into his hair, clutching handfuls of it between fists. "I'm sorry. I can't think straight anymore." His voice was siphoned of life.

"Would have been so perfect." The doctor hunched in the chair, his eyes scurrying back and forth in their sockets. "If you were the girl's father, Elsa would understand her going away. She would be sad, but she would understand. She wouldn't hate me for sending her away."

Dr. Carlton tapped the glass to the table, each word increasing the beat. "I told her over and over again she was getting too close, that it was just a matter of time before the child would go. But she had it in her mind that I was going to come around and we could adopt her." His voice grew rough. "That's not an option."

Ghan's eyes blinked in question and the doctor read him. "I hate this place. *Hate* it." His open lips were wet, trembled at the corners. "We're leaving the day my contract is up. I can't afford another mouth to feed and I don't want a single reminder of this place, especially an orphan."

He leaned forward again, his face tight with clarity. "I need the authorities to take the girl, and when I do, Elsa will hate me." He let out a short, hollow laugh. "I've grown to scorn that little girl. Sometimes I think I actually hate her. Isn't that sick? But you see, don't you? You see I don't have a choice?"

The men grew silent as thoughts replaced speech. A blazing sun lowered outside and peeked in the top of the pub entrance, caught the edge of an old mirror nailed to the wall. The doctor's profile reflected in its glass and he was nothing more than a picture on the wall—detached and flat—an artist's tribute to a lost man. Silently, Dr. Carlton pulled out his wallet, dropped folded bills onto the table and left Ghan alone.

The sun dipped and turned the mirror to a rectangle of white blinding light. Its blaze exposed a thick line of dust in the air, turning each dot to silver. Ghan's thoughts turned to the child and a hollowness filled and turned soft.

They would take her away. They would rip her from that home and put her back out in the dust. Alone. She had no voice, no voice of sound or say. He thought he had saved her. She would have died. But death is quick; it ends. She didn't ask to be saved, didn't ask to suffer from burns or bounce from place to place, hand to hand, like a used gunnysack.

Every sound in the pub fell to a dull drone. The breeze of the child wafted around him; the light of her rolled into his thoughts; the freshness of her washed away the grime of the bar stink. No, he saved her and there was no regret.

The butterflies came from the eaves then and fluttered to his shoulders, flapped an image to his mind—an image of him whistling toward work, the little girl riding on his shoulders, hugging his neck, laughing, reaching for the delicate butterflies that danced around them. He held her stockinged ankles gently and she knew she was safe; he knew she was safe. The picture softened the creases in his forehead and lost him in the silver dust that enveloped his sight.

A body entered the bar and eclipsed the sun. The quiet broke with drunken greetings. The sparkled dust vanished and the orb of light dulled back to a gray mirror. And in that mirror, his face peered back— a hard face with dark eyes and high forehead, with patchy stubble over scars; a warped face, uneven with one ear, a nose wide and crooked. The butterflies hid from him, fled as quickly as their wings could carry them. He saw a new picture now. He saw an angel perched atop a monster. Saw a man who fumbled under her weight as his crippled leg twisted with each step. Saw the gray paint-chipped walls of his dank boarding room she would have to share with him. Saw the fear in her eyes as drunken miners fought under his window amid crashing bottles. Saw the way the single miners eyed any female out of diapers.

He saw many things now, saw them clearly. Saw he shouldn't have come back here. Saw the ridiculousness of the new shirts and the time off from work. Saw that this part of his life needed to end—this dream needed to fall and drift away. His body turned hard again and filled heavy as lead. It was time to go.

Ghan looked at the child's face asleep on the pillow—he knew he would never see her again.

The stairs creaked loudly under his weight and he cursed them as he made his way through the dark. Like a slow-breaking dawn, the hall brightened in one corner with a kerosene lantern. "Yeh leavin'?" asked Mirabelle.

He rubbed his cheek, tried to look casual. "Forgot a shipment's comin' down from Murrin Murrin. Thought I'd help out," he lied.

"Well, I'll grab yer money. Yeh paid for the week."

"Keep it."

"At least I owe yeh for the repairs yeh did around the place."

"I won't take it." His voice left no room for argument and Mirabelle nodded.

They were silent for a moment and then Ghan mentioned the person on both their minds. "She'll be gone soon. He's sendin' 'er away."

"I know." Mirabelle straightened her back quickly. "It's for the best."

Ghan nodded. Awkwardly, he handled a wide envelope in his hands, wrinkling it at the edges, the money clinking inside. "Could yeh see this goes wherever she does?" He handed it to Mirabelle. "It ain't much, but maybe it'll help."

In the shadows, he couldn't make out her expression, but when she spoke her voice was softer, like a woman's. "I will."

He could leave now. The child would not weigh on him, pull at him like his dead leg. Hell, maybe he'd have the butcher take the limb off now once and for all—the less of him in this world, the better.

CHAPTER 6

❧

She waited in bed for Elsa, but the woman did not come. Her empty stomach hissed and spit with a churned ache that grew since the first rays of dawn. She folded her arms against the pain, dropped her feet to the floor, made her way down the stairs draped in silence. A dress hung on the coatrack at the bottom of the steps, a small white cotton dress, pretty and crisp, its tag still on the sleeve. She tasted something sour in her mouth.

A familiar sound tinkered down the hall. She followed it to the kitchen where Mirabelle labored over the sink scrubbing a pot. She watched the woman quietly, half-peeking from behind the doorjamb. Mirabelle washed the pot hard, over and over again even though no grime spotted the metal sides. Her elbows moved roughly and hair strayed from her bun with the effort. Then she stopped and, with a sudden burst, flung the soapy scrubber at the window. Mirabelle lowered her head between shoulders that didn't look so strong anymore.

The stomach acid stung and she leaned closer to the wall. Mirabelle turned and jumped when she saw her standing in the room. The woman's eyes were tired and red.

Mirabelle straightened and rubbed her hands on the wet apron double rolled around her waist. She sawed thick slices from a loaf of bread, then grabbed a bowl of peaches and did not look at her face. "Make sure yeh eat it," Mirabelle said softly.

The bread crumbled dry in her mouth. She didn't want to eat but finished every crumb, the food fueling the fire instead of extinguishing it. Mirabelle came over and gently placed her hand on her shoulder, her voice too soft. "Come, let's get yeh ready, eh?"

As she held Mirabelle's hand, her body numbed and chilled—the pull of the hand, the vacant look, the silence. Mirabelle led her to the sitting room, undressed her and slipped the new dress over her tiny shoulders. From the closet she pulled out shiny black shoes with silver buckles at the straps. Mirabelle dressed her absently, her lips pursed, her eyes avoiding her own. "Won't be so bad. Yeh'll see." The woman's voice cracked. "It's for the best." A rush of blood pumped to her temples with the words.

Mirabelle's fingers were unsteady, clumsy as she slid the stiff shoes over her stockings, then rubbed out the fabric creases on her arms. She looked her in the eye and spoke with finality. "Come. Let's show Elsa how pretty yeh look."

The new shoes sounded hollow as they entered the bedroom. Elsa sat up in bed, her shoulders shaking as she sobbed into a handkerchief. When she saw the girl, she wiped her nose quickly and tucked the cloth under the pillow. A smile spread across Elsa's lips and she spoke in chopped English, "Oh, so pretty! So, so pretty!"

Elsa motioned for her to come closer, arms outstretched.

The front door slammed.

Floorboards and steps creaked. The voices of men hummed below.

Elsa pulled her close in a frantic embrace, fresh tears in her hair.

A rush of sound filled the room.

Panic surrounded, crushed against her flesh and throbbed in every corner of her body. Elsa squeezed her violently and her chest hurt for air. A wave of heat flashed through her insides and her mind snapped closed like a clam, every part of her retreating, curling tighter and tighter together. Muffled sounds bounced against the blinded shell—crying, yelling, begging.

Her arms pulled from two different directions; her feet lifted off the ground in a sudden sweep. She pinched her eyes.

She was carried quickly through the house, down the stairs and out the door, which slammed away Elsa's screams in one hard whack. Strong arms held her tight; a man panted in her ear while her face pressed hard into the scratchy fabric of a uniform. Every thought closed amid the earsplitting throb between her ears. Senses livened—the smell of horses, the sound of boots against the dirt, the taste of blood as she bit her lip—everything else deadened.

The man dropped her on a smooth leather seat and she blindly scrunched into the corner. Wheels propelled and jostled her head between seat and carriage door. Every inch burned and throbbed. From under her eyelids, distantly, she caught a glimpse of the new shoes strapped to her feet, already scuffed and spotted with red dirt.

She left the lonely desert town behind in a cloud of dust—a town that would give her little more than a name: Leonora.

PART 2

CHAPTER 7

❧

A blur of hands, of people and homes, of men in uniform, dotted the months. Another journey and a policeman unlocked the buggy door. "Out yeh go." Grunting, he pushed his hat high upon his forehead, the rim cutting a pale line into his red skin. "Come on, child; we ain't got all day." He took her by the hands and swung her to the ground.

A tree stretched across their path, its bark stripped, the torn roots reaching toward the sky like bony fingers. Broken glass littered the stones at her feet, gleamed white between blades of grass. Next to the church, a pile of debris—stacks of broken chairs, loose bricks caked with mortar, books fanning out with moldy centers. The policeman dropped her hand. Her mouth went dry. The sea roared in the distance, drowned out her thundering heartbeat.

A priest exited the wide church doors. Dressed in black from shoes to chin, he seemed to float across the gravel like a dancing shadow. "Good morning, Constable," he greeted flatly.

"Mornin', Father McIntyre." The officer scanned the tarps and broken windows of the orphanage, rubbed his round belly. "Och, the cyclone did a number on yeh, Father. How yeh going to fix it all?"

The priest sighed, tapped his shoe. "I've written the Bishop. The money will come."

"Hope yer right. Geraldton took a beatin', but whew..." The policeman wiped his forehead with the back of his hand and set his gaze on the decimated pile of twisted trees. "Weren't nothin' compared to this. Yeh got the brunt of it, I'm afraid." He scratched the inside of a nostril absently, then scraped his knuckle across his nose, snorted away the talk of weather. "Anyway," he said, tilting his head at her. "Got another one for yeh."

"So I see." The priest's face was stiff, his tone stern. "Would have appreciated a bit more notice. You said she wasn't coming for another month."

The sweaty officer shrugged. "Outta my hands. Child's been through two foster homes already. Drivin' 'em crazy way she don't talk. I've been stuck with her for a week."

She swallowed, dropped her eyes to the pebbles at her feet. The burn crept up her stomach and spread to her face.

Father McIntyre cleared his throat, then knelt on one knee. Gently, he tapped her chin until her eyes leveled with his. The burn faded. His face was soft and calm. His eyebrows sloped without tension. He took her hand, held it in his warm palm. "We're pleased to have you. It's Leonora, right?"

"Not her real name," the policeman interjected as he picked at the nostril again. "Named after some bush town. Call her whot yeh like."

The priest's gaze did not waver, but his lips pinched. He pressed her hand and his mouth relaxed again. "I think Leonora is a beautiful name. Shall we keep it?"

With the request of speech, her mouth filled with cotton. She stood as still and quiet as stone. But unlike the cold stares and short huffs of the others, Father McIntyre's smile widened. He leaned in and spoke solely to her ears: "This is a good place."

She scanned the broken church, the ravaged grounds. The priest followed her gaze and nodded. "We'll get better, Leonora. Time heals all wounds." An old Scottish accent curved the words, their sincere lightness loosening her throat and shoulders.

"We'll take good care of you." He stood then, his graceful black body reaching into the Heavens as he held out his hand. "I promise."

CHAPTER 8

❧

Father McIntyre carried his morning tea outdoors. A slight breeze blew from the sea, bringing the familiar brininess and timely certainty of waves crashing against the cliffs. The thick indigo sky greedily held on to the last of its stars, each one gradually disappearing in the widening line of morning light. There was vibrancy to this hour—God's time; God's place.

The boys' dormitory lay quiet, the tarped roof barely strong enough to keep the dew out. The storm had blown out every window; thin wood bandaged the openings. Little feet still had to walk upon broken glass embedded in the grass. The girls' hall hadn't fared much better. The dormitories branched off the church in wings and the storm had clipped them.

Father McIntyre turned the corner to the outline of mortar and old bricks that was once his personal library. The devastated site still pitted his stomach. A lifetime collection of books—Shakespeare, Dickinson, Poe—blown to sea or impaled on trees, soaked beyond recognition. *Only paper and ink*, he reminded himself. The children were not harmed, not a single one. Flesh and blood had won out. Flesh and blood—the paper and ink of life.

He finished his tea as the light of dawn plucked away the last star and flooded the cliffs. He thought about the little girl who arrived earlier in the week and his throat closed. Another orphan. A child without a voice but with the light of purity in her gaze. The brass bell chimed and he listened with closed eyes—eyes of reverence. For this was the call of those within, the ones who could not speak for themselves, the nameless and the lost—a beacon of anonymity.

Seven rings. His sliver of quiet over. The children would be done with breakfast now. Chores would begin. Soon the noise of little voices and feet would surround every inch of the orphanage and his work would begin.

By noon, the sea's scent enveloped the fields, escorted Father McIntyre over the stone trail, mingled with syrupy, rotting nectar that curved through the orchard. Apple trees, wizened in branch and plucked of fruit, clustered so close limbs intertwined and sewed the line of trees together. Picking season was over, the last bushels of stoned fruit carted to town, the rest blown out to sea from the storm. Birds, now free from competitive fingers, pecked at the old pulp that hung from pits and stems. Wasps and fruit flies crawled over the ground, their wings wet and bellies besotted on the sweet juice.

Father McIntyre stepped gingerly over the smashed fruit. An older boy with rolled-up sleeves stood midway up a ladder, steadying his balance as he pruned the limbs with shears. A smaller boy sat at the base, inspecting a rotten apple for ants.

"Dylan!" the priest called out. "Have you seen James?"

The boy on the ladder turned, rested the shears on his shoulder. "In the barn. Last time I seen 'im."

"He's doin' his chores!" the bug inspector chimed helpfully.

"You finish yours?" Father McIntyre asked.

"Yes, sir."

"Good boy."

He moved evenly over pebbles bleached white and carried from the sea, his black frock starkly bold above them as he made his way to the barn in the lower paddock. There Father McIntyre quietly leaned against the old, warm wood and watched the boy push the shreds of hay into the back of the stall. The broom, still too long for the child, slipped in his hands as he cleared the ground around the horse's hooves.

James was growing up—still a child, but less and less one every day. Father McIntyre stepped into the barn, the heat trapped oppressively within the rotten wood. James rubbed his forehead against his sleeve, then gently petted the mare's nose. The horse reared, stepped away violently.

Father McIntyre grabbed the harness. "Whoa! What's gotten into her?"

James looked up in surprise. "Don't know. She's not herself."

"Did you check the stall for snakes? Lost that little nanny goat to one last week."

James's eyes lit up. He exchanged the broom for the pitchfork and shoveled through the high pile of hay. A long, brown snake erupted from the disturbed mound and slithered through his legs. The horse panicked, batted her front hooves into the air.

"I've got him cornered!" James shouted.

Father McIntyre shivered. "Don't get near that snake, James! Just finish him quickly!"

The boy's face opened with pure bewilderment. "I can't hurt him, Father." With one quick scoop he caught the snake between the pitchfork prongs, carried the wriggling creature to the door and flung him to the grass.

"For Pete's sake, James!" Father McIntyre held one hand to his chest. "Don't ever do that again. The world can live with one less snake, you know."

James knit his brows deeply. Bits of grass and seed stuck to the sweat on his forearms and crown. Father McIntyre shook his head, laughed at the boy's weighty seriousness and patted his hair, sending puffs of hay into the air. "Fearless. Always have been."

James rubbed the horse's nose softly and she calmed. He began work with the pitchfork again, pushing the disrupted hay back into place.

Father McIntyre stopped him. "Come outside and sit with me for a bit."

"What about my chores?"

"They can wait."

Father McIntyre and James left the strong smell of animals and hay behind and sat outside against a sun-soaked boulder. Father McIntyre handed him a brown package. "Happy birthday."

The boy held the gift in his hand. "We're not supposed to get presents."

The Father chuckled. "There are some exceptions. Go on, James. Open it."

Reluctantly, the boy untied the twine and pulled off the paper. His face did not change as he stared at the thick leather Bible.

"It's a new book, not a used one from the church," Father McIntyre explained. "Look, I know you wouldn't have picked this for yourself, but"—he struggled for the right words—"maybe you'll look to it for answers. Maybe not now, but someday."

James looked at the book in his hands. "Thank you, Father."

Father McIntyre couldn't decide if he wanted to shake or hug the boy. He settled on pinching his chin. "Why do you always look so serious, my son?" James didn't answer, nor did the Father expect him to.

Father McIntyre followed the stone trail with his eyes, his crow's-feet wrinkling in memory. "I taught you to walk on this path." He pointed near the end of the barn. "That smooth spot there. As soon as your legs were strong enough, we came down here every day and practiced. You would grip my index fingers with your whole fist, hold on so tight that my fingers turned white." He looked at his fingers, still seeing it. "You were so determined to walk. No sooner were you crawling than you were trying to stay upright on wobbly legs."

The sun glowed warmly and etched the boy's amber crown in gold. "I remember when they put you in my arms, not more than a week old. You turned bright red and screamed so hard I thought you'd burst." He rubbed his hand through his hair, his eyes wide with the memory. "I was so scared. My hands trembled till I thought I'd drop you. Hadn't been here more than a month myself." He smiled softly at James. "You and I grew up here together, my son. Held each other up along that path."

He watched James's profile and wondered at the thoughts the boy kept hidden. He was a fine boy. A fine, wonderful boy and he loved him like a father would a son—not an ordained father but a natural one.

James had a good life at the orphanage; this he was sure. He was fed, educated, taught to speak properly, without the slang used by other children. He was never bullied, a favorite of the nuns. But the boy had no friends and showed little interest in making them, more at peace with the animals or alone. A hollowness had lived in James since birth, and in nine years Father McIntyre still hadn't a clue how to fill it.

He pulled James to his feet, gave him a wink. "Go on. It's your birthday. Chores can wait until tomorrow." He knew where the boy would go. "James!" he called out to the figure already speeding toward the sea. "Remember, not too close to the cliffs!"

CHAPTER 9

James leaned against the trunk of the weeping peppermint tree, the shade wispy and uneven. His chin pressed on one bent knee while the other leg lay straight. His toe peeked from the shoe's crack like a worm fresh from the ground. He pulled the toe in and the crack closed. A ball broke clumsily through the branches, nearly landing on his head.

"Over 'ere!" a boy hollered from the field. "Send it back!"

James chucked the ball into the sky.

"Yeh want t'play, James?"

"Naw." James resettled under the tree, moved his attention back to his hide-and-seek toe. He traced shapes in the soft brown dirt with a crooked stick. The drone of children hummed all around, melting like the drum of insects.

Meghan Mahoney's shadow fell across his foot as she sneaked past, snickering with two other girls. "There she is!"

James sighed and poked harder at the ground, wishing their voices were far enough to merge with the rest of the insects.

"Leonora! Hey, Leonora, whot yeh doin'?" Meghan's voice, sweet as rancid butter, surrounded the little girl hidden in the shade.

"Oh! I forgot. She don't know how t'talk. Poor thing! Would yeh like a lesson? I'm a very good teacher." The girls giggled. "Repeat after me: 'I'm a dumb, ugly girl.' Say it wiv me: 'I'm a dumb, ugly girl.'"

James kept his chin tucked to his knee and did not look, didn't need to. He could see Meghan's freckled face clearly enough behind the voice as she tortured the new girl. He dug hard into the dirt until the stick cracked in his fingers.

"S'not talkin', eh? How 'bout singin'? Got a good song. Made it just for yeh.

> *"Leonora, Leonora,*
> *under the sky,*
> *'er parents left 'er to die,*
> *then laughed like the kookaburra!"*

The words sickened James's insides like sour milk. He shot daggers at the girls, caught a glimpse of Leonora's eyes as they flickered to his. There were no tears, no anger—only softness. A swift heat ignited his nerves. James chewed his bottom lip, his limbs tight. He could stop it. But it would be back tomorrow and the day after. It would be worse because they loved a fight. Their eyes sparkled for it. They'd pick harder. He closed his eyes, focused on the rustle of willowy leaves until the laughter died and Meghan and her crew bustled away.

He sat idly now, his toe tucked back into its hole, his stick broken in the dirt. The silent girl in the shadows sat and settled her chin upon her small fist. And James hated this place—the only home he had ever known—and he wanted nothing more than to leave it. He couldn't sit any longer and there weren't enough sticks in the world to break. Springing from his seat, he ran from the field, ran over the path that swung around the church, ran so hard his head bent forward and his legs blurred through the wildflowers and boulders that traced the way to the cliffs.

The smell of the sea smacked as he crested the hill and stood at the very edge. He settled atop a patch of brittle grass, sharpened to points and entrenched in sand. His legs hung over the sheer mountain ledge, his toes dangling hundreds of feet above the swirling waves. James leaned back and dug his elbows into the ground, closed his eyes and raised his chin to the clouds. The orphanage disappeared. The roar of water drowned the voices, the taunts; the briny scent of fish and sea flushed away the smell of sweat and dirt and mildew. The callousness, the cruelty of the orphanage lingered for a moment before the currents tore and diffused it.

The sea stilled him. The bounce of water far below hypnotized and quieted his mind. The steeple bell chimed two hollow rings and a weakness tugged his insides. He did not belong at this place. He knew this before he was old enough to *know* it. This was not meant to be his life and yet it was his life and he didn't understand and it made him want to crack sticks and throw rocks into the sea until his shoulder hurt.

From his waistband, James pulled out the Bible Father McIntyre had given him. The Father said it would give him answers, and one came, but certainly not one the priest would approve. James opened the cover and rubbed his hand over the tiny printed words, the paper thin and opaque. Slowly, he pinched the corner of the paper and tore it straight down its seam. He grabbed more pages, ripping evenly so they hardly frayed. The last few pages fell out on their own and James rubbed his finger over the naked seam, bare but for a few red strings. The limp cover collapsed into the back, the substance gone.

James gathered the ripped pages, held them for a moment, the edges flapping in the warm breeze before being released over the cliffs where they danced upon the wind, waved like milky hands and glided down to the frothy ocean. Beside him, a cypress tree with worn and knobby roots hung to the edge of the cliff and James picked through a pyramid of stones at its base until he found the buried black book. In the sunlight, the gold-embossed lettering glowed white and his heart raced just as it had the first time he found it in Father McIntyre's library. The name "O'Connell" shone brilliant. His name.

The Father had hidden the book from him, but the cyclone had returned it, the wind leaving the book fanned and exposed in the rubble until he'd snatched it.

Now James blew away the bits of dirt that filled the veining leather creases. He placed the book into the shell of the Bible and pressed hard. Not a perfect fit but good enough not to be questioned. Her words were safe now, protected in God's cover. He tucked his mother's diary safely under his shirt.

CHAPTER 10

Seventy-five miles north of Geraldton, near Kalbarri, the orphanage hovered above jagged cliffs that gave no hint of human inhabitation save the serpentine dirt road roughed out by convicts more than a decade before. Green fingers of hopbush worked daily to reclaim the road, their roots creeping over wagon ruts and lines sluiced by years of winter rain; immovable boulders blocked every turn. But few needed to pass along this route. The people of the north, the wild country, stayed in the north; the people of the south, the sun country, stayed in the south.

So this road met the Bishop's experimental petrol-fueled car with great amusement. Pointed rocks poked at the thin rubber tires and bounced the iron frame precariously over hidden roots and ruts. The whole of the orphanage watched the steel and rubber creature. Not even age precluded a gaping mouth as the battered car pulled up to the level lot of the church amid a cloud of dust and exhaust. Through the blanket of smoke, a man floundered with a gearshift, each jolt bringing loud screeches from the engine and more smoke farting from the tailpipe until he pulled something hard and the engine closed down with a whine. The passenger's door opened and an arm clothed in black smacked away the fumes.

Father McIntyre reached a hand into the smoke. "Welcome, Your Grace."

The Bishop stepped from the car, leaned against the car looking ill, then chuckled. "That journey is not for the faint of heart." He beat at his cope. Sprays of dust clouded and stuck to his red, sweaty face.

Putting his palms to the small of his back, he arched his spine in a long, tight stretch, his stomach bulging. Another man fumbled with bags tied to the trunk platform and then, with hands draped with vestments, joined the Bishop's side.

Father McIntyre's lips parted. Recognition reached his body first and his face drained.

"My new assistant, Deacon Johnson," introduced the Bishop.

"Hello, Father McIntyre." The man addressed the priest calmly, but his eyes were questioning and apprehensive. "It's good to see you again."

The Bishop looked up in surprise. "You know one another?"

The Deacon did not take his eyes off Father McIntyre and answered gently, "We were at the seminary together in New South Wales. I was his tutor for many years."

Father McIntyre tried to remind himself that the man had once been a friend and he let that memory obscure the others until the blood returned to his face and his chest opened again. "Deacon Johnson," he greeted formally. "It's been a long time."

"Good we started here," noted the Bishop. "Always helps to see a familiar face."

"We're not your only stop?"

"Hardly!" the Bishop huffed. "We've almost a dozen other missions to visit." He slapped a hand to the Father's shoulder. "You're not the only one in need of money, you know. Now, if you don't mind, I'd like to clean up and have a rest." The Bishop walked past the children, did not greet them with expression or voice. "Besides, I'm sure you and Deacon Johnson have a lot of catching up to do."

Father McIntyre watched the retreating figure, fully conscious of the Deacon's weighted gaze against his profile. He clasped his hands behind his back, breathed the briny sea into his nostrils before speaking. "It was a long time ago, Robert. There's no need to speak of it."

The Deacon's round cheeks twitched. "I know, but I feel I should—"

He stopped the man's sentence with one piercing look. "It was a long time ago."

CHAPTER II

❧

On this day, the waves did not crash but lapped and licked the stones of the cliffs. The pages in the book open at James's knees hardly rustled in the calm. He read little of her diary, absorbing each word in both style and meaning to create some picture of his mother. At the end of each page, he hesitated to turn to the next, for each page opened a window to his past, both the good and bad of it. He was in no rush to read the diary. He was an orphan. He knew how it ended.

James closed the book and placed it under bent knees, embracing them with his arms as he followed the sounds of the tide. Then a movement shadowed a boulder. A stick cracked. His skin iced. He waited, became as still as the rocks. Pebbles crunched to his right and he sprang upright. "Who's there?" he hollered. James tucked the book into his waistband and bent slowly for a rock, raised it into the air, readied it. "Who's back there?"

A figure emerged from behind the thorny arms of a Murchison rose. James lowered the rock and dropped it from his fingers. "You shouldn't be up here," he warned.

Leonora stepped from behind the prickly wires. Her shoulders rose and settled with nervous breathing and her eyes circled with worry. "You shouldn't be up here," he repeated. "The cliffs aren't safe." James stepped forward and she retreated with as many steps.

"I'm not going to hurt you." He walked quickly, but she moved quicker and the full sea and its distance rose up behind her. "Stop!" he shouted, but she did not understand and her feet backed into the space where the grass could no longer grow and the sand met the crumbles of the cliff edge. James did not see or think but bolted forward and grabbed her arm just as her ankle gave in against a loose rock that rolled to the sea. He pulled her roughly from the edge and did not let go until she squirmed her whitened wrist from his grip.

Adrenaline pumped hard and he didn't know quite what had happened except that she was there and did not fall over the edge and he couldn't quite believe it. They stared hard at each other, their chests heaving. Leonora's eyes flickered to the rosebush.

"What is it?" he asked. "What's over there?" She didn't answer, watched his every move as he crawled under the prickly canopy. She grabbed his arm and made him stop, then pointed to the ground. There, near his next step, was a cluster of sticks, a mound of petals and leaves. In the center, a small yellow and gray bird, her wing jutting out awkwardly, blinked with slow, pale lids.

Leonora still held his arm, squeezed it vaguely, a great begging holding her face. He knelt against the sandy base and pushed the stems away, holding them carefully between the thorns. "I won't hurt her," he whispered.

James caressed the bird's lead-colored head. "She's a western yellow robin. Her wing's broken, though.

"Wait here." James shuffled from the brambles and returned a moment later, his fingers soiled and holding a wriggling earthworm. He placed it on the ground. The bird tilted her head one way and then the other, pecked, held the worm longways in her beak and then in three choking jerks ate it.

Leonora turned to James and her eyes were bright with gratitude. She smiled cautiously. James smiled back. He never smiled and he didn't understand.

CHAPTER 12

"The tarps are all we have to protect the dormitories." Father McIntyre pointed to the wounded building. "It's a temporary fix. Certainly won't get us through another winter." Bishop Ridley nodded and continued walking, leading the tour more than following it, taking the steep slope toward the rows of dwarf fruit trees.

"The orchard will come back, but it will take time. Some of the trees were pulled out from the roots." Father McIntyre took his elbow. "Watch your step, Bishop," he said as they stepped over an open hole. "The cherries did much better—"

The Bishop interrupted, "How many children reside here?"

"Twenty-eight."

"And staff?"

"Three nuns and a cook."

The Bishop studied him. "And you."

"And me, yes."

The Bishop walked with fingers joined loosely behind his back. Father McIntyre slowed his gait to match, though he was impatient to show the Bishop all that needed to be done. The fence posts to the farm peeked up from the valley and Father McIntyre wasted no time. "In the past, shearing brought in—"

"How many children . . . I'm sorry, Father, I didn't mean to interrupt."

"No, please continue."

Bishop Ridley scanned the sky. "How many children have been adopted?"

He tried to dodge the question. "How many? I guess that depends. The orphanage has been here since before I started."

"How many since you started, then?" the Bishop asked.

Father McIntyre wiped a sweaty palm against his hip. "None."

The Bishop's jaw dropped. "Not a one? In all this time?"

"This is not a wealthy state, Your Grace. Times are hard. We aren't exactly easy to get to." He meant it to sound light but knew right away his error.

"You make a good point." The Bishop raised his eyebrows, his mind busy. "This place is remote for an orphanage. Perhaps it would be better utilized as a seminary. Young priests need the solitude. Children need the opposite."

Father McIntyre swam through waves of nerves and stopped. "May I speak frankly?" The Bishop nodded, curious.

"This is more than an orphanage. For these children, it is a sanctuary, a *life*. For most of them, this is their only chance." Father McIntyre stared deep into the man's expressionless features. "They receive vocation training ensuring they will not turn wayward as the unskilled do. Each child will leave this place with the ability to support himself and become a decent working adult and, no doubt, a strong advocate of the church." He did not speak with emotion but with profession and he held the Bishop's eyes so they could not look away.

"We do not ask for charity but for an investment," he continued. "These children work and study hard. We sustain ourselves from the farm and orchard and only ask enough to get work started again. The storm has brought us a challenging time."

"You wrote for money before the storm ever came, Father McIntyre." The Bishop flared his nostrils skeptically. "Several times, I believe."

"That's true. But I've only asked to benefit the children. To give them every opportunity."

"You're a dedicated man," said the Bishop blandly. The priest was not sure if it was a compliment.

The men did not continue to the farm, for the need was gone. Nothing he could show the Bishop would outweigh his words. Around the turn, they sought the bench under the shade of a waning sun and Father McIntyre did not feel like filling in the spaces any longer. The sun weighed on his eyelids and a twinge of a headache started at the temples. He was bored with the Bishop, bored with his disinterest, and he looked forward to the morning, when he would leave.

A group of boys played ball in the field, their activity a welcome distraction. Father McIntyre relaxed and smiled at the way the children fought for the ball, their feet quick and carefree; he smiled at the laughing faces, the joy children brought into the world, his world. He looked at the Bishop's profile to see if he smiled, too. But the Bishop didn't, and for the first time Father McIntyre saw plainly the thoughts in the man's unmoving features, the wheels that ground past the present and sped toward the future when children did not run in these fields or take shelter in this place. To Bishop Ridley, the orphanage was a minor distraction—a lost cause.

Father McIntyre entered his office with a quick push of the door, forgetting it was occupied. Deacon Johnson jumped with the noise, his hand on his chest. "You nearly gave me a heart attack!" He chuckled at his own surprise. "I was just finishing up the accounts. Forgot where I was for a moment. Numbers will do that to you."

Father McIntyre slouched into the chair, his face heavy and dull. "I trust you found everything in order?"

"Yes. Your records are very thorough." The Deacon frowned. "What's wrong, Colin?"

Father McIntyre intertwined his fingers, picked at his thumbnail. "Bishop Ridley never planned to give us any money, did he?"

The man pinched his lip. A slight blush entered his cheeks. "No."

"Then why come?" the Father almost shouted. "Why bother with the journey, with the pleasantries, when he could have ignored my letters as he has in the past? Why have you look over the books when he has no plans to add to them?"

"The Bishop plans to close half the parishes," he answered softly, his eyes unblinking. "He came to decide which ones should go."

The words kicked Father McIntyre square under the ribs. He leaned his back against the chair and looked at the ceiling, digesting the words and trying to think through the pain in his abdomen. He dug his elbows into his legs, rubbed his eyebrows with his fingers. "What can I do?"

The Deacon placed his glasses on his nose and opened the ledger. "The numbers are not good. But you know this. You were running at a loss before the storm, and now . . ." He looked at the Father with gravity. "If it doesn't turn around, the Bishop will close the orphanage."

Father McIntyre scoffed, "Turn it around, he says!" Hopelessness flooded his chest and he twisted his mouth. "Is there nothing that can be done?"

The Deacon's pupils rose above his glasses and he held up a finger for patience, then flipped through the lined pages of the ledger. "There's a number here I wanted to ask you about." He turned the ledger toward the Father and pointed. "Under the word 'Leonora.'"

"That's not our money." He pushed the ledger away. "Belongs to a child here."

Deacon Johnson cocked his head. "What do you mean?"

"There's a girl here. Her name is Leonora. When she came, there was money set aside for her future; it belongs to her."

"She's a ward of the church," the Deacon corrected. "The money belongs to us."

"Someone cared enough for this girl to set aside money." His jaw set. "I won't touch it."

"You don't have a choice."

"I do have a choice," Father McIntyre retorted, then checked his tone. "You don't understand. This girl is . . . special."

"How so?"

"She doesn't speak."

The Deacon grew stern. "Colin, this is not a place for children like that and you know it. There are state hospitals for that sort of thing. She should have never been placed here."

"She's not retarded, for Pete's sake! The poor child has been through things we can't imagine, abandoned, shuffled from one place to another. It's no wonder she doesn't speak. No one has probably ever listened to her." He pinched his knee. "A child like that has no future. She needs that money to survive. I won't allow it to be touched."

The Deacon studied him and the Father's insides bubbled. "Don't you dare look at me like that, Robert. Don't you analyze me!"

"You can't save the world."

Father McIntyre turned his head away, but the past was seeping toward them.

"You put too much pressure on yourself, Colin. It's not healthy."

"Stop it!" Father McIntyre ordered.

"I know you." Deacon Johnson leaned forward, his eyes watery, helpless. "You lose yourself in salvation. I still have nightmares about what I saw, what you did to yourself."

"Stop it!" Father McIntyre clamped his eyes and covered his ears with his hands, pressed until he heard his pulse, but it was too late; something red and sick was entering and weaving its way through the floorboards and inching through the roof eaves. He glanced at the thin white scars across his wrists. He tore his hands away and folded them against his stomach.

"Do you forget? It was me." The Deacon pounded his chest with an open hand. "It was me who found you!"

"Damn it!" Father McIntyre hammered the desk with his fist. "How dare you bring this here! How dare you soil this place, my place, with those . . . with that hell." He looked around wildly. "This is my place. *My place*, do you hear? You have no right to bring that back." He paced the floor, caged, blood pumping too hard and quick. He turned back to the Deacon and held out his wrists, his white hands reaching out from the black sleeves, Christ-like. "I spill no blood, do you see? I have skin long healed." He suddenly spoke calmly. "You have no right to cut them open again."

Father McIntyre returned to his seat, his pupils round and black. "I'm not the same man you knew. That was a different life for me."

"Yes, I see that!" the Deacon cried. "I saw that the moment I stepped out of the car. But when I saw your face here, the stress, the hopelessness . . . it took me back. Just because we age doesn't mean old demons can't strike."

"My demons have long been dealt with, Robert. I'm among angels here."

"Then let me help you keep it that way," he urged. "There is an answer here, at least a temporary one. You need to use that girl's money."

Father McIntyre's neck flopped against his collar.

"Listen to me." The Deacon danced in his seat. "If the orphanage closes, where will she go? She'll be sent to a hospital or put in a work home or worse. You said yourself she has no future. Here the child is safe. Here she will be fed, nurtured, schooled as will the other children. An individual's need must be sacrificed for the betterment of the whole. You see? You have no other choice.

"Let me help you, Colin. If you're no longer a liability to the church, I can sway the Bishop to let things stand. But you must understand this money is only a bandage. This place is stagnant; there are no children leaving. You need to find adopters, donors, it's the only way."

Father McIntyre lowered his eyes and nodded, the fight gone.

Bishop Ridley and Deacon Johnson left at first light. The smell of salt air, no longer tainted by the car's trail of exhaust, entered Father McIntyre's veins, freshened the blood.

Father McIntyre stepped upon the path to the sea, sought shade below the pepper tree and closed his eyes. He pressed his palms against the blue-black dots of hair beneath the surface of his chin and cheeks, felt their points under his fingertips. When he opened his eyes, James was there, standing with his strange seriousness and silent dignity. The priest smiled at the boy, patted the ground. "Sit. Sit."

James folded his legs, bent his spine over the triangle of limbs.

"Haven't seen you much lately. Everything all right?" he asked. James nodded.

Father McIntyre focused on James's face, the frowning young lines. The Bible stuck out from the boy's shirt. He tapped James on the knee. "So, tell me what's got you reading the Good Book so intently these days."

James lowered his chin, shadowing the grass with the oval of his head. "I don't know."

"Then read me a passage that interests you. Surely, you've found some favorites."

The boy did not move; his chest did not rise or fall.

Father McIntyre laughed, plucked the book from the boy's waistband. "Fine. I'll choose one." He pulled out his glasses, opened the book to the middle. At first, his eyes blindly stared at the page, confused by the slanted, elegant handwriting. He flipped several more pages with his index finger, saw the dates listed in the corners. He closed the book, turned his face away. "How long have you had it?" he asked, his voice dim.

The boy's silence was long and pained. "Since the storm."

"Have you read it?"

"No," James answered. "Well, some."

"You shouldn't have kept it."

"Yes, Father."

"And I shouldn't have kept it from you."

James's mouth fell. Father McIntyre put the book in the boy's hands. "I was wrong to keep it from you." He gazed at the child. "I never read it, James. I hope you believe me. This was never meant for anyone's eyes but yours." The two sat among the rustle of sparse leaves for several minutes.

"Do you think . . ." James ventured, then stopped, bit his bottom lip.

"What is it, son?"

"Do you think I have relatives . . . in Ireland?"

He thought of that for a moment. "Hmmm. It's possible."

"My father was from there. Maybe I have uncles?" His voice pitched higher. "Maybe they would bring me to live with them?"

Father McIntyre pursed his lips and tapped his foot. "There's no way to know that, son."

"You could write a letter." The boy's expression changed and there was hope. "He was from Limerick. It says so in the diary. You could write the town or the church."

Father McIntyre ground his heel into the dirt and he was suddenly angry and he was too tired in mind to know that it was wrong to be angry. "Aren't you happy here?" It was more accusation than question. "Haven't I cared for you as a real father would? Haven't I taught you and loved you as a real father would?"

James's face fell and his chin pointed to his chest.

A pit filled the Father's stomach. "I'm sorry, James." He covered his eyes with his hands and rubbed away the anger. "I'm so sorry. I had no right to say such a thing." He squeezed his temples. "I'm not well today. The Bishop's visit . . . the stress of . . . I took it out on you. I'm sorry." He pulled at the boy's arm. "Do you forgive me?"

"Yes, Father." But the great hurt still clung to his voice and face.

"I'll write the letter, James. Just as you asked. I'll do it today. I promise."

James looked up and hope entered again, cautiously this time. Father McIntyre took the boy's face in his hands and cradled it. "I'll write the letter, James. But please don't get your hopes up. Ireland's a big place and O'Connell is a common name. I'll write the letter. But please, my son, don't dream too much."

James nodded, but the dream had already taken root.

CHAPTER 13

❧

They met at the cliffs every day—Leonora with bread and James with beetles and worms. They padded the nest with new, green leaves and refilled water in hollowed sticks. At times the bird beat her dead wing for flight and at others sat upon tucked legs while the meal was fed to her.

James plopped next to a scraggly yellow-blossomed wattle and leaned on his elbows, his knees bent at the cliff edge and his bare toes pointing down toward the sea. Leonora's legs crossed at the ankles as she swung them gently against the sandstone wall.

The two small bodies sat in quiet company under a sky rich and thick with periwinkle, mimicked by the ocean in both expanse and depth. Hundreds of feet below their toes, unfiltered rays played across the sea as light dances over diamonds, the ocean moving lazily, peacefully along its natural current, meeting the cliffs with laps that hardly splashed. Pelicans and seagulls bobbed effortlessly along the ebbs and flows, their bellies fat and tired from feeding in the clear water. And the children settled into the environment just like the birds and lizards and insects, as if they had always been there.

From the corner of his eye, James caught a glimpse of Leonora's long hair, the way each strand held the sun. She turned to him and smiled and the warmth spread across his skin until he had to turn away.

"Ireland's got cliffs like these," James announced too loudly. "Only white. White as powder. They're made of chalk. Did you know that? No different than the stuff they use on the blackboard. Father McIntyre's got a whole book about the place."

Leonora leaned on one hand planted in the grass, listened with full eyes to every word.

"They call Ireland the Emerald Isle 'cause of all the green," he continued. "The grass grows greener and brighter than anywhere else on earth. The houses there are white like the cliffs." He looked far off over the sea. "Must be so beautiful with all that green and white. Must look like a field of mushrooms." They settled their thoughts on the image.

"Ireland's got loads of sheep, too. Not brown ones like here but soft white ones. They got piles of potatoes . . . got so many in the ground you can't hardly put a spade down without digging one up. You've never seen potatoes like Irish potatoes, Leo. They're near bigger than my foot!" He stuck out his foot dramatically and her irises shone.

"Someday I'm gonna live there. Gonna build myself a little white house right atop those white chalk cliffs and I'm going to fill that green grass with sheep. Gonna fill it with so many sheep that when I look out my window it looks like clouds floating on a green sky. I'll shear them myself, too. I've been practicing. Probably have a patch of potatoes, too. Got to. Might even be the law that you gotta grow potatoes." He squinted and his eyes flickered with the thoughts forming in his mind. Leonora followed suit, trying to see what he saw.

"Every night I'll have stew so thick with meat and potatoes it'll be hard to get the spoon in. In the corner of the kitchen I'll set a butter churn. I'll churn it myself, I will. I'll slab that butter an inch thick on my bread and eat it at every meal." He looked over at Leonora and lowered his eyes in embarrassment at all his talking, but she only smiled, and when she smiled she brought his out of its dormancy and it didn't feel so odd anymore.

"You can come with me, you know. You can spin the wool. I saw you do it with Sister Margaret. I'll shear, you'll spin and we'll go into town and sell it and then get fat on butter."

Leonora rested her head on her shoulder and listened to his voice like it was a song. In the distance the church bell rang dully, and James's brows fell heavy again.

"I gotta get out of this place." He held his knees and rocked, looked out over the water. "Something about this place turns people mean and I hate it. Sometimes I feel like I could get mean and I don't want to." He looked at her desperately. "I don't ever want to turn mean, Leo."

A final ring rose from the bell, then died in the air. He watched her profile for a moment, noticed the odd way the sun etched the lines of her forehead, nose and chin as if they glowed. Then he threw his legs back over the edge of the cliff and laid his head into the grass playfully.

"Know what your problem is, Leo?"

Her face grew worried.

He smirked and closed his eyes. "You talk too much."

A few days later, James and Leonora met at the curved trail of the church. A rush of sprayed pebbles and laughter met their ears and Michael Langley and two other boys plowed over the stones, whipping past them. Michael turned, held his neck as if choking before running clumsily down the path.

James watched them disappear. "Ignore them, Leo. Bunch of idiots." When he turned to her she was still as stone, her eyes glued to the sea. Realization hit him slowly, but she knew already and a flash of heat shot through his veins. He tried to speak, but his throat tightened. "No, Leo," he whispered.

Like a snapped rope, she tore to the cliffs, but he was stuck with heavy feet, mired in dread. "Leo, no!" he screamed, and pulled his muscles to hurry and catch up.

He found her in the only place she could be, in front of a pyramid of boulders and a wild rosebush. He stood several feet behind and she did not turn around. Her body was stone again. James breathed hard through his nose and his lips stretched against his teeth. "Don't look at it, Leo. Don't look."

Leonora finally turned, her face pale. Her lips were open and her chin crinkled. Her eyes were wide circles of bewilderment and horror and grief so deep it physically pained his chest. James stepped forward. "Leo . . ."

But she turned from him and ran hard along the cliffs and he did not follow. His eyes fell to the ground, to the clump of yellow feathers that ruffled in the wind and stuck to the edges of the rosebush, and anger welled inside—an anger he'd never known, an anger that clawed his insides and made him dizzy with hate. He turned toward the orphanage and beat the path with a steady, determined pace.

CHAPTER 14

F ather McIntyre's cassock draped over his thighs as he pulled his legs uphill, the exertion laboring. The evening descended and the sky turned indigo. A thin slice of moon paled above the steeple like a lizard's eye.

Growing winds reminded him the ocean was near. Father McIntyre focused on his stilted breathing, surprised by how out of shape he had become. His black shoes navigated the rocks, temporarily flattening any long grass that grew between. A small wool blanket swayed in his arms. He crossed the line on the path between comfort and vertigo, but he huffed through it, knowing if he stopped he'd lose his nerve. He owed the child at least this much.

Father McIntyre found the little girl sitting against a gnarly gum, her head buried in her arms. He stilled for a moment to calm his breath and then approached, gently covering her shoulders with the blanket. "It's all right, dear. I've got you now." He picked her up into his arms and tucked her head into his neck. She was light as a feather.

Father McIntyre carried her away from the cliffs and the vertigo lifted. A few stars peeked through the darkest line of sky as he brought her into the church and settled her into his office chair.

"James told me what happened," he said quietly. "I'm sorry, Leonora. Children can be cruel. Deeply cruel." They were words that would mean nothing and he struggled for inspiration, swept his mind for words that could console. He lifted her chin. "Leonora?"

Her pupils rose slowly and met his and his heart pulled. He stared into aged eyes that had seen too much sorrow for one lifetime—old, sad eyes trapped in a beautiful sweet face that held no hate, though it had every right to. Father McIntyre knew those eyes, knew them so well that he saw himself in their reflection. A deep sadness overcame him and tears formed. Memories trickled to the surface and he could not pull away from her pain, his pain. He knew what he had to do, even if it meant opening a part of his past long locked away.

He fell into thought for several moments, his features grave as he gathered enough strength to proceed. He sighed, found the key tucked in the desk drawer. He took down a long wooden box from a shelf and brought it back to his desk, unlocked it. He hadn't looked inside since he was a child, but he never forgot for a moment what it held.

His bottom lip twisted as he held his jaw tight and pulled out a square photo. The paper, sepia with age and ripped slightly in the corner, had creases marking years of folds. His thumb covered one of the faces and he moved it slowly, uncovering his face as a young boy. Father McIntyre placed the photo on the desk. "This is a picture of my family—my mother and father, my two younger brothers. That's me with the hair sticking up." He pointed without joviality.

The sound of a rifle fired in his mind and he jumped invisibly. His nostrils flared; he could almost smell the smoke. "I was just a little older than you."

Leonora, still as a statue, stared at the picture.

"About a year after this photo was taken . . ." He paused. The rifle blasted again and he closed his eyes. "My parents . . . passed away." He swallowed the lump filling his throat, but it didn't pass. He remembered the feel of the gun as he tried to push it out of his father's hands; the coldness of it and then the enormous heat as it smashed his mother across the wall. An icy rush washed over him. He had watched paralyzed as his father turned the gun on himself and fired. "They went to Heaven," he said softly.

Father McIntyre pushed the gun, the faces, away and spoke clearly. "We were all alone, my brothers and me. We had nothing. No money. No food. No parents."

Her eyes were on him now, watching him closely from under lowered lids.

"I was sent to live with my uncle and his wife. My two little brothers were sent to an orphanage." Fresh pain stabbed as he remembered seeing their tiny, scared faces—two faces he promised to protect and never saw again.

"In less than a week, I had lost my parents and my brothers. In a matter of a week, my world crumbled." His gaze bore through her and fell far away. "I didn't understand. My whole world, my life, my family, swallowed up. I wanted it all to stop . . . the insanity to just stop. I didn't want to move. Didn't want to breathe. Didn't want to speak." He looked at her intently and said softly, "So I didn't. I folded into myself and I stopped talking. I just stopped."

Leonora's tiny hands tightened on the blanket folds.

"It wasn't something that I chose to do and my life was much harder because of it, but I just couldn't. Every time I wanted to speak, something closed. My uncle would scream at me to talk, hit me. The kids at school tormented me to no end. The more I was abused, the deeper my voice hid. I wanted to disappear, to fade away." He stared above her head as he spoke, as much to himself as to the child.

"I suffered greatly until that was all I had left in my life—suffering. I didn't want to exist anymore, Leonora." His face twisted and his eyes burned with restrained tears eager to fall. "And I almost didn't." He remembered the razor, the sharp pain from its blade and the calm. He remembered the bright blood and the hope, the flow of death. "I almost disappeared."

His gaze carried to her face, the sadness weighing in his dark eyes. "I don't want you to suffer as I did, Leonora."

Their eyes locked and a communion forged that went beyond age or gender—went below skin and resonated to the organs and blood. Beyond his pain and the memories, something screamed in victory. For this was what he had lost, the soul's connection to another, and the fire lit and spread across him to the parts that had begun to numb and take him over, and it overshadowed the blood and the pain and the death.

A tear filled the corner of the girl's eye where it sat heavily before releasing down the side of her nose, over her cheek, and then swept to her neck. It was the first time he had seen her cry and he smiled gratefully, for if she allowed herself to feel she could heal.

Father McIntyre rose from his desk and knelt, taking her little hands in his. He worked through a constricted throat and pleaded, wanting her to understand the significance of his words. "I know your story, Leonora. I know what happened to you in the desert. I know things have happened to you that should never happen to a child. Things that shouldn't happen to anyone."

Panic entered her face and he was afraid she might try to flee. He held her hands tighter. "I don't know why you were left, but I do know that it was no fault of your own. Only God knows why people make the decisions that they do. What's important is how you deal with the pain. Don't let it consume you. Don't let it turn to hate and consume those around you." He smiled weakly. "You have better days ahead of you, Leonora. This I promise you."

Warm tears fell from her face onto his hands and he squeezed her fingers gently. "I know you feel alone, Leonora. But you are not! You weren't even alone in the bush. God was and continues to be with you at every moment, protecting you, watching over you. Don't you see? You were meant to survive; you were meant to be found."

The warmth of truth seeped through his veins. "You were meant to survive. There is so much light in you, Leonora! I don't want you to fade into the darkness; God doesn't want you to fade into the darkness.

"You are loved, Leonora." His eyes rimmed with tears as he emphasized each word. "You . . . are . . . loved."

As he held her hands, something broke inside of her. A cry, almost inaudible, released from the depths of her soul. Father McIntyre's chest burned as he pulled her to him, holding her in his arms while her body shook with the force of sobs, her tiny body crumpling. In choked whispers, he repeated over and over in her ear, "You are loved, dear. You are loved."

Time did not move as they held together in the small and cluttered office. Only after her shoulders had stilled and her eyes no longer spilled heavy drops upon his sleeve did he pull away from the embrace. He put his hands on either side of her face and tilted her head until her exhausted eyes met his. He smiled. "You're still here, Leonora."

When he thought she was ready, he rose and held out a hand. "Come with me. There are some people who want to talk to you." Wearily, she took his hand, and they walked into the hall. The sky was fully black through the windows and the only light came from the open door of his office and the wider ones opened in the rectory. He brought her to the doorway. She froze and would not go farther when she saw the boys sitting in the pews, their backs toward her and heads down but for one.

"It's all right, Leonora. Trust me." He squeezed her hand and moved her down the line of pews. "Michael," he ordered fiercely, "stand up!"

Michael stood and turned around, his head bent. "I'm sorry, Leonora." He raised his head quickly, revealing a bloody nose and swollen left eye.

Thomas rose next. His left eye closed nearly shut and he missed a front tooth. "Thawwy, Leonowa."

Patrick stood, tried to blink beneath his bruised and cut left eye. "Sorry, Leonora."

"Go on to bed now!" Father McIntyre snapped. "You'll be doing Leonora's chores for the next month."

Leonora sat next to the boy in the last pew. His right hand was bandaged from fingers to wrist. A line of red bled through the gauze at the knuckles. And she leaned in and placed a small kiss to James's temple.

CHAPTER 15

And so they healed.

Supplies came first—lumber, mortar, bricks, nails, shingles—the tools to patch the orphanage. Plants and animals came second—trees, seeds, sheep and chickens—the tools to sustain it. Next, wooden crates hauled new textbooks from Australia, not from England, textbooks where Australia's history didn't end in the early part of the century, where more discoveries than the first Swan colony filled its pages and the maps proved that yes, Western Australia was a territory. Leonora's money, though not a lot, had gone far and Father McIntyre held no more regret in using it.

And so they healed.

James's hand mended and its wound left no scar, but the memory of his knuckles against bone had changed him. He hated cruelty, violence—it made him sick to his stomach—but this was different; this had been justice and he'd known nothing of it before. He had always felt the jabs and punches of inaction, a helplessness that soured and left him weak. But justice tingled his blood.

His mother's diary still held tight to his back at every moment, though gone was the fear of its discovery. And in the parts that he read the etchings of a mother and a father had begun to take form and they spoke to him with guidance. His mother was closest when he smiled or smirked or sat quiet without scowl. This woman was made of sun and warm breezes and the perfume of flowers. His father was closest when he worked or studied hard, when he grunted under the weight of filled burlap or galloped the horses at top speed. This man was made of earth and strong wind and the scent of freshly scythed grass. But he never felt his father so close as when he clobbered those boys and his father whispered in his ear, not with malice or with hate, but with righteousness. And when it was done, and his hand lay cut and open, there was approval and pride. For a man, a *man*, stands up for those who can't stand or speak for themselves.

And so they healed.

James was quiet next to Leonora and even the waves seemed hushed below their dangling feet. She scanned his profile, searching for the reason of his silence and with clear worry that she was the one who had caused it. But she needn't have worried. His silence was active and slightly embarrassed and had everything to do with the butterflies dancing in his stomach.

James stood suddenly and reached inside a hollow log cradled between roots. He returned with hands behind his back. He stared at the ground between them for a moment before thrusting out a hand, a brown-papered package held in his palm. "It's for you, Leo."

James bent to his knees and watched as her thin fingers pulled at the light rope that gathered the paper in a neat pinch. The brown paper opened and she did not move, did not blink.

"I made it," he hurried, then swallowed. "I've been working on it for weeks." His nerves twitched under the silence. "Do . . . do you like it?"

Still she did not raise her head or flicker an eyelash and his chest fell. He was a fool! A pile of sticks—tiny sticks intertwined with yellow feathers into a scrawny nest. He wanted it to remind her of the bird, the happy memories. He had even smoothed a small, white stone to a perfect egg and placed it in the middle. But it was fragile and rudimentary and laughable.

He blushed. "It's stupid. Never mind." He grabbed for it, but she pulled it to her chest defiantly and her eyes were stretched and wet.

He sat back then on his heels and the butterflies left his stomach and he knew she saw the beauty in the gift. She carefully pulled the brown paper away and let it float to the ground while she cradled the round weave of sticks and feathers delicately in her palm. She picked up the tiny stone egg and held it to the sun where it reflected perfectly in the light. She touched the yellow feathers tenderly, a slight smile upon her lips with a beautiful memory. When she looked at him again, her eyes were two glistening pools of wonder and gratitude.

Then the winds hushed and a new sound, never before part of the sea or the cliffs, a sound as delicate as flower petals and as beautiful as the tiniest songbird, wafted from the softest of souls. Leonora's lips parted. "Thank you."

And so they healed.

PART 3

CHAPTER 16

The medic's tent differed little from the diggers' save for size. Cream canvas, squared with four corner poles then peaked in the center with two more, could have been a tent for a traveling circus except that tickets were limbs and not a soul was begging to get in, just out.

Ghan hobbled to the tent, pulled back the heavy curtain door that flapped half-opened. The smell of ammonia, alcohol and lye, a three-ringed antiseptic nightmare, hit as a wall and he nearly turned back, but his wooden peg leg was stuck an inch in the mud.

"For the love a Jesus!" he cursed. The ground sucked like a wet kiss as he pulled the end free. He scanned the mud for its source, looked at the pitched roof for a leak, then asked to no one, "Where the 'ell all the water come from?"

"They sprayed the tables off," said a man smoking in the corner on a small wooden chair. A wool blanket hung from one shoulder and crossed his chest.

"Yeh, Bianchi?" Ghan asked. The man nodded, his face dripping with sweat.

"Crikey, yeh must be roastin' like a pig in that blanket."

The man's eyes were all pupils as he took another drag of the cigarette. His hand quaked violently. But it was cold terror that wet his face, not heat. *Poor bastard*. Ghan's stomach turned queasy. The canvas held in the humidity, suffocated the fresh air and reeked with sweet, rancid blood. He wanted to vomit.

Ghan's wooden leg picked blindly over the wet spots and clopped on the dry until he could safely sit down next to the man. Ash spilled from the stuttering cigarette onto the blanket, but the bloke was too lost in pain and fear to notice.

"Yer arm?" Ghan asked. No need to mince words.

The man nodded, glanced at the blanket's raised bump.

"Took my leg 'bout a month ago," confided Ghan.

Bianchi looked at the wooden leg and swallowed. He took a hard inhale of tobacco smoke, sucking his cheeks all the way in, and then threw the stub into the mud where it simmered. "I can't do it," the man said, defiant.

"Yeh gotta choice?"

"Maybe."

"Whot happened?"

"Burned," he said, paling further. "Nearly all the way through."

"Then ain't much left, is there?"

The man shot him a look of anger, then helplessness, his face gaunt with pain.

"Yeh got no choice," Ghan explained. "If yeh want that pain t'stop, yeh got no choice. Can't walk round wiv that arm sizzlin'." Bianchi smelled like a half-cooked chicken on an old fire pit. Ghan held his breath from the stink, couldn't look at the table or the tools. *Damn that doc for leaving them out on display like that.*

"The doc is good. It'll be quick," Ghan lied. "'Fore yeh know it, the sizzlin' stop an' yeh'll be good as rain again."

"But it's my arm. *My arm!*" The black pupils widened and Bianchi leaned in with panic. "Gawd damn it, a man's gotta have his arms. I got kids! How'm I gonna feed 'em?" He looked at Ghan's wooden leg with disdain. "One leg ain't stoppin' nobody. Yeh can still move; yeh can still work. Just gotta piece a wood 'stead of bone there now. But a man needs his hands, gawd damn it!"

Ghan narrowed his eyes. "Yeh done whinin', yeh pussy?" The man drew back with the verbal slap. "Got news for yeh, Bianchi. Yeh ain't got no arm. Know whot yeh got? Yeh got a stub of a match left hangin' there, so stop cryin' for somepin yeh ain't got anyway!" The young man's lips parted and drooped, the corners stuck with dried saliva.

"Yeh'll still work, Bianchi." Ghan tempered his tone. "Those kids of yers still get fed. Morrison's already got a place for yeh in the pickin' line. Not so bad, that pickin'. Done it m'self. Borin' as all 'ell, but safe. Won't need t'worry 'bout no more burns." The man was listening intently and Ghan continued, "They'll give yeh a hook or somepin. Won't be pretty, but yeh won't be crippled. One hand's all yeh need for pickin' anyway."

Bianchi's fingers rose to his mouth before he realized he didn't hold the cigarette any longer. He drew his hand into a fist and dropped it back to the blanket. "Does it hurt?"

"Naw." Ghan shrugged. "Not so bad." Blood ran from his face and he worried he might vomit all over the wool blanket. The sound of saw against bone ground in his ears.

Strange thing about pain, he thought. *Always worse when you know it's coming.* Ghan knew pain like a lifelong foe, but this kind of pain was different. He'd lost parts to explosions, to brawls with hard right hooks, but you never saw it coming, didn't even feel anything when it was happening, only felt it after the surprise wore off. But when a man plans for pain, waits for it and watches for it, sees the person who's going to give it and the tools he's going to use, the pain starts before anything even happens.

Ghan wasn't going to show this man his pain before it happened. Bianchi would see it soon enough. Any luck, the man would faint before the cutting started. "Doc has morphine," Ghan lied again. "Yeh'll hardly feel it."

Morphine. That's what the doc said it was. *Won't feel a thing.* Last thing the butcher said before he rammed a bullet between Ghan's teeth. *Morphine, my arse!* Gave him something that made him feel drunk but didn't numb the pain, just made him feel drunk and out of control, out of his mind with pain but too drunk or stupid to do anything about it.

The memories and the pain came back too quickly and his stomach cramped and kicked. Ghan rose stiffly. "I'll get the doc. Be over 'fore yeh know it." He fled the tent in jagged steps, galloped to the nearest tree and vomited.

CHAPTER 17

Morning dew held silver upon the grass, sparkled spiderwebs and dampened the soles of Father McIntyre's shoes as he met the postman in the arc of the road. He smiled at the sound of the fairy-wrens, their chirps waning with the morning light, fading away and evaporating like the mist in the sun. "Beautiful morning, isn't it, Mr. Cook," Father McIntyre greeted.

The postman pulled his head out of the canvas, his neck skinny, his face dark as cowhide. "Mornin', Father. Didn't hear yeh on the stones." He lifted a stack of letters tied with twine and handed them to the priest. "Saw yer ad in the paper." The postman scratched inside his large ear, then inspected his finger. "Gettin' many bites?"

"A few," he said sullenly. "Have two families coming this week to meet the children."

Mr. Cook scrunched up his face. "That's a good thing, ain't it, Father? Gettin' 'em children adopted is a good thing, no?"

Sure it's a good thing, Father McIntyre answered in his mind. Just like the cliffs and the ocean were good things. But they all made his head spin and his stomach drop. "Yes." Father McIntyre gave a weak smile. "It's a good thing."

Footsteps barreled onto the gravel. "Did it come?" James huffed between breaths.

The postman grinned, settled his hands on his hips. "Expectin' somepin, son?"

Father McIntyre patted James on the shoulder and rolled his eyes.

"He's been waiting for a letter from Ireland. I told him not to get his hopes up."

"Ho! T'day's yer lucky day, m'boy!" Mr. Cook clapped his hands. "Saw one in there. From Limerick, I think."

Father McIntyre's stomach dropped again. He shoved the letters into the crook of his arm, locking them with his elbow.

"G'day, gorgeous." Mr. Cook tipped his hat at the silent girl who joined them, then turned his attention back to the priest. "Be on m'way, now. See yeh in a few weeks, Father."

"Please open it, Father!" James begged as he held Leonora's hand, squeezing it in pulses.

With a sigh, Father McIntyre untied the pile of letters, shuffled until he found a thin blue envelope with an Irish stamp, the paper soiled and smudged. He ripped the glue that held the back flap and pulled out the card, read the words and blanched. He read them again, his eyes bobbing left to right, his jaw clicking near his ear.

James followed the priest's movements. "What'd it say?"

Father McIntyre closed his eyes. "I'm sorry, son."

"What?" The boy blinked fiercely and tightened his grip on Leonora. "What did it say?"

"There's no one there, James." He couldn't look at the boy. "I'm sorry."

"But the l-l-letter," James stammered. "It . . . it was . . . they sent it."

"The letter was from a priest I know outside Limerick." Father McIntyre exhaled and his eyes shifted under the lowered lids. "The O'Connells are all gone. They've either moved away or . . . passed. I'm sorry, son."

James dropped Leonora's hand.

"James . . ." Father McIntyre reached for the boy, but James jumped from his touch. He spun on his heels, splaying gravel as he ran, his head and shoulders plowing forward like a bull with a sword through his neck.

Father McIntyre's own sword lodged in his heart as he watched the boy hurl across the trail, felt Leonora's grief-brimmed eyes upon his skin. "He'll forget with time, Leonora." His voice was hollow and distant but crisp as ice water. "He just needs time."

Leonora stepped away, her feet angled toward the cliffs.

"Just leave him be, Leonora." Father McIntyre reached for her. "Give him space." But she was already gone.

A great loneliness hung in their wake. He should have never written the letter, and guilt spit cruelly. And so the priest did not rush but walked soberly and carefully upon the bleached pebbles until he reached that invisible line that he did not have the fortitude to pass. There, from the ridge where the sea is first seen and teases in a line above the cliffs, he saw James with toes pointed at the edge of the world, his arms clasped around his knees. Leonora stood behind.

James turned to her and shouted harshly through the sound of waves, pushed her away. The girl did not move. James leaned toward her and shouted again, his face red and wet with tears and anger. But still she stood, her arms hanging loose and immobile. James pounded the ground with his fist and then turned back to the sea and buried his head into his knees.

Leonora moved now. She inched beside him and lowered to the ground. Her tiny, thin arms wrapped around the boy's shoulders. James struggled against the embrace and she tightened her hold, her arms rigid as steel as she held him as a mother would a child. She rested her head atop of his and held his spine up. This waif of a girl did not let go but held his shoulders so they did not break and she took his burdens and carried them against her own sloped shoulders and her thin spine. And there upon the cliffs where the sea worked daily to beat the sandstone to crumbs, there could be no distinction of one child's grief from the other's.

A terrible thickness crowded the Father's throat and his nostrils flared to keep the tears at bay. This child comforted James when he could not. He brought James suffering and this child brought him warmth. The thickness softened in his throat, but the lines of his jaw grew rigid. Father McIntyre turned away from the children petulantly. To console was easy; to cause a child pain for his own good, for his own future, now that took brute, hard strength.

Father McIntyre stomped down the path, stomped away the tenderness, the warmth and the innocence. He kept his head down as he entered the church and slammed the door to his office. He dropped the pile of worn and traveled letters onto his desk, spilling them out of the loose twine. James's face, the boy's raw and open grief, pinched his mind. He covered his face with his hands, rubbed his eyes to rid them of the image. He should have never sent the letter. He could have spared the boy this pain. Father McIntyre pulled his fingers down his face. James would heal in time, he tried to remind himself. Maybe he'd even thank him one day.

The Father sat in his chair and leaned back, rocked against the natural bend of its frame. The fingers of one hand danced against the knuckles of the other until he stopped abruptly and snatched the open letter off the top of the pile. He read it again, carefully this time, and the petulance swirled to anger. He was angry he had written the letter. But he was angrier they had written back. Angry they were alive and wanted James.

His prejudice bubbled now. Some poor Irish farmer wanted James. His James. They shared a name and now they wanted him. For what? To plant potatoes and pull a donkey cart? Pull him out of school and work the brains right out of him? That was not the life for the boy— not for James. Not for his James. Name or no name, blood or not, the boy belonged here.

The letter was sent more than three months ago. His eyes settled on the last line, read it again and again until his blood chilled. They were saving money, coming to Australia.

Father McIntyre held up the letter, pinched the corners with thumb and index finger and tore the paper to pieces, sprinkled the scraps into the wastebasket. "Over my dead body."

CHAPTER 18

At the turn of the century, Perth could not compare to its splendid rivals across the continent, but to Ghan this was the biggest city in the world. And as he left the bush behind and passed the houses that grew in size and frequency and proximity to one another, he entered the city as a man braces for a hurricane, with body stooped and eyes shielded.

In no time, the buggies and weighted supply drays and the formidable Cobb & Co stagecoaches swallowed up the humble noises from his horses and wobbly wagon. The momentum of the city shook from all sides, assaulting Ghan's senses until direction blurred. The reins pulled tight, wrapped under his strained knuckles as he worked to hold the panicked horses against street-savvy carriages and trams that honked like geese and veered close, blasting exhaust, gray and heavy, into their nostrils.

Ghan grabbed his hat, wiped his face with it, traveled the streets until he found the Dayton Hotel, as large and grand as a ship, a line of black buggies lining the entrance. He took his place in the queue.

A man dressed in a dark gray suit with tails and a large top hat ran from the gilded doors, blowing hard into a whistle. "Get out of here!" he shouted. "Where you think you're going with that thing?"

Ghan grimaced at the red-cheeked man, the whistle an inch from his lips again. "Pickin' up my passenger!" Ghan hollered.

The man scoffed, "No guest here is riding in the likes of that! Go on now. I don't have time for games. Move this bloody thing out!"

"Not leavin' wivout my passenger," Ghan said stubbornly. "Go on an' look him up. An American—last name Fairfield."

"Fairfield, you say?" He turned and blew his whistle until a sweaty bellboy came fast as a lapdog. "Go see if Mr. Fairfield's expecting anyone?" Then he turned back to Ghan and pointed his finger. "Five minutes, then I'm calling the police."

Before the deadline passed, a man with a white suit, white hat and trim, neat white beard sauntered from the wide doors looking at a pocket watch. His arm linked with a thin woman who was a full head and shoulder taller. The whistle blower bowed to the couple and bent to hear the man, nodded with innocent surprise before pointing sharply at Ghan and blowing madly into the whistle. The other buggies pranced forward, made a U to the end of the line. "Christ, 'ere we go," Ghan muttered.

Before Ghan could descend, the bags were loaded on the wagon. The tall woman, dressed in blue silk with layers of fabric in darker shades of the same, was stiff, looked older than she probably was. A white-gloved hand pressed against her lips. She didn't try to hide her disgust and glared at her husband, pulled her arm out of his.

"Now, now," Mr. Fairfield said appeasingly.

"Don't 'now, now' me! Where's your carriage?" She didn't give him a chance to answer and tapped the shoulder of the top-hat man. "Where's his carriage? I would think your hotel would have better sense than to leave the lane open for vagrants."

Instinctively, he put the whistle in his mouth like a pacifier, and she slapped it from his lips. "I want an answer, not a whistle from your blow toy!"

"Eleanor, please," Mr. Fairfield soothed as he took her hand. "We spoke about this. They'll never give me a fair price if they see me riding in on one of those coaches. Besides, it's only a short trip." He prodded Ghan with peaked eyebrows. "Isn't that right, sir?"

Ghan cleared his throat. "Be there by nightfall."

The man winked gratefully, turned back to his wife. "You see, dear?"

Her lips twisted back and forth. "I don't like it. I don't like it at all, Owen." She set her eyes on Ghan and turned her mouth in unbridled revulsion, spoke as if he had no ears instead of one. "You don't even know this . . . *this man.* He could rob you blind, then leave you stripped at the side of the road. Then what would you do? For God's sake, Owen! I'll be a nervous wreck." Her American accent was rough and stern, loud like a man's.

"I'll wire you from the train station. All right?"

She stuck out her chin. "You'll wear your hat? I won't be seen with a human beet as a husband, you know."

"Of course, dear."

She tapped her foot. "You'll wire me from the station?"

"Yes, dear."

"Four weeks? Not a day more?"

"Not a second past."

Mr. Fairfield craned his neck and kissed her on the cheek. "Goodbye, dear." Then the whistle man took his hand and helped him onto the deck next to Ghan.

Out of the corner of his mouth, Mr. Fairfield whispered, "Just drive." Ghan stirred the horses quickly and the American mocked surprise with the sudden thrust, gripping on to the sideboard. He blew a kiss to his wife. "Love you, dear. I'll wire you at every stop." Ghan peeked back long enough to see Mrs. Fairfield pull her lace collar higher up her throat and scan the street, mortified she might be associated with the old wagon and cripple.

Ghan ignored his passenger, held his breath as he worked the horse through the choking streets. Sweat poured from his forehead as he dodged men and beasts and the moving, burping metals weaving around them, his concentration so tight between his blinders that he only saw what was directly in front. The outskirts of town grew steadily, widening and revealing more sky above buildings, buildings that were finally beginning to shrink instead of tower.

The two men rode in silence through the changing lanes of city and country. Ghan's eardrums opened from their clenched state and welcomed the fresh air, where sounds did not bounce over one another and boom in between buildings and hooves. The wagon crested a small hill and its slight rise made the city feel a million miles away. Ghan finally allowed his lungs to expand in the wide space. His body slumped and he pushed his hat high upon his head.

"Don't care for the city, do you?" asked his passenger. Ghan looked up, startled. Mr. Fairfield sat erect, watching him. His back did not touch the seat and his hands kept company on his lap. The man laughed. "Your shoulders were creeping past your ears, man."

Ghan consciously lowered his shoulders, relaxed his muscles. "Just not used to it."

Mr. Fairfield stretched like a lazy cat in the sun. He unbuttoned his jacket and threw it into the wagon bed, then unsnapped his stiff collar with a sigh and threw that into the dirt. He rubbed his neck. His fingers found the turn of the thick onyx cuff links and plucked them off, shoving them deep into hip pockets. Left to right, he rolled up his sleeves, then pulled out a pouch of tobacco and pile of papers. He sprinkled the tobacco onto a sheet, rolled it tight and licked the seal. "Smoke?" He offered it to Ghan, who shook his head again.

"Yer wife's right." Ghan eyed the man's white forearms. "Sun'll burn yeh crisp."

"I'll manage," he said good-naturedly. "I'm not supposed to smoke, either. She says it makes me smell like a chimney." He rubbed a sulfur match on the splintered wood and brought the blue flame to the pinched end of the cigarette. "I plan to smoke every inch of the journey."

"Fair dinkum. Yer right as a man," Ghan said.

"Spoken like a true bachelor, Mr. . . . ."

"Ghan."

"Ghan, huh? You a Turk?"

"Naw. Used to drive the camels like the Afghans."

Mr. Fairfield nodded and continued, "Of course, my wife is right about most things. But sometimes a man doesn't want to be right. He wants to be wrong and wants to try and get away with it like a snot-nosed adolescent. Silly, I know. Childish, but I can't help it. At the end of the day, I take my scolding and a kiss on the forehead." The feebleness of voice was left back in Perth and his accent was light and carefree, if not husky. He smoked between easy smiles. "You ever been to America, Ghan?" he asked.

"Naw. Never been outside Australia."

"Well, I've been around the world several times over and I'll tell you something, Ghan: Australia and America are about the most similar two countries can be."

Ghan tried to soak in the comparison.

"It's true," Mr. Fairfield explained. "Our two countries are the infants of the world, half sisters, really. We share the same mother England, but she got loose hips and invited men from Europe to father the rest of us until we're such a melting pot you can't tell who's got whose blood anymore. Except for the natives, of course."

Ghan listened to the accent, the flow of speech, the quickness and confidence of the man's tongue, as much as he did to the words. Maybe it was three days without company, but Ghan liked the way this man talked, liked the blend of words, their foreign dance.

"Australia and America are huge," continued Mr. Fairfield, addressing an invisible sea of listeners. "Got our towns and best land in the east and west, and dry land—the wheat and desert—in the middle. We both got the best beef cattle in the world and the toughest men herding them. No difference between our cowboys and your drovers—tough, sun-baked men as quick and handy with a whip as with a whore. Those are men who are men, who make mateship a religion. I'm a lady comparatively." Mr. Fairfield stopped suddenly and cocked his head. "I'm not chatting your ear off too much, am I, Ghan? Give me the word and I'll shut up."

They were quiet for a minute before the man started up again, languidly this time. "It's nice being in a country where they speak English." Mr. Fairfield turned to Ghan. "Know what makes our accents so different? Australians always sound like they're asking a question and Americans always sound like they got the answer." He laughed hard. "Yes, sir, Americans got an answer for everything."

The American put his shiny calf leather shoes on the footboard. "You've never heard of me, have you?"

Ghan shook his head.

"Would it surprise you to know that most people have? You see, Ghan, I'm a very rich man," he said without affectation. "Never set out to be rich, though. Studied to be a geologist. Always had a fascination for rocks and earth, the streams of minerals and the pressures that can harden rocks into diamonds or soften them to oil. Seems I had a knack for sniffing out hot spots. Before I knew it, I had a copper mine in Utah, a coal mine in Pennsylvania and a silver mine in Nevada. Got mines all over the world now.

"So, that brings me to why I'm here with you," Mr. Fairfield explained. "I'm looking to expand in Australia. I've been watching this gold rush with open eyes. Saw the same thing happen in California not long ago and I know where this is leading."

"Afraid yer too late," Ghan noted. "Bush is already burstin' wiv big minin' companies. Can't be too much gold left."

The American nodded in agreement. "Exactly, my friend. I don't want the gold. All these men working with their picks are blind to anything but the gold. Let them keep it. I want the nickel, the ore, the stuff that don't shine but the stuff the world needs way more than gold."

Mr. Fairfield pulled an elbow back, inspected him. "What's your manager like? Mr. Matthews."

Ghan rolled his eyes. "Bastard's a piece a work."

"How so?"

"Lazy. Mean fella." A sly look crept across his face. "Guess yeh can't blame 'im."

The man leaned forward expectantly. "Do tell!"

"Well, Mr. Matthews got a big ol' house not far from the mine an' his wife is always comin' down sayin' this or that is broken—pipes, waterspout, door hinge. Always wiv the whinin'. So, Mr. Matthews gotta dig up a miner from the pit an' send him to the house."

The American scrunched up his face. "Can't the guy fix his own place?"

"S'not his house needs the fixin', yeh see." Ghan gave a sharp wink. "Mrs. Matthews gets the servicin', if yeh know whot I mean."

"You're pulling my leg."

"Strike me down dead if I am! Each bloke sent to the house comes back skippin' like he got a mouthful o' sugar. She ain't picky, either. One day, Matthews sent one-eyed Earl over an' when he got back, his one eye was stretched so full wiv twinklin', yeh thought the scarred one gonna pop wide open!"

"That's a good story, my friend." Mr. Fairfield closed his mouth, clicked his tongue against his teeth and raised his eyebrows mischievously. "A very good story."

The men sat silently for a spell, sucking in thoughts and breathing them back out through the nose. "Mind if I ask yeh somepin?" Ghan scratched the stub of his missing ear. "Why'd yeh bring yer wife wiv yeh? Ain't she gonna be all alone?"

"She's heading to an orphanage up the coast from Geraldton." The skin of the man's face sagged, his voice quieted. "We're adopting a little girl."

CHAPTER 19

❧

Eleanor Fairfield arrived at the orphanage with an entourage of high, stiff collared and scissor-trimmed mustached men. The three lawyers surrounded her in a triangle of dark gray suits, but the woman rose in the middle, long and thin, dressed in green emerald from ankle to throat, a ribbed line of white lace blooming under her chin, and it was not hard to tell who held the power.

"Mrs. Fairfield," greeted Father McIntyre as she emerged from the group. "Welcome."

She offered the priest her hand, gave a limp bend of the wrist as a handshake. Scanning the priest, she made obvious note of the wrinkles in the cassock, the day-old stubble. "Father McIntyre," she acknowledged. "This is Mr. Newton, Esquire."

The two men shook hands and she did not bother to introduce the other two lawyers clutching matching black leather briefcases locked with brass clasps. Father McIntyre swept the way with his hand. "Shall we?"

Eleanor Fairfield rivaled Father McIntyre for height. She was not an old woman, but she held the toughness of old meat in the set jaws of her face, and had there been no expression she could have been described as pretty; however, a rigid line ran from her hairline down the bridge of the nose and spread to curveless lips, squeezing away any natural beauty.

"What part of America are you from?" asked Father McIntyre, trying to make up for his slovenly appearance.

"Pennsylvania. Pittsburgh."

"Ah, yes. I've heard of it." He smiled dully as he pulled two wooden chairs to wing the leather ones already planted in front of the desk.

"So," he began formally. "I understand you would like to adopt a child from us. A girl, is that right? Do you have an age in mind?" The words had become mechanical.

"I'm interested in meeting Leonora."

"Leonora?" Father McIntyre blinked.

"We've been researching the children available for adoption all along your West and believe she is best suited."

"Why is that?"

"It's not important," she said, flicking her hand. "Is she bright?"

"Yes." He tensed with her tone. "Very bright."

"Is she pretty?"

"Yes."

"Good." She leaned her shoulders back slightly. "I'd like to meet her now."

Father McIntyre cleared his throat. "I must tell you, Mrs. Fairfield, there's an adoption pending for Leonora."

"Why wasn't I aware of this?" she snapped at Mr. Newton. The man twitched and glared at the other lawyers, each slumping. Mrs. Fairfield rolled her eyes, turned back to the priest. "No matter. I'd like to meet her."

Father McIntyre found himself standing and moving like a trained puppy down to Sister Louise's class. He opened the door in interruption, nodded to the nun and motioned to the little girl in the back row. "Leonora, please come with me." The children watched her closely as she passed between desks and took Father McIntyre's hand.

Back in the office, he introduced her gently: "Leonora, this is Mrs. Fairfield. She was interested in meeting you."

Eleanor Fairfield raised her chin above the lace and passed her eyes over the girl. "Turn around, please!" she ordered.

With shuffled steps, Leonora turned in a small circle.

"She's pretty," the woman assessed with certainty, not compliment. "How old are you?"

Mrs. Fairfield cocked her head at the child's silence. "I asked you how old you are."

"She's eight." Father McIntyre smiled softly at the girl. "She's very shy, Mrs. Fairfield. She rarely speaks."

"Well, I suppose that could actually be a benefit. A quiet tongue is better than a loose one." She passed her eyes over the girl again. "All right. You may go." She waved a hand in dismissal. "I've seen enough."

Leonora searched the priest. "Thank you, Leonora," he said. "You can go back to class."

When the door closed and the child's footsteps had faded away, Mrs. Fairfield folded her hands. "I'll take her."

Father McIntyre disliked the woman, the fact settling affirmatively in his lower abdomen. "I already told you, Mrs. Fairfield. . . ." He paused indulgently. "Leonora is unavailable."

Her eyes glinted. "You did not say she was unavailable, Father McIntyre. You said she had an adoption pending. Be clear with your words, sir," she warned.

"To me," he said with his own warning, "they clearly mean the same thing."

"Has a contract been signed?"

"Yes."

"How much did they pay?"

He squirmed before the words came. "A good home for a child is payment enough."

"Huh!" She smiled for the first time. "Then she is quite available." She tapped her purse. "I'll pay twenty-five thousand dollars for her."

Father McIntyre froze, his eyes growing helplessly.

The woman smiled again. "That's a lot of money, isn't it, Father McIntyre? The church would give a priest a hefty promotion for bringing in that kind of money, don't you think?"

His Adam's apple rubbed against his collar. "I have no interest in personal ambition."

"Of course not!" She laughed and met the crinkled eyes of the lawyers. "No man of God ever has eyes for himself."

His face set sternly. "Believe what you want, but the children are my only interest."

Eleanor Fairfield nodded slowly, a thin grin curving the corners of her mouth. "Then I suppose it would not interest you that you may be out of a job soon. Bishop Ridley is looking to close the orphanage." Every pupil tracked the priest's face in the dense silence.

Father McIntyre's feet chilled below the desk. He did not breathe; his body did not shift; only his eyelids batted spastically.

The glint grew in her eye with the priest's pallor. "You've either made some enemies in high places or done little to please your superiors, Father McIntyre." She petted the pearl buttons of the purse like it was a cat. "I'm sure twenty-five thousand dollars would show the Bishop that the orphanage is worth saving."

"The orphanage is made of stone and mortar," he answered quietly. "And can crumble into dust at God's whim." He brought ice to his gaze and continued through clenched teeth, "A child is worth saving. Leonora *is* worth saving. Your money's no good here, Mrs. Fairfield. Leonora's happiness is not for sale."

"Ah, such godly sentiment! I'm very touched, Father McIntyre." A throaty cackle escaped the woman as she dabbed at an imaginary tear. "But what about the other children here? Surely, their happiness, their security, is worth something." Her eyebrows rose sadistically. "Or perhaps . . . you hold special feelings for pretty little Leonora?"

Father McIntyre's lips blanched. "How dare you—"

"I speak purely of devotion, of course," she interrupted, then swatted the air to clear it. She tilted her neck, studied him calmly. "Believe it or not, Father, we both want the same thing for Leonora even if our means might differ. I can provide her with a life most children could only dream of. She will have wealth. She will get a superior education. She will see the world and have a family name that is rich in heritage and esteem." She paused. "You should be thanking me, Father. You know the fate that awaits orphans, especially girls like Leonora."

A flicker of kindness lit her face only to be smashed by something that had no patience for empathy. "Let's assume for a moment, under some grace of God or blind stupidity, you deny us adoption rights for Leonora. You could keep her within your protective sight, but the age limit for residence is sixteen, so then what? Her options are to be married off to some vagabond with no future or to work as a barmaid in a seedy pub."

"You forget about the couple who want to adopt her," he reminded.

"And *you* forget that the people who come here are poor. She'll be put to work. It'll be a hard life for the child."

The room fell silent. Father McIntyre felt the words, the truth of Leonora's future, like a pulse. A bead of sweat trickled from his temple and rolled under his ear. The hands of her destiny were shifting and he held the crank.

Eleanor nodded as if he had answered a hanging question. She relaxed her shoulders, tamed her voice. "The contract for Leonora's pending adoption is of no issue. Mr. Newton will find the holes in it and you won't face any liabilities even if the adopters decide to argue, not that they would have the money to fight it legally anyway. It's a non-issue really. Tell them whatever pleases you. It's no concern of mine." She flapped the words off in the air like a bad smell.

"My lawyers will draw up our own contract and you will sign it, along with the Bishop," she continued. "I'll be staying north of Geraldton for the next month. You can come there to sign the papers. At that time, all records on the child must be relinquished with no copies left behind. Are we clear?" She did not wait for an answer. "I'll send a tutor who will work with her until we depart in a few months. Leonora has two months to drop the accent and learn ours perfectly. She'll be taught proper etiquette and our family history. We haven't much time."

"What if she can't meet your demands?" he asked bitterly.

"Why, Father," she cooed. "Have ye no faith?"

CHAPTER 20

❧

Leo wasn't at breakfast, hadn't been there all week. James looked at the empty chair every few seconds to see if she appeared, looked at the wide main door for her entrance, but she didn't come, and her absence hung like dust-speckled cobwebs. He knew where she was—stuck in that tiny office with that mealymouthed tutor. The room was nothing more than a converted supply closet, only now it held a desk and two chairs, the mops and brooms shoved to the side.

James spoke as rarely as Leonora now. There was nothing to talk about and no one to listen. He floated through sleep, through waking, did not speak of Ireland, tried not to think of it. The old talk of emerald grass, of wool and chalk cliffs, of sheep and warm fires, seemed the talk of silly toddlers, of treasure chests and fairies, and he wasn't a child anymore.

This was his life. He felt the deadness of it, the black corners that boxed him. His thoughts were empty now and they had been so full not long ago. So full there was little room for any others, and now they were gone and the void tasted sour in his mouth and thumped like steel drums in his chest.

James gave a final sigh to the empty chair before returning his plate and fork to the kitchen. The gray tutor shuffled into the dining room, grabbed a plate from the cook and sat down. He'd never seen her eat outside the office and his heart galloped. James took off quickly and ran past the two classrooms to the end of the hall.

Without knocking, James threw open the door. Leonora shot up from the chair and backed against the brooms. "Sorry, Leo. I didn't mean to scare you." He waited for the shock to leave her face, waited for the smile that took away the deadness, but she just stared.

"Hurry, Leo. That pigeon lady's having breakfast." He held the door open wide. "Let's go before she gets back."

She stood perfectly still, her eyes wide. James approached. "Don't worry; she won't get mad. We'll be back quick."

Leonora leaned farther into the brooms and shook her head.

"It'll be fine. I promise." He grabbed her hand. A small cry left her lips.

"What's wrong, Leo?" Icy fingers tickled the backs of his legs. "What is it?"

She hid her hands behind her back. Gently, he reached for her right elbow and pulled her arm to him. Her hand was in a fist and then she opened it, slowly, palm up.

It took a moment for the red lines across her palm and fingers to register. His heart thudded hard and rough as he reached even more gently for her other hand. An open cut bumped across her knuckles, the palm raw as the other.

White rage, sharp and cold, pumped through every vein as he stared at the tiny beaten hands. He looked into her face. "Don't!" she begged.

But he was already gone, running blind with fury, down the hall. He did not look for the tutor but ran to the rectory, to Father McIntyre's small office, and pounded on the wood door with the side of his fist. There was no answer. James pounded again. He heard a shuffling behind the door but still no response. James pressed his shoulder against the door to force through the bolt, but the door opened easily; it was not locked.

Father McIntyre came through the bedroom door, his hair matted on one side. "Is all that banging really necessary, James?" He plopped down at his desk. "Why aren't you in class?"

James slapped away the question. "Why didn't you answer the door?"

Father McIntyre gathered a pile of papers and collected their corners. "I was resting."

"That's all you do," James seethed.

Father McIntyre looked sharply at him. "I don't appreciate your tone, James."

The white rage took over and James landed both palms fiercely on the desk, their sudden smack sending the priest inches off his seat. "Wake up!" James shouted.

The priest sat stunned, then slowly rose. "Don't raise your voice to me, young man!"

James stuck out his chin, his eyes deep and black and blind. With one hand, he picked up the desk lamp and hurled it against the wall. The glass shade shattered against the floor, spilling thick, clear oil around the shards and open wick. "How could you?" James's breath came quick and fierce through his nose, the rebellion raking his body.

Father McIntyre gazed dumbly at the mess on the floor, his expression as broken as the lamp. He searched for clarity in the oil. "I don't know what you're talking about." But then, through the haze, Father McIntyre reached for the boy, suddenly lucid. "I'm sorry, James. Please, don't hate me!" he begged through a warped smile. "I was only trying to protect you."

"Me?" James shouted, aghast. "This has nothing to do with me!"

"It has everything to do with you, my son! Don't you see?" The disconnect was growing. Nothing about his words made sense. "I had to think of your future, protect you. The letter . . ."

"What letter?" James shook his head, pushed aside his own question. The Father was talking like a fool. James closed his eyes in disgust. "You're supposed to protect her, not me!"

Father McIntyre clamped his lips tight, swallowed something that had tried to escape. He met James's eyes and this time he was awake. "Tell me what you're talking about, James."

"Leonora," he said with palpable pain. "How could you let them hurt her?"

Possessed, Father McIntyre tore down the hall. James tried to keep up as they headed to the storage room. They could hear voices behind the wall. Father McIntyre pushed the door open with such force that both Leonora and the tutor jumped.

"Let me see your hands!" he ordered. Leonora was immobile with fear. The priest checked himself, calmed his voice. "You're not in trouble. Please, let me see your hands."

With eyes turned to her feet, she raised her cut and bruised hands. Father McIntyre held them as if he handled shredded glass. His upper lip rose above his teeth and his face burned red.

"Leave now!" he ordered the tutor.

"I had no ch-choice," the woman stammered. "She has much to learn in little time and can be painfully slow. Some days she hardly speaks!" She eyed the girl accusingly. "Mrs. Fairfield gave me strict instructions."

"You're fired."

"Mrs. Fairfield hired me and only Mrs. Fairfield can fire me." The woman's voice wobbled with fake authority.

Father McIntyre dropped Leonora's hands and faced the woman. "Leave now before I take the switch to you, Mrs. Applegate." He picked up the stick next to the desk and waved it perilously close to her cheeks.

Mrs. Applegate grabbed her purse to her stomach, her face ashen, and turned abruptly, her heels clicking against the floor as she fled through the hall like a blown dust ball.

Father McIntyre seemed to forget he wasn't alone. His eyes flickered left and right and he mumbled under his breath, swinging the switch against his shoe. He turned then and noticed James, dropped the stick to the ground under the boy's gaze. "James, ask Sister Louise to wrap up Leonora's hands."

"I'll wrap them." James's voice was hard and deep. He moved in front of Leonora, shielded her protectively. "I'll take care of her."

CHAPTER 21

❧

"I'm going to Northampton." Father McIntyre pushed savagely past Sister Margaret and weaved between children. He did not pack a bag, no water or food. He did not saddle his horse but rode bareback, kicked her sides roughly, sending pebbles flying under hooves.

Father McIntyre had been drowning in the muddy water, the pull of sledge beneath his feet stronger than his will, but now anger pulsed and dangled a branch into the water and he clutched it with both hands. The brown mare barreled past the church onto the cliff road. Vertigo swirled. Father McIntyre kept his eyes closed, turned his head away from the endless waters. He hugged the horse's neck as if it were a ledge, its hair reaching into his nose and whipping his face. And he stayed this way until the crash of the sea weakened.

He thought of Leonora's little hands, red and swollen, and he unbent his spine, kicked the horse harder. His black cassock flapped loudly above the hooves, the sound resolute as they flew. Balled fists held the reins—the hands of a man, not the hands of a child; whole and clean hands, not cut and sore. He was not a child, he was a man, and it was his job as a man to protect a child.

In Northampton, the priest's legs were stiff and heavy from constant clutching and his thighs twitched like a cow trying to rid herself of a fly. For a moment, his reserve wobbled, but he forced the picture of Leonora's hands to his mind as he entered the red-carpeted lobby of the Duxton Hotel, saw her knuckles as he took the wide steps two at a time. He needed the anger to keep him strong and alert.

He breathed hard, closed his eyes to channel her wounds and gave three hard knocks to the double pine doors of the Fairfield suite.

"Bring it in!" Eleanor Fairfield's voice rang from inside.

He pounded again. She opened it swiftly and snapped, "I said you can bring . . . !" Her eyes widened. "Why, Father McIntyre, this is unexpected! I thought you were Housekeeping back with the laundry. Please, do come in."

The sitting room was plush with Oriental carpets and polished oak. A large, gilded mirror owned half a wall. Mrs. Fairfield lowered into a high-backed chair, a queen on a throne, and motioned to the horsehair sofa. "Please, Father McIntyre, have a seat."

"I'll stand," he said coldly. "I won't be long."

"All right." She studied him carefully, sleepily. "So, to what do I owe the honor?"

"I've come to talk about Leonora."

"So I guessed. However, I was expecting you later in the week. No matter. My lawyers just finished the paperwork, so you can sign the contract today. It will save you another trip." She reached for a brown leather case and placed it on her lap.

"There won't be an adoption." The words smoldered, heated the lining of his mouth.

"Is that so?" Eleanor Fairfield raised her eyebrows and the corners of her lips tipped in amusement. "And why is that?"

Father McIntyre tried to hold his temper, but his ears burned and his bottom lip trembled. "I won't allow a child to be beaten!" he growled.

Her brows dropped, all levity erased. "What are you talking about?"

"I saw her bloodied hands!" His teeth chattered. "I won't tolerate child abuse!"

Eleanor Fairfield pushed her back into the chair and stared at the right wall, ruminative. When she turned back, her face was drawn and serious. "I'm a hard woman, Father McIntyre, but not a violent one. Mrs. Applegate hit her?"

"Don't play games with me, Mrs. Fairfield. She said you gave her strict orders."

"Yes, to teach her, Father McIntyre!" she defended. "To teach her, not hurt her."

Her anger mirrored his own, sapped him. He tried to push her. "I fired the tutor."

"Good." She nodded. "I'll find a replacement."

The fight waned. He needed the rage, the fire. "I believe the result will be the same, Mrs. Fairfield. Your expectations are too high for the girl."

With that, the softness left her face and the glint returned. "I can assure you, Father, I want her bruised no more than you do." She leaned forward, defiant. "However, I'm surprised by your passion on the subject. 'Spare the rod, spoil the child'—isn't that the saying, Father? I've always heard the church was a strong proponent of corporal punishment."

"The only outcome of abuse is fear and a broken spirit."

"Mind you, most of the world thinks differently," she toyed. "I have to say, you impressed me with your vigor just now. I don't have much trust in priests. Find them quite selfish and out of touch." She clapped quickly with wrists held high. "Let's start fresh, shall we?" She pointed again to the sofa. "Please, have a seat and let me get you a drink."

His legs were suddenly weak from the gallop, the anger. He drifted to the sofa, his figure dwarfed by the large camelback. "I'll have tea." He wasn't sure who the enemy was anymore.

"Tea? No, have a drink with me. A real drink and a chat."

The priest took the brown drink from her hands and did not ask what it was.

"You've never inquired about my husband," noted Mrs. Fairfield as she took her own drink and sat back into the throne, crossing her long legs leisurely. "Don't you want to know if he's a good man? After all, he's also adopting Leonora."

"So," Father McIntyre asked flatly, "is he a good man?"

"Yes," she answered. "He's smart and good and kind. Kinder than me. You would like him. He's in mining, in case you were interested."

"I'm not." It felt good to pinch her ego. Father McIntyre leaned back, his whole mind and body alert to her moves. He sipped the liquid slowly and she smiled as if his silence tickled her.

"So, tell me, Father . . ." Mrs. Fairfield gave a quick laugh to a passing thought and sipped her own tall drink. "What did you tell the couple that wanted to adopt Leonora?"

His fingernails bit into his knees. "I told them she didn't want to go with them."

"Huh!" She laughed and held her glass up in a toast. "Brilliant! Blame it on the child. A noble choice." Her tongue played in her cheek. "I'm guessing you aren't a very good liar, Father McIntyre, which of course can be a virtue or a curse. So, tell me, did they believe you?"

"No." He released the pressure on his knee. "I don't think so." He raised his eyebrows and turned back to his drink. Through the glass he could see his fingers, warped and bloated, could see the shadow of her form in the bottom as she watched him. "Why is it so important that Leonora be the one?"

Her foot dangled from the dress, the hem flirting with the air. "Because she's a ghost."

"I'm not following you."

"She leaves no fingerprints. She has no past, no history, no name. If she disappeared tomorrow it would be like she never existed at all. *Poof!*" She snapped her fingers. "No one would know she was gone."

His expression turned hard as granite. "I would."

"Yes," she said, smiling. "And I've taken precautions that you'll never share that information."

"The contract?" he scoffed, nearly spilling his drink. "A name signed in ink is only as strong as one's word. A man's word may change over time. Even a priest's."

She laughed. "I'm not an idiot, Father McIntyre. My lawyers tear through contracts daily. I know of how little worth they are. No, my assurances go much deeper, I promise you."

Mrs. Fairfield stared into her glass, seemed to search for words within the liquid. "My sister recently passed away."

"I'm sorry," he said automatically.

She shot him a look of buried pain and snarled, "Don't be sorry for me." She composed herself, rubbed the folds of her dress. "Anyway, she was in Sydney when she passed, a mental facility. She hanged herself." She said the words calmly, but her neck lengthened. "I was the one who sent her there. Thought Sydney the farthest civilized place I could find, and I was right."

With a sudden switch, she smiled and raised her glass. "I invented a story, Father McIntyre. I was quite elaborate in my telling, too. All about my beautiful, brilliant sister living the exotic life in Australia. I even created a daughter for her." She pinched her lips. "I don't make many mistakes, but that was one of them. When my sister died, everyone wanted to know what would happen to the child. 'The poor darling!' they cried. 'Surely, you'll bring her home!' they cried. 'A child must be raised with family!'"

Eleanor Fairfield put the drink to her lips and finished it, rattled the empty glass in her hand as if calling for a waiter. "And that, Father McIntyre, is why I'm adopting Leonora. She will be my long-lost niece and the only history she will bring is the one she is taught."

Father McIntyre's mouth fell open. He wondered if she was joking, but the truth sat in the frigid, set lines of her face.

"Ah," she said. "I've shocked you. You think I'm a woman without a heart."

Eleanor studied him, then reached for her checkbook. "I promised you twenty-five thousand dollars. If it helps you sleep at night, I'll make it thirty thousand."

The corrosiveness of the money severed all restraint, and before he realized it he whipped the pen out of her hand and threw it at her feet. "I'm not in the business of selling children!"

She stood and faced him, her tall frame matching his own.

"That's where you're wrong, Father. You sold Leonora just like a slave, auctioned her off to the highest bidder."

"How dare you!" He tried to find an excuse, felt his own mind cripple. He stammered, "The ch-children . . . I was trying to help—"

She cut him off and paralyzed him by the poison of her words. "You teach them and train them and then sell them off to people too poor to hire proper help." She pushed him into the murky water. "Your intention might be godly and noble, but the outcome is the same." She tore the branch from his hands. "You throw them to the wolves and pat yourself on the back as they're eaten!" She held his head under the waves.

He stepped back. The room closed and he couldn't remember where the door was. "Why?" he asked, desperate. "Why are you saying these things?"

She inched toward him. "Because beneath those black clothes, you are a man. You may indeed be a good man or you might be a bad man, I quite don't care which. But once dressed in that suit, once leashed with that collar, you become something greater than a man, don't you? You become a man of God; you become a treasured child of the Heavens. What a prized and fortunate human you are. The ultimate hypocrisy! You see, naked you are a man, as weak and flawed as any other. Clothed you are a priest!" An old scar revealed itself in the rawness of her tone. "I dislike hypocrites and I hate priests!"

The water filled his lungs and plugged his ears until every part throbbed and drowned. In his mind he ran from the room with fury, but in truth he fled slowly as a coward and the door slammed against his back.

CHAPTER 22

Father McIntyre slept through the first bell, then through the second. When the mid-morning toll hollered from the church eaves, he buried his head into the pillow before using every will to rise. He was already late for his meeting with Deacon Johnson.

His pants were wrinkled from sleep, but he did not change them and lifted his soutane from the floor, slid his arms through the sleeves, the fabric thin and coarse. Sluggishly, he buttoned the long row until his fingers fell to open loops. Two buttons were missing. He rubbed the gaps and wondered how long they had been absent, wondered if they had ever been there.

In the office, Deacon Johnson sat behind the desk, situated his glasses upon his nose. He didn't look at the priest and his face contracted. "You met with Mrs. Fairfield."

"Yes."

"How's the new tutor working out?"

"She's not drawing blood from the child," he said. "That's all I care about."

"You understand the terms of the contract?"

"Yes."

The man leafed through the pages, thick as a book, fanning them through his fingers. "The Fairfields have generously donated thirty thousand dollars to the church."

Father McIntyre shook his head in disgust.

Deacon Johnson grew quiet, his neck splotching pink. He pushed the contract to the priest. The Bishop's signature slanted low and sleek, the Deacon's squat and illegible. Father McIntyre dipped the pen in ink. He scribbled on the empty line and slid the papers back.

"Where are her files?"

"First drawer." Father McIntyre offered no more assistance, watched indolently as the Deacon rifled through his personal files.

Deacon Johnson played his fingers over the tabs and pulled out the gray folder, flipped through the few pages within its cover, closed it, then dropped it into the metal wastebasket. He lit a match from a small cardboard box, placed it to the papers like a kiss. Flames wrapped the corners, curling and blackening. The name *Leonora* twisted for an instant before engulfing in blue fire, reducing her small history to smoldering ashes.

Father McIntyre's body stiffened, his mouth hard. "A little dramatic, don't you think?"

White smoke clouded, but neither man pushed it away, just let it linger and spread until diffused. Only the burnt smell remained. Father McIntyre remembered Eleanor Fairfield's words: *Like she never existed at all.* Poof!

The Deacon turned his gaze from the ashes to his hands without moving a muscle in his face. "There are to be changes, Colin. The need in this country continues to burden our resources. If we are to have any impact, real spiritual impact, we need missions and priests to run them. It shouldn't come as a surprise to you that the Bishop envisions this site as a seminary." The Deacon rubbed his temples. "The Fairfield money will be used for that purpose. Two new buildings will be constructed, the rectory expanded. The road will be widened from Geraldton."

The room was stale, moistureless. Father McIntyre's throat parched. "And the children?"

"Some will stay; the rest will be placed elsewhere."

The words were hanging, their meaning indigestible, simply lodged somewhere between his head and chest. "Why keep any of the children here?" he asked bitterly. "Why not move them all, send them to work the fishing lines, send them to tuck dynamite in the mine shafts?"

"It was one of Mrs. Fairfield's conditions." The Deacon sighed, his face crimson. "As long as Leonora's anonymity is maintained, the orphanage remains in some capacity."

Father McIntyre laughed then. Sick, choked laughter that erupted and teared his eyes.

"She's brilliant. Simply brilliant."

Deacon Johnson shrank from the priest's gaiety as one avoids the ill of mind.

"She twists the knife, then makes me grateful she hasn't pushed it through my heart. Brilliant." He saw her mind clicking and he was awed by his opponent. He laughed absurdly. "You see," he spouted, "she had no guarantee that I would keep my silence about Leonora. She knew I could sign a contract—knew we could burn any physical trace of her, but there were too many gaps for a loose tongue. So, she cut it off, you see? Ah, her brilliance shines like a hot pitchfork, doesn't it? If she dangles the children, just enough, it alone guarantees my silence."

"You're overanalyzing, Colin. She just wants what's best for the church and her new daughter."

"Her niece," he corrected sourly. "Her long-lost, dear niece."

Deacon Johnson's cheeks sagged, the skin flaccid. "You don't look well, Colin."

"I'm not." He stood to go, spent. "I'm not well at all."

"Colin." The Deacon's voice rose. "Sit down. There's more."

Father McIntyre crushed his nose against the door, turned and sank back into the chair. "Of course, there's more!" he cheered.

The Deacon's face was soft now, tired as his own, and his heavy cheeks drooped farther next to his receding chin. "Do you know Father Brennan?" he asked quietly.

"No. Should I?"

"He's a Roman Catholic. One of the priests at Saint Rose. He does a lot of work with the poor, immigrants. He's a good man."

Father McIntyre waited, distracted, not understanding the Deacon's point.

"A couple came to see him," the Deacon went on. "Newly arrived from Ireland. They had your name with them." He paused for a moment. "Said they had written you but never heard back . . . about James."

His body grew brittle as glass, and had there been a breeze, he might have shattered.

The Deacon continued cautiously, "Name was O'Reilly. The wife's maiden name is O'Connell. Like James's." The man raised his eyebrows, joined his hands together on the desk and swirled his thumbs atop and under each other. "I know how you feel about the boy."

It was all breaking now. Shards ripped across his chest. His mouth opened and closed like a fish in open air, but not a word leaked out.

"It's his family, Colin." Pity hung in every crease of the Deacon's face. "It's where he belongs."

"You don't understand." Father McIntyre's voice cracked. "James is not like the others. He's kind. He's smart. He's..." His eyes searched wildly to say something sensible. "He's better." Father McIntyre beseeched his friend for understanding. "James could be a doctor, a lawyer. This isn't his destiny, Robert. Please. He's better than that, better than those people."

"They're blood." The Deacon reached out as he would in a sermon. "Colin, you've given everything to these children, saved nothing for yourself. You're only a man. Do you understand? Only a man. You can't change what's out of your hands."

Father McIntyre blinked, his eyes dry. It was done. The decision had already been made.

Deacon Johnson rose slowly from behind the desk, leaned his spread fingers on the edge. "I'll be taking James to them myself, if that helps any. They're setting up the home now, not far from the Southern Cross. I've been called to do a funeral out that way, so the timing works." He tapped a knuckle on the wood. "We leave in two days."

Father McIntyre lowered his head into his hands, let the world go black. He listened to the Deacon's footsteps, felt the hand pat him lightly on the shoulder, heard the creak of the door.

"Do you want me to tell the boy?" the man asked before he left.

"No." Father McIntyre's voice was hollow and dead. "I'll tell him."

CHAPTER 23

James knelt next to a row of saddles and rubbed the lanolin into the darkened leather, his hand soft as a baby's from the oiled cloth. The sound of boots drew his attention to the path and his brows pulled. Father McIntyre's form was tall and dark against the blue sky. This was a man he did not know. The priest who used to laugh and smile at the wind had disappeared. James pushed the cloth faster against the saddle.

Father McIntyre stooped and inspected the work. "Isn't this Hugh's job?"

James stopped and bit his cheek, his brow tightening further. Hugh had been adopted three months ago. "I don't mind," he answered coldly.

Father McIntyre touched his shoulder. "I need to talk to you, son."

Son. He wasn't his son. He wanted to smack the hand off. "Yes, Father."

Father McIntyre sat upon the ground, clutched knees against his chest, his face gray and drawn like a lamb soaked in the rain. "I just want you to know," the Father began. "I just want you to know that I've always tried to make the right decisions for you and the children." He looked far away, his lips pale pink, nearly white. "Especially for you, James." The priest paused, held up his neck, blinked past grass and sky. "I lied about the letter."

James didn't understand. *The letter? The* letter. Recognition finally entered.

"You have an aunt, James," Father McIntyre sighed. "Your father's sister."

Sweat beaded down James's neck and along his forehead. He was too shocked to be angry, too shocked to feel anything except the pounding of his heart.

"They've come to take you home."

"To Ireland?" The question fell out.

"No. Australia. They moved here for you."

James's skin was live and pulsing. Hope and relief expanded his rib cage. The windows opened, the doors thrown wide, and only one thought formed in the breeze—*I'm going home.*

"James," Father McIntyre interrupted. "There are things you should know." The priest tried to look past the hope in the boy to the part that needed to think clearly. "They are poor people." And then he whispered, "It may be a hard life, James."

James didn't care about money. He didn't mind work. He didn't understand any of the tone in the Father's voice.

"You don't have to go, James," the priest pleaded.

"I want to go." His voice was unwavering. "I want to go home."

Father McIntyre bowed his head. "You leave tomorrow."

At this, a hand seemed to grab James's throat; his heart sped again and did not leave lightness in his chest. Without thinking, he pulled at a goldenrod bloom, the bright pollen falling between his fingers, staining them yellow. *Yellow. Gold. Sun. Light.* His stomach went inside out. *Leo.*

CHAPTER 24

James was leaving. Leonora saw it in his round eyes, in the talking brows that always spoke his thoughts; she saw it in Father McIntyre's face, in the shadows that he dragged. The priest's light flickered like a candle near a draft and she could not look at him without shrinking from his pain like a slug under salt.

If the sea and the sun and the cliffs were beautiful, they only paled next to James. For she loved him as only a child can love another, with arms stretched so wide and open that the expanse of the world could fit in the embrace and there would still be room to spare. Her heart nearly split in joy for James, to know that his family had come, that he should get the life he deserved, and until the morning that was enough.

Then it came. The dawn. She met him in the hall. Did not have eyes or thoughts to the Deacon or to the Father waiting by the door— only James, his clothes packed in an old work shirt, the sleeves tied as a handle, his knuckles white with clutching. He saw her, too. For a moment, neither moved, only stared, breathed.

"I'll check the carriage over," said the Deacon. "A few minutes, James. That's all."

There was panic in James's eyes. Leonora squashed her own as she took his hand. He looked down at her fingers, his nostrils flared. She squeezed his hand, pushed the burn away.

He shook his head then, almost angrily. "I don't have to go." He looked at her quickly, then away as if she hurt his eyes. "I'll stay, Leo. I'll stay if you want."

She bled like a bruise below the surface, blue and black pain that spread under her skin while her face remained unchanged. She pulled him by the hand and he followed. The burn grew hot and rough inside, but she would not acknowledge it, sent it to her toes, told it to wait. She walked him into the hazy morning. *Step, step, step.* Absent, dreamed movements; it was all a dream—the thick mist, the gray horses strapped to the carriage, the parsons black as shadows.

Leonora pulled James to Father McIntyre, the man's eyes rimmed red. She let go of her friend's hand but stood close. Father McIntyre reached out blindly, his hands shaking, and hugged James tight. A cry left the priest's throat and then he pulled away, his face, his body twitching.

James glanced at the Deacon already sitting in the carriage with reins in hand, then turned to Leonora. She smiled through the fire, held him steady with her eyes, held him up by the arms with only her will. His voice cracked. "I can stay, Leo."

"Go." Her pitch was high, nearly too thin to hear. James blinked in a daze and turned to the carriage. He was stuck in the dream, too.

His back had only just turned when the first tear dripped from her eye, trickled down her cheek and landed on her lips still poised in a smile.

James sat in the beaten leather seat. The Deacon smacked the reins and the horses found their rhythm. James's back swayed with the carriage. He did not look back and for this she was thankful, for the burn threatened to take over if he met her eyes.

The carriage crept through the haze, turned gray. James's brown hair muted but was still visible against the back of his neck. Then the white took over and he disappeared in the mist.

Leonora turned to Father McIntyre, a granite statue. The priest was gone, swallowed up in black instead of white. In his place stood cloth and skin and eyes, all stone, blank and flat.

The darkness came for her now and something far and deep shrieked in terror. The burn from a life not so long ago, from an early-morning dawn, returned. She knew those lost eyes, that tremor in bony fingers, the drawn face of a broken man. She remembered another broken man, another father who had dropped her hand and vanished into the very air. The tears released. Tears that flowed thickly around her eyes, blinding them and soaking her cheeks and the collar of her dress. She wanted to scream, wanted to shake his arms: *Don't break! Don't leave me!* But the man did not hear her sobs, did not see her, and turned blindly to the church as a ghost.

Alone in the silence, again. The waves hushed, the birds absent. The trees did not wobble a leaf and there Leonora stood with the panic circling about her chest. She could break and she felt the cracks and she shook her head plaintively. Leonora squeezed her eyes tight, knew how easy it would be to just give in, to crumble in the dust until it all disappeared, but part of her fought hysterically, the fear of vanishing worse than the pain.

She pulled through the despair to the one face that was not broken—James. She focused every thought and feeling on him. He was going home. She pictured him in the arms of his new family, in a life where his brows were never knit, and she smiled through the tears. If his life was happy, then she would not break.

Leonora's body opened again, the grief still whole, but she was still there. She reached for every beam of goodness James had brought her and she clutched it to her ribs and scratched through every other memory to collect the crumbs and remnants of him and she tucked them secretly and hoarded them in case they tried to escape.

Leonora stood tiny and straight against the expanse of the seaside land and did not break. But the lesson had been taught well and she would not forget. It joined the threads and pulled tight and knit hard into the fabric of her being.

They all left her in the end.

Chapter 25

❧

The night sky domed from one end of the earth to the other as Ghan set up camp with the American in the emptiness between Woolgangie and Coolgardie. In the moonlight, the flat plain glowed ice blue, the few spindly trees silhouetted blacker than the sky beyond. Stars were not diamonds on this night, but solid orbs that hung as low as the horizon.

"Never seen a sky like this. Not ever in my life." Owen Fairfield gazed with head tilted back, his palms held against the base of his spine while Ghan set the two tents. One lantern haloed the camp as he broke mulga scrub into the burning pyramid. There was no wind and the fire burned straight, sending white smoke toward the stars.

"What do we have for eats?" asked Mr. Fairfield as he rubbed his hands together.

"Same as last night." Ghan dug through the canvas bag and pulled out a knife, a pot, a couple cans and jars. "Beans an' salt pork."

"Start cooking, then. I'm starving."

Ghan chuckled. "Can't believe yeh like this slop."

"Man can only eat so much stinky cheese and goose liver, my friend."

Ghan warmed with the reference. "Wait till we get to Lake Douglas. Fix yeh some brown trout an' crayfish. Roast it over the coals whole. Bet yeh ain't never tasted anything so good."

"Mouth's watering already." The man clapped his hands. "Got any coffee?"

"I'll probably burn it. Just warnin' yeh."

"Blacker the better." The man sat down on a half log that Ghan had set near the fire. "This is your life, isn't it, Ghan?"

Ghan sawed the tin can with his knife until bean juice splashed his fingers. "S'pose it is."

"You're a dying breed."

"I know." He dumped the beans into the blackened pot.

"When you think we'll get to the Pilchard Mine?"

Ghan searched the sky for the North Star. "Day after next. Mid-afternoon."

Fire licked the dry twigs, sent light flickering over their faces. An owl called out in the night, waited for an answer, called out again. The bush air was cool against their backs while sweat glistened body parts close to the flames. Mr. Fairfield raised his eyebrows mischievously. "I've been thinking about that story you told me about your boss: Mr. Matthews. About his wife gallivanting with the workers." He shut one eye in focused thought. "You think Matthews knows what his wife's been doing?"

"Still tryin' t'figure that one out." Ghan chuckled. "Don't know if he's just too stupid t'see it, or if he don't care. Missus ain't much t'look at, but still wouldn't want Earl's gums suckin' on my wife!"

Ghan put the pot on the fire and the flames sizzled yellow against the juices and hardened quickly against the sides. He picked up the slab of salt pork and sliced off chunks into the beans. The cooked salt and sugar tasted good even in the nose.

Ghan stirred the beans and ladled them onto two tin plates. He handed the scalding dish to Owen, who set it on the ground quickly. Then Ghan took the smaller, clean skillet and added the coffee grounds and poured water from the bag. "Have t'make it in the skillet," he explained. "That's why it burns."

Owen wasn't listening, his eyes thoughtful and dark, slit like a snake's. "I'm going to buy the Pilchard Mine."

Ghan swallowed. The man was going to buy a mine. Just like that. Buy a bloody mine. Said the words as calm as if he were buying a pair of socks. "Owners are Swiss," Ghan offered weakly. The words came out mumbled.

"What's that?" Owen leaned in.

Ghan was suddenly jittery. "Hardly ever in Australia, is all."

"No matter. I'm in Switzerland frequently," Owen said lightly.

"Whot if they won't sell?"

"They'll sell." He met Ghan's eyes and they were cold, odd in his pleasant face. "I always play fair, at the beginning. I'll offer a fair price. The gold is gone and they know it. If they're smart, they'll sell at my first offer. But sometimes these guys get greedy. They'll smell the blood in the water and try to keep me from getting the meat that's hanging. I'm willing to entertain them for only so long and then I lose patience."

"Then whot?" Ghan listened with tight muscles.

"Then," Owen said as he picked up a fork of beans, "it gets ugly." If a voice could be a color, his would be black. The tone was too much of a contrast to his easy banter and Ghan stirred the coffee briskly, the syrupy bubbles popping over the sides, the burnt smell of coffee filling the smoke. He took it off the fire to cool.

"Every man has a weakness, Ghan. Some have more than one. Purity is an angel's halo in a Rembrandt, not a man's life."

Now that the food had cooled, Owen shoveled it in quickly between words. "If a man is being difficult, I find his weakness and exploit it." *Scoop, chew.* "Sometimes it's gambling or drink." *Scoop, chew.* "Sometimes it's women." *Scoop, chew.* "Sometimes it's young boys."

Owen Fairfield scraped his plate clean. "Seems the richer they are in money and power, the more degenerate the vice." He pushed the plate away and took a cup of coffee. "I find the chink in the armor and use it—it's not pretty." He looked sad for a moment, then triumphant. "When I'm done, they sell for a song and are grateful they got out alive with skin intact."

Owen finished his coffee and spit out the grounds, wiping his thin white mustache with the back of his hand. "Every man's got a weakness, Ghan. Even you."

Despite the scalding coffee, a chill raised the hairs on his arms. Old training turned tinges of fear to defense. He rubbed his wooden stump and insult rose. "Yeh talkin' 'bout my leg?"

"No, my friend. Rest easy. Your leg has nothing to do with it," he answered easily, moving the conversation up and down like a wooden yo-yo.

"Work," he said. "Work is your weakness. You need work like a man needs breath in his lungs. You got no family, no girl, nobody but yourself. You'd do any kind of work just to do it, just to keep breathing." Owen stood, stretched to the sky, then took out his bedroll and laid it against the log for a pillow. "It's a noble weakness, Ghan, so don't take offense. Noble, but lonely."

Ghan chewed on the words but not long enough to awaken anything deep. The American turned to him and said sleepily, "I like you. I could use a man like you in my corner. You're better than working for transport. You're loyal, honest. I'll remember that, Ghan. I will. Hell, maybe I'll bring you back to Pittsburgh with me."

Ghan did not know praise and he tried not to let it tickle his stomach like a feather. But the praise tasted good and sparkled over the horizon. Praise didn't mean anything from a stupid man, but coming from a man like Owen Fairfield, it meant something. Ghan spit out his bitter coffee grounds, but the words still tasted good in his mouth and he grew bold. "Whot's yers?"

"My weakness?"

"Yeah."

"My wife." He gave a resigned laugh, closed his eyes to the stars. "Always has been."

If the Bailen Mine was a village, the Pilchard Mine was a city. The town swelled around the pit, a wide-open sore in the land, descending in rings like a flat rock skipping upon water. Shacks, humpies and tents freckled the outskirts. Everything grew from the mine—the telegram and post office, the market store, two restaurants, a blacksmith, a livery stable. The mine paid the workers; the workers paid the businesses. The businesses were funded by the mine, so the money went right back to the deep pockets that started it all.

Two boardinghouses kept the drink. Pubs weren't allowed within the immediate miles of the mine. But drinking was a vice that could be contained, not eradicated, and the boardinghouses had their rooms in the basement with the cards and the drink. Ladies for hire were brought in every Wednesday by train.

The stores were open but traffic light. All the men were underground. The acrid air settled in the nostrils and the back of the throat. The metallic clang of the mine's poppet vibrated through the ground. Ghan's horses flared noses, their gait nervous.

"Drop me off at the main office!" Mr. Fairfield ordered.

Ghan followed the steel hammering. The smell of raw ore and rock thickened the air, made a man's teeth hurt. There was no beauty here. Gray-blue smoke eclipsed the sun. Hard dins made the chest thump in unison. No flowers. No birds. Only tools. Rusty metal. Men.

"I'll be here awhile." Mr. Fairfield buttoned his white coat and Ghan stopped the wagon so he could get off. "Park the wagon on the main street," he directed without looking back. The man was a sight walking into the office, strong and confident, nearly mean in intensity.

Ghan parked the wagon and stretched his leg, took off the peg, let it throb unrestricted. He didn't mind waiting. Waiting was easy as moving. A minute's a minute whether you're sitting or walking. He took out an apple and munched into the warm skin, each crisp bite cracking the sound of pounding metal in the air. Ghan figured the meeting would take most of the day. *Might as well rest a spell*, he thought lazily. Owen never said where they were headed next. Might need to drive all night. Ghan chucked the apple core to the dirt and climbed in the back of the wagon, rested his head against his swag and fell asleep to the mine's brittle lullaby.

Ghan woke with a dry mouth. A line of drool stuck to his whiskers. When he wiped his cheek he felt the indent left from the edge of the bedroll. He drank deeply from the water bag, tied on the wooden peg leg and pissed behind a tuart tree. He brushed the horses, filled the feedbags and waited against the wagon.

No sign of Mr. Fairfield, or anyone else for that matter. He looked toward the manager's office and smirked. "Give anything to be a fly on that wall," he said out loud. Ghan scanned the storefronts. The boardinghouse looked decent, its full verandah screened. There were tables and chairs set up for the restaurant. He was getting hungry.

If the meeting went well, maybe Mr. Fairfield would want to celebrate, Ghan thought. Seemed like the kind of bloke who would.
Maybe they'd spend the night. *How about that for a kid from the Sydney
slums? Staying in a fancy hotel on an American's dime! Probably eat a steak
in the dining room.* Of course, he'd be just as happy under the stars.
Then again, he argued with himself, *fine living like this doesn't come
around every day.*

This rich American liked him and it felt good. He was getting used
to it, didn't feel so odd anymore. Almost like the man thought he was
smart, nearly treated him like an equal. Kind of a glow about it. Who
knew where this could lead. Plenty of mines he could show the man.
If he did it right, if he showed him the real story like he wanted, hell,
he could pick his work. As mines went, Bailen was on the bottom
rung. Pilchard would be good. Nice to be in town. He could work at
Pilchard. *Hell, there's always Pittsburgh. Never had options before.* The
faint smell of hope, sweet and foreign, tickled his slanted nose.

A young bloke came out the side door of the brick manager's office,
jogged head down to the wagon, a grin on his lips like he was listening
to an old joke. Ronnie Peters. Ghan met him a few times during transport. Snot-nosed office assistant trying to make his way up.

"G'day, Ghan." The half boy, half man waved.

"G'day," Ghan answered, shoving his hands into his pockets.

Ghan watched the boy's face for clues from the meeting, but Ronnie just scratched his head, widened that shit-eating smirk. "Damn,
that bloke got stories!"

"Been travelin' wiv him awhile." Ghan nodded, proud in familiarity. "He's full of 'em."

Ronnie reached an arm over the side of the wagon and hefted out a
bag, set it on the ground before reaching in for the big leather satchel.

"Whoa," Ghan warned. "Those belong to Fairfield."

"I know." Ronnie pulled the heavy bag to the ground and reached
for the next. "Told me to bring 'em in." He grabbed the last one, placed
it on the pile, then slapped Ghan on the shoulder. "Yer free t'go, mate."

The kid's voice waffled between insult and stupidity. Ghan leaned
back into the wood of the wagon, crossed his arms at his chest. "Naw.
Gotta wait 'ere for Mr. Fairfield."

Ronnie cocked his head. "Yer done, mate. He told me t'send yeh on yer way."

Ghan spit on the ground and grinned at the kid. "Must of heard wrong. Got another week on the road at least. Probably just wants t'stay in town for the night."

"Yeh his mother now? Heard him just fine." Ronnie scowled. "He's in there smokin' cigars an' sippin' scotch. He says, 'I'm not moving any more north. When a man sees what he likes, he doesn't go any farther.'" The boy's American accent was piss-poor.

Ronnie beamed. "Naw, I heard every word. Bloke talked t'me like a mate. 'Ronnie, my boy!' he says. 'Bring me my bags and send that poor man home!' Then he says, 'I swear if I sit on that rickety wagon one more minute my nuts gonna crack like a walnut!'" Ronnie laughed hard at this, rubbed a palm over his eyeball, then picked up the bags, strained under the weight.

Ghan swallowed something rough and jagged in his throat. A tightness crimped his belly. *Poor man.* That's what he called him. *Send that poor man home!* Heat inched from the tightness and flushed into his face and he shrank against the wagon. "He say anything else?"

Ronnie thought for a minute, shifted his weight from one foot to the other. "Oh yeah, said yer ear givin' him the bloody creeps!" He hoisted up the bags. "Christ, cover that thing up, mate. Gives everybody the bloody creeps."

Ghan watched the half man wobble across the street, followed his movements hollowly until he was obscured in the building. The words punched his gut, quick jabs that repeated with each replay. For a second, he thought he had heard wrong, chalked it up to a cocky kid, but he knew the rhythm of Mr. Fairfield's speech, felt its flow in his weakening limbs.

The office door slammed and laughter filtered out before the men. Mr. Bradley came out first, Mr. Fairfield next, white and clean, his arm around the man's shoulder. A fat cigar hung in the corner of his mouth, the soaked tip bloated as he spoke. Another two men followed and then Ronnie, galloping in their dust.

The men veered in Ghan's direction and he sighed with relief, pulled himself together, postured like a soldier waiting for a salute.

But then the group turned, crossed the street toward the boarding-house, the party giving him no more notice than the wagon or the horses or the dirt. Their laughter trailed off, then swelled again as they entered the boardinghouse.

The flush throbbed quicker this time. The air pushed dry and hot and his mouth filled with spit. Ghan looked at his foot, the leather boot as red and dust covered as the ground beneath it, the sole worn down on one side from years of crooked walking. The stick leg posed beside it, skinny, hard and ugly—useless as the dead tree it came from; useless as the man who perched on it.

The street quieted; the drone meshed with his pulse. Behind the walls of the boardinghouse, down in the basement, Ghan knew it was not quiet. Whiskey would slosh, fill the air sweet, mingle with sweat and ripe breath. Stories would be shared, grown and added to; jokes would dirty by the sip. Laughter would fill the cracks, drown out the sound of clinking glass.

Ghan's bones were tired. The pull to stay, to see it out, to hold out for something shining in the haze, made moving hard. But he cursed and rolled a fist, thought about smashing it into his own nose. Wouldn't feel it anyway; wouldn't change a damn thing.

The horses were quiet as they waited for him under the sun. A man could beat a horse and it would still wait for him. *Not right how people treat animals. Not right what people do.*

Ghan gave a last, quick glance to the boardinghouse and then pulled himself onto the hard seat, shifted the pit from his chest to his gut. He heard Ronnie's words again, except the voice was Mr. Fairfield's: *I swear if I sit on that rickety wagon one more minute my nuts gonna crack like a walnut!* The heat flushed again. *That ear giving me the bloody creeps!* Ghan sat still for a moment, looked at the white scars along his arm, bold and round in the light. He picked up the reins and gently stirred the horses, turning them back to take him home.

Ghan stuck the key into the hole, turned and pushed, but his shoulder landed flat against the hard door. He jiggled the key again, tried to turn the knob. *Damn it.* He was so goddamn tired. His bottom was numb and hot from the wagon; his stump ached like it was pinched between two thumbs. Now he'd have to hunt down that lazy Pole to let him in.

On the gravel, he favored the good leg while the wood leg stuck out like a thorn. Ghan found the Pole at a table outside the butcher, playing cards with three other men. Not a single one raised a head as he limped over. "My key ain't workin'," Ghan announced.

Lupinsky chewed a fat cigar squeezed in the side of his mouth, the stub so short it was nearly flush with his lips. He threw down a queen of diamonds, chuckling. The man to his right rolled his eyes, threw down his cards.

"I says my key ain't workin'!" Ghan snapped. *So help me, if that Pole don't get up I'm going to turn this table over.*

Lupinsky looked up at him now, his fat, round face poked with greasy black shoots. "No vrent, no vroom," he answered with a shrug. The Pole spread out his flush and laughed as the third man shoved his cards away.

Damn manager late on the bills again. Jesus Christ, all I want to do is to lie down. Ghan pushed on across the street to the brick office at the edge of town. With each step, he pressed his lips together against the pain and focused on resting his head against the cot.

The cool was instant in the small office. Ghan wiped the sweat off his neck with a stained handkerchief. Andrew Morrison, the assistant manager, came in through the back door buttoning up his fly, then noticed Ghan with a jump. "Crikey, yeh scared the crap outta me!"

"Just got back," Ghan stated. "Had to drop that American off at the depot."

Andrew suddenly looked down at the floor, scratched his chin nervously. "Crikey."

"Matthews late on me rent again," Ghan grumbled. "Pole done locked me out."

The scratching increased. The man's fingers clawed the back of his neck like he had fleas. "Whot yeh go an' do, Ghan?" He stopped scratching and put his hands up. "Why yeh go an' blab all that stuff to Fairfield?"

Ghan's leg trembled, the peg clicking the floor like nervous finger taps. "Whot the 'ell yeh talkin' about?"

Morrison sat down at the edge of the desk, his shoulders hunched, his hands holding his knees. "Yer a good bloke, Ghan. Hardest-workin' bastard I've ever known. Told yeh that b'fore, an' I'll say it again. Nearly kills me I got to be the one t'tell yeh."

"Tell me whot?" he asked. "If yeh need me outta the boardin'-house, just say it. I don't mind livin' in the camp."

"Ghan." The man leveled his eyes, the tone and look raising the hairs on the back of his neck. "Matthews came down yesterday hot as piss. Said you've been waggin' yer tongue to that American bloke. Never saw 'im so angry, like somebody shagged his wife or somepin."

Morrison's eyes lingered on Ghan's face. "I'm sorry, mate, but yer fired."

CHAPTER 26

James gone. His son. And in his place, a hole with sides that did not mold together in scar tissue but widened with each breath. And the hole dripped blood, soaked the footprints left by each of Father McIntyre's steps.

Life moved slowly now in the blackness. Nothing the priest did was without great effort and he dragged from one useless moment to the next as a sleepwalker, existing now at a great distance. Noises and chatter from the children were hollow, echoing as if from a cave. Food had no taste, and if he ate he didn't remember doing so.

The priest turned into the barn and closed the red door behind him, his eyes adjusting to the dim light. In looking for something familiar, he found only a cut wound. James was all around this place. The pitchfork leaned against the wall and waited for the boy's hands to lift and work it. The hay piles were disorderly now, stale, since none of the boys were as thoughtful as James in their duties. The horses were quiet. They missed him, too. The void of the boy was everywhere and it choked the priest.

Shadows hovered above doorways, in corners. Cobwebs hung and joined the eaves with silk, and beside them all Father McIntyre sat fully aware of his own blackness. Sun filtered in particles through the cracks between the boards, forming white lines across the floor. Emptiness. His face twisted for tears, but none came. Tears needed feeling to push to the surface, and his insides were numb and cold as an empty well.

Father McIntyre turned his palms up, stared at the blue veins that connected his hand to his wrist. He touched the scars that lay healed and horizontal. The lines sickened and warmed him all at once. For a moment there was longing. For a moment there was a future where the pain would stop. Then, in a fury, he pulled his wrists into the sleeves and crossed his arms, tucking his fists in his armpits. He closed his eyes and rocked against the shadows.

April 9, 1902
Afternoon

No record would be written or kept of her departure.

The coach, six horses deep, must have been the finest Northampton had to offer. The driver's suit and hat showed no signs of dust or grime. The Fairfields were not present. Only Mr. Newton, Esquire, awaited the party.

Mrs. Fanning, the new tutor, short and squat, not much taller than the girl at her side, lifted a hand for the lawyer's support as she entered the open door of the carriage. Leonora waited at the wheel, both hands holding a small suitcase. She was dressed in a pale blue dress, white cashmere stockings and black patent-leather shoes that did not have a single crease. Her hair was pulled back in one long tail, tied at the top with matching blue ribbon.

"Good-bye, Father McIntyre." He did not recognize the voice. Leonora's Australian accent was washed away, the words American now, even and perfected. There was no whisper or shyness in her tone. She had learned well. She hadn't had a choice.

Father McIntyre was the mute now. He did not reach to embrace her shoulders. He did not promise that all would be all right. He did not ask her to trust him. He wanted these reassurances from her, but she was already gone. The carriage left before he even knew it had pulled away.

With her departure, the darkness swelled thick and fat. The light left and followed the little girl like a sieve. It did not matter that no clouds dotted the blue sky; it did not matter that the sun's smile was wide and open—it was a round rip in the blue that scalded his vision.

The shadows crept from the ground, carried numbness to his toes, through skin, across his chest, stalled his brain. No thoughts told him to turn from the drive; no intention moved his shoes over pebbles. He didn't hear the crushed sticks underfoot.

Flashes, memories, replaced sight. Old sounds played in his ears. A shot of gunfire hatched, its dull rhythm reverberating. It came again, bounced his joints.

Blown to bits. Bit by bit. The carnage of his world unmasked in one full sweep. His mother's body shattered. His father's holed and gaping. His brothers ripped, their chasms manifesting into real wounds, then death. And here he hid, like a whole, selfish fool. Hiding behind walls too thick to crush, yet it all gets in. It comes digging underground or seeps through the rafters. It enters, and just when you feel secure it blows you to bits.

His legs moved in long strides up the winding path, the salted air pungent and thick in his nostrils that breathed in air with quick, tight spurts. Father McIntyre passed the invisible line that had always stopped him before—the line that said the sea, the never-ending cliffs, would be in view. He came closer and his stomach sickened.

His face was damp with salted water—from tears or from the sea, it did not matter. The memories were around him, poking with dead fingers. He closed his eyes against the wind, pushed forward, felt the warmth of a future without pain, and he moved faster.

Father McIntyre did not heed the wind, did not stop to mull regret or ponder excuses. He stood at the edge of the world where the earth hovered with the sea and the air. He stretched his arms above his head, the wings of his cassock flapping violently, begging his body to soar. And he stepped upon the sky. . . .

Part 4

CHAPTER 27

James slid the hat rim toward his nose, his eyes retreating from the relentless sun. At fourteen, James had spent over three years now living with his aunt and uncle in the Wheatbelt of Western Australia. And in these years, the rain did not fall. Spits. Teasing splats. But not rain. Had the land only given drought, life would have been easier. A man does not try to work a desert; he moves away, says good-bye to a dead land and searches for one of life. But not this land, the land that hovers between green and brown, a place where rain can hit in sheets and then, a mere mile to the east, only the smell of rain falls. This was life in the Wheatbelt—a flirtatious dance between bounty and lack.

Rain. It was easy to blame life's hardships on the whim of the sky, but James knew better. He had known this for years. The fault lay with him.

James gripped two hands to the left plow handle while his uncle, Shamus O'Reilly, clutched the right. James matched the man head to head in height and so their shoulders came level to the crossbar. His weight did not match that of the burly O'Reilly, though, and so his side tilted forward and lagged. He ground his heels into the rock-laden earth until his legs shook with pushing.

"Come on, boy!" Shamus shouted. "Put ye shoulder into it. Go!"

The old workhorse pulled, jerking her head up with the drag of the dull plow. Slowly, foot by foot, the stubborn tool furrowed lines, grinding up last year's brittle wheat stalks and chopping up the spinifex that seemed to grow anew each morning.

"All right. 'Tis enuf fur now." Shamus let go of the plow in exhaustion, bent forward. "Give 'er a rest, James."

James unhooked the horse, her coat slick with sweat under the leather straps.

"We'll finish after we eat." Shamus stretched out his back, the joints of his solid frame and thick arms cracking. "Be a late one. Plowin' got t'be done tonight even if we work by lantern. Got t'harrow an' seed an' roll by end o' week." He squinted at the sun and growled, "Late as 'tis!" Then he pointed his chin at James in challenge. "Yeer up fur it, boy?"

"Yes, sir."

They walked across the deep furrows, a history of lines that had taken up full days and weeks and the skin off their palms to form. The smell of bacon carried from the kitchen stovepipe before the little brown house came into view. Home was no bigger than a shearing shed, its wood so dark from kitchen smoke that it looked charred. The corrugated steel roof was ridged in silver, then valleyed red with rust. The porch stuck out lopsided, supported with planks of wood to keep the roof from collapsing. A water tank flanked the side of the house near the detached kitchen, and behind that the fowl house squawked behind a wire fence.

Tess O'Reilly met them at the door with a hidden smile. "'Bout time! Yeer lucky I didn't feed yeer meal t'the pigs!" Her threat was nothing more than jest as she shepherded them to the table and filled their plates with eggs and bacon. The tea was hot and thick with sugar. It was the beginning of the month. By the end, there would be only one egg per plate, only a small slab of pork, and the tea would be bitter and black. Meals indicated the days of the month and the rent payments clearer than any calendar.

Between mouthfuls of food, Shamus rehashed the details of the morning's work, sighing and shaking his head with emphasis in case his wife did not grasp the magnitude of his efforts. And Tess would scurry around the kitchen, listening and adding little sounds of expression to show that she did indeed grasp the magnitude of his efforts. And when he inevitably began to curse the blasted Australian land, she would click her tongue soothingly and reach over his shoulder to replenish the eggs, and as she did she would smile and wink at James.

Tess was a small woman and, at first glance, seemed startlingly frail, all the more because her skin was almost translucent against long onyx hair. But her eyes, bright green saucers, eclipsed her body until that was all one saw. And these were the eyes that watched James always, welcomed him into her life with joy stretched in her pupils. Sometimes, when she didn't think James could see, Tess would touch her lips, then touch her heart.

Shamus frowned and pushed his empty plate across the table. "Back to it."

"Not now," Tess protested. "'Tis the hottest time of the day. Ye'll faint within the hour."

"No choice." Shamus motioned for James to follow. "Don't rush with supper, Tess."

Tess wagged a finger at her husband. "Ye make sure the boy rests, Shamus."

Shamus's mood soured with the inching degrees of mercury so that by the time they reached the plow and re-hooked the horse, he was dark with mute cursing. They toiled silently over the last, infinite stretch of field. The heat brought weariness to their work, sapping their strength doubly while productivity halved. Shamus's lips twitched with growing anger and internal diatribe. James shut his mind to everything but work, pushed with all his body, the sweat spilling over his eyes and stinging them with salt.

"Push it!" Shamus shouted to the plow, to James, to the horse, to the endless ground.

A sharp metal clang stopped the plow cold, sending James to his knees.

"Fur the love a Jasus!" Shamus bent his head to the plow turn, reached in with both hands. "Bloody hell!" He wrenched himself up and tore off his hat, beat it against the red plow, the color of his face.

"Axle cracked! Clean through!" he shouted, and stormed away, his back bent, hands tight at his waist, before stomping back and giving the plow a hard kick with his foot, the thud so dull it almost mocked him. The horse shuffled nervously.

"Would it kill ye to do one bloody thing right!" Shamus suddenly turned on James.

"I told ye to stop grindin' the feckin' wheel into rocks!" Shamus brushed past him, mumbling, "Wouldn't be in this feckin' country if it weren't fur ye."

James did not follow Shamus to the house, stood quietly for a minute with the weight of lead on his chest. He moved to the horse, scratched the backs of her ears before peeking down through the plow spokes. The axle leaned on the ground, broken and rusted through. He turned back to the horse and stroked the velvet of her nose. She breathed heavily, too old for this kind of work. James unclasped the harness, letting the plow fall forward into the dirt, and walked her back to the house. He pumped fresh water into the trough, sat and watched her drink, the sun a rippling orange reflection in the water.

And it was here in the silence near the flimsy house, beyond the work of the field, his muscles numb with pain, that the void of a missing friend filled the corners of the endless sky and reminded him that this was the life he had chosen.

CHAPTER 28

On this day, Leonora's eleventh birthday, the rain of Pittsburgh did not end in rainbows. It blackened with night, stained the bark of the great oaks, dried in gray streaks down the slate roofs like sooty tears and pivoted from steady pours to ashen sniffles.

Leonora pulled the covers up to her neck, watched the bloated splatter against her bedroom window, dancing finger taps upon slick glass. Eleven—a number, an age—a birthday to celebrate—a fake date—another stomachache. The guests had departed, the chatter and footsteps silent.

A light rap knocked against the door, but she didn't answer. "Are you awake?" her uncle asked through an open crack.

"Yes."

"Good." He closed the door behind him and lingered at the knob. "I didn't want to leave without saying good-bye."

Owen Fairfield's figure moved through the room. He sat at the foot of the bed. He reached for the lamp and turned the brass key, lighting a square above the covers. His white beard was short and clean and perfectly lined at the jawbone and mouth. He looked quickly at the gold pocket watch in the vest of his gray twill suit, his traveling attire. White suits never lasted more than a few hours in the coal-laden air without him having to change.

He tried to lighten the mood, tried to get her to look at his face. "You had such a busy day, I thought you'd be asleep."

She smiled weakly. He smelled of pipe tobacco, slightly sweet.

"Eleven!" Owen Fairfield shook his head. "Eleven years old, I can hardly believe it. Seems like just yesterday you were a little girl and now you're halfway grown." He pointed a finger at her, his eyes crinkling with affection. "You're making an old man out of me, darling."

Her uncle peered around the room, looked up at the coffered ceiling. "You didn't open any of your presents."

The shame of what she had done brightened her cheeks and she turned away.

"It wasn't your fault, Leonora." He pinched her chin. "You have nothing to be embarrassed about." He looked down at his hands then, twisted his wedding band around his finger. "She's too hard on you. Always has been."

He stayed quiet for a moment before pulling out the watch again, then snapped it shut and tucked it back. "Car's waiting for me," he said without rising. "I'll be gone six months at least. China and Japan." He frowned. "Traveling's not what it used to be; things are tightening. Hard to explain. Like the whole world's being pulled in different directions like elastic. Used to be a lot simpler, friendlier. World's changing, darling, and I'm not sure it's for the better." Worry lines changed to smiles as the weight of the words struck him. "And here you are, eleven! Changing right in front of my eyes." He pointed another finger at her. "No more growing while I'm gone, you hear me?"

She nodded.

"I'll bring you back a silk kimono, one that picks up the gold in your hair and eyes." He winked. "Maybe a jade tree. You and I got a thing for the rocks, don't we?"

Her uncle leaned over and kissed her on the forehead, looked like he wanted to say more but then left the room—an incomplete sentence. A few minutes later, the beams of the Rolls-Royce splashed against the window before turning down the pine-lined drive.

Leonora wrapped her arms around her belly. The room widened in emptiness, the canopy bed loomed and the gaping mouth of the marble fireplace wheezed a cold draft. The house was icier without him, like a scarf removed from an already-chilled neck. Not that he was attentive or playful, but instead a distraction between her and Eleanor. With Owen gone, her aunt's anxiety and missing of her husband always turned to hard focus, singular and defined, to Leonora. Nothing she could do was right and so she spent her days hoping to evaporate with the morning dew.

In the darkness of the large room, Leonora's mind was too busy, the day too full with unpleasant moments that kept replaying, drawing in scenes from the past like moths to a flame. So, with bare feet, she climbed out of bed and went out to the hall, felt the way down the thick walnut banister.

The fireboxes were out and the wood floors chilled as Leonora tiptoed past the closed doors of the kitchen and shrank into a corner, tucking her nightgown around her ankles. The room was cold, but the noise behind the walls was a heat that warmed from the inside out. She opened her ears to the lone area of activity in the house. The sounds of clean dishes clinking mixed with laughing voices over scrubbing pots and the pounding of rolling pins.

The kitchen nourished with more than food. Words stirred within the walls; emotions flowed freely. Real words. Real feelings. Not the contrived small talk and lies that filled her day or the relentless tutoring of facts, history and numbers drummed into the creases of her brain. So many words spoken in a day—words that must be remembered; words that had to be recited, but never words that meant anything.

A door slammed on the servant side and a woman moaned. "You're still here?" Bertha's voice bellowed. "Thought you turned in for the night."

"Huh! To be so lucky." Leonora recognized the voice of Mindy, the table maid. "Had to polish the silver twice!" the woman grunted. "Once before the party and again after. Even the pieces nobody used!"

"Well, sit for a spell and have some tea before you go!" ordered Bertha. A stool screeched across the floor. "Mrs. Fairfield asleep?"

"Far as I know. Course she'll be up for her midnight feeding soon, sucking the blood out of kittens and babies." The cooks laughed. "Cake looked out of this world, Bertha. Spice cake?"

"Carrot. There's a whole one left. Take a piece."

"You heard what happened?" Mindy snickered.

"Everyone heard what happened. Was it so bad?"

"Worse. The girl threw up all over herself just as she was blowing out the candles! Should have seen Mrs. Fairfield's face—her eyes bulging and her face red as a tomato!" The woman snorted. "Leonora be lucky if she lives to see twelve."

Heat grew sharp to Leonora's cheeks, burned her ears. She felt sick just thinking about it.

"Poor girl," Bertha tsked. "Got a room full of people she don't even know telling her how pretty she is, asking her questions. More grown-ups than children. See all those presents with the blue wrapping paper? Crystal and silver! What's a child going to do with that stuff?"

"Not for her at all, you know that," answered another voice. "Kissing asses. Every guest had lips puckered for a taste of the sweet Fairfield behind—tasted better on their lips than your carrot cake, Bertha." There were throaty chuckles before she continued, "Can't blame the girl for barfing. Can't be easy knowing you ain't got no friends."

"You'll hear no pity from me!" Mindy snapped. "Mark my words, Mrs. Fairfield will have one of us fired over this. I'm telling you, that girl is like a curse. Her maids and tutors don't last more than a year. Soon as she warms up to them, they're gone. Get too close to that one and you get burned."

"Poor thing's just lonely. Child wouldn't hurt a flea," said Bertha, her voice mellowing like her arms were crossed against her stomach. "I pity her. They got her scheduled with lessons from morning to night. She's not allowed to have any friends or playmates. And look who she's got to live with? An uncle who drops a present at her feet and taps her on the head as he leaves and an aunt who'd freeze the devil's tail with a look."

"So terrible is it?" Mindy scoffed. "Imagine never picking up a dirty dish or having to cook a piece of toast."

"No shame in hard work and you know it. Would you want her life?" The maid fell silent.

"Of course not." Bertha's tone deepened. "It's no life for a child. I wouldn't wish her life on a dog."

The teacup moved to the counter and Mindy's feet tapped against the tile as she got off the stool. "Well, the girl might seem sweet and innocent now, but Leonora'll grow up mean as Mrs. Fairfield. You'll see."

Leonora cowered into the wall, replayed the words over and over, half-conscious of the waning sounds of the kitchen. The lights switched off, snapped away the beam of white near her feet. The servant door closed and the key rattled as it locked. It would be the last time she would hear the voice of Bertha, the cook who would sneak her extra desserts and squeeze her with fat, warm arms, the last time she would hear this kind woman defending her. For her aunt had already decided to fire Bertha, blaming Leonora's sickness on the cake, too rich for a child's stomach. Leonora remembered the maid's prediction: *Get too close to that one and you get burned.* The guilt and shame rose swift and hot.

What little warmth left and the cold from the empty kitchen seeped into her bones, shaking her limbs. She rose unsteadily and inched blindly back through the hall and up the staircase. As she passed her aunt's room, she slowed her pace and held her breath, the familiar fear rising. But another sound crept upon her and she stopped, listened. Hiccups of sobbing, low and prolonged, seeped from behind the closed door.

Leonora could not move, the feeling akin to seeing a rose blooming in the dead of winter, the oddity of it stunning and strange—the reality of a fleeting moment of grace and truth even stranger. Without thinking, Leonora touched her fingertips to the door, and it swung inward. Eleanor sat hunched before the fireplace, her face buried in her hands, her shoulders shaking. The moment was so soft, the woman's pain so real, that Leonora's eyes welled, her heart breaking at another's suffering.

Leonora inched silently to her side, leaned in and wrapped her arms gently around her aunt's bent neck. In Leonora's arms, in a moment of warmth and emotion, the neck fell limp upon her shoulder and a weak cry left the woman's throat. Leonora had never touched Eleanor, never felt an embrace or a kiss from the woman, and she melted into the cold skin, lost herself in a single moment of closeness that her whole soul craved. But it was only a moment. One moment to be forever lost, for suddenly the woman's neck and head jerked up as if awakened by a thunderclap. The eyes glowed black, rimmed red with tears. "How dare you come in here." Eleanor's voice cracked and her chin shivered. Leonora stepped back.

"How dare you sneak up on me!" Eleanor screamed. Leonora retreated two steps more, but Eleanor grabbed her wrist and pulled her close. "If you ever tell anyone about this," Eleanor hissed, "I'll leave you out in the dust! Do you understand me?"

Leonora tried to pull back, began to cry, her voice closed with the habitual panic.

"Do you understand?" Eleanor screamed. *"I will leave you!"*

I will leave you. I will leave you. I will leave you.

Leonora's mind went blank and she nodded furiously, kept nodding furiously even as she fled the room and ran through the hall.

I will leave you. I will leave you. I will leave you.

These were the threats, Eleanor's promises, the lullaby that sang in Leonora's ears since the Fairfields adopted her in case she dared slip about her past, made any mistake. And no one ever defended or protected her from the promise, not even her uncle. Owen upon hearing the woman's threats would always draw inward, his face sallow and gray as if the words were spoken to him. And he would leave, never defend, never say all would be all right, and for this the pain was worse. So Leonora never misspoke, stayed silent and shared her secrets only with the birds and trees and barn cats and hunting dogs who would lick away her frowns.

Leonora climbed into her bed and hid under the covers. In the darkness, she pulled out a tiny, egg-shaped stone from her pocket, curled it into her palm, ached for the friend who had given it to her, ached for a place to belong, ached for a home that didn't exist. And this night, like so many others, she held on to a memory that neared a dream, shivered in the silent darkness and fell asleep in a nightgown wet with tears.

CHAPTER 29

"Ye look right handsome, James." Tess winked as she buttoned his worn suit jacket, a Shamus hand-me-down. The lining was gone and the elbows were worn bare. New stitches stood out bright black against the rest of the faded threads. Tess wrinkled her forehead as she pulled at the sleeves and inspected it from a distance. "A little crooked." She laughed. "Mendin's never been m'strongest skill."

Shamus grunted from the bedroom, came out fumbling with a collar. "Tess, do I have to wear this bloody thing? Ye know it chokes the breath out o' me."

"Course ye do! It's a funeral, Shamus. Have ye lost all respect?"

He grumbled, "Hard to respect a man that set us on a bum piece o' land."

"Shame on ye!" The woman's voice rose with sudden vehemence. "The Shelbys 'ave been nothin' but angels to us from day one! Set us up with credit 'fore they even knew who we was. Then, Mr. Shelby come over his self an' lend ye those tools, bringin' all that food from his wife." She put her hands on her hips and wagged a finger in his face. "He told ye 'bout this land. I stood right here while he told us 'bout the dry dirt an' ye remember what ye said? 'Never a land an O'Reilly can't tame.'

"Shameful!" Tess grabbed his collar, tugged it closed, his neck reddening with the pinch. "Complainin' 'bout wearin' a collar to a man's funeral. A man who done nothin' but help us."

"I'm sorry, Tess." Shamus withered. "Yeer right. Forgive me?"

She tried to hold to the anger but softened and pressed his suit lapels. "Course I do."

Tess's face sagged then and the smile left her eyes. "Temper's a bit short. Couldn't sleep thinkin' 'bout that poor Mrs. Shelby an' those children of hers, all on their own now. Six children an' two more on the way! Shamus, can ye imagine? An' now their father gone."

"She'll live fine off the renters."

"I don't know." She scanned the kitchen, picked up the covered stew. "'Tween the gold diggings and the drought, men leaving farms left an' right. Heard the Holloways picked up an' left without a word. Didn't even clean the dishes off the table!"

Tess put her bonnet on, her skin stark white against the black. She stopped then and looked at James, looked at her husband. Tears welled in her eyes and Shamus took her hands. "What is it, Tess?"

"Look at ye two. So handsome. So strong. Mrs. Shelby lost her husband an' here I am with ye both." Her lips quivered. "God has truly shone on me."

For all Shamus's talk of renters and money, the funeral numbered under twenty and those represented were as threadbare as the O'Reillys. The preacher solemnly greeted the mourners but left an instant impression of oddity. Thick glasses magnified his eyes, his head appearing top-heavy and bobbly over his skeletal figure. He seemed a step away from reading his own rites.

Mrs. Shelby stood in front of the parson, black lace draped over her large body, her thick red hair visible under the veil. An army of children hung around her skirt folds, fidgeting feet and squirming under sun and boredom.

A boy in his teens just like James glanced at him before looking down at his feet. He moved from one foot to the other, and everything was crooked—hat, waistband, tie. The cuffs of his pants did not fall evenly, though they looked new and unmended. He peeked at James again and smirked, plucked awkwardly at his suspenders, then kicked dirt at his brother's shoes. The older boy shoved him in the chest before Mrs. Shelby shot a warning look that could freeze water.

James did not listen to the words of the preacher; no one seemed to except for Mrs. Shelby, who kept her head pointed straight, still with attention. Instead, James watched the faces of the other farmers, watched their impatient expressions, watched them flex their biceps. They all wanted to get back to the fields.

When the service ended, men began to fill in the grave, one hard shovelful at a time. The rest of the group separated into clusters. Shamus and Tess joined the renters at Mrs. Shelby's side, held hands and shared words of consolation; little girls clung to mothers' skirts and older boys joined and tried to look like men with stern faces and shoulders sloped with heavy burdens.

The uneven Shelby boy walked over to James, his gait lopsided as he tried to size him up with a tilt of his head. As if satisfied, he stuck out a hand. "I'm Tom."

"James." They shook heartily with limp elbows.

The men at the graves patted down the mound with the backs of their shovels.

"Sorry about your dad," James offered.

The young man looked down, twisted his mouth. "O'Reilly, right? You don't talk like your folks."

"I was born here."

"Oh," Tom said, fine with the answer. "You go t'school?"

"No."

"Mum says I can stop goin'. Needs me on the farm now." He stole a look at the grave and shrugged his shoulders. "Hate school anyway. See that preacher? He's the teacher. One day in class with him an' you wish he was buryin' you!"

James smiled and Tom laughed but caught himself before his mother did, pulled his mouth crookedly to the side. "Haven't seen you around b'fore."

"Been busy in the fields."

"Just you an' your dad?"

James ignored the reference. "Yeah."

"Don't you have any hired hands?"

"No."

Tom nodded and shrugged again, looked at him cock-eyed. "I could help you sometimes, if Mum lets me. Long as I get my chores done, I bet she'd let me come an' help you."

"Tommie!" Mrs. Shelby called. "Time to get back to the house."

He rolled his eyes. "Preacher's gonna hold mass at our house t'night. You got to see that man eat! Chews his food sideways like a horse an' talks preacher stuff through his chewin'—sprayin' food an' Gawd talk all over the bloody place!" Tom shuddered. "You're comin', right?"

James looked ahead at the procession following Mrs. Shelby, saw Tess and Shamus among them. "Guess so."

They walked easily, as if their footsteps had always been together. Tom chatted away affably with no toughness of speech or pretense, just simple good nature.

"Got any bullocks?" Tom asked.

"No."

"Sheep?"

James shook his head.

"What you got then?"

"Wheat."

"That's all?"

"Couple pigs and chickens, I guess."

"Hell, everyone's got those," Tom said without condescension.

James grew quiet. Tom suddenly perked. "We got fifty heads of cattle! Another hundred in sheep. Mum says we don't got money for a drover, so she said I can do it." He stopped with the half-truth and explained, "Well, not really drovin' but herdin'. You ride?"

James nodded.

"Thought so. Maybe you can help me with the drovin' if I help you with the wheat. We can camp out in the far paddocks, make a fire, dig for grubs an' eat goannas like the Aborigines!"

James grimaced and Tom laughed. "Just kiddin' . . . 'bout eatin' the goannas, that is. Those Abos eat 'em, though. Maggots, too. Eat 'em like candy." Tom shuddered.

A few minutes later, the Shelby homestead rose from a sea of green, an island swimming on barren land. Red roses crept up the pillars anchoring the verandah; lilacs and yellow wattles hedged the base. Behind the flowers, the house paint peeled in curls and a few windows hung with only one shutter, but the wide doors and porch spread open in warm welcome. And with each square foot of the one-story house, the clear poverty of the O'Reillys grew in contrast.

"How you keep it so green?" James asked.

"Aqueduct. Pumps in from the artesian well. I'll take you back one day. Stinks like rotten eggs but keeps Mum's flowers growin'." The boys entered the house, now abuzz with chatter that grew loud and constrained between walls.

"Tommie." Mrs. Shelby waved. "Show Reverend Jordan to the spare room."

Tom winced. "Means he's stayin' for a while. Gawd help me!" He made the sign of the cross over his chest. "I'll be back down quick."

James squeezed through the packed dining room. The house was worn, cozily scuffed. Faded wallpaper met chipped baseboards. Unraveling carpets settled on worn floors, remnants of many feet, many gatherings. He turned the corner and entered a room with a slight mildew odor and halted. Books lined shelves from floor to ceiling. Old volumes with broken spines and faded covers meshed between new leather ones. James ran his fingers over the books, pulled one out and fanned the pages, dust rising up and tickling his nose.

"What are you doin' in here?"

James spun around, closed the book with a clap.

Mrs. Shelby leaned against the door frame, her red hair afire above her black dress.

"I'm sorry; I was . . ." he sputtered.

Mrs. Shelby came toward him, watched him carefully from downcast eyes. She pulled the book from his hands, leafed through the pages and placed it back on the shelf.

"I didn't mean to . . ."

"Shush." She held up a finger for quiet and scanned the bookshelf, reached up on her toes, pulled out a thick green volume. "Here." She handed him the book. "You'll like this one better."

James rubbed the cover. Robert Louis Stevenson.

"Like to read, do you?" she asked, inspecting him again.

"Yes, ma'am."

"My boys have no use for it." She shook her head. "Enough children t'fill a schoolhouse an' not one of 'em wants to read a word. Only way I can get 'em close to these books is by whacking one over their thick skull," she said, and snorted, her pregnant belly rising with the chuckle. "Guess they take after their father. Tommie especially." Mrs. Shelby's face grew gray. "He wasn't a learned man but smart as a whip. A good man," she said, voice fading.

She pointed to the bookshelf, her tone strong and firm again. "These books belong to the church. They were savin' for a school library but needed the space for the preacher's quarters. I took 'em gladly. Haven't had a chance to read in years. Shame, isn't it?"

She put her hand on his head, her palm warm. "These books are just as much yours as mine. Come over an' take as many as you want. Hear me?"

"Yes, ma'am."

Her eyes scanned his suit. "How your folks doin'?"

"Fine."

"I mean with the land. It's not easy tillin'."

"We got the wheat in this week. Crows been picking at it, though."

"Need a dog. A good barker scare 'em faster than a shotgun." She nodded, frowned. "Course, if we don't get some rain for it to root, the whole crop gonna be picked, dogs or not."

A young man peeked into the room. "Mum, preacher wants to start mass."

"Orright. Be right in."

She leaned down to James. "Wants to cut into that ham is what he wants!" She snorted again. "Preacher eats like a horse. Be droolin' all through the mass, starin' at it. You watch!

"You're a good kid." Mrs. Shelby winked. "Talk proper. Be good for Tommie to have a friend like you." She took him by the shoulder and squeezed, the arm as strong as a man's, as comforting as a mother's. "Know you're as welcome here as in your own home."

Two tables lined the walls of the dining room, spread with boiled ham, turkey, loaves of bread, crocks of butter, bowls of gravy, and dried fruit. Tom handed a plate to James and poked him with his elbow. "Let's eat outside." They took their pile of food out to the verandah, swung their legs over the side. Two young men joined them on the porch. They were a few years apart in age but had hair and faces similar enough to be twins.

"Who's your girlfriend?" one asked, smirking.

"Shut up." Tom threw an apricot at him. "This is James. O'Reilly's boy." Tom rolled his eyes. "Will an' John. My older brothers."

"Irish, huh?"

James put his fork down and met Will's eyes square.

"Whoa!" Will's hands went up in defense. "Wasn't an insult. Just heard your folks talkin', is all." He shoveled a hunk of ham in his mouth. "Our dad was a Scot. Couple of drinks in him an' his accent come out so hard, you could barely understand a bloody word!"

The three boys smiled into their food, their eyes missing him. "Dad would have liked having all these people here," said John.

Will laughed. "He'd corner 'em with his yarns till they beat the door to get out!"

James listened to the banter of the boys, the communion of brothers, warm and easy.

Clink. Tom dropped his fork to his plate. All eyes turned to him. He wiped his hand across his cheek and looked at his finger in disbelief.

"You cryin'?" accused Will with horror.

Tom leaned his head back and looked at the sky, blinking. "It's raining," he breathed.

They all craned necks. Gray clouds pulled toward the homestead, pillowing and thickening with momentum. A few light drops landed on their eyelashes.

"It's raining," Will repeated. "*It's raining!*"

Full plates clattered to the ground as they rushed into the house, the chatter of the guests silenced by the charging boys.

"It's raining!"

Every mouth hushed. Chins lifted slowly, eyes turned up toward the ceiling, ears stiffened with focus, alert as roos.

And then it came.

Slap. Slap. Slap. Raindrops hit the corrugated roof. But the people did not rejoice. They stayed rigid and waited for the tease, waited for the drops to disappear and the sun to cut bright through the window again. Men gripped the edge of the table, while the women held hand to chest lest a breath send the rain away. They waited for a sign, a wind shift that would either leave the cloud in place or carry its gift away.

Then such a sound! The Heavens released and erupted atop the house. *Slap, slap, slap*—thick coins dropping into an iron can—*slap, slap, slap*—till they blended together in one glorious note. And now chests sent out held air, and eyes closed in prayer and faces thawed into smiles disguised as frowns in heavy thankfulness.

A streak of lightning cracked out the window, the clap of thunder riding its heel. Cheers and tears released unabashed. They were no longer squatters or colonials, farmers or renters, Irish or English or German, preachers or drinkers, but people of the land. And the crowd hugged Mrs. Shelby for they all knew the significance and the clear face of the miracle—Mr. Shelby had no sooner entered the gates of Heaven than he broke open the clouds and sent rain to his land.

So began the freedom and joy of the green years—the sigh of the county—the slaps on the backs between neighbors and pulling up of waistbands that said, *We made it. It's gonna be orright.* So began wheat that grew green and pumped with veins no different from blood. And the wheat matured, browned and grew gold, blew in the breeze and rippled soft as calf fur.

James found freedom in the green years. He grew to love the wheat, the white and yellow everlasting blossoms, the delicate spider orchids, the cool riverbeds that gushed from hibernation, the pink galahs that sang from the trees—grew to love them as much as the sea.

Shamus hired an Aborigine to help in the fields, and while the work still consumed each day, there was time for freedom at the Shelby library, for campouts in the bush with the boys, horse races across the paddocks, swims in the deep creek beds. There was freedom for limbs to grow and muscles to thicken as boys grew into men.

In the green years, it was easy to overlook that which was not fresh and bright and blooming. It was easy to look past Tess's pallor and the dark circles that grew purple under her eyes and the smile that faced you and then winced as it turned from view. She made it easy to believe that the lines of pain stretching down her cheeks were only furrows of reflection. If one asked after her health or stared too long in examination, she would pull a sparkle to her eyes and tsk at such silliness. And a man becomes easily appeased, for he does not want to see the thorns hidden within his Eden. No worries when the ground is lush and the rain is full!

These were the green years when the ground cracked open and sprouted from every pore, a world teeming with life—even as Tess's started to slip away.

Chapter 30

The clouds left Pittsburgh. The last drops of rain on Leonora's bedroom window evaporated with the emerging sun. The day would be dry of storms, but would remain damp.

Leonora sighed, turned her head on the pillow and faced the door, long auburn hair spilling around her shoulders. The adornments of the bedroom were the same as the day she filled her role as a Fairfield. Pink-blossomed wallpaper and chestnut bureaus had witnessed her growth from child to adult and yet she felt little changed beyond form. Her body had lengthened and slimmed; hips and breasts drew curves against her silhouette. By all accounts, she was a woman now. But her angled yet soft face implied a confidence and sophistication she did not feel.

Far away in the distance, an ambulance wailed. Her heart thumped. No one else in the house would hear the siren, a remote hum from the valley, but it caught her ear as a silent whistle would a dog's. The Fairfields were donating a wing to the hospital and she was to attend the dedication ceremony—a moment of freedom, a moment of release from the house she was nearly forbidden to leave. Her ears followed the waning trail of the siren until it whimpered and disappeared in the valley's muzzle. Her heart thumped again. If she was going to bring up her desire to attend nursing school, today would need to be the day.

"You're not wearing that!" Eleanor scolded when she saw Leonora coming down the stairs. "We're donating a wing, not taking the nurses to tea. Wear something patriotic."

Leonora changed, met back at the stairs for the next round of editing.

Her aunt glanced at the dress. "That'll do."

The black Rolls idled in the drive as the chauffeur held open the door. "Have you heard from Mr. Fairfield?" Eleanor asked as she bristled past the servant.

"No, ma'am."

"He was supposed to come in yesterday." She grimaced. "Just like him." The door closed, the women settled into seats. "Your uncle's as stubborn as a badger. Every sane man is scrambling to get out of Europe and Owen is digging his toes in the bloody soil. Now I've got to do the whole ceremony myself." Eleanor rubbed her long neck, stuck out her chin. "I've half a mind to change the locks. Let him stew in the stables for a bit."

Leonora slanted against the door, tried not to attract more attention than necessary. She knew the anger would spill her way at any moment.

Mrs. Fairfield picked at the graying hair above her ears, tucking in strands that were already well tucked. "The *Post-Gazette* will be covering the story. Try not to clam up." She waved her hand. "Don't say too much, of course. Just that we support our allies—the importance of doing our part—you understand?"

This was the opening Leonora was waiting for, but as she opened her mouth to speak her throat closed. She lowered her head in defeat. "Yes, ma'am."

Eleanor scanned her. "You were going to say something. What was it?"

There was no escape. A blush rose to Leonora's face as she stammered to form a coherent word under her aunt's gaze. "I-I-I'm . . . I . . ."

"Speak, for God's sake!"

Anger suddenly eclipsed the fear and Leonora met her gaze, swallowed hard. "I want to go to nursing school."

Eleanor laughed. "Yes, yes, Owen told me all about your little idea. He thought it as stupid as I did. We both had a good laugh actually."

The slap was instant, a sting without touch. "That's not true." The anger and disbelief swirled in her mind. "He said he supported my decision. He . . . he said he would think about it."

"Have you learned nothing about my husband over these years, Leonora? Owen says whatever serves him at the moment. He would tell you the sky was green just to make you smile." Then, under her breath, she murmured with a hint of jealousy, "Pathetic.

"Nursing school is out of the question. No woman with the Fairfield name will be working like a paid servant. A nurse is nothing more than a maid to a sick person." Eleanor leaned forward to examine her reflection in the driver's mirror. "The answer is 'no' and I expect never to hear it brought up again."

Leonora held her tears at bay, forced them with sheer will to stay down. "But I'm nearly done with my studies. What would you have me do?"

"You'll marry into a good family and have lots of babies and happy memories!" she spit sarcastically. "Now enough of this chatter." She shook her head like she had an itch and rubbed her throat. "We'll be at the hospital soon and you're all red and agitated. That's not the way to make a first impression, especially with the press." The woman's fingers scratched at her throat again. "Of course, who's to say what sort of reception we'll get after you scorned Dr. Edwards. My God, Leonora, the man only asked you to dinner."

Leonora turned to the window. The scorn was a polite refusal to the forty-year-old board director whose eyes never looked above her breasts.

Eleanor settled into her lace collar and relaxed. "Well, at any rate, the hospital is not the place to meet a husband. Trust me. Half the doctors will be shipped out soon and the ones who are left are too old or inept."

The car descended into the city, the buildings dripping with varying levels of black and gray, a mirror of Leonora's heart. The conversation, the hope, was smashed. All that was left was the urge to cry, to disappear, to melt into nothing even as she was squaring her shoulders for the latest Fairfield function.

The driver pulled to the entrance of the hospital and helped the women out to the sidewalk to the awaiting swarm of businessmen and government officials turned out for the ceremony, not out of support for the new wing, as it was not as grand as some others, but out of fear of losing favor with a family such as the Fairfields through absence.

As the photographers set up tripods and held flashes high in the air, the men pushed comically against one another lest they get cut from the frame and have no record of attendance. They fought to shake Mrs. Fairfield's hand, to promise future social dates and gush what a lovely young woman her niece had become. Leonora nodded and smiled, shook hands, let the compliments and praise fade into the pitch of voices like a foreign language.

After the crowd dispersed and their vision speckled with camera flashes, the doctors escorted the women to the new wing, touring between aisles of steel beds, sheeted in white, half-opened in crisp triangles below propped pillows.

"The war should be over long before America sends a man." Dr. Edwards spoke confidently to Leonora's bosom. "However, it's important to be prepared," he continued to Mrs. Fairfield's neck. "Besides, the English hospitals are overflowing."

"We must do everything we can to support our allies," recited Mrs. Fairfield.

The reporter from the *Gazette* scribbled down every word but paused to look at Leonora. He was a little older than she, a thin pencil mustache above his lip. "And you, miss, is there anything you'd like to add?"

She lowered her head.

Mrs. Fairfield narrowed her eyes. "My *niece* was just mentioning how important it is for the younger generation to see beyond themselves to the higher good of the masses."

"Ah," said the reporter as he kept his eyes glued on Leonora. "So, philanthropy runs in the family. Do you plan on volunteering here at the hospital?"

Just then the cage door opened and bird wings flapped in her stomach. "Yes," she almost shouted. The group stopped. Eleanor's eyes grew to saucers.

The wings flapped louder in Leonora's throat. "Yes. I'd like to volunteer—to work here. Anything to help." The voice that came out shocked her with its boldness.

"Wonderful news," said Dr. Edwards as he scanned her hips. "We'd be pleased to have you. We'll set you up with the Red Cross. When would you like to start?"

"Tomorrow." The word tumbled out. Mrs. Fairfield closed her eyes for a moment, her jaw clenched and rigid below the high cheekbones.

The reporter wrote down every word, his tongue peeking out the corner of his mouth. "Great way to round out the piece—one family making a difference in big and small ways."

Leonora's aunt did not speak for the rest of the tour, only nodded politely at Dr. Edwards's directives. But Leonora could hardly contain her joy and looked upon the white walls, the linoleum floor and echoing halls as trails to freedom.

After lunch, the driver pulled the car to the sidewalk. The Fairfield ladies presented their hands for the round of cold lips and many thanks.

"We'll see you tomorrow, Leonora," said Dr. Edwards with a wink.

"Yes. Thank you."

Dr. Edwards closed the car door, shutting out the noise from the city and magnifying the space between Leonora and her aunt. Leonora kept her gaze cemented to the window as the car turned into the street, her aunt's eyes burning her skin.

"You must feel pretty proud of yourself," Eleanor began, tugging at each finger until her gloves sat folded on her lap like a second pair of hands.

Leonora waited for the rug to be pulled.

"I admit, I didn't think you had initiative. I'm not sure whether I should be angry or proud." The woman cocked her head, inspected her. "Of course, watching you stand up for yourself is a bit like watching a blind man cross the street. Pitiful, actually."

The flutters died and the cage locked.

"However, I'm going to allow it."

Leonora's head snapped up.

"I don't have to," her aunt corrected. "I could easily find an excuse as to why you're needed at home. But I've decided not to fight you on this one." She rolled her eyes. "Why you'd want to spend time in that place is beyond me, but that's neither here nor there."

Leonora savored her fortune, tried to keep the excitement from showing, but her aunt saw it like blinking lights. "A note of warning, Leonora. I've indulged you this time. If you ever pull a stunt like that again, it will not end in your favor. I suggest you don't try to test me.

"Look at me." Eleanor tapped her roughly on the knee. "You don't talk to anyone, understand? Do your work, roll bandages or whatever nonsensical job they have you do, and that's it. You'll need to make up your studies in the evening. Are we clear?"

"Yes, ma'am."

Mrs. Fairfield's fingers tapped on her purse as they passed the first gate to the estate drive. "Knowing you, you'll fall in love with some crippled soldier. Just like you try to save those mangy alley dogs." Her disgust suddenly shifted and her body shot upright as if someone pulled her hair. She peered over the driver's shoulder. "Owen's home."

Eleanor tossed her purse and coat to the maid and walked briskly toward clinking glasses in the library. Leonora took her time removing her coat before following.

"You're late!" her aunt scolded, the reprimand too clouded in relief to be terse. "We expected you yesterday."

Owen Fairfield kissed his wife on the cheek while juggling a cigar in one hand and an amber drink in the other. "The time change, dear. Always takes me by surprise."

She rolled her eyes. "Time change!" she huffed. "You're a man who lives by the world's clock. Nothing takes you by surprise."

He smiled and kissed her on the forehead. "Ah, I've missed you, my love."

Just then Eleanor noticed the man leaning leisurely at the bar. She rubbed her hands down her hips. "I didn't realize we had a guest." Leonora followed her aunt's gaze. Her breath caught.

The man stepped forward and Owen placed a hand to his shoulder. "Ladies, I'd like to introduce you to Alexander Harrington."

Alex took Eleanor's hand and brought it to his lips, her eyebrows rising oddly. "Good evening, Mrs. Fairfield," he greeted. The young man turned to Leonora, inched close, picked up her hand and kissed it, his lips lingering and soft against her knuckles, sending goose bumps across her arms and up her legs. "Hello, Leonora." He dropped her hand and slid his eyes over her figure. "It's a true pleasure."

Eleanor Fairfield watched the interaction with growing enthusiasm, her lips twitching into an inexperienced smile. Owen squeezed the young man's shoulder again and announced, "Alex has been managing our mine in Bombay."

A maid brought white wine on a silver tray. Eleanor shoved a glass into Leonora's hand, prodded her to drink, then turned back to their guest. "And how are you finding India?"

"Hot." Alex smiled, revealing rows of white, straight teeth. "Depending on the time of year, it can be wet or dry, but always hot." He smirked, his lips well formed and sensual. "India's hard as she is beautiful. Not another place on the earth like it. Thanks to the British, I can still enjoy some normal comforts. Of course, everything's scarce with the war."

"You won't be returning anytime soon, I hope?" Eleanor asked coyly.

"That's up to your husband."

Eleanor dangled her glass between two long fingers, cocked her head. "How old are you, Mr. Harrington?"

"Twenty-seven."

She ran her finger along the rim of the glass, the wine making her amused, her eyes skeptical.

Alex crossed his arms and returned the look, unflinching. "By your expression, Mrs. Fairfield, you're either impressed or troubled. I can't tell which."

"Both, actually." She smiled. "I'm impressed by your ambition. However, I'm disappointed in my husband."

Owen raised his eyebrows against the accusation. "And what have I done?"

"To waste such a handsome and charming man in the pits of Bombay!"

Alex was startlingly handsome. He stood a full head taller than Leonora's uncle, even taller than her aunt by several inches. In his winged collar and ascot his skin was smooth with a hint of tan, his dark hair upswept and rugged, almost windblown, adding a casualness to his form.

"It's not like he's picking rock, darling!" Owen scoffed, then conceded with a bow, "I promise to have you assess the physical attributes of all my workers from now on."

Alex turned to Leonora, his eyes falling on the scoop of her dress. She stretched the fabric to her neck before catching her aunt's scowl. Eleanor motioned to the maid to refill Leonora's wineglass and then addressed her husband: "Your niece has decided to volunteer at the hospital." The statement sounded strangely like a compliment.

"Is that so?"

"What sort of work will you be doing, Miss Fairfield?" Alex asked, his dark, nearly black eyes holding her face.

"I'm not sure," Leonora answered. His gaze became too strong and her face heated. His lips curved to a grin and she was grateful when the maid stepped between them.

Owen raised his empty glass. "Scotch, please."

"Not before dinner, Owen!" Eleanor ordered.

He ignored her. "Alex, will you join me?"

"Not if it displeases the lady." The young man's tone rang with authority and Leonora was amazed. Governors and business moguls alike kowtowed to the Fairfields and here was this man with unsettled hair who did not pluck a word or stall in self-consciousness.

"Actually, I think the evening calls for champagne," Eleanor decided. "Mr. Harrington has put me in a celebratory mood." And indeed, his presence had a joviality about it. Usually evenings were indigestible, choked between excruciating silence and nagging quips. But tonight there was levity and Eleanor Fairfield bubbled subtly like the champagne now uncorked.

"A toast!" Eleanor raised her glass. "To my husband's homecoming, to our guest, Mr. Harrington, and, of course, to our country!"

Leonora drank her champagne, felt the effervescence tickle against her tongue, felt it blend with the white wine already in her stomach, and she found herself flush with gratitude. Tonight brought the banter of her uncle's relaxed speech. Tonight brought a man who drew her aunt's attention away from Leonora's shortcomings. And tomorrow the hospital, freedom from the confines of the house. Tonight there was air. Leonora could breathe, really breathe, this evening, and she turned to Alex and smiled without realizing it—her smile unwavering this time, simply grateful. He raised an eyebrow and his dark eyes danced over her features.

Eleanor Fairfield relaxed into the alcohol, her face loosening, almost pretty. "So tell me, Mr. Harrington, what line of work is your family in?"

"Banking. Investment firms. Commodities. That sort of thing."

"And how's business?"

Owen sucked on an ice cube. "My wife wants to know if you're rich."

Alex laughed. "Working for your husband, no. No disrespect, of course."

"None taken." Owen patted him on the back, then eyed his wife. "Now leave the young man alone, dear."

"It's all right," said Alex. "I have no qualms about talking money. In fact, I admire her frankness. Most people try to find a man's story by his manner or dress or education, or by gossip. I appreciate the forfeiting of games—it makes for a much more interesting and honest evening, I think. Besides, I take no pride in the wealth of my family, just as I'm not ashamed of my own lack of it." Alex leaned casually, his body inching closer to Leonora's. "My father passed when I was quite young; my mother a few years ago. My stepfather is a rich man, it's true, and money has been set aside for me if I need it. But I don't need it, nor will I ever use it." His whole figure shifted and tensed, his eyes hard and steady. "I intend to be a very rich man, but plan on earning every penny myself." He grinned arrogantly. "That's why I feel so fortunate Mr. Fairfield has taken me under his wing. I'm learning from the best."

"Nothing you don't deserve." Owen spoke between bites of ice. "Productivity magnifies around you. Don't know how you do it. Could teach me a few tricks at this point." He plopped another scotch-soaked cube in his mouth. "That's why I'm bringing him to the mills. Want him to see where all that ore is going."

"I hope that means you'll be staying here," Eleanor insisted.

"I don't want to impose."

"Nonsense. We certainly have the room." She turned to Leonora and clicked her teeth with her tongue. "Don't we?"

"Then I'd be honored. I expect we'll be seeing quite a lot of each other." Alex grinned at Leonora, his comment singularly defined.

Eleanor nodded with slit, glowing eyes. She took Owen's drink out of his hand. "Come check on dinner with me."

"I'm sure the cooks have it covered, dear."

Eleanor rolled her eyes, pulled her husband's hand, tilted her head toward the young people. Leonora blushed hotly and lowered her eyes to her hands, tried to sink through the carpet.

Alex reached into his jacket pocket and brought out a small silver case, flicking it open with his thumb. He displayed the line of cigarettes. "Do you smoke?" She shook her head and twisted her hands.

"Good." He took out a cigarette, smacked it twice against the silver and put it in his mouth, shoving the case back in his pocket. "I find it unladylike." He cupped his hand away and lit the tip, sucked in, shrugged. "I'm old-fashioned that way."

They were quiet for several minutes. He peeked at her. "You aren't going to have your aunt throw me out for smoking, are you?"

"No fear of that," Leonora said softly. "You charmed her. That's not an easy task."

Alex leaned back and placed his hand on his heart. "Ah, she speaks!" He smiled widely. "Your aunt is a strong woman and I respect that. A man knows where he stands." He looked at her steadily. "But the bigger question is, have I charmed you?"

Leonora swallowed, but a smile tipped her lips.

"That's more like it!" he teased. He smoked casually, watched her. "How long have you lived with your aunt and uncle?" Alex asked.

"Since I was eight."

"Mind if I ask what happened to your parents?"

The words were drilled and rehearsed. "They died in a fire."

"I'm sorry." His face mellowed.

She drew upon the champagne's warmth to dull her nerves and drown out the guilt of the lie. "My uncle likes you. You must be very good at your job."

"I am," he said with unabashed confidence. "But my credit is limited. I've learned everything from your uncle." He shivered playfully. "Wouldn't want to be on his bad side."

"Oh, he's a teddy bear."

Alex stopped short. "With hidden claws, my dear! I've seen him tear men to shreds."

Now she stopped. "Are you saying he's violent?"

"No. Not violent. But ruthless." He turned to her shocked expression and grinned. "It must sound like I'm speaking ill of him, but it's a compliment. Really. He's an amazing man. A master negotiator. He can give a man a choice, acts like the decision is completely out of his hands, when, in truth, there is only one answer and it always—always—works out in his favor, just as he intended." He glowed in admiration. "Your uncle's got a true gift."

Leonora grew silent. Alex ground out the cigarette in a crystal ashtray. "Here I am with a beautiful woman and I'm talking business. Feel free to yawn." He smirked mischievously, then shoved his hands in his pockets. "Tell me, Miss Fairfield, are you seeing anyone?"

The nerves sparked again, her heart thumping. "No."

"You sure? I'm quite certain I saw a line of suitors standing outside the gates!" he teased.

She rolled her eyes, tried to suppress her smile.

"No husbands I should know about? Hmm? Wouldn't want to step on anyone's toes."

She laughed then—a real laugh with a real smile. She glanced at him and his eyebrows rose with pleasure. "Good," he said as if she had answered. Then he moved to her side, inched his shoulders closer and stared boldly, his face and manner sanguine. He whispered in her ear, "Then you won't be angry if I try to steal a kiss."

"Dinner's ready!" Owen hollered from the hall, nearly loud enough to cover the hammering of her heart.

"Just stand here and hold the pan steady," ordered Nurse Polansky. Tall and blond with a hint of a Polish accent, the nurse looked better suited to the Milan runways than a patient's bedside, but her hands moved aptly and surely over the man's body, raising his eyelid to make sure he was asleep. Taking the scissors, she cut the line of bandages that reached from his knee down to his covered foot, the gauze opening wider with each steady snip.

Leonora felt the blood drain from her face. The skin crumbled black below the gauze, and the smell of wet, rotting flesh rose from the bed. Nurse Polansky removed each square slowly, placing the crusted bandages in the quivering bedpan. Drops of blood beaded from the man's disturbed skin. Leonora closed her eyes and the room spun; bile rose to her throat. "Go," the nurse said firmly, taking the pan and turning back to the patient.

Leonora sped from the room, covering gags until she reached the bathroom. Gripping the toilet with both hands, she vomited until there was nothing left, and still her stomach spasmed for more. She slid to the floor and covered her eyes, reached for the toilet paper and wiped her cheeks. Finally, she walked out to the mirror, her face white, her hands still trembling as she splashed water over her face and patted it dry.

Nurse Polansky didn't look up when she returned. She finished wrapping the man's limb in a fresh bandage, cleaned up the remaining scraps, then motioned with a curved index finger for Leonora to follow. From the nurse's expression, she would be sent back to rolling bandages.

In the common room, Nurse Polansky scrubbed her hands to the elbow, dried them and folded the towel next to the sink. She turned to Leonora. "You're the Fairfield girl, aren't you?"

Her heart sank. "Yes."

"Why aren't you working downstairs with the other volunteers?"

Leonora flushed as she remembered the way the women teased her, called her princess and mocked her cruelly. Nurse Polansky seemed to read her thoughts and nodded. "Do they know you're working up here?" she asked.

"No." She waited for the dismissal.

The nurse opened a drawer and handed her a name tag that said Clara D. "Make sure they don't find out." Leonora looked up gratefully.

"And there's a young man in room three eleven who wants your help writing a letter." The nurse gave a wink. "I think he likes you."

Leonora found the room at the end of the hall and recognized the young man whose arm was amputated a few days before. He couldn't have been more than her age. The stump from the elbow was thickly bandaged and held in a sling. He watched her sit next to the bed and pick up the notebook and pen. She met his gaze and asked gently, "How are you feeling?"

He shrugged one shoulder. "About the same. Gets so I can't remember what it's like not having something in pain." She sat before him intact and yet she knew exactly what he meant.

Leonora tried to change the subject. "Where are you from?"

"South Carolina. Spartanburg." The accent was drawn and smooth. He was freckled, not handsome, but cute, cocky like a farmer chewing a piece of straw.

"And who would you like the letter to?" she asked with poised pen.

"My mom." He smirked. "You married?"

"No."

"Got a beau, then?" His eyes began to glass over.

She knew where this was going, for Cupid held no chance in the face of morphine. "No. Now, what would you like the letter to say?"

"Will you marry me?" The young man looked at her dreamily, and she put down the pen.

"That's the morphine talking, I'm afraid." She covered him up with the sheet for the sleep that was coming his way.

His speech began to slur as he protested, "A man knows when he's in love."

"You don't even know my name."

"Course I do." He craned his neck and squinted at her name tag. "It's Clara. Clara D."

"That's not my name."

"Sure, it's not! See it right there. Not nice to tease a cripple, Clara! Now come on . . . what d'ya say? Will you marry me, darlin'?"

She patted him gently on the good arm. "I'm very flattered, but I won't be marrying you or anyone else, for that matter." The words took her by surprise, for she meant them heartily.

"Sure," he said sarcastically before closing his eyes lazily, giving up the fight against the morphine and her hand. "I know you, Clara. You'll marry. The good ones always do."

* * *

Several weeks later, the moon was new, but the gas lamps bordering the rose gardens spilled ample light along the gravel path. Each segment haloed in the glow before waning gradually into the contrasted darkness, until the garden seemed a place of its own, surrounded by the black of the universe, the stone mansion nowhere in sight. The perfume of roses clung to the warm air and enveloped the skin and senses. Leonora held a silk shawl lightly in her wrists, the back of it drooped along the small of her back.

"There you are." Alex emerged from the shadows. "Your aunt's been looking for you. Party's about to start." He watched her face and edged closer. "What's wrong?"

"I don't do so well . . . socially." She shot a furtive glance at the house, twisted the shawl.

He laughed and kissed her temple. "Ah, but you've never had me as a date before."

His body radiated warmth, made the rest of the air feel cold in comparison. She neared him, the smooth fibers of his jacket brushing against her arm. His thumb touched her little finger, tickled the skin. He took her hand and pulled her gently to a stop. "Is there something else? You've been quiet ever since you got back from the hospital."

"Do you think the war will last long?" she asked, her lips frowning.

"Yes. Fighting like this doesn't end quickly; blood's too thick."

The thought settled dully in her chest. Images of wounded British soldiers who had been shipped to the states for critical care fanned in her memory, bundles of pain more than human bodies, and now the cruelty was to continue with new boys, new pain that spread man's ruthlessness like the plague.

"With war, there are those who suffer and those who prosper," he preached. "I, for one, have no intention of being on the suffering end." Alex touched her cheek with the back of his fingers, traced a path to her jaw before sweeping them under her chin. Without seeming to move at all, he appeared closer, leaned in slowly, touched his lips against hers, lips as full and soft as petals. He put his hand at the small of her back and pressed softly, guiding her body against his. Her arms reached around his waist and held tight to his jacket, her caress spurring him closer, his lips moving surely. Her body, unaccustomed to touch, soaked in his fingertips as they moved up her spine and etched lines across her shoulder blades.

His kiss grew fervent as he parted her lips, slid his tongue around hers, forced her mouth open. The sensations came too fast and she pulled away with a jolt.

With empty arms spread and mouth still open, Alex stood stunned. Then he shut his mouth, covered it with one hand, his body laughing. "I don't believe it. You've never been kissed, have you?"

She turned away, hoped the earth would swallow her whole.

"Aw, darling, don't be upset." The laughter stopped, but his voice was full of merriment. Alex came up from behind and held her shoulders. "I'm sorry I laughed. Truly."

When she didn't move, he kissed the back of her neck. "I find it lovely, actually." He whispered near her ear so that all the tiny hairs of her face tingled with his breath. He kissed the side of her neck. "It's quite enchanting." He kissed the ridge of her collarbone. "Irresistible."

Alex turned her toward him and kissed her lips again, treading more slowly, grazing her lips instead of pressing them. "We'll just have to take this slow, won't we?"

He leaned in and kissed her softly on the throat, moved his lips up her jaw to her earlobe and whispered, "As slow as you like . . ."

By Fairfield standards, the party that evening was a small affair, though the guests held most of Pittsburgh's wealth in their palms. The Monroes and Edmontons were old money multiplied by generations in real estate and banking. New money in resource management, inventions and construction plumped the pockets of the Beekers and Sotherbys. Judge Richardson attended with his gaggle of girls who flirted with any male over seventeen and scowled at any female regardless of age. Then the select higher brood of Mr. Fairfield's steel mills, young men without immediate wealth but its future acquisition a certainty, for no one stayed poor long under Owen Fairfield's wings.

Leonora wore another new dress to go with the others that kept showing up in her wardrobe—Italian, French tags, lower necklines and clinging fabric, silk stockings and slips that made the body feel more naked than clothed. Cocktails were served in the sitting room while maids bobbed invisibly between circles of guests, refilling glasses at every sip. These parties were not new for Leonora, nor was the anxiety surrounding them, for they were insistent reminders that she lived on the periphery and did not fit into any group. But this party was different, for Alex stood so close to her side that a line of heat grew between them, so close that the sour whispers of the Richardson girls and the winks of the mill men could not reach her. His lean, strong body shielded her from Eleanor's pointed criticisms, while his erudite conversation saved her from the tedious chore of small talk.

"Alex!" called Owen Fairfield from a ring of smoking men. "Come join us."

"I've been summoned." Alex winked at Leonora. "Don't talk to any strange men while I'm gone."

Lithe as a cat, Eleanor Fairfield slid to fill his spot, one arm folded at her waist, the other balancing a wineglass. "It's going well then?" she asked. Leonora nodded.

"He's very attentive. I doubt he's taken his eyes off you all night." She pointed her glass to the Richardson girls. "Look at them nearly panting in the corner. Shameful. Of course, their mother's no better. *Tsk-tsk.* Why does that woman insist on wearing cream when it washes her out completely?

"Look at the effect he has on the men as well." Now Leonora's aunt pointed the wineglass at the group of black tuxedos. Owen was bright with story, his hand clasped to Alex's shoulder. "I daresay my husband has a crush on him!" She laughed. "Do you see how the men straighten around him, fix their hair? Remarkable." And she was right. Alex rubbed his fingers through his hair and two of the young men imitated him with comical timing. His manner combined arrogance with casual posture, the beguiling smile erasing any insult. As if his ears were burning, Alex turned to the ladies and took leave of the men.

Eleanor inspected her niece quickly. "Don't screw this up, Leonora."

Alex returned to Leonora's side, placed a hand on her waist and kissed her temple to the open pleasure of her aunt and the chagrin of the young women and men jealous in their own way. "This room is becoming lopsided with beauty," Alex said brazenly. "Not fair really."

"You're a charmer, Mr. Harrington." Eleanor pinched his cheek affectionately before making her way to her husband.

Alex scanned the guests. "I'm having a hard time thinking of anything other than that kiss. You've put me in a pickle." He took a sip of his drink, grinned and rubbed a thumb against her back. "I might have to take you in my arms right now and do something very improper."

After cocktails, they joined the others in the banquet hall and took their seats. Gerald, the butler, as experienced and subtle in his role as a ghost, poured wine so not a glass was less than half-full. Angela, the new table maid, struggled with the tray of soup bowls, each filled to the top. She served Mr. and Mrs. Fairfield first, then nervously placed a bowl in front of Leonora, who looked up at her and smiled with reassurance. The woman took a noticeable breath and steadied.

Owen Fairfield's nose was red from drink as he slapped the table, continuing some story he found extremely amusing. ". . . of course, they didn't expect a Yank to know a lick about polo, but our boy here"—he pointed across the table to Alex—"our boy here beat them clean, then handed them their balls!" The men erupted in laughter.

"Owen!" Mrs. Fairfield gasped.

He raised his hands innocently. "It's polo, dear."

Alex leaned back and laughed, bumping his head against Angela's arm, sending the soup she was serving down the center of his shirt. He bolted upright, nearly knocking the chair over. "Jesus Christ! You clumsy b—!" he shouted, his fury immediate and violent.

Leonora froze, his anger stopping her cold. He caught her look and loosened his jaw. "It's all right." He picked up the napkin and began wiping off the mess.

"It is not all right!" Eleanor scolded. "Did she burn you?"

"No, I don't think so."

Eleanor growled at the quivering maid, "Get out and pack your bags!"

The maid began to cry, her eyes flitting from face to face. Leonora rose and took her by the shoulder. "It wasn't her fault."

"She's right," Alex said, composed, adjusting his neck. "It was my fault."

"Nonsense!" Mrs. Fairfield addressed the butler: "Gerald, get her out of here. Now."

Helplessly, Leonora let go of the maid, watched her hunched figure depart.

"Please accept my apology, Mr. Harrington." Eleanor rubbed her neck. The rest of the guests stared awkwardly into their soup. "Leonora, take Alex upstairs for a new shirt."

Leonora ignored Alex as she stormed from the room, did not slow down as he tried to catch up. She stomped upstairs to the last room, throwing open two walnut doors like shutters.

"You think this is my fault, don't you?" he asked as she opened one closet after another, pushing full hangers aside. She played deaf, scanned a line of shirts and pulled out a white one.

"I'm the one who got scalded by hot soup and you're angry at me?" he shouted.

Leonora inspected the tag at the collar and shoved the starched shirt to him. "Here. This should fit." She moved toward the door and he grabbed her arm.

"Don't be cross. Please?" he begged. "Besides, you can't leave me up here. I'll be hopeless to find my way back."

She kept her back to him but did not attempt to leave. Alex removed his jacket and laid it on a dimpled ottoman and began fumbling with his collar and tie. "Damn it," he mumbled. "Could you give me a hand? These blasted buttons are caked with soup." She turned, dubious.

"Please? Your fingers are much smaller than mine."

Plastered with acorn soup, the man looked quite helpless. Leonora stifled a laugh.

He grinned. "Seeing you smile like that makes a third-degree burn almost worth it."

Leonora stepped toward him and undid the first three buttons under his neck easily. At his chest the button stuck with the soup and she twisted and struggled to free it. The shirt opened in a V at his chest and she swallowed. Her fingers worked on the next button. As she was fully aware of him watching her, a blush rose to her cheeks as her fingers brushed his stomach. She moved a button lower and her hand began to shake. She knew he was smiling just by the way he was breathing. She plucked the button and turned away.

"There's one more," he said smoothly. "You forgot the last one."

Leonora bit her lip, turned back to the shirt, pulled at the button above his belt until the shirt fell open. A line of dark hair grew between his muscles and thickened above his waistband, sending a wave of heat down the backs of her legs. He followed her gaze, looked at his stomach, his muscles rippling with the bend. "You're a nurse." He smiled. "Is the burn very bad?"

"I'm not a nurse," she said, averting her gaze.

"Well, you spend enough time with them." He peeled off the shirt and let it fall to the floor, his broad shoulders as disturbing as the chiseled chest.

She blushed hotly. "You'll live."

Alex finished dressing while she tapped her foot and tried to calm her pulse.

"All better, eh?" he said, moving close. Brushing an arm past hers, he opened the door and bowed. "Thank you for your assistance, Leonora."

As they walked down the hall, he leaned a shoulder against her back and whispered in her ear, "And, for the record, if you ever have soup spilled on you, I'd be happy to reciprocate."

CHAPTER 31

Work in the dry years exhausted James with infertile ground, sowing hope and despair in equal profits, but work in the wet years exhausted him with brute labor. For as soon as the sun exchanged spots with the moon and the tea was as dark as the sky, the work began, and did not finish until the dingoes howled. As a man, James was tall and lean, his muscles long hardened. Still his limbs ached until they quivered, and a dinner fork felt like lead between his fingers. But the growth, the life, was enough to raise weary eyes before the rooster's call, gave the strength to work, and he was nearly disappointed when the day had called to a close. The land fed them, housed them and paved the future, and they drank the green like champagne.

From the woodpile James carried as many logs as would fit in his arms to the house. Tess was buried to her chin under quilts next to the stove. Her eyes lit bright at the sight of him and she stood, dropping the blankets to the floor and holding the chair for support.

"'Tis late." Tess reached for one of the logs in his arms, but the weight was too much and the log slipped out of her fingers to the ground. Fumbling, she bent to retrieve it and brush the splinters between the floor cracks. "Clumsy tonight," she said while keeping her eyes averted. "Here I am tryin' to lighten yeer load an' I'm makin' more of a mess."

"It's all right." James knelt, gently took the log from her hand, then opened the damper on the stove and added the new wood to the fire, stoked it with a poker. He wiped his forehead. Outside, the air was hot; inside, the room was an inferno.

Pots banged at the sink and he turned to see Tess wrestling with the wrought-iron skillet. "Shamus comin' in soon?" she asked, trying to keep her voice level.

"Soon." James picked up her blankets and folded them back on the chair. "Trying to work while the moon is full." But the man worked whether it was light or dark, obsessed. To a man like Shamus, hard work healed all. He worked to keep from seeing Tess's face, hoping his tilling would bring life back into his wife as it did to the plains.

From the pantry Tess found potatoes, and began shaving them with a small knife. "Shame on me, not havin' dinner waitin'." There were tears in her voice.

James came next to her. He was a full two heads taller now. He removed the knife from her fingers. "I'm not hungry."

She hid her face. "Don't lie t'me. Ye haven't eaten all day." A tear dripped on his hand.

James held her by the shoulders, the bony knobs round against his palms as he steered her back to the chair. He covered her with the blankets. "I'll make tea."

She grabbed his hand. "Ye'll have one, too? Ye'll sit with me?"

James smiled and turned to the stove, boiled a pan of water and brought the steaming tea with two scoops of sugar. He sat on the floor next to her slippered feet and sipped the boiling drink. Sweat leaked out of every pore, the tea hot and solitary in his stomach.

"Yeer so much like him," Tess said quietly.

It was hard to focus on anything but the heat and gnawing hunger. "Who?"

"Yeer father."

James peered into the black tea, his brows scrunching toward the bridge of his nose.

Tess's fingers tucked his hair behind his ear with the lightness of a feather. "He'd be proud o' ye." She laughed softly then. "The way yeer forehead creases an' yeer eyebrows knit when yeer thinkin', it's like he's sittin' here with me."

She smoothed down the quilt across her knees. "Wish I had known him better. I was just a girl when he went off. But I remember watchin' him with his books an' his writing. How serious he was, how smart! At night, he'd sneak out to his meetings, dressed in his wool coat, tall an' swift on his horse. Like this gallant Irish knight! I was in awe of him. We all were."

James's throat burned. A question stuck. "Was he a good man?"

Her eyes saddened as she searched James's face. She put her fingers through his hair. "Aye, James." She nodded fiercely. "He was a *great* man. Don't ever think fur a minute he wasn't."

He turned away, but she knew what was in his mind. "James, men were arrested in Ireland for stealin' bread. Boys even! Takin' from their mum's side, fur poachin' a little cow's milk fur a dyin' baby. Yeer father never stole. He was arrested for his words, James. That's all. Fur his words that he spoke an' fur the words that he wrote an' distributed. He spent his last days defendin' the ones who couldn't speak fur themselves." Tess lowered her voice. "Or were ye askin' 'bout he an' yeer mother?"

James held tight to his cup, the heat spreading.

"He loved yeer mother, James. Sometimes love doesn't come bundled neatly." She took his chin in her hand. "Take no shame in it."

The door banged. A hard shadow fell across Shamus's expression as he saw Tess and James so close. Tess dropped her hand.

"Sippin' tea while I'm slavin', are ye?" he snapped at James.

Tess stood up, quivered. "Don't speak to 'im like that! Poor boy hasn't even eaten."

"Makes two of us." Shamus peeled off his shirt to his singlet, pried off his boots and chucked them outside. "It's bloody roastin' in 'ere."

James went to the sink and started peeling the potato left on the counter. Tess's eyes followed him in apology.

Shamus leaned back in the chair, his mood calming. "Tess, ye should see the bales! Goin' t'need a team just to get 'em all to market."

Tess sat down at the table and patted her husband's arm. His eyes fell to the bony fingers; he looked away. "Think we might get a second harvest, too. What d'ye think, James?"

James plopped the lard into the pan and began frying the potatoes. He added the side meat, the grease hopping into the air. "Shelbys starting a second, won't be as big, though. Tom said they're selling the east corner. Hundred and fifty acres."

"That right? Why they sellin'?"

"Didn't say." James didn't know why he lied. But he remembered the expression on Tom's face about selling the property; looked like it nearly killed him. James wasn't going to share the Shelby money problems with Shamus.

"That's what happens when ye leave a woman t'run a business. Sells the best parcel just when the land is givin' back."

James and Tess exchanged a glance. Only Shamus didn't see the wisdom in the Shelby logic. James handed a plate to Tess, but she pushed it away. "No, thank you, James."

Shamus's face fell. "Ye got t'eat, Tess. Please!" he begged. "Just a bite or two."

She poked at the potato, took a few bites into her mouth. She turned away with tears in her eyes and pushed the plate. "I can't." She got up and slipped to her room.

James brought his plate to the table. "She needs a doctor."

The man swallowed and cut into his meat. "Doctor don't know a bloody thing. Ye heard what he said last time. Not goin' to pay t'hear a man's lies."

James lost his appetite and the food grew cold. "She's sick, Shamus."

Shamus stopped chewing and growled, "Course she's sick!" Then he sighed and chewed slowly again. "That's why we're goin' t'take care o' her till she's all better."

Days passed filled with harvest. And when clothes and hair smelled of cut grass and the kookaburras drowned the night with their lulling cackle, James would read to Tess from books borrowed from the Shelby library. With green eyes glowing, Tess drank the words, carried them into her dreams and slept pale with lips upturned. Shamus listened, too, but his eyes darted with the jealousy of the illiterate, his posture sagging with disgruntled admiration.

The last week of October brought sun till supper and rain till breakfast. Boots sank ankle deep into morning red mud and dried stiff by noon. Wheat bowed their tips with the weight of rain, their stalks bent as willows, then slowly rose rigid with the tug of the sun. At times, the wheat seemed to unbend right in front of a man while he watched.

By the last day of the month, the rain fell early and dampened the stalks so that the sickle only dented and could not cut fully. Still, Shamus pressed on through the hanging rows with stubborn slashing and cursing. But the rain pelted and landed so hard in the mud that drops bounced back up so both the sky and ground seemed to rain at once. The horse moved each hoof out of the mud with a long sucking sound and the wagon wheels sank with each step.

"Furget it, James!" Shamus finally hollered, his face slick with water. "Mud's too deep. Call it a day!"

James unhooked the harness and led the horse back to the barn. A stream of water poured from the center crease of his hat. His skin was soaked even under the oilskin coat, the rain dripping down the collar. On the verandah James kicked his boots off and threw the coat and hat on top, then walked into the house shaking the water out of his hair.

"Shhhh." Shamus put a finger to his lips and motioned toward Tess asleep on the bed in the next room. The two men sat across from each other at the table in silence as they ate the leftover stew both were too tired to reheat.

The bed creaked. Tess sat up, her face contorted with fresh pain, her gaunt cheekbones angled with shadows. Shamus turned away, swallowed a chunk of lamb without chewing.

"James"—Tess tried to clear her voice—"will ye come sit with me? Read t'me a little."

Shamus's dark eyes leveled and his mouth twisted to the side. "Ye heard 'er." He stabbed a potato in half with his fork.

James sat on the spindled chair and picked the thick volume off the night table. Emily Brontë. Tess leaned into the thin pillows and pulled the quilt to her chin, the material dwarfing her in its folds. Her black hair and green eyes stood out too boldly, magnified against the white of her skin while everything else seemed to be fading away.

"Read the one 'bout the earth is still," she said lazily. "Ye know which one I mean?"

" 'How beautiful the earth is still'?" he asked.

"Aye! 'Tis the one." Her breath came rapidly, the few words heaving her chest. She lay back down and spoke calmly. "Please."

James read the black lettering on nearly translucent paper. From the corner of his eye he saw Tess writhe. "I'll get Shamus." He stood, but she grabbed his arm.

"No, please. Just stay with me. Please." She closed her eyes for a moment, sank into the pillow. "'Tis passing."

James glanced past the door, saw the back of Shamus's head, his elbow moving food from plate to mouth. When James looked back to Tess's face, she was staring at him. Tears began to spill from her eyes, shining them until they looked like giant green emeralds.

"I'm sorry," she whispered.

Fire shot through his chest. She reached for his hand and squeezed tightly. "I'm so sorry t'leave ye." Her voice broke. "Will ye forgive me?"

"Don't say—" James balled his hands into fists, trying to force his nails through his palms, anything to stop the fire from spreading.

"I need ye t'promise me something," she begged.

James turned away and tightened his mouth, but she grabbed his chin, forced him to look at her. "Promise me ye'll remember that ye were loved. Ye *are* loved. Always."

A tear escaped his eye and dripped hot down his cheek, the very burn of it angering him.

She stroked his cheek, brushed away the trail of the tear and smiled weakly. "Now." She leaned back into the pillow and patted the top of his hand, closed her eyes. "Read to me."

Through the fire, he opened the book, the weight pressing into his numb hands, almost too heavy to hold. He began to read, one sentence at a time, his own shaking voice unfamiliar.

"'*A thoughtful Spirit taught me soon, / That we must long till life be done; . . .*'"

Tess's nails dug into his hand, her body arched.

"'*That every phase of earthly joy / Must always fade, and always cloy: . . .*'"

Her hand untightened, rested limp against his. James's eyes lowered to the end of the poem, the lettering stretching with blurred vision. He choked and read:

"'*The more unjust seems present fate, / The more my Spirit springs elate, . . .*'"

Her hand slid from his and hung over the bed.

" *'Strong in thy strength, to anticipate | Rewarding destiny.'* "

James closed the book, his breathing lone in the room. He rose and did not look down at the woman—there was no need.

James stood in the doorway. Shamus still sat at the table, his back turned. His plate was clean of food and pushed to the center of the table, in wait for someone to clean it. His arm moved back and forth as he scrubbed an oiled cloth over a rusty gear. He glanced back at James quickly before turning back to his work.

And then Shamus stopped. His body stilled, his elbow poised above the gear in suspended motion. With barely a shift of his neck, his face turned, his chin fell, his lips quivered. In that instant, his face morphed from that of a man to that of wild agony.

The gear slipped from his hand and landed with a hollow *ding* on the floor, spinning around and around and around until it fell flat. Shamus tried to stand, gripped the table while his chair fell to the ground with a bang. He pushed past James into the bedroom.

Behind James, the face of agony turned into the sound of agony— pleading snorts into hair, light slaps against skin, shaking flaccid limbs: the heart-stabbing sounds of a burning man trying to wake a corpse.

A moment of silence, then howls of pain, and James ran from it, ran from the house, ran into the wall of rain to the fields, his feet splashing and sinking. He burst into the rows of wheat, the soggy pedicels whipping across his face and arms, and ran blind until the mud held him by the calf. He slumped down and held his scalp with his hands, clutched through flooded hair, and still he could hear the cries stuck between his ears . . . cries that seemed to rise from the very earth.

The months following Tess's death passed in horror. War raged across foreign battlefields, across the home front. There are men who die of wounds and there are men who live with wounds. Tess died and Shamus bled from every pore.

The round table was cleared of plates, of food and tools, the worn wood noticeably smooth with use, the dark grain spreading from one end to the other. And, in the middle of this table, the brown bottle stood. Red wax circled the top and hung in hardened drips along the neck, the seal cracked. The bottle was amber almost to the bottom, where it darkened with an inch or so of liquid. James picked up the bottle, swayed it so the liquid sloshed, the light of the lantern reflecting in spurts. And there it was, in his hands, the war, and he would remember the details of the bottle as if it were an event, not an object.

Shamus emerged from the bedroom, his chin wet and quivering, his eyes red and swollen. James set the bottle down, glass against wood, the sound stamping a memory that would last a life. And then he waited.

The hit came quickly to his jaw, twisted his head with snapping force, painting the world black. Something broke inside that was not made of bone or cartilage or blood. The second hit landed on his temple and knocked him out cold to the hard ground. And so the war came and beat him senseless.

The first hit was the worst but not the last. James never hit back, never ran from it, took it until the blackness ended it. And he would have stayed if Mrs. Shelby hadn't forced him otherwise.

For Shamus, that day brought a late binge and a readied fist, not a knockout punch but a near one. James was at the table still cleaning his dripping nose when Mrs. Shelby barged in unannounced. "Brought yeh some dinner!"

A haunted silence hung in the kitchen among the three. Shamus stood at the counter, his knuckles bloody. Mrs. Shelby turned to James and her eyes bulged, her face as red as the tomatoes in her basket. "You son of a bitch," she snarled at Shamus.

Shamus took a swig of whiskey. "Mind ye business."

Mrs. Shelby gritted her teeth, angry tears welling in her eyes. "Yer wife be rollin' in 'er grave at the sight of yeh!"

The mention of Tess brought his eyes to black. "Ye don't mention me wife! Not 'ere! Ye hear me! Ye all killed 'er with this land, just like James did by draggin' her 'ere!"

Mrs. Shelby plucked the bottle out of Shamus's hand and whacked him across the head, breaking glass over his skull, cutting his skin with razored shreds. She grabbed James's hand with vise strength. "You won't ever lay another hand on him again, Shamus O'Reilly!"

As Mrs. Shelby pulled James down the steps, Shamus flung open the screen, banging it hard against the side. He held his hand against the bleeding side of his head. "Ye leave 'ere, ye never come back! Do ye hear me? Murderers! All of ye!"

Mrs. Shelby dragged James to the buggy and yanked him to the seat. "Close yer ears to it, James." She tried to stay heard over Shamus's threats. "The rantin' of a madman. You pay him no heed!" With one hand she found a handkerchief and pressed it against James's nose, and with the other she picked up the reins and beat the horse to a gallop. And even above the clatter of hooves on stones, harness buckles flapping and old buggy wheels grinding, they could still hear Shamus's curses, even as the house disappeared in the swallowing twilight.

CHAPTER 32

Before the Americans joined the fighting, the prospect of war held the breath of the country the way an autumn frost stiffens grass for snow. Ears tuned to radios took hope that Europe's war would not become America's war. Woodrow Wilson, in speech and pomp, appeared of like mind and so the hope remained.

But there were others who knew the war was growing. Leonora knew, for she heard the murmurs between Alex and her uncle, saw the shadows that lined their faces as they spent more time at the mills, the way their mouths twisted at telegrams.

The people of Pittsburgh raised their noses in the air and sniffed the tainted, first scents of war. Leonora saw the subtle, silent fear in the female help as they wondered at this strange threat of a draft, their thoughts occupied with sons or new husbands or brothers as they dropped the silver and carried the china with unstable hands. Leonora saw the faces of stable boys, the close way men spoke to one another, looked at their feet and then off into the distance like they smelled fire. She noticed the ripple of violence in the air, moving and gnawing like a hungry beast, spurring deep lines in foreheads and jaws clenched against the unknown.

Then, on April 6, 1917, America declared war on Germany. The skin of the country rose like gooseflesh with a mix of fear and excitement. The bravado of the American boys rang in the streets, as they spouted their strength over that of the Krauts. But these were boys who did not know the cold of the trenches, the weight of a bayonet or the sight of another man gutted.

And no sooner were the young men sent out—dropouts from Sewickley, miners from McKee's Rocks, tutored boys from Shady Side—than boys returned in broken pieces. Outside the hospital body bags and gurneys made quick bursts from ambulance to sidewalk to building, while two streets over a longer procession filled the road as a parade of boys, brown clad, steel hatted and armed, waved farewell to the people lining the streets.

Emotion filled the faces of the people as the boys walked off intact. Mothers memorized their children's features, wondered if they would scar or warp, and they saw not the faces of the young soldiers or the men they had become but the innocence and frailty of the children the women had borne. Fathers saw their sons as older than they were, as men, as extensions of their own arms. They looked with pride and pain and questioned, *Did I make him strong enough? Will he be brave enough?* And so the war began and brought casualties before good-byes were even spoken.

In the hospital, along the rows of torn bodies, Leonora saw the rainbow of war—each macabre hue—the yellow of typhoid and sclerosis, the black of gangrene, the white of pneumonia—the recurring colors that foretold amputation or death as inevitably as a sentence. The duties at the hospital were gruesome and left Leonora rattled and consternated. And she hated it and loved it all at the same time. For even in the horror, the sights were stark and real and, despite the smell of death, there was life and intrepid hope in the sterile rooms.

And there was healing. For here Leonora found a piece of herself that did not belong to the Fairfields, had not been warped in lies or transformed by false impressions. Here she brought smiles to those who cried, gave hope to those who had none and held the hands of soldiers who woke each night screaming with hidden horrors. And this belonged to her and yet was not about her. She gave and gave freely and opened her heart to a greater good that lit with hope. This was not bought or held upright through forced conditions but flowed from her soul and brought gooseflesh to her arms that she was still here, she was alive, she was intact and could serve a purpose that was real. Here she did not shrink and wish to disappear; here she wished to shine and offer what *she* had to give.

Leonora was deep in these thoughts as she changed the bedsheets and jumped slightly when Nurse Polansky tapped her shoulder. "Someone's downstairs looking for you," she said, smiling oddly. "He's tall, dark and handsome."

Leonora's hand came to her throat. She patted her uniform, picked at lint that wasn't there. She was surprised by her sudden resistance, annoyance that Alex was here. This was her sanctuary and she felt him strangely as an intruder.

"Wouldn't keep that one waiting," the nurse reminded. "The Red Cross ladies are panting at the window."

Leonora nodded, hurried through the hall and down the metal steps, while trying to shake off her petulance. As she rounded the corner, she found Alex observing a watercolor hanging on the wall, his hands laced behind his back. Her hands were dry, but she still wiped them over her white skirt.

"I've been looking everywhere for you." Alex gave her a quick kiss on the cheek.

"What are you doing here?"

His eyebrows went up. "Well, I thought I might get a warmer reception than that."

"I'm sorry." She looked furtively down the hall. "I just didn't expect to see you here."

"Apparently." He picked up the name tag, his finger lingering on her breast. "Clara."

Quickly, she reached up and unclasped the pin, putting the name tag in her pocket. "The Fairfield name has a strange effect on people." She pointed to the family's plaque on the wall.

He sighed and nodded, for this he understood. "Why aren't you with the volunteers?"

"They were shorthanded upstairs."

"Oh." He put his tongue in his cheek. "With the soldiers?"

Her heart galloped with his tone. "Yes."

"You think that's appropriate? You're not a nurse, after all."

"I know." Her insides shrank. "Alex, why are you here?"

His face calmed, he reached for her hands. "I need to go away for a while."

Alex shifted his eyes to the nurses in the hallway and lowered his voice. "My number in the draft came up. Your uncle is trying to pull some strings, saying I'm needed here. It's true actually. England and America can't get enough iron. Anyway, it's best if I go away until the whole thing is cleared up. I'm fairly confident your uncle will make them see that I'm more useful at the mills." He chuckled. "Certainly more useful than getting shot on the front lines."

Leonora grimaced at the light reference, thought about the wounded young men upstairs. Alex mistook the look for worry and stroked her cheek. "I want you to come with me."

It took a minute for his words to register, for the dread to enter. "What?"

"I'm not ready to say good-bye to you yet."

She floundered and found comfort in an unlikely ally. "My aunt will never allow it."

He laughed again. "She's the one who suggested it. Your uncle will be our chaperone."

Leonora looked longingly at a group of nurses chatting at the front desk. "Alex, I can't just abandon the hospital. They don't have enough hands as it is."

"Yes, yes." He pinched her chin and clicked his tongue. "How would they ever manage without you?" He leaned in happily. "Besides, it's already been taken care of. I spoke to Dr. Edwards. Said they had more bandage rollers than they knew what to do with." He looked very pleased with himself.

"You did what? How—"

"Between you and me, he hardly remembered you volunteered here."

"You had no right!" The words flew out quick and heated.

"You're angry?" he sputtered.

"Of course I'm angry!" A few heads from the hall turned their way. "You had no right to go behind my back without speaking to me first."

He grabbed her roughly by the elbow and his pupils dilated. "You should be thanking me!" he hissed, keeping alert to listening ears. "Anyone in their right mind would be begging for an excuse to get away from this place. You can smell the death as soon as you walk through the doors. I'm not happy with you being here; neither is your aunt." He hushed again, his voice taking on a hint of smugness. "It's really not . . . proper . . . for someone of your background."

"I'm finished talking, Alex." She turned, but he took her hand, gently this time.

"Look, I'm sorry if I upset you. I should have talked to you first. You're right." He gave a quick bow. "In my defense, I truly thought you would be pleased." Alex's mouth frowned in earnest. "I'm a bit on edge, Leonora. Things are moving faster than I expected. It's important I leave as soon as possible." The half smile returned. "I'll make you a deal. Come away with me for a few weeks and I'll convince your aunt to let you continue to work at the hospital when you get back. She was planning to have you quit."

"She can't force me to quit, Alex."

"Maybe not, but she can have you fired." Spite flickered, turned up one side of his mouth. "Your aunt and uncle give this place enough money they'll do whatever they wish. What's one volunteer to a new wing of a hospital, after all?"

Once again, the shackles of her family's name cut into her flesh, choking any freedom. She looked into Alex's handsome face, searched for a glimmer of understanding or compassion, but found the eyes empty, disinterested. She turned her face from him and her gaze landed on the watercolor hanging on the wall. Her lips parted, and for a moment time slowed and the noise of the hospital faded. The painting brushed the strokes of the sea, of a perfect sky and sheer cliff sides that seemed to rise from the very earth, from an ancient time, from an ancient land. A warmth flooded her chest, and for a second she was there, her feet dangling over the cliffs, sitting next to a friend who always chased the demons away.

Alex shook her arm. "Leonora, did you even hear a word I just said?"

And time began to move again; sounds invaded the silence. The painting turned back into an amateur imitation of a pastel landscape and she pushed the memories away, pushed the ache down to her fingers and then gripped them into fists. She looked at the nurses and the patients moving through the hall. The hospital was all she had in this world and Alex's ultimatum leaned only one way. Resignation settled. "When do we leave?"

CHAPTER 33

The Shelbys folded James into their home and family as if he had been naturally born into it. There was no mention of Shamus's abuse; there was no pity, no words of transition, no questions. The extent of the Shelby kindness and warmth made renowned bush hospitality seem like snobbery in comparison. And in turn, James offered the only reciprocation he could—work.

Each morning, James, Tom, John and Will set off for one paddock or another, their stomachs full from Mrs. Shelby's cooking, their sleeves rolled down against the bite of dawn. Even between their eight strong arms, work outnumbered them. Help was seldom hired, only afforded for the busiest seasons of shearing and harvest. And each night, they returned orange with dust, dirty and smelling of sheep or grass or fur or whatever the job had been for the day. The work was as hard as at home, but here there was chortling and joking, so much that James's side hurt more from laughter than it did from labor.

Under the guise and training of the Shelby men, James learned to cull dingoes and rabbits through trap and bullet, learned to brand the calves and castrate. With quiet fortitude, he held his stomach and learned quickly that he hated the cruel tasks beyond description. And, after some hearty ribbing from the brothers, learned he would never have to do them again.

Instead, in an equal exchange, James took over the stock, a chore as loathsome to the Shelby boys as branding had been to him. What had previously taken the work of all three brothers James now did alone. Expert riding bareback or saddleback, he steered with a touch of the reins or nudge of the knee and could charge a horse, against all its instinct, straight into a ring of angry bullocks without touching a spur to fur.

James trained the unruly dogs, overbred mongrels with more dingo in them than shepherd. They followed him with wild, alert faces so that he only needed to nod, wink or raise a brow in command. And after a day exhausted with work in the paddocks, he lavished such great affection on them that the dogs would curl and whine with an ecstasy that mimicked pain.

The whip became another appendage. With it looped at his hip in rest, he could flick it out quick as a lizard's tongue. But James used the whip as warning, not instrument, the crack more menacing than its touch, for he could round the bulls and the sheep without a snap to their hides. So James worked the farthest paddocks, mended fences along the way and drove the cattle from one area of grassland to another.

And he loved this land that grew and stretched under feet and hooves, the land that opened endlessly until it seemed to slope as the curve of the earth. Through the spotted shade of the box gum forest, green and yellow parrots sat in ornament along the branches. Red kangaroos, tall as men, clustered by the hundreds in rust-colored expanse, chewing leaves and licking paws to stay cool. The land was noisy with life but silent in purity.

On searing afternoons, he'd strip down for a bogey in one of the deep creeks and swim from one end to the other. Then, floating on his back, the sun warm against his bare chest and the water cool against his back, he would watch the platypuses slip off rocks and ripple the glass surface next to his body. After the swim, he'd dress back in his clothes that lay cooking on a slab, drying his body instantly.

Beyond the forest, the grassland grew to his waist and the cattle chewed to bliss and here he would spend the night in the open air, under the stars, only his bedroll between him and the earth, and he would drift into the stars as he did with sleep and find it more a home than anything built out of slab or timber.

During these years with the Shelbys, James did not go back to Shamus, tried not to think of the man darkened and lost in despair.

Mrs. Shelby, saint and forgiving soul that she was, dropped off food once a week on the old porch steps, never mentioned if it was eaten. Tom retrieved the horse for fear of starvation, but without comment on the homestead. Shamus was a ghost, only accounted for by neighbors who dragged him home from the pub or plucked him sleeping out of ditches along the road. "Never saw a man fall to drink so fast," one man would say, and another would nod: "Irish got t'drink their grief." James would burn under the shame, under the pitying glances.

Over time, James's long body had become used to the ill fit of the Shelby couch, his legs awkward and hanging over the worn side. James scrunched his fist under the pillow, flitted in and out of a dream. Something poked his arm—a wheat stalk, a branch maybe. Stuck in the confines of sleep, he brushed it away. Another poke, a blurred dream. He grunted and flopped his arm over his chest.

"Jamesie," whispered the poker.

James jolted, dropping the book that was fanned on his lap to the floor with a thud. "Charlotte? What are you doing up?"

The little girl sucked in her bottom lip, wiped her nose through choppy sobs.

James reached for her hands. "What's wrong?"

"I-I-I had a bad dweam," she stammered, a snot bubble forming in one nostril.

James patted down his shirt until he found a handkerchief and held it to her nose.

"Can I-I-I . . . stay with you, Jamesie?" she asked with new tears.

He sat her on his knee, hugged her shoulders. "Course you can." He kissed the top of her red hair. "Want to tell me about the dream?"

She shook her head and leaned against his shoulder. Her chest quivered as she tried to hold her cries. James stroked her arm.

"Do . . . do . . . you ever have bad dweams?" she asked.

"Sometimes."

"How you make 'em go away?"

James thought for a moment, kissed her on the head again. "I try to think of happy times. Beautiful places, good days . . . that sort of thing."

She raised eyes that were round and wet and open. "Like what?"

He smiled. "I think of the sea."

"Tell me 'bout it." She smiled. "Please?"

"Well," he started. "There's a place, not too far from here, where the earth meets the sea. Cliffs as big and golden as a mountain seem to rise right out of the ocean, like a giant took a bite out of the side of Australia. The water is as blue as the sky and nearly as big." He closed his eyes for a moment. "When the sun shines on the water, it's like a field of diamonds all glittering at once. It's beautiful, Charlotte. Almost as pretty as you." He pinched her chin and she giggled.

"I never been t'the sea," she said.

"I'll take you someday. Promise."

Her little face grew serious. "You'll always stay with us, right, Jamesie?"

"Long as you'll have me."

Each cheek dimpled. James rubbed her arm and rocked her gently until her body loosened with sleep. Then he untwined her arm from his neck and laid her on the couch, covered her with the quilt and took his pillow to Tom's room, where he stretched out on the floor. He tucked his hand under the pillow and shifted his hips on the hard floor, didn't realize he had fallen back asleep until the wood boards vibrated and his eyes opened in the dark.

"Get up, ladies!" John jabbed him in the ribs with his boot. James twisted onto his belly and buried his head into the pillow.

John moved over to Tom and pulled the quilt off. Tom grabbed it, his hair in full distress. "Bugger off!"

"Get movin'. Mum needs us to take the wheat down to the weigh station."

Tom grunted. "What d'you need us for?"

"You know they always pay more when we got two pretty girls with us!" he teased.

"Stop messin'. Why we need t'go?"

"You an' James need to pick up the new harness. Came in by rail yesterday." His tone was serious now. "John an' me will take care of the wheat an' then you can meet us back there. Got to leave now else we'll be comin' back in the dark."

Tom swung his feet out of bed and rubbed his hand through his mop of hair. James rose from the floor and stretched, his back cracking.

"Oh, an' wear that little pink number with the bows. It really brings out your eyes!" John laughed and ducked from the pillow thrown at his head.

James changed quickly, pulling his suspenders up with a snap. Tom moved slower, grumbling as they went outside. Will and John already had the wagons coupled. The sun was just rising over the horizon and a slight morning chill clung to the air. One by one, the bales of wheat were jabbed with hand hooks and loaded onto the bed. It was heavy work and the dust flew in their eyes and noses. James rubbed his face on his shirt as the last bale was hauled on top. Will got the ropes and each man paired to secure grips across and under the wagon.

"Boys, come in for breakfast!" Mrs. Shelby called from the door.

"No time, Mum. Need to get to the weigh station b'fore the crowd," John answered.

"Don't argue with me! Not makin' that drive without something in your stomach." She turned back into the house.

John sighed. "We eat quick, got it?"

The smell of fat-soaked sausages filled the room. The boys gulped the black coffee and finished their eggs and meat without a word exchanged. The roosters sounded a morning call behind the house— they weren't the early risers this morning.

"Be back by dark, Mum." John kissed her quickly on the cheek, leaving a greasy print.

"What you think napkins are for!" She wiped her cheek with her apron. "You boys be good. Don't let them stiff you on a good price for that wheat." She went back to clearing the table for the next round of hungry mouths.

Will and John sat in the front of the wagon behind the horses. James and Tom took a seat on the wheat. The ride was rocky, the wheat shifting under the weight and the sway of the wagon. There was little talking, each man set with his own thoughts. Tom stretched out sleepily, his boots crossed at the ankles, his teeth nibbling a strand of hay.

By 10:00 am, they passed the McGinnys' sprawling house with netted verandah, tennis court and fruit-burdened orchard. A new crop of wheat greened the top sphere of the homestead.

"Seen the McGinny girls around?" Tom asked.

"Jesus, Tom. Sun's not even up an' your pants are perked!" Will teased.

"What?" Tom raised his hands innocently. "Just asked a simple question."

James threw a clump of hay at him. "Horny bastard."

"Besides, you don't have a chance with 'em." John laughed. "Only got eyes for James. All three of 'em."

Tom rolled his eyes dramatically and in his best falsetto chimed, " 'Oh, James, he's so handsome . . . so mysterious!' " He fluttered his eyelashes.

James smirked. "Can't blame a lady for having taste."

The men remained quiet the rest of the hours, drowsy and lazy above the lulling wagon motion. As they approached the Southern Cross, a few drays and horses and several tramps passed, each tipping a hat and giving a hearty, "G'day."

Tom yawned, smacked the hay off his pants. "Want to drop us off at the station first?"

The men exchanged a look. Will nodded in signal. John cleared his throat. "When we get to town, you an' James need to weigh the wheat an' pick up the harness."

"Why?" Tom shoved between them, his elbows touching. "Where you goin'?"

"Got some business t'take care of."

Tom scoffed at the secretive tone. "What business?" The boys were silent. "Come on. Out with it," he pressed.

"We're enlisting, Tom," John answered quietly.

The creaking wheels ground against the furrow; the hay slid and brushed across splinters.

"What?" Tom gulped. "In the army?" Dead air confirmed it. "Does Mum know?"

"No."

"When you gonna tell her?"

"Tonight."

"She's gonna flip!"

"That's why we have to do it b'fore we tell her. Otherwise, she'll chain us to the house."

Tom leaned back against a bale, his eyes wide as the words sank in. Then he sat up like a lightning rod. "Oh no, you don't! Not without me an' James. You're not goin' without us!"

"You know the army don't take women." Will meant to make light, but his tone fell flat.

"We're goin' with you," Tom said with finality.

Will pulled the horses to an abrupt stop next to the road and turned around, his face stern. "Look, Tom, you can't go 'cause Mum an' the girls need you. They need both of you. We'll make a small wage in the army that we'll send home, but it won't be enough."

"Then you stay. James an' me will go."

"It ain't gonna happen, Tom. Mum can't take care of the fields without you an' we need James for the stock. You know that. Besides, you're Mum's favorite. Anything happen to you, it'd be like losin' Dad again." John said it without jealousy and no one argued.

Tom sat sullen, his mind busy trying to plead its case. "Makes no sense! Money from the army can't be more than you make at home."

John sighed. "If this dry spell turns into another drought, which all signs are pointin' at, the army'll be about the same pay. Look, Tom, we're enlisting, so we're not arguing with you, just tellin' you the facts. You're the eldest now, so the accounts will be in your hands. We're in a bad way. No sugarcoatin'. We didn't make taxes last quarter an' we're still payin' down the interest from the year before."

"But the last years were good ones, saw the figures myself."

"Dad had some bogus bonds, no fault of his own. Then the bank failed. We started at a deficit. After he died, we never caught up. I'm not gonna whine about it like a poor bum an' you can't, either. It's just how it is."

"It's not just the debt," Will added. "Look, we're not war chasin' or fancy for diggin' trenches in Turkey, but it's the only way. Government's dividing crown land to the returning soldiers. Mum, holdin' a lease an' not payin' the taxes, has to be top of the list for cutting up the homestead. If she's got two sons back from the war, it's as good insurance as we got that we can keep it. At least if we want to sell the land, we get the profits before the government does."

"Look, Will an' me been around this whole thing two, three times over and we got our plan," said John. "Sulkin' ain't gonna pay the debts, so better start swallowin' it now."

John turned to James. "You're part of this family, too, and Mum needs you." He cocked his head at Tom. "Talk to him. It's the only way."

Tom was still pissed when they curved the ring around the market, the price they got for the wheat not helping. Crops screwed a man one way or another. In drought, a man can't grow enough for profit; in the wet, a man grows too much and floods the market and drowns the price.

The *ding* of metal against metal vibrated up from the new railroad line near the center of town, grew louder as they walked. Tom was brooding, halted in mid-stride, twisting his lips. "Damn it. Should have fought for more money." He turned on his heels. "I'm goin' back."

James shoved his hands into his pockets. "He's not going to budge."

"Then it's gonna feel bloody good kickin' him in the teeth." As if to prove his point, he kicked a rock, spiraling it into the air. It wasn't the price of wheat that burned.

James finally asked, "Why you so hot to go to war?"

"Because I'm fuckin' stuck, mate! I've been on the same patch of dirt since I was born." Tom rarely angered, but his face grew red, then balanced. "I love the land. I do. But scares me t'death to think of never leavin' it. Just birth an' death with only cows an' wheat an' a few girls to pass the time in between." He looked at the horses and the old wagon, empty now of its cargo, his eyes bitter. "I'd leave in a heartbeat if it weren't for the money."

They walked down the main street, heads low. The sun beat upon their backs, lines of sweat streaking their spines. The railroad shimmered ahead, the glare blurring the metal till it showed white. A row of Chinese swung the giant mallets above saucered hats. Their bodies, bone thin, pounded in synergy, one set raised, the other hammering, over and over again like the pistons of a steam engine. The sharp *ding* bit into the eardrum, throbbed into the foot's arch.

James felt Tom's weariness and the burden of Shelby debt as if it were his own. The hands of poverty tightened around his neck and squeezed with shame that he wasn't able to help the family that sheltered him. "Evict us. Shamus and me," James blurted. "The land is sitting idle while you're paying taxes."

Tom dismissed it without a pause. "Nothin' doing."

"We've taken charity long enough. Rent the land or sell it. I'll drag Shamus off myself."

Tom grew angry. "Doesn't matter, James! Nobody's rentin'; nobody's buyin'. Land's going to sit there whether your dad's there or not. Besides, with you gone, who'd run the stock? You're worth more than that bum piece of land, three times over."

The men watched the Chinese hammer under the blistering heat. Tom rattled the loose change in his pockets. "I need a drink."

"Me too."

They stepped over the fresh rails, the ground undulating beneath their boots, and passed the co-op to the pub on the corner. Made of old steel drums, bolted, taped and welded together, the pub stunk with confined sweat and spilled beer and was filled with bushmen and farmers—one set coming from the east, the other from the west—converging around sharp liquor.

"Two whiskeys!" Tom ordered, scanned the crowded tin can. "There's Flanegan and Berkshire." He raised his glass in greeting to the rough jackeroos from the Baratta Station.

The men grinned as they approached. "Wonderin' when we'd run into yer ugly mugs!" the giant Flanegan hollered, a trail of whiskey slurring his words.

"Don't sweet-talk us," Tom sported. "Your girlfriend's gonna get jealous."

They all shook hands, firm and worn palms slapping. Berkshire was quiet, but his smile was silly, his pupils bobbing in ale.

"Sell this mornin'?" Tom asked.

"Sell? Robbed more like it!" Flanegan growled. He was the biggest bloke in the county by a head, a fiery Irishman who held the shearing record for a hundred miles—a man famous for his limited talents: shearing, drinking and brawling.

Berkshire shrugged. "Bloke's got us by the balls."

"Yeah." Flanegan pursed his lips. "Where's yer brothers, Tom?"

Tom beat the ground with his boot. "Signin' up."

"No shit!"

Tom swirled his drink until it splashed over the rim.

Flanegan eyed James. "Still livin' off the Shelby fat, eh, James-o?"

"Still drinking your baby's milk money, eh, Flanegan?" James poured the whiskey down his throat in one gulp.

"Damn right!" the man spit darkly. "Sittin' right along wiv yer dad." James slammed the empty glass onto the bar.

"Just jokin'!" Flanegan smacked James roughly on the shoulder, nearly knocking him over. "No worries, eh, James-o?" He hit him in the arm without restraint, his eyes violent above his cock-eyed grin. Flanegan wandered off.

James motioned for another drink, brought it to his lips, drank it empty.

Tom watched his friend. "Easy, mate. You're not a drinker."

James ignored him, ordered a third. His arm still ached with Flanegan's punch and he absently ran his fingers over the spot. He watched the brown bottles of beer and whiskey poured along the bar, saw the bottle that had sat on Shamus's table. He rubbed the bruise harder and remembered the look on Shamus's face when he hit him, remembered the drunken gaze that looked no different from Flanegan's. The buzz of the pub bounced around his ears and he drank, closed his eyes to the pounding thoughts that grew louder and the memories more violent, drank still more. The throng of hammering from the railroad reverberated under the pub, the monotonous ting of metal throbbing his brain like an impending headache.

Flanegan stumbled back through the bar, splashing whiskey from his glass over Tom's sleeve. "Watch it!" Tom bellowed.

Flanegan slunk between Tom and James, dropping a heavy arm around each neck. "Two drinks fer my mates!" he hollered, his skin wet with sweat and alcohol.

"See those coolies workin' the line?" Flanegan slobbered. "Look like stinkin' women with those braids." His lips were slick. "Hate coolies. Half a mind t'beat 'em wiv those mallets."

James squeezed the glass in his fingers, thought it might crack. "Leave 'em be."

"Whot's that?" Flanegan rattled his head, cocked his ear.

James met the drunk's gaze straight. "You don't beat a man for wanting a better life."

Flanegan paused and then leaned his head back in hard laughter. He whistled and laughed again, so loudly that a few men turned and listened.

James looked at Flanegan through his own growing whiskey cloud. He looked at the sausage fingers, short and stubby as Shamus's. He tasted blood, his own blood, as he bit his lip with clenched teeth. All the good was leaving, like voices fading down a well, and in their place the flood of anger rose and gripped what it could for growth.

Flanegan raised his glass, his pupils dilated and unfocused in the dim light. "A toast!" he yelled in smeared, cutting speech. "To the coolie-lovin' mooch . . . may 'is dead mother be proud!"

James smashed his fist into Flanegan's broad nose before the glass touched his lips. The man's head stayed tilted with the blow, still stunned. Then his neck twisted, his eyes wild in disbelief. "Why, yeh son of a—"

James pulled back, belted another blow to his jaw. Flanegan fell through the men, the crowded bodies breaking his fall and thrusting him upright. James jumped at him, the skin across his knuckles breaking as he punched the bones of the man's face—as he punched Shamus, the drought, the charity, the debts, the deaths, the plow, the loss, the pity and the void. And Flanegan returned the blows, fist for fist, grunt for grunt, across tables and broken glass.

In a rush of adrenaline James heard Tom curse, "Aw, Christ!" Heard men hold him back and shout, "Leave 'em be. 'Tis a fair fight!" And then another voice: "Fair or not, get 'em outta here 'fore they break the place!"

Between punches, their bodies were shoved out into the sun, where they landed in the dust. James rose, but Flanegan kneed him in the side, sent him to the ground with stupefying pain, then raised him by the shirt collar and held him tight as he landed two pummels to the side of the head. The fighters grabbed at each other, their fists slipping in blood, but now unobstructed by the pub confines, Flanegan used his full strength. And with one final blow to the head, James didn't see the ground, just fell into blackness as his head bounced off of it.

* * *

"Roll up your coat and put it under his head," John's voice echoed from a long tunnel.

James tried to open his eyes, but the right one sealed tight, the other opened a crack, the narrow slits of light instant intruders. His head felt as large as a watermelon.

James saw stars. Real stars that stretched and bounced, then doubled and blurred. He closed one eye, the other still glued shut, and the blackness spun in his head and the sour whiskey swirled in his stomach and tipped the earth. He rolled on scraps of hay till he nearly fell off the dray's boards. James threw up over the side, his bruised ribs tortured with each hurl.

"Sunshine's up," said John from the driver's seat.

James rolled on his back, his head bouncing over the unweighted wagon, each thump an anvil to the skull.

"Sit up." Tom pushed his shoulders from behind. "Look good in purple, James."

James squinted and pressed his hand to his ribs. Tom grinned, a bloody handkerchief against a split lip, his nose crusted black at each nostril.

"What happened to you?" James croaked.

"Fell onto Flanegan's fist." John chuckled.

Tom laughed, winced as the lip reopened. "Not gonna sit by while they make pulp outta my mate."

James thought he might throw up again. "I can fight my own battles."

John laughed. "Yeah, we can see that."

"Good thing Tom's an idiot. He saved your arse," Will added. "We come back from the office an' Tom's bleedin' like a busted pipe but got his arm around Flanegan and Berkshire, singin' their hearts out."

Tom crooned with tone-deaf acumen:

> *"On hill and plain the clust'ring vine*
> *Is gushin' out with purple wine . . .*
> *And cups are quaffed to thee and thine—Australia!"*

He held his heart in mock sentiment and placed a hand on James's shoulder, and even in his pain James cracked a smile. "See! Irish can't stay mad when a drunk is singing to him. Even a drongo like Flanegan." Tom stuffed the handkerchief deeper into his nostril.

Hours later, under a full moon, the wagon pulled into the homestead. James held his head between his hands, trying to keep it from exploding. John pulled up and looked at the lights in the window. "Here we go."

The brothers dragged James toward the house. John pulled the door open with his foot and let it slam behind them. The children were at the table eating, their forks hovering in their fingers as James came into view. Gracie cried out. Mrs. Shelby spun from the stove, her mouth open before pinching closed. "Girls, go get some towels!" she ordered. The children sat dumb with staring.

"Out with you!" she hollered. "Scoot!"

The children knocked into one another as they fled.

John cleared his throat, hit James on the back. "Aw, Mum, should have seen James here. Took on the biggest bloke in the county! Brute causin' a load a trouble b'fore he stepped in."

"Put him here." Mrs. Shelby pulled out a chair and filled a pot of water, the boys fidgeting under her rare silence.

Will spoke up nervously. "Yeah, bloke had it comin'. Looks worse than James for sure."

Mrs. Shelby pushed past them. The three brothers glanced at one another and waited.

"Go help the girls." Mrs. Shelby knelt in front of James, picked up his chin and examined his face.

"He's orright, Mum," Tom noted. "More blood than anything else."

She whirled her head. "Get out! All of you!" Mrs. Shelby watched them leave. "Raised a bunch of idiots, I did." She turned to James, began cleaning his cut cheek, applying pressure against the opening. "You proud of yourself?"

James winced under the sting of words, of water on open flesh.

"Feel good to you, eh?" she asked. "Taking your fist to somebody's face? Getting your own smashed in? Drown yourself in drink. Makes it all better then, eh?"

James looked at her with his one bloated eye, then lowered it.

"You're better than this, James." She sank the cloth back into the water, the blood clouding it pink. "I'd expect this from my boys. Not from you. Your mother be turnin' over in her grave."

He pulled his face away. "Tess wasn't my mother."

"I know." She paused. "I was talkin' about your real mother."

"How'd you know?"

"Any blind fool could tell!" she fumed. "You're about as different from Shamus in feature an' temperament as a man could be!"

She picked up the cloth again. "I got to know your auntie pretty well. Knew Tess was sick 'fore Shamus did. She told me you weren't their son by birth, how they adopted you."

His face loosened, his body grew limp, the weight of whiskey heavy against his thoughts.

"That woman loved you, James." Her voice faltered. "It'd be torture for her to see what you did to yourself—what Shamus did to you."

"She's dead because of me." A cracked rib stabbed his lung; he didn't flinch.

"That's a lie! Tess had cancer, James! All over her insides, you hear me? She had six miscarriages because of it. You were the only thing that kept that woman alive as long as she was. You! She knew she was dyin'—knew she was dyin' before she left Ireland. Said you were the only thing that kept her fightin' for life each day. You!"

Mrs. Shelby took his battered face roughly in her fingers. "You listen to me, James, an' you listen good. You have a choice in this life. You can let the anger an' the grief eat your insides out. You can drink that anger till it poisons everybody around you. That's what Shamus done. He's a damn coward, James!"

Her hand turned gentle and her eyes glistened, but she spoke firmly. "You got choices, James. What are you gonna bring to this world . . . peace or suffering?"

She wrung out the cloth in the pan, the water dark red now. "Go on to bed."

James hobbled to the library, collapsed onto the couch. Breathing came from the room's corner and he turned to see Charlotte, sobbing.

"Why'd they hurt you, Jamesie?" she asked, her chin wrinkled as an old apple.

The tears stomped his heart. "I was an idiot, Charlotte. Nobody's fault but my own."

The little girl frowned so greatly that her whole face pulled down. "I got scaret when I saw you. Real scaret. Thought you was dead."

Shame lit through him like a match and he looked down at his torn, bloodied hands and he saw the choice, saw it clear and bold, felt it down to his marrow.

John and Will entered the room and turned the girl by the shoulders. "Off to bed, little one." Charlotte nodded and left.

"Mum alone?" asked Will. James nodded and the boys squared their shoulders and went to the kitchen.

James lay on the sofa in the dark, his head pulsing with words and pain. Voices wafted from the kitchen, too muffled to discern. John spoke mostly, Will on occasion. Mrs. Shelby's voice lay mute.

By and by, the chairs scratched the floor. The kitchen door opened. John and Will's footsteps climbed the hall to their room, dull and burdened. The house grew still for a long while. Finally, another chair scratched, followed by the sound of soft shoes on carpet. The lamps in the hallway wound low, turned off. The hinge to the front door squeaked, and through the library window James saw Mrs. Shelby step out onto the moonlit verandah. With her back turned, the woman leaned against the railing, her large weight sinking to her palms. Her head tilted and rested on the porch beam. Her hands clasped her mouth. Below her burning hair, a neck bent and wide shoulders crumpled.

CHAPTER 34

"How long will we be gone?" Leonora broke the silence of the car ride, tried not to let her missing of Pittsburgh taint her pitch. She couldn't stop thinking about the hospital and the soldiers left behind; the way the nurses had rolled their eyes and turned their backs to her, another wealthy volunteer leaving her duties at the wink of a boyfriend. They didn't know she hadn't had a choice.

"Just until your uncle gets this draft nonsense resolved." Alex's face darkened, spawned a new quiet between them.

A few moments later, Leonora leaned forward, perked at the changing landscape. New York City loomed in the window of the Rolls-Royce.

Alex inspected himself in the side mirror, straighened his tie.

The driver parked in the arch of a towering limestone hotel, the sloped awning licking the air like a metal tongue. Alex nodded to the doorman while young men with buttoned coats and strapped caps bustled for their luggage. Alex led her through the lobby by the elbow, passed under a chandelier as large as a sparkling pond, then up the sweeping stairs. "You've been here before," she noted, surprised.

"A few times." He winked and escorted her to a thickly engraved door. "Your suite, Miss Fairfield."

The room contrasted perfectly in color and texture: dark wood and gleaming white marble; stone and silk; pillows and tiles. Every angle and corner filled with three-foot vases of roses, birds-of-paradise, cannas and jasmine—the smell of which left her light-headed. Gossamer panels hung from the bed's tester, and so many pillows lined the bed that only a foot of comforter showed at the base. The shuttered windows were open, revealing the balcony with more silk curtains blowing gently into the room.

"Do you like it?" Alex asked.

"I don't think I've ever seen anything so lovely."

"We'll see about that." He pulled a black velvet box from his jacket.

"What's this?"

"Open it."

She opened the box to find two diamond-studded earrings. She touched her throat. "You shouldn't have, Alex."

"Call it a thank-you. For coming away with me."

"It's a very expensive thank-you."

He kissed her cheek, looked at her intently. "I'm glad you're here."

She smiled and kissed him back, her eyes sparkling. "Me too." And she was. He was handsome again, kind. The conversations about the hospital and the motives around the whirlwind trip faded into the softness of his eyes and she couldn't remember why she had been so angry with him.

He led her to the bed. "It's been a long trip. Why don't you rest a bit and we'll meet up later." He pointed to the silver tray on the nightstand. "There's fruit and rolls. Champagne."

"Where are you going?"

He smiled at the disappointment in her voice. "Business, darling. I've got a lot of people to connect with." He popped a strawberry in his mouth. "A few friends are going to meet us for dinner. They're all anxious to meet you."

Alex bent his neck and kissed her, found her lips willing. He stirred closer, held her hips in his palms before releasing her quickly. "I better leave now or I won't be leaving at all." He sighed, then kissed her forehead. "Get some rest, darling," he directed, and left the room.

Leonora leaned back on the pillows, the softness of his lips still fresh as she closed her eyes. The noise of the city rode on a breeze, filtered through the gossamer. The scents of the flowers mellowed to a warm cologne, and somewhere between her massaged senses she fell asleep before she even knew she was tired.

The breeze tickled her cheek, moved down her neck, smelled of drink. She opened her eyes to find Alex kissing her throat and jumped.

"Sorry if I scared you. I knocked. I swear," he said innocently.

She smiled nervously, bluntly aware of his body lying on the bed next to her, then looked over his shoulder at the night sky. "What time is it?"

"Eight o'clock. I'd have let you sleep, but everyone's waiting downstairs."

Leonora hurried off the bed and opened the closet. "It'll just take me a minute to change."

Alex leaned back on the bed and watched her languidly. "Take as long as you want."

Playfully, she pulled him by the hands to his feet. "In private. Now, go!"

After she dressed, they strolled outside under a full moon to the sweeping stone patio. Arborvitaes lined the edges, their sculpted green points shielding the space from the frenzied lights of the city. Ragtime hummed from an invisible source, its syncopation making the very breeze dance. Laughter, high and shrill, echoed from a long, rectangular table. Cigarette smoke drifted and fogged the stars. Empty bottles of wine were collected by the waiters and new ones uncorked. Chatter rippled, flowed over the slate.

"Finally!" One of the men stood from the table, a cigarette dangling precariously from his mouth. "We started to think you'd forgotten about us!" he said with a smooth British accent melted down with drink.

Alex's manner shifted instantly, loosened like he had traded hard shoes for slippers, and his eyes turned mischievous. "This, my dear, is Edward Warton."

"And you must be Leonora." Edward lifted her hand and kissed it with an air of familiarity. "You're as lovely as Alex described." Suddenly, he pulled her against him. "Why don't you take the seat next to me and we'll see if I can't change your favor in beaus."

"Not likely," said Alex as he rescued with one arm and with the other wrestled his friend in a headlock. Leonora tensed under their game.

"Boys!" A woman from the table clapped her hands and scolded, "Don't be greedy with our guest!"

Alex let go of Edward and whacked him on the back, brought Leonora to the table for introductions. "Leonora, this is Molly Brighton, of Brighton teas no less." The woman rose grandly, her face almost shielded by the tilted, oval-rimmed hat. In one hand hung a cigarette in a black holder that nearly reached to her elbow, in the other a martini glass with drunk olives, a smile of red lipstick stained on its rim.

"Why must you always introduce me that way! It's my father's affair, not mine. I'm not exactly a tea toddler, you know."

"Quite clearly!" Edward chimed. Molly elbowed him flirtatiously. Her dress dipped down, showing the deep crease of her bosom. She was not beautiful in feature, but quite astonishing in figure and manner. It was hard not to stare.

"And this is Margaret and Robert Farthington." The middle-aged couple, tighter in face, rose from the end of the table. "Robert runs a diamond plant in Arkansas," explained Alex.

"I see you're acquainted with our stock." Mr. Farthington winked. Leonora touched the studs in her ears. "They're beautiful."

"Then we have the brothers, Ralph and Ronald Hancock. The laziest, wealthiest bastards in New York. What does your family do anyway?" Alex asked, amused.

"White slavery. Opium. Sex. The usual affair," answered Ralph with a straight face until the table snickered.

Leonora inched closer to Alex and smiled wanly. Every exchange seemed like a carried-over joke that went over her head. Alex pulled out her chair and everyone sat.

Ralph searched the room and his brother's gaze followed narrowly. They were good-looking men, tan and lean, but their faces looked in a permanent state of contempt even when laughing. Ralph snapped his fingers at one of the waiters along the wall. "I'm fuckin' starving."

Molly tapped her ashes into a silver tray, blew a trail of smoke out the side of her mouth. "Have another drink, darling," she consoled

Ralph, then turned languid eyes to Alex, tilting her head. "It's so nice having our Alex back. We've missed you, darling."

Leonora's stomach turned uneasy, but Alex seemed unaffected as he leaned smoothly into his chair.

"And how long will we have the pleasure of you in New York?" Molly glanced at Leonora. "Both of you."

Alex took a sip of wine, irritated. "Depends on the blasted draft."

"Horrid thing, the draft!" Mr. Farthington chimed, his wife nodding dumbly. "Picking men from numbers! Lining them up side by side as if one were equal to the next."

Molly leaned her head back, cackled. "A table of cowards! Amen." She sucked on her cigarette.

"Hardly!" Mr. Farthington blustered. "Someone's got to watch out for the economy. If we all spill our blood, what's the use of fighting?"

"Cheers." Ralph and Ronald raised their glasses.

Edward leaned in, his beak nose flaring at the side with amusement. "Talk all you want of drafts and blood, but we're all prospering from this war and let no man, or woman, deny it."

Molly raised her glass for a toast. "To war!"

Leonora stifled a cough with her handkerchief. The tobacco smoke made her eyes water and her throat itch. With every sentence uttered, she felt more and more the uninvited guest. Alex seemed aloof, so engaged in drink and banter that he nearly waved her off with the smoke.

Alex ran a hand through his hair, then rubbed his finger along the edge of his glass. "Soon as I get the word that all this draft nonsense is cleared up, I'm heading back. No offense to my dear friends, of course."

"None taken!" Mr. Farthington laughed. "I've been wondering, though. Why did Owen let you out of India? You're his best manager."

Edward snickered and winked at Leonora. "I'm sure there are more important partnerships in the pipeline." Alex and Edward exchanged grins. "Where is the tiger anyway?"

"Tiger?" Leonora asked.

Alex laughed. "The white tiger—your uncle." Then, addressing the group, "He's in Harrisburg pulling the strings."

Leonora turned to him, confused. "I thought he was going to meet us here in the city?"

"He will, dear." Alex tapped her knee. "The good man wanted to give us a night to settle in first, give us a chance to be alone." Alex's gaze rested on her lips. "Nice of him, eh?"

"Kind of chaperone every man dreams of." Edward licked his lips, the comment sending a cold draft up her dress.

Waiters lined to the table and began laying out a spread of bread, beef tenderloin, gravy, potatoes and Yorkshire pudding. "Makes it hardly seem there's a war on, eh?" Edward flapped his napkin, draped it across his lap.

"Here's to the poor saps in the trenches!" toasted Ralph.

"May their stupidity bring us glory and wealth!" chimed his brother.

The table erupted in laughter. Leonora dropped her mouth, scanned each guest. "That's horrible." Her words rose above the noise of the table. All chatter ceased with the tone.

Alex cleared his throat and smiled to his friends. The top part of his jaw clicked. "It was a joke, darling." He leaned in and kissed her on the cheek, hid his lips in her hair. "Just shut up and eat."

They were all strangers, especially Alex, and Leonora wanted to be alone, wanted to be back in that room where everything seemed beautiful and he had been kind, a place where no ugly words had been spoken. She stood to go. "Excuse me."

Alex grabbed her wrist. "Where are you going?"

It was Molly who spoke. "Oh, I'm afraid we've offended dear Leonora with our callousness!" She scanned the table with mock reprimand. "Watch your manners, children. Please sit, Leonora. We were just having a bit of fun. We'll behave better now; I promise."

Leonora sat down. The waiter held the tenderloin in front of her, knife ready. "No, thank you." Alex looked at her coldly but kept quiet.

Molly ignored the plate before her, seemed to feast on the sudden change in mood. "I like her," she announced. The woman's lips rose pointedly to one side. "Much sweeter than the others. Prettier, too."

Alex stopped chewing and glared at Molly, wiped his lips with his napkin.

"So, Leonora," said Molly, leaning in. "You must share your secret. How did you tame the wild Mr. Harrington?"

"That's enough, Molly," Alex warned, no longer smiling.

She ignored him and moved in closer, confidentially. "You are familiar with his reputation, I'm sure."

Alex stood then. "Ralph, take Molly home. She's had one too many."

Ralph took her by the shoulders. "Come on; we'll get you a cup of your dad's tea."

"I'm not going anywhere." Molly shooed his hands away. "I'm simply trying to get to know this lovely lady. Besides, I'm sure she'd like to hear some stories of our friend."

Alex dropped his napkin. "That's enough." His anger was palpable and a nervous shuffling took place. He moved to Molly and with a few other men, despite her protests, escorted her out.

Mrs. Farthington shot a look back at them, swayed against her husband's shoulder. "I do believe Molly is jealous." She breathed in her husband's ear and he turned away disgusted. "She's always had a bit of a crush on Alex, hasn't she?"

The men came back soon with Molly nowhere in sight. Conversations and laughter started again, but Alex was distracted, his face dark. He ignored Leonora completely, not even pulling out her chair when the meal ended.

Alex walked her up to the room, did not speak. At the door, he turned. "Don't ever do that again. Do you hear me?" His lips were thin with anger.

Her heart pounded. "Do what?"

"Embarrass me like that."

"I wasn't trying to—"

He stepped forward until she retreated against the door handle. He spoke each word with measured threat, his top lip twitching, "Don't make me look the fool, Leonora. Ever."

Through the open shutters of the New York hotel room, phases of night, of uprising stars and veering moon, kept her company through the hours of fitful sleep. Dreams bordered on nightmares, sucking in the sounds from outside and distorting them with anxious will.

By morning, she was only dully refreshed, her body jittery. The smell of garbage and old urine snaked above the streets, rose between the stately buildings. The haze from exhaust washed away the dawn. Leonora dressed, found the tea and fruit the butler had unobtrusively left in the sitting room.

A siren wailed a farewell song, for she planned to leave this morning. She tried again to close the leather suitcase against the pyramid of flung clothes. She moved her thoughts to Pittsburgh, and while the home and her aunt brought her no joy, the hospital reached to her like a beacon and she held on to its wide wings as if they were a waiting embrace.

The door to the sitting room slammed. Her nerves iced. A long silence paused until the knob to her bedroom turned and Alex walked in, closed the door and leaned against it, arms folded. He was clean shaven, his hair still damp from bathing, but dark circles lined his eyes. "Good morning," he greeted formally. "Going somewhere?"

"Home." Even as she said it, the word didn't fit. She had no home. The Fairfield mansion was only a building of cold stone and contempt. A wave of sadness suddenly left her weak.

"All right." Alex moved to the sofa and, to her surprise, pressed against the suitcase until it locked effortlessly. He picked up the handle and set it on the ground. "But not until I have a chance to apologize."

He sat on the sofa, pulled down his tie, unbuttoned the collar and then massaged his eyebrows with his fingertips. "Sometimes I forget how naïve you are." She shot him a look and reached for the suitcase.

"Sorry, bad word choice. Sensitive. That's what I meant." He patted the seat next to him. "Sit. Please?" It was not a command but a request and she set herself reluctantly, straight spined on the edge of the velvet.

"Your sensitivity is one of the things I love about you. The innocence of it." He turned to her with soft eyes. "You have to understand that I work around men all day. Not men like your uncle. Men as hard and rough as coal who'd sooner smash a rose with their fist than smell it. It's easy to forget the sensitivities, the gentleness, of women. I'm sorry I mocked the soldiers." He put his hand on hers. "We come from very different places, Leonora. We're going to have to meet in the middle sometimes."

Leonora stared at the hand on top of hers, felt the warmth of his touch, the warmth of his eyes. There was so much coldness to her life, and the pull to that warmth, to anything not made of ice, drew her heart forward.

"Let's start over." Alex stroked the fight away. "Promise me you'll give me a few more days to make it up to you. If you're still unhappy, I'll drive you home myself. Is that a deal?"

She nodded and turned her hand over, squeezed his fingers, let the heat eclipse the cold. Maybe this was how men and women worked. She had never dated before, never known a kiss before Alex's. Perhaps all men had moods that swung; perhaps she *was* too sensitive.

Alex sighed and raised her hand to his lips, held it out in front of him, turned it over and etched a line down her palm, the touch so delicate her fingers twitched. "You have the most beautiful hands, Leonora. White. Smooth. Perfect." He rubbed his thumb over hers. "They remind me of my mother's."

His face fell with a memory and her heart opened to his sudden raw pain.

"She died when I was away at boarding school," he began. "My stepfather never contacted me. I didn't find out she was dead until I came home for holiday."

"I'm so sorry, Alex. That's terrible."

"Par for the course." He sank his head into his hands and scratched his scalp methodically until he began to laugh. The shift frightened her with its bitterness. "A proud name—Harrington. My mother scrambled to acquire it, then drank herself to death to forget it."

And then she recognized it. The cold. He had known it, too, had felt it in his life just as she had. And in that moment she understood him. The anger fell away like a feather upon silk. He only needed warmth to chase away the ghosts, the bitterness. He could be kind; she had seen it. He just needed warmth, her warmth.

Leonora reached around his waist, but he was too absorbed in his thoughts to notice. Her heart pounded; he looked as wounded as the torn soldiers in the hospital. She kissed his cheek, tried to turn his face toward her to distract him from the pain. She pressed her lips against his fervently until she felt them soften and bend against her mouth. She slipped her arm under his jacket and slid her nails down his spine. His mouth became urgent with the touch and he raised his shoulders, took her face in his hands, slid his lips to her neck and ran his tongue to the base of her throat. He pulled at the fabric on her shoulder until he found her slip strap and tugged it down her arm, his nail scratching a line of red.

Pressing his face against the crook in her neck, he reached for her breast, squeezed it roughly, pushed it upward until it came loose from the fabric. Her mouth went dry as he sucked it in his mouth and found the nipple. She stiffened. He felt the tension and took it for pleasure, pulling at the nipple with his teeth. Crying out, she tried to pull away, but he clasped his hands to her back, swung her to his open knees and pushed her against him. A hard bulge pressed against her inner thigh. The warmth disappeared and she began to panic under the hands molding her breasts and tried to push away.

A loud knock rattled the room. "Alex, you in there?" Owen Fairfield's voice rose and fell pleasantly.

"*Fuck!*" Alex growled into her breast before raising his head. Leonora took the pause to tuck her body parts back into her dress and pull up the straps.

"Anybody home?" called the voice again.

Alex placed his finger to Leonora's lips, waited until her uncle's footsteps receded. Alex grunted, adjusted his pants, the mood broken. "Your uncle's timing is perfect, isn't it?" He smirked, his words flowing lazily. "Help me with my tie, darling? Sounds like he wants to talk. Hopefully, it's good news."

Taking the black tie with shaking fingers, she formed a knot and glided it under his chin. He stood, scanned her body before drawing her against him. "You'll remind me where we left off?"

She placed a hand on her forehead, stared at the floor. "I'm just going to rest. I'm feeling a bit under the weather."

"You do look pale." He kissed her lightly. "Rest, darling. Tomorrow's a new day."

She stood in front of the closed door for several minutes. She touched her left breast gingerly, still sore from his fingers and mouth. Inside her body, a pulling had begun; straws of feelings gathered and tightened until they were no longer vague memories and sensations but one emotion. And with the gathering, a truth formed and trailed a subtle power—a knowing. She thought of Alex's face, how it looked in anger, in mirth, in desire, and the faces melded until she saw him, saw one face. Her nerves settled under this knowing, for she cared for Alex, at times felt great affection for him, even desire. But she also now knew with all certainty and a hint of fear that she did not love him.

Over the next few days, Alex kept his promise and when he wasn't at a meeting with her uncle he doted on her with attention and affection. If he gathered with his friends and stayed up late with drink, he kept it hidden. And, three nights later, Alex escorted Leonora to a private terrace atop the hotel. The sky rose lavender above the city. Lights flickered from candles, orange and yellow flames elongating across the marble terrace, reflecting the silver urns of fire in a mirage of imitation. Simmering rose drifted and thickened the air like brandy, left Leonora breathless as she scanned the gossamer canopy over their table, the shower of white lilacs hanging over every ledge and railing, softening each angle.

Alex wore a black tuxedo and white bow tie and had never looked more handsome. He pulled out her chair. She could smell his rich cologne with the movement. The waiters disappeared. The weather was neither hot nor cold, but balmy enough to tickle the light fabric of her dress around her crossed ankles. It was perfect.

Leonora's skin suddenly chilled. It was too perfect, too planned, and what should have been obvious before she even left Pittsburgh became startlingly clear now as Alex rose to his feet, drifted toward her and took her hand. Each of his movements stood out strangely magnified and she watched it all play out before her as helplessly as a dreamer. Her chest sank in steady increments that matched his descent to one bent knee.

"Leonora." He spoke with sureness and clarity. "I know that we have not known each other for any great length of time, but I knew as soon as I saw you that I had found my wife."

The word *wife* brought a fresh wave of panic. She tried to stop the widening of her eyes, tried not to look horrified, but her face was frozen.

"Your beauty and grace, your refined dignity and purity . . . it leaves me breathless." He squeezed her hand and smiled. "I want nothing more than to spend my life with you."

Alex reached one hand into his pocket and pulled out a black velvet box, opening it slowly to reveal a large oval-cut diamond set in gold and flanked with emeralds. "It belonged to my mother. I can't think of anyone's hand more worthy to wear it." He took a deep pull of air in just as her own lungs stopped. "Leonora Fairfield, will you marry me?"

No. No! The word screamed. She closed her eyes, felt such a fool for not seeing this day was coming. She did not know how long she was silent—a second, a minute—before the words came out. "I'm sorry, Alex."

He cocked his head, the smile still plastered to his lips. "What?"

"I'm so sorry." She tried to squeeze his hand, but it was cold and stiff.

"Sorry?" he repeated, still trying to grasp the word. Alex pulled his hand away, shook his head like his ears were filled with water. "You're saying no?"

She nodded slowly.

"Why the hell not?" he shouted.

Her mind swam in a million directions and yet he stared at her, waiting for an answer. In her silence, his face drained of any tenderness and hardened.

"I know it doesn't make any sense, Alex." She floundered for words that wouldn't hurt and came up empty.

Alex's eyes narrowed and his knuckles cracked into a fist. "Is there someone else? So help me, I'll—"

"No! Alex, no." She shielded her eyes with her hand and pressed her temples. "I just can't marry you. I'm so sorry."

A prolonged pause showed real pain in his face before a seething ripple clenched his jaw and flared his nostrils. Leonora's throat closed. "Please don't be angry."

"Shut up!" he spit, and raised a hand, pounded it against the air as if it were a wall. "Just . . . shut . . . up!"

Alex looked over the rooflines and snorted. "And would you mind telling me what the last three months were about?" His eyebrows rose to sharpened peaks. "Was this all some kind of game to you?"

Her hands writhed; she lowered her head. Alex flicked her chin up. "Damn it, look at me! What? Did you get a thrill leading me around by the dick all this time?"

The foul speech was rough, violent, and her lips began to tremble. "Please don't say that."

"Then why?" he shouted. "Why won't you marry me?"

This is why! her mind whimpered. She opened her mouth to speak, but no sound came out. Everything began to shut down and she was a child again, mute, too scared to move.

Finally, Alex pursed his lips and nodded. He pulled his shoulders back and rubbed his palms across his lapels, straightening them. He looked at her then, his lips twisted in disgust. "You're a fool, Leonora. A damn bloody fool."

He turned to walk away but stopped at his pulled-out chair, kicked it flying into the air before it landed wounded and shattered across the tiles.

Leonora looked down from her hotel room balcony. Window shutters closed with a click behind her. She took her elbows off the wrought-iron banister, did not turn around. The sweet smell of pipe tobacco joined her before her uncle did. Owen Fairfield smiled over the sea of traffic and took a deep breath of the air.

"I'm not marrying Alex."

"So I've heard." Owen chuckled. "I suppose he reacted well to the news?" When she didn't answer, he grew serious and stepped closer to the balcony, leaned on his forearms and made a pyramid with his fingers. "I'm very disappointed."

"I don't love him."

He was quiet for a moment. "The problem with the Western world is we look for fairy tales, Leonora. In India and Asia, almost all of the marriages are arranged. Did you know that? They say those unions end up happier than in countries where men and women choose their own mates." He looked at his hands. "We carry the word 'love' cupped in our palm as if it were something that falls out of the air and needs to be caught. Sometimes it happens that way. Sometimes. But most often, love needs to be grown, added to, watered." He smiled then with a thought. "Eleanor didn't marry me because she loved me, Leonora. I knew that then and I know it now. But the love did come, over time. Just like it will with you and Alex. He's a good match for you, dear. And he loves you. You might not feel the same way now, but you will. I promise."

"It's not just that." She struggled to find the right words and was surprised by the ones that she chose. "There's a cruel side to him."

"Alex? Psssh! We've kept you too sheltered, I'm afraid. A man must have a few harsh veins, my dear. He's not a man otherwise." His tone grew stern. "You're young in more ways than years, Leonora. Some decisions are better left to your aunt and I."

She looked at him, aghast. "Are you trying to force me to marry him?"

"No. Of course not." Owen moved his gaze pensively over the buildings. "I can't force you to marry anyone. It's 1917, not 1617, after all."

She put her hand on his and sought his eyes. "I'm sorry I've let you down, Uncle. But I've made up my mind."

He turned to her, his face deep with pity. "It won't stop, Leonora."

"What won't stop?" she asked, not sure if she wanted to hear the answer.

"Eleanor's obsession to get you married. She can and will make your life very, very miserable." He sighed deeply. "This is important to her, Leonora. You marrying Alex. She will take away everything from you, dominate your life until you're clutching the first proposal that comes your way, just to escape. Alex is a good man. The next offer might not be as promising."

She cringed at his words, the truth of them, knowing her aunt's wrath. Even worse was her uncle's passivity, as if he had nothing more to do with her treatment than the paint on the wall.

Owen read her thoughts, the soft parts around his eyes wrinkling, aging him. "I'm a weak man, my dear—weak when it comes to my wife. I love her, Leonora." He put his hands on her shoulders. "There are things about your aunt that you don't know—things about her past, about what she has endured in her life. I don't think you could ever imagine what she's been through." He shook his head. "She would die if I told anyone and I'll keep her secret to the grave. Even from you, I'm afraid."

His eyes moistened. "I'm only sharing this with you because I would do anything to keep her happy. Anything. When she is upset, she panics and the old memories flood her." Owen combed his beard with his fingertips. "I'm not a fool. I know she hasn't made life easy for you. She can be cruel. If you don't marry Alex, I won't be able to protect you."

You've never protected me! Her head swirled; her stomach hurt.

Suddenly, his whole figure transformed. He chuckled and seemed at peace again and she couldn't keep up. "My dear, life is about compromise. It's all about choices, weighing the benefits against the losses. It applies to business but works equally well in relationships." He paused, his eyes boring into her. "If you agree to marry Alex, I am prepared to offer you something in return."

The gears in her mind sped. What could he possibly offer that would make her change her mind? "The hospital?" she sputtered. "You think I would agree to marry Alex just so I could continue working at the hospital?"

He laughed heartily. "You dear girl! I'm talking about holy matrimony! Working eight-hour shifts cleaning bedpans? Huh! That would hardly be a fair trade. I never understood your devotion to begin with. No, I can offer you something much bigger, more important, than that."

She shook her head, frustrated, tired of having her brain manipulated. Then he shifted again like the phase of the moon and stepped toward her, placed his palms on her cheeks. His voice came out very soft. "Don't forget I *know* you. I knew you before you became my niece. I know your history." His eyes burned. "I know where you came from."

Panic filled her. The mere mention of the subject chilled her blood. Her eyes blinked and she wanted to run away, the fear completely automatic after a lifetime of threats.

His voice quaked with remorse. "We took so much from you, dear child. But I can give you something back." He pleaded, "If you marry Alex, I can give you a piece of your past. A part of you that you lost . . . that we took away from you so long ago. I don't believe you will be disappointed.

"Remember, with Alex you have a chance, a real *chance* at happiness." Owen pulled out his gold watch, checked the time. "Just think about what I've said. The choice is yours."

CHAPTER 35

Mrs. Shelby peered out the window, her jaw dropped in horror. "Fire."

James and Tom stepped closer, followed the trail of Mrs. Shelby's gaze in the twilight. They all knew the direction from which the smoke came.

"Damn fool," she whispered. "With this dry he'll set the whole bush ablaze."

James grabbed his hat.

"Let Tom go!" Mrs. Shelby ordered.

James shook his head. "I'm going. Alone."

Mrs. Shelby looked at him a moment and nodded, then reached behind an old squatter chair for the rifle. "Shoot it twice if you need us."

James took the gun and strapped it to his saddle with the whip, then set off down the dirt road, the dust clouding the Shelby homestead.

The dry had lasted and marked signs all along the route. Stingy grass held green near the roots while the tips gave up and dried to razor points. Where puddles had once formed under the ghost gums, cracked earth now veined. Hoofprints paved the trail with bumps, for the trek of the beasts to find the deepest water holes had lengthened.

James focused ahead to the smoke billowing white and swirling under the stars, clouding their points. The smell of charred wood strangled the air. The horse raised and lowered her head. James clicked his tongue, moved the horse at a trot past the rows of dead fields, the forgotten stalks blue in the moonlight that defined the O'Reilly property lines. He rode past the rusted plow, tilted on the edge, inert since the day the drinking began so many years ago.

The growing smell of flames signaled the fire was beyond the ridge. Black smoke mixed with black night; orange sparks rose and flickered. A small sigh left his lips. It wasn't the house. Flames would have licked the sky; the sound of cracking beams would have reached him by now. He crested the next ridge and touched the gun to make sure it was still there.

A few minutes more and the house became visible. The misery of the shack and the poverty of his childhood sank down to his heels. One half of the shack was black as night; the other glowed, illuminated by the bonfire. The horse stepped back with the heat and James dismounted, tying her to a tree. The gun showed hot with reflected flames. He reached for it, then took his hand away and walked empty-handed toward the fire.

Junk lined the ground under and around the fire—bottles, a flat tire, a hand drill, a broken chair. A wheelbarrow lay on its side, the front wheel in the flames.

The screen door slammed. Shamus stumbled out of the house, his arms filled with pots and spoons and hand towels up to his chin. He walked right up to the burning pyramid and dumped it on top, hardly flinching from the raised flames. He turned back to the house.

"What are you doing, Shamus?" James asked from the shadows.

The man turned and peered blindly past the light. "Who's that? Who's out there?" Then with a laugh, "Couldn't be me dear lost boy, could it?" Shamus walked toward the flames. His face lit white, his eyes dark rimmed and black. His beard hung scraggly against his neck.

James fought every urge to turn back and walked forward until he faced him.

"There he is! Surprised I ain't starved yet, eh?" Shamus opened his arms to give James full view of his body, his clothes dirty, his shirt ripped at the stomach. "What? Took me wife, now checkin' t'see if the ol' man's still 'ere?"

James bit his bottom lip and looked heavily at the man he didn't recognize. He held no more anger toward Shamus, only a rough pity. "Let's put the fire out, Shamus. I'll make you some dinner. Help you get cleaned up."

"'Twas ye who killed her, ye know!" Shamus growled, and stomped closer. "Only fittin' ye help burn her memory."

The sparks reflected in the man's dark, wet pupils. The smell of him—drink, vomit and excrement—was hard to stand. James turned his face away.

"Can't face it, can ye? Can't face what ye done, boy! But I'll remind ye, I will!" Shamus stumbled backwards, turned and hurried back to the house, returning with a bureau drawer between his arms. He threw it on the ground and bent forward, his body almost falling with the gravity. He held up a book. "Brontë shit! Last words she heard 'fore ye killed her." He threw the thick volume onto the flames and reached back to the drawer. "See these photos." He fanned them across his face. "Dead. Dead! *Dead!*" Shamus screamed, and flung them onto the fire.

"Stop it!" James went to grab the pictures, but they were already curling in flames. His breath came quickly now and his fingers folded into his palms, his nails cut into the skin.

"So, am I finally gonna see some fire from ye, son? Eh?" Shamus beat at his chest, clawed at it. "Come on, boy! Show me if ye turned a man yet."

James closed his eyes. "I'm not going to fight you, Shamus."

"Fight me? Huh! Fight me?" he screamed into the night. "With yeer sissy hands? I beat ye till I was too tired t'move me arm an' what ye do? Fight back? Naw! Ye laid there like a hacked chicken!"

The anger shook him, shook him so hard that his muscles nearly broke in two. "I'm not going to hit you," James exhaled the words, a command to his own hands.

Shamus glared at him, his top lip twitching. Slowly, he reached back into the drawer and held up a small black book. "Well, well! Finally found it!" He laughed and raised the book in the air, waving it back and forth. Flames highlighted the gold lettering. James froze.

"Yeer precious Bible! But it ain't the word o' the Lord, is it?" Shamus opened the book and thumbed the pages with dirty fingers. "'Tis the word of yeer whore mum!"

His mind went black. James lunged for the book, struggled to pry it from the man's claws. But Shamus was a man possessed, fought till his arm was free to chuck it to the fire.

"*No!*" James pulled it from the flames, tossed it to the ground, kicked out the embers.

Shamus laughed, held his side. "Stomp it all yeer like, she's still burnin' in Hell!"

The fire of anger moved to James's chest, thrust down his arm as he pushed the filthy body away. Shamus wobbled on his feet, stepped back, lost his footing and fell into a pile of trash.

James held the book tight in his hands, squeezed it to calm his pulse and stop the rage pulsing through his veins. He walked to the horse, tucked the damaged book into the saddlebag, then removed the rifle. He pointed high into the air and shot—waited a moment—shot again. The sound reverberated through the night. He wrapped the rifle back into the whip, his energy sapped. The anger left with the crack of the gun and all that remained was weariness.

James walked around the fire to where Shamus lay. "Get up." He lowered his hand to pull him up, but the man's arms stayed still.

James knelt down and slapped the man's hairy cheeks. "Get up, Shamus."

James reached under Shamus's head, curving the man's limp neck. A long sucking sound came from under his hair. A gush of warmth flowed over James's fingers, ran down his wrist and into his sleeve.

James dropped the man's head and fell back. A square scrap of wood lay next to Shamus's ear, the pointed nails black and dripping. "No." James looked at his hands, red and tightening with drying blood. "No!"

Blood flowed in a black puddle toward his boots and he scooped at the horrid liquid, pushed with his fingers to stop it, grabbed Shamus's head to force it back in. "*God, no!*"

Shamus's face tilted distortedly to one side, staring at him with far-away eyes. James let go, dropped the head into the ground with horror, crawled backwards on his palms to get away from the blood that chased him. His hands convulsed as he raised them to his face, covered his eyes. But the smell of iron blood was too strong and he pulled his hands away, rolled them into fists and shoved them under his legs.

The fire snapped and burned near his right shoulder; on the other side, his body shivered with the cold body sprawled only inches away. "*No.*" James crossed his arms at his knees, pressed his forehead hard against them and closed his eyes to the fire, the blood and the death.

"Stand up, James." Mrs. Shelby had her arms around his shoulders. He didn't know how long she had been talking to him, how long she had been there. He looked up suddenly at her face, her steady eyes. "Get up, son," she said softly.

James stood slowly, his legs cramped. The smell of smoldering fire and wet wood was everywhere. He noticed the pile of debris smoking behind her, the staring moon. He remembered where he was and the nightmare slid back. He jerked his head around, but Shamus's body was gone, a dark rust stain etched in the dirt.

Tom came around the corner to his mother's side, a shovel in his hand. He didn't look at James, asked quietly, "Where you think?"

"The far field." She pointed with her chin. "Put the plow on top t'keep the animals away."

Tom stepped behind the house and Mrs. Shelby put her arm around James again. "Tom's takin' care of it. Makin' it go away." She tried to walk with him. "Let's get you home."

James stayed rigid and looked at the spot again. He turned to her, his throat raw. "I pushed him." He blinked with the memory, flexed his hand with the feel of pulling at the book, pushing Shamus in the chest. "He burnt everything. Her pictures. Everything."

James saw his hands, brown with blood up to the elbows. "He fell. But . . . there were nails," he rambled. "I didn't mean to . . . tried to stop the bleeding . . ."

"James . . ." Her voice was distant, came from a far tunnel.

"He fell on the nails . . . the blood."

"Look at me, James." Mrs. Shelby's voice was soaked with tears and he looked up and met her eyes. "You did not do this!"

He shook his head, but she squeezed his shoulders. "Listen to me, James. Listen to me! Shamus died the day Tess did. He was just waitin' until his body caught up."

"I shouldn't have left him," James muttered. "I should have helped him."

"You couldn't save him, James. That man had only one ending comin' to him. This, *this!*" she cried, and pointed to the bloodstain. "Was an accident. That's all. Shamus was gonna end his life one way or the other. Through drink or gun. *This* was not your doin'."

Mrs. Shelby pulled him to her, pushed his head against her shoulder and hugged him. "This ain't your doin', son. This ain't your doin'."

CHAPTER 36

❧

The rain lashed the side of the New York City hotel, deafening against the stone. Despite the width and depth of the balcony, the water spilled to the very edge, only inches from the open doors of Leonora's suite. It was early afternoon, but the sky was nearly black, muting the shades of the buildings to gray. Not a soul was out. No lightning or thunder bombed the sky, only the solid sheet of rain.

Leonora was glad to keep the doors open—a window in the stifling walls. She sighed and folded her hands over her stomach. From behind, Alex put his strong arms around her. "Are you cold? I could close the doors," he offered.

"No. I like watching the rain."

Alex kissed her cheek. "I like watching you."

Her uncle had met with Alex first, told him she had taken ill. Not used to the city, he had said. Women were fickle creatures. Emotional. Feverish. Must have caught a bug from the help. Owen had calmed Alex so completely that when she finally accepted his proposal he did not bat an eye at the reversal and slid the ring on her finger like it had always been there.

Alex's hands inched around her waist, clasped at her stomach. He rested his chin on her head. Humid air damply textured the room so it became warm and heavy, almost tactile. Alex's thighs pressed against the backs of her legs; something hard stirred at the small of her back. He pulled aside her hair and kissed the back of her neck. "Have you heard of the Kama Sutra?" he whispered behind her ear.

She glanced back quickly. "No."

"It's an ancient Hindu text. About pleasure." He twirled her hair in his fingers. "Sex, to be specific."

A blush moved up her neck, through her cheeks. His fingers pressed in pulses.

"Describes the many ways a man and woman fit together. The details are quite graphic." He kissed her neck again. "Sixty-four positions in all." His lips moved down until they reached the collar of her dress. "I'd settle for just one." Gripping one hand to her waist, Alex reached up with the other and nimbly undid the top button on the back of her dress.

"Alex . . ."

"Shhh . . ."

Leonora did not protest, tried to control her breathing as he went down the line of buttons, moving his lips over each inch of exposed skin, his breath hot against her back.

Alex twisted her to face him and pressed his lips against hers, his tongue darting in her mouth as he pushed the sleeves off her shoulders. His body shoved against her and she stepped back with the pressure until her back touched the wall. She wanted to slink down, escape through the door, but realized with a hollow pang that he would soon be her husband. Worse things were yet to be endured, and so she did not struggle.

With her body steadily affixed against his rib cage, Alex pushed the dress easily down the silk slip and over her hips to her feet, then kicked it away before she could reach it.

"Alex, I can't breathe!" she gasped against his open mouth, but he did not hear her. He pushed his palms over her breasts and moaned into her neck. With one bent knee, Alex pried her legs open while his right hand slid under the hem of the slip. She recoiled and turned her head from him, reached down to grab his hand away, but it was moving upward, squeezing the flesh of her thigh. His finger etched the lines of the garter belt, his nails clenched in the skin.

Leonora struggled then, didn't care that he would soon be her husband. She shimmied her elbows under his chest, pushing futilely against his weight. "That's enough."

He chuckled against her neck. "No, it's not."

Her heart pounded with his inching fingers. "We're not married yet," she stalled.

His teeth touched against her skin as he smiled. "Times have changed, darling. There's a war on, you know." He brought his other knee between her legs. "This might be our last chance."

Alex's thighs pinned her hard to the wall. "I won't think less of you; I promise. Besides, you owe me. You've caused me quite a bit of distress of late." He looked up at her then, sharply, before returning to the quest under her slip.

Leonora twisted her hips, which were widening without her will. Alex slipped his hand between her legs, moved it up her inner thigh and into the edge of her panties. With a thrust upward, his index finger entered her. She froze. He met her eyes, held her gaze, smiled in satisfaction, moved his finger in and out of her. She whimpered and flung her body back against the wall, but there was no retreat. The more she struggled, the harder and rougher he pushed. She closed her eyes, paralyzed.

Abruptly, Alex stopped, clutched her buttocks with two hands and carried her a few steps to the bed. Her mind could not catch up. Before she realized she wasn't tied to the wall any longer, her slip was off and he was on top of her, straddling, while he peeled off his shirt and unbuttoned his pants.

Leonora shook her head, started to plead with sounds, unable to utter words any longer. Cold panic seized and she turned desperate. She leaned up and pushed him in the chest, beat at him with tight fists. Alex grinned, pushed her shoulder down with one hand and removed his pants with the other. Terror swept across her as his penis came into view, stiff and throbbing. She reached for his face, scratched his shoulder, tried to scream, but her throat closed.

Alex grabbed both her wrists with his left hand and held them above her head. The next moment, his full weight topped her, sinking between her thighs. And then with a groan and a swift thrust, he was inside. She arched her back with the force, biting her lip from the pain. His bare chest rubbed against hers as he rocked against her body, her pelvis spreading in cracking aches. Her mind closed down and quivered in the corner; her eyes shut tight. And it went on and on for short or long periods, she did not know which, until his body suddenly stiffened. A wounded moan left his throat. He shuddered, pulled out and lowered his head to her torso.

Alex rolled to his back, stared at the ceiling, his slick chest rising and falling, his penis limp against his thigh, hanging like a dog's panting tongue. Lazily, he turned on his side, propped up on an elbow. He looked at her and smiled, tucked a strand of hair behind her ear. "Are you all right?"

She swallowed, molded her sight to the plastered ceiling.

"It only hurts the first time. You'll see." Contented, he rubbed a palm over her breast, stomach and hip and spoke to them. "God, you're beautiful."

Her chin trembled as she fought back tears.

"Ah . . . the virgin remorse. Don't be ashamed, darling." He rubbed her arm with the backs of his fingers. "Waiting for the wedding night is a bit outdated, don't you think?" He circled her nipple with his finger, his voice low. "At least now you can't change your mind."

Leonora turned her neck and faced him, his eyes shining with a hard glint.

"Wouldn't want you backing out of our wedding with the next fever, would we?" he said. The look passed in an instant and he grinned, kissed her gently on the forehead. "Good night, Mrs. Harrington."

Leonora turned back to the ceiling. Her chest rose and fell slowly, the rest of her body still and naked upon the cotton sheets. Soon Alex's breathing mellowed in sleep. The curtains floated into the room and then sucked back to the balcony. The rain had stopped. Warm, moist air grew thick. The buzz of insects stretched from under bushes and scraggly city trees. And her future took shape—one prison for another. Inside her heart a light flickered, and she begged it not to go out, cupped it with her hands and cradled it against the darkness.

The melancholy song of a siren rose from the window. Leonora listened to the wail, did not move as warm tears released from her eyes and streamed down her cheeks to the sheets.

CHAPTER 37

❧

Shamus's funeral would be held in drought, under blue, piercing sky—a canopy of dry tears.

James sat on his haunches, his worn boots creased permanently at the toes, the hems of his moleskin breeches stained orange with dirt. He rubbed his fingertips across the ground and picked up the fine dust, rubbed the granules with his thumb before letting the powder fall from his palm. He stood, his tall body stretching from its folds, his back broadening under the white, ironed shirt, only now relaxing from starch. He wiped his hand on his trousers. With legs straight and slightly open in a V, he was the tallest form for a mile under the cloudless blue sky. The sun beat mercilessly atop his leather hat. Only mulga scrub, spinifex and the occasional lizard brought any life to the spot. Life but no comfort.

Mrs. Shelby stood to James's left, covered in black, a worn dress now faded with memories of those long buried. Tom stood to his right, their postures even. The ring of red-haired girls flanked him. John and Will were away at war but their presence still strong. The Shelby circle stood close, a buffer against the outside world as they had always been.

The preacher offered the only shade in the high noon, his imprint stretched on the ground in front of the tombstone. The ground below his feet lay unbroken, no fresh mound of disturbed dirt, for the marker was only that—a reminder of a life that was; a reminder of who was buried far out in the fields, unmarked.

"And so we mourn the passing of Shamus O'Reilly," the priest heralded before sprinkling holy water on the ground, the dust sucking God's moisture in quickly. "May he rest in peace."

Two white tombstones. Side by side. Tess O'Reilly. Shamus O'Reilly. Mrs. Shelby tucked her hand through James's arm—orphaned twice in one lifetime.

The preacher clicked the gate of the cemetery, a useless bit of metal to keep the ghosts tucked in and the living pushed out.

"Come back an' eat." Mrs. Shelby touched James's elbow. "Leave this day behind. No mass, I promise."

"I've got some things to clear up at the house."

Mrs. Shelby nodded and squeezed his arm, then turned to Tom. "You still heading out?"

"Yeah. It'll be late."

"Be good, Tommie, or so help me . . ." Mrs. Shelby pointed a finger in his face.

Tom smiled and batted her hand away. "Always."

"Orright," said Mrs. Shelby. "I'll ride back with the preacher. Children gettin' rowdy. Better feed 'em before they start killin' each other." Mrs. Shelby patted James's shoulder. "You go back to that house an' do what you have to. After that, you put this day behind you, son. That place ain't your home no more. Your home's with us now. Always has been."

James bent down, kissed her cheek. She squared her shoulders, yelled out to the children, "Pile on! We're headin' back."

James watched the wagon grow smaller, the empty land grow wider. He turned to Tom. "Where you off to?"

"The Cross." Tom kicked the dirt and looked up shyly.

"Yeah?" James grinned. "What's her name?"

"Ashley." His eyes bounced with the name. "From the dance a few months back."

"I remember." James crossed his arms and eyed his friend. "Also remember we didn't see you for two days after."

Tom laughed and raised his eyebrows. Then he turned his face to the cemetery and grew serious. "Want me to come with you? Just say the word, mate."

"No, thanks," James said. "Just need to be alone. Do this myself. Long time coming."

Tom nodded. "See you back home then."

"Be good." James pointed a finger at him, just as Mrs. Shelby had done.

"Always." He smirked.

Once Tom left, James walked past the cemetery, lowered his hat over his brow. The sun beat from the front, so he kept his head down, watched his boots spray red earth with each step. The buzz of cicadas rose from the ground and hovered until it seemed no other sound existed.

To the east, a thin line of wheat bordering an acre of Livingston property shimmered in brushed gold. A breeze blew, perhaps as far away as the sea. The gold strands rippled as thin and smooth as hair. Warmth flooded his chest as the memory of a friend, of hair and sea and light carried on a wind from very long ago. But then he blinked, raised his chest, shoved his hands into his pockets and turned the wheat back into wheat.

On Leonora's wedding day, Eleanor Fairfield tapped her foot harder and quicker as she assessed her niece. "Thank God for veils. You look like a ghost." She adjusted a few strands of Leonora's pulled-back hair.

"Did you find those diamonds?" Eleanor snapped at the maid.

"Yes, Mrs. Fairfield." The woman handed her a rosewood jewelry box.

Eleanor raised the lid and grimaced. "I swear, you're like a five-year-old child, Leonora." She picked up a small, round stone. "Stashing gravel with diamonds!" She flung the rock across the room. Without moving her head, Leonora watched its path until it rolled under the bed.

Roughly, Eleanor pushed the diamond studs through her niece's ears, looked her over one last time. "That will have to do. We're already late." Her aunt opened the door to leave, then turned back. "Well?"

"I just need a minute," she said softly. "Please."

Eleanor rolled her eyes and bustled into the hall, her voice trailing orders as the maid followed at her heels.

Leonora scrambled to the bed, scrunched the wedding dress around her knees as she bent down and reached across the floor, rescued the stone that was as smooth and perfect as a tiny bird's egg. She rubbed the surface, saw the kind smile of a dear friend and felt an old warmth that went beyond the sun's.

James stood upon the sloped porch of his old home, the splintered wood buckling under his weight. Tobacco spit stained the walls like splattered blood; broken bottles littered the floorboards. He opened the screen door, the hinges screeching from rust. Flies were everywhere. Disrupted, they buzzed at the intruder before settling back into favorite corners. The curtain wall that divided his room from the others was torn, the mattress on the floor hollowed out from rats.

Shamus's room lay gutted, the iron bed pushed against a wall, no blankets or pillows. The striped, thin mattress was stained from rusted springs, soiled with yellow spots. Drawers were gone. No remnants of good days remained—only scars of the bad days, the bad years.

James left the house and went to the small shed in the back, pushed the cans and tools aside until he found the kerosene. He twisted the cap, doused the base of the wood frame and the steps along the porch with short, quick splashes. The wood was dry and old; the fuel, a guarantee. James lit a match against a stone, the blue flame hissing with new life.

Leonora stepped from the car, blind to who carried the gown's train or put flowers in her hand. Life moved through the veil in a foggy haze.

Music began. Violins and cellos stretched bows across taut strings; resin powdered under bridges. Pachelbel's Canon in D Major. Voices and chatter hushed within the hall. Her uncle took her elbow, whispered in her ear, "You're breathtaking, darling." And her feet moved. One step at a time. One step closer.

James threw the match at the kerosene-soaked timber, stood back, his spine firm, his thumbs tucked in belt loops. He watched the fire fill the space under the porch, wrap around the boards.

* * *

Leonora looked through the smoky veil. Alex took her hand. The priest spoke. "Do you take this man to be your lawful wedded husband?"

Fire inched up the posts, the weak fibers collapsing quickly into a fountain of sparks. Spastic flames licked each beam, blackened fissures sizzling under their tongues. The fire reached inside, disintegrated the flimsy curtain shreds.

Leonora answered, "I do."

The porch collapsed. The charred slats of the house crumbled.

"Ladies and Gentlemen, I introduce you to Mr. and Mrs. Alexander Harrington."

Smoke choked James's throat.

Tears burned her eyes under the veil.

Flames of regret—embers of pain.

CHAPTER 38

James returned to the Shelby homestead, the hour late. A magpie, its caterwaul hauntingly human, cried out from the trees. A lamp took form in the kitchen window. Home.

James put the horse in the barn. A tiny glow bobbed near the verandah. It was Tom stooped on the steps, his shadowed figure smoking. James sat down next to him and stretched his long legs, the vibration of the horse still in his thighs. The smell of tobacco was heavy around his friend. Cigarette butts littered the stairs. He studied Tom for a minute and his brows lowered—Tom didn't smoke.

"Burned it down?" Tom asked quietly. James nodded.

"You orright?"

"Yeah," said James. "It's done." He bent his head back and stared at the stars. "Figured you'd be out all night."

Tom sucked at his cigarette, one eye closing with the pull. He paused for a moment, then exhaled the smoke from his nose in a long stream. "I'm in trouble, mate."

James waited, watched his friend darken.

"She's pregnant."

The men grew silent, the weight of the words drowning out the magpies.

"You going to marry her?" James ventured slowly.

"Wish it were that simple." A low laugh broke from Tom as he reached around his knees and rocked, the cigarette pinched between two fingers. "Already got herself a bloke. Married."

"Christ."

"I didn't know," he blurted. "I swear to God, she never said a word."

"Who's the bloke?"

"Don't know." Tom raked his fingers through his red hair. "Crazy son of a bitch, is what I hear. Works the chain gang up in Queensland. A deputy or somepin."

"Does he know?" James asked.

"Not yet."

"She planning on telling him?"

Tom picked up a stone and hurled it into the night, hung his head in exhaustion. "I guess that depends."

"On what?"

"On whether I pay up. She wants money, James." Tom picked up another rock and threw it past the first one. "Thinks we got money. Us bein' squatters and all. I told her my dad didn't leave us a pot to piss in, but she don't buy it. Says I'm going to pay one way or another."

"Doesn't make sense. She'd have to admit what she did with you."

Tom sucked at the last bit of tobacco, his fingers shaking. "Ashley's a fool, but not stupid. Thought of everything." He laughed coldly, his voice scared. "Says if I don't pay, she's gonna tell him I forced myself on her. Gonna tell him I raped her."

Tom blinked fiercely, his face sick. "I'd never do that to a woman! You know that. I got five sisters. The very thought of somebody doin' that to a woman makes my insides curl." He grimaced. "And here she is waving a word like 'rape' around my face like it's a bloody streamer!"

Tom dropped his head into his hands. The cigarette butt fell to the ground and smoldered. "What am I gonna do?"

James ground out the stub with his heel, stared hard into the dark.

"Got no money," Tom choked. "Hell, I'd pay in a second just to get her off my back, but I got nothin'." He shook his head. "Swear I don't care what the bloke does to me. He can string me up from the nearest gum branch an' I'd take it smiling. But I can't have Mum livin' with this shame. Kill her worse than Dad dyin'. Kill her worse than the boys goin' off to war."

James stood, felt the weight of Tom's eyes as he walked in a clipped circle, hands on hips. "Let's say you pay. She's still pregnant. How's she going to explain that?"

"Says once she gets paid, she's gonna visit her bloke. Make him be with her so he thinks it's his." He spit at the ground. "She's damn twisted, James. Evil and twisted right outta her gawddamn head." Tom blew out the side of his mouth. "I think she planned it all along. Picked me out special. Just a dumb squatter." He sighed. "Not half-wrong."

James looked at his friend, his brother. His voice steeled. "We'll get the money, Tom."

The man's lost eyes met his. "We don't have—"

"I'll find the money." James extended a hand and pulled Tom up. "I'll find it."

CHAPTER 39

The elegant rooms of the Fairfield manor overflowed with guests. Leonora stayed quiet, smiled faintly at the well-wishers, her insides numb to words and sounds and sentiment. Alex loomed large and confident in his black tux as he made the rounds of greetings. He juggled a full tumbler agilely as he kissed hands, hugged shoulders and kept his fingers glued to his wife's waist.

Waiters herded the lingering crowd to the ballroom to take their seats for dinner. Leonora and Alex sat at a small table draped in gold silk, centered with white roses.

Owen, dressed in a pure white tuxedo, stood and tapped his fork against his champagne flute. The room quieted. "It's with great honor that we welcome you to our home on this wonderful day—the wedding of Alexander Harrington and my beautiful niece, Leonora."

Leonora stared at her pale hands in her lap as if they belonged to someone else.

"But even as we share our congratulations and our love for this happy couple, we must also use this opportunity to say our good-byes."

Leonora looked up. Owen and Alex exchanged grins. "As many of you know, Alex has become like a son to me. His business acumen, as well as his devotion to my niece, has been a great source of pride for my wife and I. And with that pride comes a deep trust. Alex has graciously agreed to step into the family business and will fill my shoes overseas."

A live wire pulsed, itched her palms. Air came quick and short to her lungs.

"Please join me as we wish Alex and Leonora health and happiness in their new home." Owen Fairfield raised his glass, met Leonora's eyes deeply and tilted the glass solely to her.

Her breathing stopped.

"Australia!"

PART 5

CHAPTER 40

❧

Ghan picked his way along the road furrows, the hour early as a sparrow fart. Frost crunched under his steps as he hunched his body against the cold, his hands taking turns holding the bag strap and warming in the front pockets. Only the nights and mornings brought the piercing chill. By noon, he'd be sweating through his shirt.

Ghan stopped, pulled off his boot and clawed his swollen, blistered toes. *Damn chilblains.* The more he scratched, the more they burned and swelled. Every season brought its own itch—fleas in the summer, lice in the spring, foot rot in the wet, chilblains in the winter—least he only had one foot to scratch. Ghan shoved his boot back on without relief. No time to dawdle. He had work today.

The sun peeped above the plain. Toes would be warming soon. Work came. Work went. He had a good run with the sandalwood that lasted a few years. Just tie the trunks to a few wily goats, pry at the roots and pluck the trees out straight. He could have done that work forever, but the forest cleared fast. After a few years, nothing was left but some lonely craters. Leaves a man hollow when he sees acres and acres of land barren and holed. No birds; no wallabies. Nothing. But somewhere a rich lady got a nice-smelling sandalwood box sitting atop her bureau.

Grounding wheels perked his ears and he turned. A small dray pulled up, the driver bulky and red, his worn coat buttoned to his chin. "Where yeh headin'?"

"Southern Cross."

"Hop up."

* * *

"Here's the map." Mr. Fletcher, the co-op owner, handed him the scrawled piece of paper. "Yeh can read, can't yeh?"

"Course I can!" Ghan spit. Course he couldn't read a lick, but a map's a map and he could read one as good as any fancy sook could read a poem.

"Team's ready," said Fletcher. "Need 'em back in two days, yeh hear? No slackin'."

"No worries."

"Good people, the Monahans. Steady customers. Lost a boy in the war. Don't put 'em out, yeh hear? Need this team back in two days, yeh hear me?"

Say it again an' yer gonna hear my fist in yer jaw. "Yes, sir. Two days." Ghan was getting too soft—but a man's got to eat. He crumpled the map into his pocket and pulled himself up to the seat behind the two yoked bullocks.

"Put the animals in the barn t'night, yeh hear?" Mr. Fletcher hollered out. "Yeh hear me?"

Yeh, I hear yeh, yeh naggy son of a bitch. Bullocks be sleepin' cozy in the barn while I'm freezin' my arse in the paddock. "Yes, sir!" Ghan hollered back with a polite tip of his hat.

The roads from the Southern Cross branched out in fingers, and once he passed the outskirts of town he unwrinkled the map, caught his bearings and headed through the thumb.

Ghan passed a small cemetery on his right, no different from the others that dotted the inner land: a bent iron fence, humble white stones marking forgotten names, forgotten lives. A few hours later, he passed the remnants of a dead farm and a burned-down squatter shack. A few charred beams stuck from the soot-stamped ground. A wheelbarrow lay on its side, half-brown with rust, half-black with burn. The old water tank stood untainted. With the sound of the bullocks, a feral cat slinked with bowed back out of the empty chook house and sprinted into the rows of old wheat stalks. *Shame,* Ghan thought to himself, *good land sitting empty.*

By dinner, the Monahan station came into view. One by one the children poured from the house, yelling in shrieks that the supplies had come. They swarmed the wagon before he could pull to a full stop.

"G'day," the station men and family men and women greeted in a round. "Thought O'Shaye deliverin' the load?" they asked while their eyes flitted over the crates.

"Measles."

"Goin' round. Seems to every few years."

Quick as bees to syrup, the people swarmed and climbed upon the boxes, the wagon creaking under the weight. Women searched until they found the bolts of gray calico, boxes of needles, threads and buttons. Men began unloading the supplies with grunts and veins popping in their necks. The children sniffed out the tins of barley sugar candy as if they could smell it straight from the packing straw.

A little girl with braids hanging down her ears held up one of the metal candy tins. "Can we, Mum?" she begged.

"Orright," Mrs. Monahan allowed. "But one apiece. No more." She rolled her eyes. "Be gone 'fore the week's out."

The men carried away cases of dried fruit, bags of white sugar and rice, chests of tea imported from China, tons of flour. A strong field man picked up the crate of rock salt and headed for the barn loft. Crockery, men's work clothes, medicine, seeds and spices were unloaded and accounted for.

"Come in and join us for supper," invited Mr. Monahan as he handed off the last box. "Piece of sugar candy in it for you. If you can pry it out of their sticky hands, that is."

"Thanks, but got some tucker from town. I'll just set up out here, stay outta yer way."

"Nonsense. Missus'll take it as a personal affront." Mr. Monahan turned away. "Don't wait long or food's gonna get cold."

When a man isn't used to hot, good food he's stubborn to eat it, because once he tastes it he remembers how much he's missed it and how it's going to be a long time before he tastes it again. So Ghan ate, spoke when spoken to and tried not to enjoy the food too much, tried not to close his eyes and cry from the sheer joy of butter and sugar and fresh beef on his tongue.

That night he slept in the barn, up in the loft, shoved between the crates of rock salt and gunnysacks of seed. As far as places to sleep, it wasn't half-bad—not bad at all. By the time the sun squeezed through the termite holes, Ghan was up and on his way back to the co-op.

Mr. Fletcher inspected his pocket watch as the team drove up. He took a look at the animals, nodded with approval. "How'd it go?" he asked.

"Got everythin' they ordered."

"Course they did." Mr. Fletcher put his hand on the rump of the bullock and leaned casually, his thin arms oddly long. "Good people, the Monahans." He turned back to business. "O'Shaye's still sick. Up fer another run?"

"Take as many as yeh got."

Fletcher poked his tongue against his cheek. "Orright. I'll load her t'day. Come back tomorrow an' we'll send yeh south t'Corrigin."

With the day now free, Ghan headed down the curve of the railroad. A row of Chinese, only pegs above slaves, droned and slumped over the rails. Ghan found the pub farthest from the center of town. Living off the land like he did, he treated himself to a nip now and then, especially when he finished a job. But only a nip; any more and the old anger shot back, and he was too old and worn to fight.

Ghan entered the pub, his foot sucking on the sticky floor. Barely past noon and men lined each side. A barman, arms folded at his chest, leaned against the cracked mirror that reflected the bottles, tried to fool a man into thinking the bar was well stocked. A mustache drooped from his lip to his jawbone and stretched as he talked.

Ghan pulled out a stool. The young man sitting next to it scooted over so he had room to sit at the counter. The barman raised his chin.

"Schooner," Ghan ordered.

The man poured a pint of ale and splashed it on the counter but kept his fingers tight around the glass. "Yeh got money t'pay fer this?"

"Didn't come in here beggin', did I?" Ghan snapped.

The barman squinted, reluctantly let go of the glass and turned to the man next to Ghan. "More water?" he asked mockingly. The young man smirked and ignored him. The barman went back to his mirror and his chat.

The ale was piss warm but hoppy, warmed his belly right up through the veins. Ghan sipped it slowly, no rush to go, no place to go until the next morning. Waiting. Waiting for work.

Another young man entered the pub, a redhead faded by the sun. He sat down a seat over, nodded to the man next to him as a mate would. They were shaved and clean, tan from outdoor work but not slovenly like the shearers and roustabouts.

"You talk to her?" the dark-haired one asked.

"Said she'd give me a month before she tells him." The redhead scratched an ear. "One stinkin' month."

The barman walked over. "Whot yeh need, Tom?"

"A job," he answered bitterly, then shook his head. "Whiskey."

The man poured a shot. "Thought you made out pretty good last couple seasons."

Tom sipped his drink, stared into it. "Not good enough."

The quiet, dark-haired man spoke up, stretched his shoulders back. "Tom's thinking we should head to the diggings." He smirked then. "Thinks we'll find the great nugget a thousand other men just over-looked."

Tom rested his elbows on the counter, slouched his weight. "Better than sittin' around watchin' the grass dry up."

"Listen to James," ordered the barman. "Diggin's no place for boys like you. Beats the hell outta a man, changes 'im, turns 'im mean an' hard like the rocks he's poundin'."

Tom laughed. "You're like a bloody poet."

"Diggin's no joke!" he retorted. "An' no place fer you boys. I knew yer dad well, Tom. Know whot he used to say to any farmer wantin' t'go out there? He'd say, 'Impossible fer a man who works atop the land t'work under it wivout losin' his mind.' Trust me, stick wiv the land, mate. She'll give yeh trouble, but she won't fuck yeh."

Two sweaty men came in the front entrance. The barman gave them the silent nod, moved down to meet them.

Ghan listened to the talk. Not eavesdropping, just listening the same way he listened to the glasses clinking on the table and the boots shuffling against each other. The barman was right. The dig-gings would eat these two clean boys for breakfast and spit them out in chunks.

Ghan glanced sideways, stole a closer look. James, the one with the water, had a steadiness about him, a toughness without the show. *Good-looking kid—even a bloke could see that and not feel like a poof.* Brows were knit, looked like that was his natural expression, the thinking type. The other guy was the typical country kid, loose in posture, sulky but quick-witted.

Ghan finished the last warm gulp. He'd set up camp, have some lunch, turn in early after the sun set. He pushed the glass along the counter and stood. The barman came back, took the glass. "One shilling."

Ghan reached into his pocket, fished around with his fingers. He took his other hand and dug deep in the other, his fingers twisting around the fabric, a hole widening in the seam.

The barman watched him steadily, licked his top teeth. "Problem?"

"Got it here, somewhere." The pockets were empty, but he kept digging, trying to manifest the coins that were there this morning. "Must 'ave dropped out."

The man smacked the counter hard with his palm. Chatter halted, all eyes turned. "Knew yer were a bum when yeh walked in! This ain't a fuckin' charity ring! Now yeh pay that shilling or I take that peg off an' beat the money outta yeh!"

"I ain't a bum!" Ghan snapped, but at that moment he was. "Just need to trace m'steps."

"Yeh'll leave an' stiff me fer the tab, yeh will!"

"Ask Mr. Fletcher! I ain't no bum!" spit Ghan. "He's got me deliverin' for 'im."

"Told yeh he was a lyin' son of a bitch!" the barman announced to the group. "That's O'Shaye's job. Been doin' it for two years." He rolled up his sleeves and reached for a long stick across the back counter, pointed it at Ghan's chest. "Listen, cripple—"

The young man next to him pushed the stick away. "Back off!" James threw a few coins onto the counter. "It's covered."

The barman flitted his eyes back and forth between the two men and tapped the stick on the bar. "Don't go bailin' out these bums, James. They gotta learn."

"He ain't a bum," James defended. "Now leave him be."

Tom rose, paid for his own drink, pushed the money at the stick. "Besides," he taunted, "should be payin' him for makin' us drink that horse piss. Buy a cooler, yeh cheap bastard."

Some of the men laughed. The barman lost his anger. "Yeh got some pluck, Tom." He put the stick back under the mirror. "Just like yer dad."

Ghan pulled out the lining of his pocket and showed it to James. "Must have dropped out." He rubbed his scraggly beard, the shame hot in his ears.

James patted him on the shoulder. "No worries."

Ghan couldn't soothe the burn of the handout, and when the two young men left the pub he followed. "Hold up! Give m'yer post an' I'll get the money back t'yeh. Get paid tomorrow. Can ask Mr. Fletcher at the co-op yerself. I ain't a bum." The words repeated in his head over and over again. *I ain't a bum. I ain't a bum.*

James smiled, waved him off. "Only a drink, mate. My treat."

That man did him a good deed—saved him from getting his few teeth knocked out. Ghan hurried on his peg leg and stopped them again. "Heard yer lookin' for work."

"Yeah." Tom stepped forward. "Know of any?"

"New chap comin' to run the mine outta Coolgardie. American fella. Word is he bought a couple of bush stations an' needs workers— drovers, stockmen, shearers, jackeroos, managers, the works." Ghan pulled himself up. He wasn't a bum. "Know 'bout it 'cause I brought a load of wood up there. Buildin' everything fresh. Get in there first, yeh could probably pick yer job."

That young man, James, had that thinking look again, his face intense and alert. "Where'd you say the station is?"

"Up near Leinster. Part of the old Miranda Creek Station."

"Appreciate the tip." James reached out a hand. "Did us a good service, sir."

Ghan puffed out his chest. *Sir, he said.* He shook the hand offered and the shame melted away. *I ain't a bum.*

CHAPTER 41

❦

"Bronson said he'd move into the old manager quarters," said Tom haltingly. "Keep an eye on you an' the girls."

Mrs. Shelby's face turned fierce. "Already said I can handle a gun as good as any man."

"I know. Everybody knows," appeased Tom. "But if people hear there's not a man here, you might have t'use that gun. Bronson'll stay outta the way; you know that. He'll just sit on his stoop with his gun. More show than anything. Gives the poor bloke a purpose."

When Tom finished, they waited, the silence expanding uncomfortably across the table. Tom's nerves frizzled. "Course, that's only if we get the job. Long shot for sure, but we'd be kickin' ourselves if we didn't try."

Mrs. Shelby had aged; the corners of her eyelids drooped. Gray wiry strands lined the roots of the red hair piled and pinned on her head. She shifted her eyes to Tom, to James and then back to Tom. "Why you so desperate for money all of a sudden?"

Tom squirmed in his chair, reddened. "Taxes, Mum. Girls getting' older." He floundered, "Drought comin'."

"You're in trouble, aren't you." It wasn't a question. Mrs. Shelby pulled in her bottom lip, stretching the skin on her chin. A great pleading held her eyes. "What you do, Tommie?"

Tom's mouth fell open. The blush drained and left his face pale.

"Nothing that can't be undone," James interjected. "We're going to make it right, Mrs. Shelby. But we got to get work. Good work."

The woman nodded in quick spurts, raised her head and sucked air in through her nose. "Orright. I'll speak with the renters about share-cropping." Mrs. Shelby pointed to the office, avoiding her son's face. "Tommie, go fetch the books."

Tom slinked away, the shame turning his gait crooked. "Boy's got no sense." The weariness grew and sagged her jaws, aging her further. "Is the trouble bad?"

"Yeah."

"Take care of him, James." Mrs. Shelby closed her eyes. "Make things right."

"I will." James nodded. "Promise."

"Coolgardie!" the conductor shouted above the roar of the steam engine.

"That's us." James grabbed his pack from the seat.

Through the steam and smoke and wheels still burning from movement, they stepped off the train into a town of metal and looked up into a sky loud and crowded with roaring pistons and distant clangs. Rows of railroad tracks, lined with filthy ore cars, veered in clogged veins from the heart of the station. The smell of soot and oil and coal clung to the air. The clash of train cars coupling and grunting sent the eardrum retreating like a turtle's head in a shell. Miners, blackened and rough, dotted the platform and weaved between the cars. A mix of accents—Italian, Polish, Ukrainian—blurred with Australian slang, guttural and nearly indiscernible.

Two dark-eyed men sat atop a donkey cart, their cheeks swollen with tobacco. They snickered at the new arrivals, pointed to their pressed clothes. Tom hiked his bag up his shoulder in case he needed to hit someone with it. "Feel like a fish outta water about to get gutted."

James crossed a set of tracks and approached the men. "G'day," he greeted curtly.

The man to the right spit on the ground, left a red phlegm splotch near James's boot. "Waitin' fer a buggy, sweetie?"

James ignored him. "You work at the mine?"

"Me an' everybody else 'ere."

"Heard there's a new manager coming in. You know anything about him?"

The threat in their faces left as they took on the look of men who suddenly found themselves a fraction superior with knowledge. They stretched their necks to meet the sought counsel. "'Arrington. Yankee bloke. Loaded son of a bitch."

"Got a station around here?"

The men laughed. The left one spit. The tobacco landed on the foot of the donkey, who shuffled and kicked it away.

"What's so funny?" Tom asked.

"Yeah. He's got a station. More like a country. Over three million acres, they say."

The other man, not to be outdone, leaned in and added, "Bloke's got a hundred thousand head of cattle on hold. Got horses, too. Bringin' 'em in from Middle East somewheres."

"Sawdi 'Rabia!" chimed the other man.

"They hiring?"

The man shrugged his shoulders, his help burned out.

"Know where we can catch a ride?" Tom asked.

"Ask at McKellar's pub. Usually get a hitch there."

"Thanks." James tipped his hat and the men went back to stretching, chewing and spitting, watching the metal bang across metal.

"Think he was jokin' about three million acres?" Tom asked.

"Guess we'll find out."

The driver of the old dray swayed in his seat from drink, singing a mix of three songs tied into one. He pulled the gray packhorse to a stop on a lone road, one side wired waist high with a fence that went on as far as the eye could see. "This 'ere the start of the property," he said. "Hole in the fence give yeh a shortcut to the house. Far as I can take yeh."

Tom and James stepped out to the red earth. Spinifex dotted the landscape, rose like hairy moles on sunburned skin. They climbed through the fence and walked ahead, stayed focused on the direction of the sun. After an hour, they passed a rusty windmill. Tom paused, stared up at the still blades. "Think that drunk had any idea where he was sendin' us?"

James laughed, wiped the dust and sweat from his forehead. "Nope."

"Christ, we're screwed." They stopped then, looked around, every inch of land the same. "We're bloody lost." Tom chuckled.

"We're dead, mate."

"We'll be shriveled like raisins." Tears streamed down Tom's cheeks with tired, thirsty roars of laughter.

James pulled out a canteen, drank through a spread smile, then handed it to Tom. "So much for clean clothes, eh?"

Tom examined his shirt littered with dirty, red handprints. "I'm a bloody mess." Then he scanned James. "How the hell you keep so clean?"

James clicked his tongue. "I'm a gentleman."

Tom shoved him in the shoulder, leaving a picture of his palm near the collar. James ignored him and perked, his eyes squinting into the distance. "Looks like a car." He pointed to a small dust cloud that moved in a parallel line. "Must be the place."

They moved quickly, keeping their eyes locked on the trail of dust so as not to lose it. From the horizon, buildings slowly emerged over the level ground like sprouted seeds. First an old whitewashed barn. Then a dented windmill, its shadow pointing east. Another barn popped up followed by a twenty-stall shearing shed, a ringed stable, three water towers. Beyond that, the big house loomed with fresh yellow brick and a gleaming iron roof. A screened verandah edged its girth, mounted by a metal bullnose that stuck out like lips.

James and Tom patted down their shirts and pants, wiped faces with clean handkerchiefs. A workman straddled the peak of a new roof, the stable big enough to hold thirty horses. James hollered up to him, "Looking for Mr. Harrington!"

The man pointed his hammer, spoke between nails held in his teeth, "Jist got back."

Dropping their packs behind the barn, they headed to the drive, past the new Ford, its chrome covered in dust. The front door of the house opened. A man stepped out, yelled behind him, "Just tell them to get it here!" the American accent quick and direct.

The man wore beige riding pants and a starched white shirt opened far down at the collar and rolled up at the sleeves. He paused on the steps, lit a cigarette, his cheekbones prominent as he breathed in the tobacco before noticing the two men. A smile rose to his face and he clapped in drawn applause, the new cigarette hanging easily and expertly from his lips under a thin mustache. "It's about time! I was expecting you two days ago."

Tom shot James a furtive glance from the side, raised his eyebrows with the unwarranted familiarity. "Train schedule was off," he offered tentatively.

"Not surprised." The American stepped up in high black boots, the foot dirtied to the ankle, the calf still shiny with polish. "Of course, it takes so long to get to the telegraph office, it's hard to know what to expect from one day to the next." He looked them over and laughed. "You're filthy. You walk here?"

"Got a ride from Coolgardie," Tom explained. "Bloke dropped us off a little short."

"Should have taken the train to Gwalia. Would have saved you hours. Didn't you get the directions?" he asked sharply.

Tom rolled his eyes and shrugged his shoulders.

"Oh, well." He smirked. "Half my orders get lost out here, sucked up in this bloody desert." He nodded then, pleasantly. "We'll get you settled in a bit." Then, letting the cigarette rest loosely in the side of his mouth, he stuck out a hand. "Alexander Harrington. Call me Alex."

James reached out and shook the man's hand, their grips firm. "James O'Reilly." He cocked his head to Tom. "Thomas Shelby." Tom stuck out his hand and leaned forward in nearly a bow, caught himself and stepped back with a manly puff of his chest.

"I'm surprised." Alex squinted, studied the new arrivals intently and sucked in a long drag. "When Mitchell told me about you, I pictured a couple of sunburned roughens. Seem young to be station managers."

Tom choked, shuffled his feet and opened his mouth to set the record straight when James stepped up. "You kind of surprised us, too," he said casually. "Seem young to own a station this size. No disrespect."

"None taken." The man put one hand in his pocket and grinned. "I'm relieved actually. You'll bring some energy to this place."

Alex dropped the simmering butt, used his boot to cover it with dust. "Position pays six thousand a year with a five-hundred-dollar advance. Divide it any way you want."

Tom's mouth fell open. James shot him a look and Tom clapped it shut.

"I know the base is a little less than you made before," Alex added. "But there's bonuses if we make our numbers and, if you work hard, you'll be bringing in a heck of a lot more than you were in New South Wales. I'm a firm believer in incentives." Alex clapped his hands once and rubbed his palms together. "Let me take you around and get you acquainted." And then as an afterthought, "You need to clean up first? Get something to eat?"

"Ate on the way," James answered easily. "Might as well get started." He stepped in front of Tom, his face still naked with bewilderment.

"Good." Alex clapped again. "Pick your horse."

Once saddled, the three riders trotted past the two-story homestead, the steel roof pearly and blinding. French doors leading out to the verandah lined every few feet. Fruit trees, new and recently planted, hung limp and thin as willows in the sun. A wiry rosebush tried to grasp its stems to the side of the house, but besides that the vegetation was slim.

"I had the old house leveled," Alex explained. "Everything's new—the barns, the water towers—everything. Once we get settled, we'll work on the landscape. There's a lot to do."

Alex kicked his horse. He was a good rider, strong and postured. The men rounded a corner to a wide riding arena. A cluster of Aboriginal men, odd and uncomfortable in Western clothes, leaned against the fence posts; a few sat crisscross on the dirt.

Alex pulled his horse to a stop. "I've got twelve Aboriginal stockmen, hand-me-downs from the last station that was here. Live about five miles that way in a bunch of shacks, like a shantytown. I've only been out there once. Would have cleared them all out, but the neighbors tell me they'd stick around regardless, sleep under the sky as easily as they would under a roof."

Leaning back in the saddle, Alex raised a long leg up and bent his knee, rested his elbow against it. "Can't understand a word they say, can't even make out if it's English. But heard they make good stock-men, as long as they're led and directed, that is. Cheap, too. Seem happy enough working for sugar, tea, meat and tobacco." He looked at James, then Tom, then back at James. "But you're the ones that got to manage. If they're not pulling their weight, they're out."

A couple of white men lingered past the ring—one sinewy, his neck tight and stringy; the other a bit taller but with short, stubby arms. "Who are they?" Tom asked.

Alex shrugged indifferently. "Beecher and Russell. Roustabouts that I hired from another station. Quiet, seem harmless enough. Take orders but aren't thinkers. I needed someone to take care of the horses right away." He scratched his neck. "Keep them or fire them, it's up to you."

Five horses centered the arena, their muscles slick and defined as they stepped within the perimeter. "Beauties," Tom said. "You planning to breed them?"

"That's the plan. Should get some good racers out of them."

"Got some wild ones out there, too," Tom noted.

"Stallion's a beast. Won't let anyone near him. Have to bring some-one in to break him." Alex clicked his tongue, put the horse in motion again, rode between James and Tom over the flat, low-lying country. "Property is three million acres," he announced.

Without looking, James knew Tom was gripping the reins with white knuckles and probably sweating through his shirt. "How much stock do you have?" James asked.

"Ten thousand sheep right now. The bullocks are coming in a few months. You'll need to meet the drover halfway. Bringing them from up north—hundred and fifty thousand head."

They rode in silence a few miles more to a granite range, a large pool of freshwater reflecting the jagged walls. The men dismounted, let the horses drink. Alex leaned against a tree and lit another ciga-rette, offered two, then tucked them back in his pocket when de-clined.

Prickly moss lined the water, the yellow flowers round like pom-poms. A salmon gum bloomed with parakeets, their chatter bouncing off the stone, magnifying. Tom reclined atop a boulder, finally at ease. "Got a beautiful piece of land here, Mr. Harrington."

"Alex," he corrected. "She is indeed." He looked over the land with ownership.

James skipped a flat stone across the water. "You're taking over the Coolgardie mine?"

"That's right."

"Long commute."

"Have a place in Coolgardie, too. I'll divide my time," Alex noted. "Besides, this place is more for my wife. I don't want her anywhere near those mining towns." Alex tapped the cigarette in the air. "That reminds me. In a few days I leave for Perth to pick her up." He looked at them carefully. "I'm trusting you to keep the place running and watched while I'm gone. I kept the managers' quarters close for that reason. You'll find it half a mile toward the creek. There's running water, electricity."

The American flicked his burning smoke to the pond, pulled out a black flask from his pocket and took a long drink. He pointed it to Tom, who took it gratefully, dropped his head back and gulped. Alex took the flask back and handed it out to James. "You're next, my friend."

"I don't drink."

"No?" Alex sucked in his cheeks, then dismissed it. "To each his own." He wiped his mouth with a fist and put the flask back into his pocket. "You boys married?" he asked.

"Naw," Tom answered. "Don't need the distraction."

Alex laughed hard. "Smart. Very smart." He pulled his horse from the water's edge.

"Your wife American?" Tom asked.

"She is."

"Bush can be hard on a woman." Tom glanced at the sun trickling through the branches. "Especially if she's not used to it."

"And trust me, she's not." Alex stroked the horse's nose, inspected the hair along the mane. "My wife's as spoiled as a child. This place will do her a world of good, toughen her up a bit." Alex winked at the men. "A good woman's like a good horse, just needs some breaking in." He settled upon the saddle and jerked the reins. "Australia'll work her better than a whip."

CHAPTER 42

~❦~

She was Australia.

Leonora pressed her forehead to the hot window of the train car, her eyes racing with the speeding land. Endless miles of red earth blurred along the tracks, stretched off to the edge of the world, and her gaze fell into its rusted hue and the white heat that shimmered above it—the land of her birth.

She was Australia. Its air was her air, its cells her own.

Leonora sat on the train as a woman. She returned to this flowing land, both a dead and living land, a named woman—branded a Fairfield, then a Harrington: names of wealth that trailed and spoke of her and said she was not a daughter of Australia but of a pedigree. But she knew.

A month ago, America waved from the deck of the steamer and sent kisses from her shores, wished her well toward the other land, just as an aunt says good-bye and gently pushes a child to her mother. After weeks and weeks upon that ship, where the wind shifted and called to her, Australia grew from the very sea, rose to greet her with sheer cliff walls and ocean pinnacles that had not changed a stone but waited patiently for her return. And secretively, she unfolded the creases, smoothed out the edges of her wrinkled Australia, but she did not breathe—not yet.

Southern Cross. Kalgoorlie. Menzies. Kookynie. The towns swung past. The train stopped at each, the firebox exhaling in rest before eating coal and chugging forward again. And then they stopped. Alex took her elbow and led her through a hard, smoking town with hard, smoking men and led her to the car. Australia slowed now and drifted and heated the car on an unshaded journey upon a lone road.

The land cut in two with a wiry fence, a fissure that extended as far as the eye's gaze could follow. Every mile, a gate stopped them. Alex let the car idle as he undid the lock, drove ahead, shut the gate and moved on through the entrances shielding one empty acre from the next.

And there it was. Wanjarri Downs. The house rose from the dirt, its yellow brick mellow and baking against the sun. Alex opened her door and put his arm around her waist, gazed at the house. "What do you think?"

But there were no words. This land was her home, her *home!* Here she could begin anew, breathe life into this house, raise a family, create new memories that would wipe away the nightmares. Life was new again and she was grateful. She reached for Alex, hugged him and felt his smile in her hair. She would forget about the past, erase any history before this moment. She would try to love him. He had brought her back to Australia and she could forgive him for the scars. She would be a good wife. Her soul bloomed. The breath was coming, filled her lungs and wanted to erupt as tears, but it was still not time.

Alex shuttled her through the house, showed her the rooms, opened up the French doors so the curtains billowed upon the hot breeze. He chatted about the land, about the mine, but her ears were dull to the words and only heard the sounds—the sound of his voice, the swish of drapes as they embraced the window frames, the echo of her and Alex's footsteps on new hardwood and the cackle of nearly a million birds from outside.

She was Australia.

The day's light waned. Alex took leave to his office. Leonora stepped to the verandah where the setting sun met with a fiery orange eye. Her body moved now without her will, her thoughts just a passenger. She watched her feet, told them to walk when they wanted to run. The dirt below her soles was red and knew her feet, dusted and coated her high heels. The birds laughed, asked in shouts and shrieks where she had been.

Leonora headed to the trees, buried herself in a cluster of ghost gums, so closely knit that their bony boughs intertwined and latticed.

And she pulled herself up into their limbs, gathered her silk dress around her legs and touched the smooth peeling bark with her fingertips, sank her cheek to the white skin. She hung to the boughs, peered with the wide eyes of a chuditch into the growing dark. Kangaroos grew from the shadows, seemed to pop up from the very spot they stood and dotted the plain with raised paws and twitching ears. Her body shook then. Her chest opened. She clung to the tree limbs and cried into its creases like an infant to a mother's breast.

And she grew from Australia again and she was made of Australia again. And she was here under the deep sky, stained by its earth and greeted by bloated flies. And Australia broke her heart with its grace, that it had not forgotten her just as she had never forgotten it. Her lungs broke with sobs and the air broke in and she breathed.

She was home.

CHAPTER 43

Tom paced the floorboards that lined the managers' quarters, the crevices between the new wood still filled with sawdust. He stopped at the window for the hundredth time. "Think he knows?"

"Hard to say." James held an empty boot between his thighs, rubbed the leather with wax.

"Been back for hours," Tom continued. "Would have come down by now if he knew, right?" He didn't wait for an answer. "What d'you think he'll do if he knows we ain't the guys?"

"Throw us out," James said calmly as he squared a soft cloth and spread the grease over the boot's creased tongue.

"Christ." Tom scratched his head. "He'll be pissed. Looks the type." He turned to James. "What should we do? Tell him first?"

"Out of our hands." James buffed the lines near the sole and around the eyelets. "If he knows, he knows. We'll find out soon enough."

"But Christ, James! Six thousand dollars! Be sick till my grave if we lose this job." Tom paced back and forth, his mouth twitching.

James picked up his other boot and threw it at Tom's back.

"Ouch!"

"You're putting a hole in the floor. Clean up your boots," James directed. "Least we can try and look halfway decent when he fires us."

"Aren't you worried at all?"

James stopped buffing. "We can run this place, Tom. I'm hoping this guy knows it." He handed Tom the tin of lanolin. "Either way, we'll have our answer soon." He glanced at their bags slouched near the door. "Wouldn't go unpacking, though."

Tom picked up a boot, set it on the table, raised and lowered the heel without paying attention to the movement. "Did you catch a glimpse of his wife?" Tom grinned.

"No," James said, disinterested.

"Only saw the back of her." Tom's face softened with a wide smile. "Bet she's a looker."

James chuckled. "What happened to your vow of celibacy?"

"Just lookin'." Tom raised his hands innocently. "Man goes crazy staring at nothin' but a sheep's arse." He sweated under his Akubra hat, stood and nearly knocked the chair over. "Can't take the waitin' no more. Let's go take our lumps."

Outside the quarters, the homestead was quiet. The sun warmed the right sides of their faces while the left sides stayed cool with morning air.

"Here he comes." Tom pushed up his sleeves, stared past James to the house, his jaw set. "G'day, Alex!" he called out, shuffling like he needed to use the loo. "How was the trip?"

Alex sauntered up the wide drive, his hands resting easily in his trouser pockets. He wore a light tan suit, white shirt and blue tie knotted thickly at the stiff collar. "Fine." The man looked around, smiled under the sun. "Gorgeous day, eh?"

Tom relaxed, wiped his forehead with the back of his hand.

"How were things here?" Alex asked.

"We made a map of the property, assessed the best feeding areas for the stock," James told him. "Wrote down the numbers, list of supplies you'll want to stock, shearing schedule, number of men needed. Should cover it."

Alex nodded with pleasure. "Good. I'm impressed." Then he leaned back, loosened his tie. "Not bad for a couple of farm boys."

Tom lowered his head and closed his eyes. James did not flinch, stared out to the distance as if he hadn't heard a sound.

"Didn't take more than a few calls to figure it out." Alex winked. "Nice try, though."

James turned to him, met his eyes square. "Never lied to you. Not once."

"True." Alex furrowed his brow and thought about this for a second. "Of course, you didn't try and set it straight, either."

James remembered his promise to Mrs. Shelby. "We can run this place."

"I'm not arguing with you," Alex said. "But there are men much more qualified begging for work." He narrowed his eyes in challenge. "Give me a reason why I should keep you."

James gazed intently around the land, at the house, at the barn, and settled his eyes on the horse ring. "Said you needed to bring someone in to train the horses."

Alex studied James's deep look with amusement. "That's right."

"I can do it."

"Is that so?" Alex laughed then. "You know horses?"

"Yes."

Alex rubbed his chin, enjoying himself greatly. "You a bettin' man, James?"

"No."

"Hmmm. Don't drink, don't smoke, don't gamble." His face opened in mock wonderment. "You're a man without a vice!" Alex clapped his hands then, rubbed them exultantly. "All right, since you're not a betting man, how about a challenge?"

James watched him narrowly, straddled his legs. "What do you have in mind?"

"You get on top of that stallion"—Alex pointed at the black body in the ring—"and stay on him for one minute, you got the job."

Tom gave up, slouched his shoulders. "We'll grab our stuff an' get going." But James was already bent under the top fence beam, easing into the arena.

Along the rough-hewn wood, Alex leaned his elbows and pulled out his cigarette case. He opened the tin, pounded the tobacco and lit the match, then sucked in deeply through a smile. "Hope you know how to fix a broken rib."

In the ring, the black stallion stood alone, raised and lowered his front hooves as James approached. The horse flared his nostrils and snorted, but James paid him no mind, walked past him to the more sedate mare, rubbed her shoulder and nose.

Alex folded his arms, covered his grin with one hand, cleared his throat. "Ummm, Mr. O'Reilly?" His eyebrows pointed arrogantly. "The stallion's the black one—behind you."

James ignored Alex and pulled the brown mare closer, stepped back until the stallion was right behind his head, the breath hot and angry in his hair. James reached into a feedbag and fed the mare from his hand. The stallion pushed James in the back with his nose. James talked to the mare with soothing words and shoulder scratches.

The stallion, rearing like an obstinate child, stepped forward and pushed James's elbow, spilling feed along the ground. James brought up another handful and, with his back turned, held up his palm. The stallion smelled the oats, huffed, stepped back and then forward, took a nibble.

Slow and easy as a spring breeze, James brought his hand around to the onyx mane. The horse balked. James turned away. The stallion came up again, then recoiled. And they played this game for several rounds until gradually and nearly imperceptibly James's hand moved across the thick muscled neck and rested on the mighty shoulders.

James did not give a hint of threat or impatience as he flowed around the horse. The stallion quieted but stretched eyes to watch him, showing the whites at the corners. Then, with one hand to the horse's neck and another to the twitching back, James closed his eyes, held his breath and in one hard jump swung himself onto the long spine. The stallion reared and James squeezed his thighs and knees hard against the ribs, held to the neck with every muscle in his hands. The horse sprinted furiously to the other end of the ring, jumped over the high fence.

A cloud of dust erupted under the horse's hooves. James buried his face in the thrashing mane, his hands white with his grip and his ears deaf with the angry pounding. Pulling every ounce of strength into his thighs until they locked hard and tight as steel, he held on—held on for the job, for the Shelbys, for Tom. And the gallop went on, blasted through trees, the limbs ripping his shirt and lashing his arms. The horse veered, splashed over creeks, splattering his face and body with mud, his inner thighs burning as they slipped over the wet hair.

Finally, after miles of terrain, the horse's breathing labored and the slick, bulging muscles twitched, began to slow. Guardedly, James raised his head off the stallion's mane and adjusted his numb jaw, his neck cracking with the turn. He released the pressure from his knees and his thighs trembled with the slack; his joints throbbed with the rush of restricted blood.

The horse trotted now and James stroked the subdued head, patted the great neck. Deep red gorges surrounded them, the sun hitting directly on the walls, blazing the stones blood orange. Stately tuart trees and red box gums stretched high, their trunks majestic and solid, the limbs flowering only at the peaks.

With a tired knee, James steered the horse to the creek and let him drink. James's own mouth was dirty and parched, but he didn't dare get off; he wouldn't have the strength to remount. When the horse was sated, they left the gorge behind and traced the hoofprints back to the lost station.

The homestead emerged as a pale dot in the landscape, grew with each tempered step. A crowd had formed at the arena. Workmen put down hammers, stood to watch the sweaty, lathered horse and the mound of dust that rode him. Tom took off his hat and waved, worked hard to calm his lips.

Alex offered James a hand as he dismounted, held him up as his legs buckled. James gripped his knees, coughed the dust from his mouth. "So"—he raised one eye—"we got the job?"

Alex slapped him heartily on the back. "You got the job."

CHAPTER 44

❧

"Next!" The man sat behind a worn table, slouched over papers and stamps. He scratched at his eyebrows and did not look up. "Name?" he ordered.

"Ghan."

The man bent forward to inspect the peg leg. "Pickin' line's full."

"Ain't here for pickin'."

The man shook his head. "No cripples." He shuffled his papers and hollered, "Next!"

"Now yeh wait just a minnit," Ghan spoke up desperately. "Been workin' underground more years than yeh've been walkin'. Leg don't stop me none—not pickin' rock wiv m'foot, gawd damn it! Got two strong hands like any other bloke." He stuck out his palms as proof, pulled them back when they started to wobble. "Leg don't matter! Always been a hard worker. Got the scars to show it. Hell, I could work wiv two pegs, ain't pickin' wiv my damn legs!" Ghan breathed hard; his lips quivered. He was hungry. So goddamn hungry. Sick and tired and hungry from not working, walking from one dead town to the next begging for work.

The man tapped his nails on the table. He was clean and white, not a man who knew life under the earth, only knew how to direct it from above like the almighty God. "Whot yeh say yer name was?" he asked.

"Ghan."

He gritted his teeth. "Yer name, I said! Yer real name."

"Claudio Petroni."

"Italian?"

Ghan nodded.

The man studied him, the disinterest fading. "Ever been part of a strike?" he asked.

"Naw."

"Ever join a union?"

"Ain't no union gonna fight for a man wiv one leg."

"Close the door for a sec!" the man ordered.

Ghan shut the door—shut out the waiting, vacant faces of the men standing in line.

"Got a new owner here—Mr. Harrington," the man began. "He's bringing in Italians to replace most of the old workers. First crew came 'bout a month ago. Hard workers, cheap. Another load arrives in a few weeks. People losin' their jobs: Greek, Slavs, even Aussies. The ones that stay are getting' their pay cut. Only keepin' them on 'cause we got t'keep a ratio of blokes that speak English. Royal commission comes out an' tests couple times a year.

"Look," the man continued roughly. "I ain't gonna sugarcoat this. I'd never think twice 'bout hirin' a cripple, but yeh got ears"—he snickered—"at least one anyway. An' that's whot we need. Need somebody that don't grab any attention, somebody t'let us know if there's grumblings—anybody plannin' somepin."

"Yeh askin' me t'spy?" Ghan spit in disgust.

"Naw. Just listen. Listen to both sides. See if anybody's talkin' 'bout the union. Listen to the Italians. They're eager now, but that fades. Gotta know in advance 'bout any troublemakers. Send 'em back 'fore they start anythin'. A bad mouth heat 'em up faster than fever."

"I don't know," Ghan mumbled. Nothing about it sounded right; left a swirling pain in his gut like eating meat that sat around too long.

"Thought yeh wanted work?"

"Course I want work." He was so goddamn tired of walking. So goddamn hungry, scavenging for food, staring at a bait line for a fish, roasting under the sun trying to trap a rabbit.

"Look." The man leaned back, the window on his patience closing. "I ain't askin' yeh t'do nothin' but listen an' give me the headsup. That's it. Yeh in or not?"

Ghan's side cramped. "In."

"Suppose I don't have to tell yeh t'keep yer mouth shut 'bout all this?" Pulling out a square of paper, the man scribbled a few lines. "Mr. Harrington ain't got patience for rousers or slackers. He wants profits. Yeh screw him an' he'll use that peg to fire the furnace." He handed him the paper. "And you'll be attached."

CHAPTER 45

Almost overnight, Wanjarri Downs erupted from a quiet homestead into a full, bustling station. Livestock—chickens, pigs, goats—clucked, squealed, and baaed in distress as they were handled from crates. Three new stallions descended the transporter, their eyes panicked and blind in unleashed sunlight. Workmen pounded on roofs, on new fence posts, dug wells out in distant paddocks. The smell of sawdust and disturbed dirt rose with the grunts of sawing men, digging men and moving men.

Leonora unpacked the china from the cedar box, wiped the wood shavings off with a cloth and stacked the china on lace-lined shelves, each plate a promise of permanency, of home. She closed the glass-paneled doors to the cabinet, rubbed the smooth wood.

"You've been smiling this whole time." Alex leaned against the doorjamb, his arms crossed. "I didn't realize unpacking brought you such pleasure."

She reached back and untied her apron. "I like it here."

"I'll never understand you, my dear." He smoothed out his hair. "This place is the size of one of your servants' quarters and your face shines like it's a palace."

"But it's ours." She reached for his hand, pulled him to a chair. "Let me make you some tea. Are you hungry?"

Alex followed her movements as she inspected the pantry. He bent his leg, put his ankle atop his other knee, picked at the fabric of his riding pants. "I've hired a cook and housekeeper. They start next week."

"There's no need to hire anyone, Alex." Leonora brought out a crock of jelly and a tin of tea biscuits. "I don't mind cooking. Or cleaning for that matter."

"Nonsense." He moved his fingers to the table, etched circles over the polished wood. "You have no idea the amount of cooking that needs to be done on a station, love."

She turned away from the familiar condescending tone. "I suppose you're right."

"Besides, this far out, guests stay for several days, sometimes weeks. Then you have the workers, shearing just around the corner. There'll be a lot of mouths to feed."

She brought the biscuits to the table, poured the tea. "What are the men like?"

"Managers are good men." He nodded with approval. "Typical cowboys, but young and smart. They'll take over the details of this place. I've got enough to worry about with the mine." Alex slung an elbow to the back of the chair, added a lump of sugar to his tea, stirred it delicately. "Should see their eyes pop at this place, Leonora." Alex snickered. "The way the men look at the horses, at the land. Property's half the size of Belgium, did you know that? Doubt they've ever seen anything like it." Alex's eyes slid over his wife. "Wait until they get a look at you."

Alex rose from the chair, the biscuits left untouched, the tea hardly sipped. He wrapped his arms around her waist, pressed into the small of her back. She closed her eyes to the familiar precursor to lovemaking and tried to resist the urge to stiffen. He had never been rough with her again, never forced himself upon her like that first time, but she also never gave him reason, for she did not fight against his urges, let him find his pleasure and was glad when it was over.

Alex kissed the back of her neck and she fumbled for an excuse, used the only one that ever had an effect. "It's not a good time, Alex. I could get pregnant." And with that, he dropped his hands. Alex didn't want children until his fortune was self-made and secure.

With an air of finality, Alex gulped down the rest of his tea, then clapped his hands. "You've been stuck in here long enough. Come out and meet the men." He took her by the elbow. "I've got a surprise for you."

* * *

Tom plopped the saddle near the open barn door. "Looks like the boss is givin' the lady a tour. Wants everybody out by the ring."

"Be out in a minute." James hammered the thick nail with two quick pounds and hung the last harness to the wood. He wiped his hands on his trousers and went out to join Tom.

Alex centered the group of men, his arm around a woman's waist, her eyes downcast. "Everyone, meet my lovely wife, Mrs. Harrington," he addressed the men, made sure each man held a touch of envy at his good fortune. "Darling, these are the men who built our home, the men who will make Wanjarri Downs the best station in Western Australia." There was an awkward silence as men bobbed and weaved, unclear if they should clap, shout or remain quiet.

James ignored the speech, wanted to get back to work. He met the glances of the other men, legs crossed or arms folded: men with hard faces, tan and full of lines, stubbly chins.

"O'Reilly!" Alex shouted. "Bring out Midnight."

James went to the barn and brought out the black stallion, calmed after weeks of training. He handed the reins to Alex.

Alex led the horse to his wife. She rubbed the black silken nose. "He's magnificent, Alex!" she gasped. The men all nodded. The stallion was a fine horse.

"Saddle him up," Alex directed James. "I'm going to take him on a run."

James pushed his hat above his eyes. "He's not ready."

"What are you talking about? You've been riding him for weeks now."

"He's used to me. Hasn't let anyone else on him."

Alex slit his eyes and looked around the group, chuckled. "I've been riding all my life; I think I can handle it. Saddle him up."

James twisted his mouth, looked at the horse for a long while. He glanced at Tom, who shrugged his shoulders and mouthed, *His funeral.*

James strapped on the saddle and stepped back several feet, kept his body alert, readied for the moment he would need to step in.

With full confidence, Alex mounted and smiled. "Told you—"

The horse's ears perked at the voice and in a wave of panic he beat his dark head, raised his front hooves up and down, reared higher with each flail. Sweat formed on Alex's face as he worked to control the horse, his flawless hair now slipping unmanaged strands on either side of his forehead. The horse whined in fury and with one quick kick from his back legs bucked, sending Alex flying onto his belly, landing in dust in the middle of the men. A few snorts of laughter leaked from the crowd while the rest stayed quiet and watchful.

His wife inched forward. "Alex, are you all right?"

He lifted his head. The woman recoiled. Slowly, Alex stood, ran his hands over his clothes, the dust sticking like glue to his front. He cleared his throat. Stifled laughter grouped from the right. Feet shuffled from the left. Alex snickered for a moment, his eyes black. With a sudden slide of his hand, he pulled a pistol from his coat. Sun on silver blinded as Alex raised his arm stiffly and pointed the gun at the stallion's head.

James braced to grab the horse, but the woman was there first, grabbing Midnight's reins and planting herself under the horse's chin. "No, Alex!"

Alex spit through his teeth, "Get out of the way!"

"No!" She cradled the horse's head. "Put the gun down, Alex!"

"Get away, Leonora!" Alex pulled back the trigger, his hand twitching. "Move or I swear I'll shoot you with it!"

Leonora. The name echoed in James's ears, shuddered down his arms and legs, and for a moment he could not see past the solitary word. *Leonora.* He snapped the name away, inched his way to the horse, brushed his hand across the coat and subtly positioned himself in front of the woman, his frame eclipsing her tiny one. The horse reared again and James pulled the reins. "Whoa!" he shouted to the horse; shouted to Alex, "Can't believe you mounted!" James forced a grin through his pounding heart. "Kicked Tom in the pants this morning just for standing close."

Tom took the cue and grabbed his crotch, his expression pained. "Poor Mum won't be gettin' any grandbabies outta me!" The men all laughed and James used the distraction to pull the horse away, relieving the woman from the bullet's aim.

Alex's arm slacked, his eyes blinked through sweat.

"Stallion's a beauty, though," James continued. "No doubt about it. Maybe win you the Melbourne Cup." Alex swallowed hard, lowered his hand, the gun still cocked.

James released the reins and walked toward Alex, gave him a manly wink. "After all"—his stomach turned sour with the words he needed to say—"horses are a lot like women: The spirited ones eventually give the most reward."

The men laughed, nodded in agreement, and Alex relaxed. He put a hand on James's shoulder. "True, my friend." Alex strode to his wife and gave her a hard smack on the bottom. "True indeed!"

Leonora slammed the door, her face still red, the humiliation fresh, the anger burning. She heard Alex come through the front door and she turned on him. "How dare you—"

Alex grabbed her arm and twisted, the sudden pain shooting up her shoulder. "*What did I tell you?*"

"What?" she cried. "Tell me what?"

"Don't ever speak to me in front of the men like that again! Do you hear me?"

"You were going to shoot that horse!" He jerked her arm, twisted it farther, the force choking her. "Stop, Alex! You're hurting me!"

"Never raise a voice to me again!" he screamed. "Never!"

"Please let go," she pleaded, her whole arm unhinging from the shoulder. "I'm sorry!"

Alex shoved her away. He walked to the mirror, straightened his hair, opened the liquor cabinet and took out two brown bottles. The front door banged in his wake, leaving Leonora alone and stunned, clutching her bruises.

"What the hell was that?" Tom asked.

James ground his teeth, his brows low as he stared at the still house.

"Crazy bastard." Tom tucked in his shirt. "Think he would have shot that horse? A thoroughbred, no less? Sure looked mad enough t'do it. Christ! I think he would have done it. Even with his wife standin' there," he rambled. "Remind me not to piss that bloke off."

Tom's lips turned slowly upward. He clicked his tongue against his cheek. "Wife's a looker, though, eh? Guess that's the kind of woman money buys."

James turned on him, his eyes hot. "Take it back, Tom."

"Whoa!" Tom stepped back. "What's your problem, mate?"

"Just shut up."

Tom laughed, raised an eyebrow. "So, red blood flows through your Irish veins after all."

"What's that supposed to mean?"

Tom's grin reached out broadly. "You fancy her."

"I don't fancy her!" James huffed.

"Known you a long time, mate, an' I know that look. You're smitten!" Tom smacked him on the back. "The boss's wife, no less. You horny bastard."

James's face grew grave. "I think I know her."

"What?" Tom was still smiling. "What the hell does that mean?"

"I think I know her." James faced him, his eyes weighted. "From the orphanage."

Tom's smile froze, his mind trying to wrap around the words. "You're jokin'." He laughed without humor, stared at the big house. "Impossible, mate. She's not even Australian."

"She is . . . was. As much as we are." James's voice dropped away uncertainly. "She was adopted by an American family. I think it's her."

"Jesus! Does she remember you?"

"Doubt she saw me." James squinted, questioned himself. "Maybe I'm wrong. I don't know. It's been a long time." He grew quiet for a moment. "I don't know."

The front door of the house opened. Alex walked down the verandah waving two full bottles. "Looks like somebody's in the mood to celebrate!" Tom scoffed.

"Not a word, all right?"

"That you got a thing for his wife?" Tom teased. "Never."

James glared at him.

"Well, she's pretty. No arguin' that." Tom stepped forward and hollered out to Alex, "Those drinks for us or the horses?"

James lay awake, rested his hands behind his head and stared at the new boards that latticed the ceiling. *Leonora.* He thought about the woman's face, thought about the face of his friend long ago and compared them until they merged and left him nervous. He remembered her fierce protection of the horse, remembered the blush that shot to her face when Alex smacked her—remembered it was his insult that had spurred it. But he hadn't a choice, for he knew Alexander Harrington now—a man who fed on applause and raged in its absence.

Footsteps thundered from the steps. Tom stumbled into the house, grabbed the door frame as if it were a boat rocking on high seas.

James chuckled. "You all right?"

"I'll be fine," Tom said drowsily. "Soon as this bloody room stops spinnin'." He leaned his forehead against the wood. "I'm wiring the money to Ashley tomorrow."

"Good."

"You saved my arse, mate." Tom's eyes wrinkled with drunken sentiment.

"Just keep it in your pants from now on."

"Told you, I'm celibate." Tom let go of the wall and raised his hand in oath, his whole body swaying. "Swear it!"

"Celibate as a jackrabbit."

"By the way"—Tom stepped back from the room, his voice fading as he fumbled to stay upright down the hall—"the wife, the looker? Maiden name is Fairfield."

The name resonated, echoed from the past, vibrated in the back of James's throat. A breeze, the gentle zephyr of the sea, clung to the rafters, wafted across his eyelashes. Her face, the verity of it, entered torpidly like a body steps into an icy pool. A glow waved down his limbs, finally settling in his chest with confirmation. *Leo*.

The setting sun poked his face. James pulled the hat over his eyes, leaving just enough space to see the horse as he rode back to the homestead. Tom, his body caked red, swept up the last remnants of the dust storm that flew in overnight. "How'd the sheep fare?" Tom asked.

"Dirty and thirsty. Didn't lose a head, though."

Tom scratched his ear. "Thinking we should head out in a day or two. Move it up."

"Had the same thought," James agreed. "Weather's going to test us." He pulled out a handkerchief and wiped down his face. "I'll go tell Alex."

James rapped on the large wooden door of the house, his knuckles stained orange from the ride. He faced the drive as he waited. A fine layer of dust covered the Model T, the rosebush along the porch. Stuff stuck like chalk to fingers, he thought. Be at least a week before it cleared.

"Hello." Leonora Harrington stood at the open door.

His boots melted into a puddle, glued to the wood slats. He forgot where he was. He scrounged for his hat, took it off too quickly. "Sorry to bother you . . . Mrs. Harrington." James cleared his throat, patted down his matted hair. "Is . . . ah . . . your husband in?"

"No. He went out this morning," she said softly. "Should be back later tonight if you need to speak with him."

James thought about leaving. He should go. *Go.* His legs forgot how to walk. He tapped his foot, made sure there was feeling in it, then suddenly stuck out his hand. "James. We didn't meet officially."

"Leonora." She smiled and shook his hand, then looked at the red dust stuck to her palm.

"Aw, sorry." James rubbed his hand on his leg. "Just got in from the back paddock. Haven't had a chance to wash up." He wrinkled his forehead. He was a mess, inside and out.

"Been half-covered myself." She laughed, opened the door wider, leaned her hip against the edge. "Still trying to clean the dust from the floors. Do the storms always come in so fast?"

"Not usually." His mouth moved normally, spoke automatic words while his pulse raced like a runaway train. "Only seen one like that before, but moved out quick. Without the wind, they can linger." And there she was again. Standing there. James forgot the storm. He forgot his name. He forgot to speak and just stared.

Her eyes flitted with the long pause. She touched her collar. "You're one of the new managers, right? I remember you from the other day."

"About that, Mrs. Harrington," he started, and took a step closer.

"Please, call me Leonora."

He couldn't say the name. "About the other day"—he swallowed—"I owe you an apology."

"No." She lowered her eyes, pulled her body closer to the door. "It's all right."

"No, it's not. That comment I made . . ." He paused and put the hat back on his head. "I saw the gun and . . . thought he'd shoot the horse," he tried to explain. "Didn't want anybody getting hurt. Certainly didn't mean to insult you. I like women." His ears burned with the last fumbled words. "I mean, I respect women."

She laughed then, the rise and fall soft as a feather's stroke.

"I'm screwing this all up." James smirked helplessly, cocked his head. "Just wanted to say 'sorry,' that's all."

"Apology accepted." Leonora smiled, the discomfort gone. "You probably saved that horse's life. I should be thanking you."

James looked over her features—the skin, the shape of her face, the hair. A steady warmth, thick with memories, flowed into his chest. He turned away, stared back to the drive to give his senses a break, line up his thoughts in some sort of order.

"Was there anything else?" she asked.

He turned back slowly, kept his gaze glued to his boot as he tapped the heel against the wood. "I knew a Leonora once." The words came out soft and gentle as an old, lazy wind.

"Really?" She tilted her head pleasantly. "It's not a very common name."

"You look like her." He raised his face up. "We lived at an orphanage on the coast . . . near Geraldton." James watched her intently now, his nerves gone. "Perhaps you know it."

Her lips opened. The blood drained straight away from her face and neck. She tried to speak and floundered, then shook her head as one shakes a soiled rug. "Are you suggesting I was an orphan?" Her eyes panicked.

Just then, the sun slid past his shoulder and lit the side of her hair, glowing a line of gold around her face. His heart kicked. The light rose to her eyes and picked up the fear and the pain in the hazel irises and he knew her. Doubt, if there had been any, was gone. James stuffed his hands in his pockets and straightened his posture. "I didn't mean to offend you."

"An orphanage?" She cringed with the words, her voice high and shaking. The sun reflected off her wet, wide eyes. "What do I look like to you?"

Her disgust cut straight and quick. "My mistake," he said grimly, tipped his hat.

"Yes, it is!"

The door slammed at his nose, his insides smacked flat.

Leonora rolled her body against the wood door and covered her face. Sobs burst from her throat, bent her spine with the force. Tears, hot and bloated, ran down her face and slicked her cheeks and wet her lips. She slid down the door to the floor and buried her face into her knees, her shoulders shaking.

Fear stung the surface—real panic, conditioned terror at the mention of the orphanage, of that life. She clawed the collar of her dress, snapping open the buttons that strangled her throat. She shook with raspy cries, quick spasms against the flood of tears. Her fingers clenched the gold chain around her neck, slid down to the small stone clasped at the base and blindly rubbed the smooth pebble, and the disbelief grew; the shock and the fear grew.

But below the fear, it was the longing that brought the ripping sobs, the missing of what had been buried and nearly lost, the knowing and the bone-breaking relief that the dream was not a dream. *James.* Leonora pulled the necklace into her palm, then slowly released her grip and stared with wavy, wet vision at the white stone. She smiled through the tears now, her lips stretching between joy and grief and fear. A short laugh, tinged with crying, spluttered from her mouth. She shook her head, jostled the disbelief to belief.

Leonora pulled her head up and the tears stopped with dread. She saw his face—saw how she had spit on him. Grabbing her knees, she rocked and tried to remember the man's features before they were hurt. He had shaken her hand, touched her. She brought her palm up, turned her hand, felt the strong grip of his long fingers, the sturdiness of them. His features blurred then and she squeezed her eyes to see the lines of his face, but she only saw the way he looked away as if his face had been slapped. She looked at her hand again. The yellowed bruise from Alex's grip ringed her wrist and she tucked her hand away.

Leonora plopped her head back against the door, drained. The curtains fluttered gently with the breeze, the light smell of roses riding on its tail. *James.* She smiled softly with the name. *Here.* The air flowed cool to her wet collar, dried her cheeks and eyes until the skin felt tight. The room grew soft with mellowed light. She whispered the name out loud: "James."

Tom sat on a hay bale examining a ledger, his hat high on his head revealing freckled forehead and red hair slick with sweat. He scribbled with his pen, chewed on the cap, then turned with the sound of clinking glasses. "Mrs. Harrington, I do believe you're an angel!"

With chin up, Leonora tried to steady her arms so the glasses of lemonade stopped spilling. Despite her nerves, she couldn't help laughing, the man's expression so easy and happy. "Thought you might be thirsty."

He left the ledger and pen on top of the bale, took the drink offered and with no more than two gulps swallowed every drop. "Heaven couldn't taste any sweeter!" He stuck out a hand. "Thomas Shelby."

Struggling to balance the tray in one arm, she stuck out her hand. "Leonora."

He pumped her arm. "Good to meet you."

"Would you like another glass?"

"Naw, that was perfect. Thanks."

She couldn't help smiling at him. He was simple and genuine, with clear blue eyes that sparkled with humor. More cute than handsome, he seemed a man who would wrestle and tickle a girl as much as he would kiss her.

Tom wiped his forehead with his sleeve. The sun beat upon their shoulders. "I don't know how you can bear this heat," she said.

"Haven't seen nothin' yet. This is winter, love. But don't worry; you'll get used to it." He looked past her, past the house. "Got a beautiful place here, Leonora. My dad would have killed for an acre of this land."

"He's a farmer?"

"Was. Died a long while ago."

"I'm sorry."

"No worries. He always wanted to raise sheep, have a station. Had a few head, but not many." Tom's lips twitched with amusement. "Dad treated 'em lambs more like pets than stock. Had 'em all named, too. Called half of 'em Fluffy."

She laughed, liked him instantly, liked him more than almost anyone she had ever met.

"Well, guess I should get back to the books. Thanks again for the drink."

"Is the other manager around?" she asked, trying to sound natural.

"James? Yeah." He craned his neck. "Back behind the barn fixin' a hole in the fence. Just warnin' you, though, he's been a royal grump." He gave her a quick wink. "Maybe the drink will sweeten him up, eh?"

Leonora carried the tray away from the barn, stepped over a few rocks toward the endless fence, the lemonade sloshing over the rim from her unstable grip. And there he was, James, sitting on his heels, a piece of wire in his mouth and a wrench in his hand as he wrestled the torn fence. She swallowed hard and walked toward him, her heart galloping.

James did not look up at the sound of footsteps or turn his head when her shadow inched across him. "I . . . I thought you might like some lemonade," she offered.

"I'm not thirsty." James kept his eyes focused on the wire as he wound it up and over the hole. His brows were knit and the tanned muscles of his forearms twitched and tightened with each pull.

"Please." Her voice cracked. "You don't even have any shade."

He put the wire down and stretched up, her eyes watching his body unfold. James took the glass from the tray and nodded, averting his eyes to a spot far into the distance. "Thanks."

She stood there dumbly holding the tray in her hands while he drank. He didn't seem to notice she was still there. She fumbled to fill in the space. "What happened to the fence?"

"Not sure," he said tersely. "Maybe a dingo."

She stared at the side of his face, the long throat, the chestnut hair trimmed neatly around his ears and at the neck, the smooth, straight nose and the distant, ignoring eyes that stung her very skin. Leonora looked down, closed her eyes and with a deep, last breath asked softly, "Do you remember what you used to call Sister McCrackenas?"

James stood there quiet. He took a long drink of lemonade. His face did not move.

She got the signal. Her face flooded red and she turned away, tried to slink away without losing her last smudge of dignity. But then a voice sounded from behind in a spot-on Scottish drawl, "Ah, ye mean thee lov'ly Mis' Crack 'n the ass?"

The laughter erupted before she knew it was coming, came so fast that she started hiccuping. She dropped the tray, the empty glass, and they bounced in the dirt. James looked at her now, a mischievous smirk on his face. He bent down and picked up the fallen items, handed them back, grinning widely as she tried to quiet her giggles.

Leonora wiped her eyes, fanned the air as if it were the heat, not the bold relief, that brought the unbridled mirth. She calmed, steadied her smile, her breathing. James watched her now, the dark eyes studying, the space between them quiet.

"Is it really you?" she whispered, her mouth unable to close. "After all this time?"

He nodded, his features still and waiting.

She remembered her slight from the day before. "I was very rude to you!" she gasped. "I'm so, so sorry."

"No worries."

"No, I was awful. I just couldn't believe it." She hurried to find the right words. "It was so long ago, almost like a dream. And then to be here—for you to be here." She put her hand on her head. "Do you know what I mean? Am I making any sense?"

James nodded and she knew he understood, probably couldn't explain it any better. The quiet crowded again, self-conscious with a familiarity that had too much time to fade and widen.

James shoved one hand in his pocket and pointed to the house with his chin. "Looks like life has treated you well."

"So it appears." Her agreement came too heavy and his face softened, the lines above his forehead gone. "And you?" she asked. "Has life treated you well?"

The lines came back and the brows dropped. "Well enough." And the space between them grew wider and the rags of conversation tattered.

Leonora squeezed the glass, pulled the tray to her chest, held it like an armored breastplate. "I need to ask you a favor." The words twisted in apology. "I need to ask that you don't mention our past . . . my past. Alex doesn't know." Her voice faltered. "It could make my life very complicated."

James looked at his boots. "Of course."

"He wouldn't understand," she tried to explain. "It'll be better for everyone."

He nodded and crouched down to his heels, picked up his tools, began rewiring the broken coils. She had hurt him again. It didn't matter the slap was delivered gently. The mark still showed.

The men rode from Wanjarri Downs in the pearly dawn. Fourteen horses, tied with packs and saddles, left in pyramid formation: James and Tom in the front, their coats buttoned high against the morning chill, the Aborigine stockmen behind them. The bodies, of man and beast, synchronized as one form, glided over the land like pulled silk.

Leonora watched them through the closed window of her bedroom, the glass muting the sound of hooves, so the horses and men moved as silent phantoms until they disappeared into the fog. They would be gone for months. Leonora touched the cool glass with her fingertips. Alex's snoring hummed from the bed. A deep emptiness filtered over the land, breathed into the house and filled the corners. And the shadows thickened and stayed. And she missed him.

CHAPTER 46

Ghan passed the dirty tents until he reached the last in the row, the canvas brown and sagging and crusted with spiderwebs. He set down his pack. *Home.*

"By Gawd!" a voice shouted. "It can't be!"

Ghan stared at a mug nearly as old and ugly as his own. "Whistler, is that you?"

The man slapped his knee and cackled. "Yeh filthy son of a bitch!" He wobbled on bowed legs, white chest hair frothing from his undershirt. "Whot the 'ell yeh doin' 'ere, Ghan?"

"Workin'. Looks like we're gonna be neighbors."

Whistler's whole face smiled, all the wrinkles shaping like curved lips. "Can't believe yer still livin', yeh ugly fart!"

"Can't kill blokes like us," said Ghan. "Get right back up by our knuckles."

"Ain't that the truth!" The man laughed. His pants slipped down from his waist and he pulled them up without a second thought.

"Yeh don't whistle no more," Ghan observed, remembering that back in the day the man had a rotten front tooth with a perfect gray hole in the middle. Every time he laughed, a high-pitched, long whistle would blow from his mouth.

"Got no teeth no more!" Whistler opened his mouth wide. "Hey, yeh hungry?"

"Always."

"Come on; I'll fix yeh up somepin. Leave the pack here. Nobody'll touch it. Good blokes overall." He stuck a finger in his ear and grimaced. "'Cept fer those damn motorbikes. Them E-talians race 'em mornin' till night, I tell yeh. But good blokes. Yeh'll see."

Whistler held the canvas flap open to this tent so Ghan could enter. A tiny stove made out of a kerosene can sat next to the middle pole. Whistler snapped a few twigs and lit the fire. He set the can of water to boil, dropped in the tea and set out two tin cans for mugs. Then he pulled out a frying pan still white with lard and started mixing the standard for damper: flour, water and sodium bicarbonate. Tea and damper—the feast of the bushman.

"Ain't got no jam," Whistler apologized. "But got some golden syrup. Quarter the price."

"So hungry, I'd eat the lard straight."

Whistler stirred the tea, bubbling and nearly black. He poured it into the cans. "Been outta work awhile then?"

"Yeah. Vets comin' back from the war. Cripples wiv medals. Can't compete."

The old man handed the scalding cup to Ghan, who held it unflinchingly with callused fingers. "They took the leg off?"

"Yeah."

"It hurt?"

"Like the devil."

Whistler shuddered. "Have t'kill me first. Don't have the guts fer the knife. Feel all sick inside jist thinkin' 'bout it." Then he laughed so hard drool dripped down his chin. "See whot happens when yeh got a fam'ly full of girls! Makes a man soft as butter!"

"How the girls?" Ghan remembered the five children, all a year apart, blond and sweet. Whistler would watch them with tears, the love just pouring out of his eyes.

"All married. Got good blokes, too. Thank Gawd! No drunks, no hitters." The man smiled with pride. "Guess how many grandkids I got?"

"How many?"

"Twelve. Wanna know how many are girls? Eleven! Gawd damn it!" Whistler sparkled even as he complained. "Eleven gawd damn girls! Like I got sweet nectar in my blood instead of steel. How a tough-arse devil like me get all 'em girls?"

Ghan chuckled and sipped his tea while Whistler heated the frying pan. Fat melted and bubbled around the blobs of dough, the smell bringing gurgles and grunts from his empty belly.

"My wife . . . yeh 'member Pippa, don't yeh?" he asked.

"Course. Pretty as yer girls."

Whistler's eyes glistened with the compliment. "Died awhile back. Long time now." He poked at the browning dough with a fork and flipped the damper over, splashing angry grease over the side. "Miss her somepin awful. Doesn't matter how long she's been gone, still hurts." He pounded his chest. "Right in here. Somepin missin'. Gawd, I miss her."

Ghan stared into the dark steaming tea, his reflection wavy and distorted. He lifted it to his lips and drank the drawn look away.

Whistler set a tin plate and shoveled the dough, the damper's bloated sides slicked with oil for only a second before drying. He drizzled the golden syrup on and the flies followed. The men ate with food in one hand while swatting flies with the other.

"Whot job they give yeh?" Whistler asked.

"Diggin'."

The man stopped chewing, the squished dough visible between his lips. "Underground?"

"Yeah."

"How long it been since yeh dug?"

"Don't quite know." Ghan squinted at the smoke leaving the hole in the top of the tent. "Fifteen . . . twenty years maybe."

The wrinkles fell in the old man's face. "Why the hell yeh goin' back under?"

"Told yeh. Need work."

"No. No. No-oo-oo!" His lips twisted defiantly. "Too long, mate. Once yeh been aboveground that long, it'll kill yeh t'go back under. Don't do it."

"Gotta."

"Naw." Whistler swallowed the rest of the dough without gumming it. "Listen t'me, Ghan. Get outta the diggin' fer that long an' it's too hard gettin' back in. The sun changes a man; the air gets in his lungs again an' he likes it. Goin' underground feel like somebody holdin' yer head underwater."

Ghan chewed on the dough, couldn't taste it now. "Ain't got no choice."

The man combed his wiry chest hairs with broken nails. "Damn, wish I could get yeh on pickin' duty wiv me. Doin' it so long, the managers don't see me no different than a machine. Got a line a mile long waitin' fer me to die so somebody can move into my spot." His face sagged. "Damn, wish I could get yeh a place there wiv me."

The last of the damper disappeared, leaving round, wet stains on the plate. The flies went to work cleaning, the worry of a swat now gone. "Come on." Whistler stood and moved out of the tent. "I'll show yeh the neighborhood."

The men swerved lazily between the tents, some all canvas, some reinforced with hessian and metal drums, some large enough to fit full families, some nearly too small for a grown man. "G'day, Mrs. Riccioli," greeted Whistler with a short bow.

A fine-looking woman with black hair pulled tight around her face stopped her sweeping. "Morning." She smiled. "You awanna eat somepin? You alookin' too skinny, Whistler!"

He stuck out his stomach. "Got t'keep m'figure fer the ladies, yeh know!" Whistler leaned to Ghan's ear and whispered, "Those E-talians always tryin' to feed yeh, specially the women. Good people. 'Cept fer those blasted motorbikes."

Whistler gave a quick wave to the woman and led Ghan up the line. "Got most of the tents divided like a map. Got the E-talians over here, farthest away. Got the Aussies clustered closer to town. Then yeh got a mix of Slavs an' Poles an' couple other blokes scattered round. All work fine together in the pit, but aboveground, they can't see past their own flags. Used to be a bunch of Germans, but they got run out wiv the war. Shame, too. They were good blokes, strong an' funny. Gave up a fight leavin'. Poor blokes got their pants licked. Wonder where a German suppose to go when everyone hates 'im. Where yeh think they go, Ghan?"

"Back t'Germany."

"Naw. Those blokes hated that Kaiser more than anybody. Must be hard bein' a man wivout a land. Must be hard." He laughed merrily then. "Gawd damn it! See whot I'm sayin' 'bout havin' all those girls? Soft as butter, I am. Melt in yer gawddamn mouth!"

They hobbled past Italian flags, flapping pathetically, half-shredded from razored dust. "More E-talians comin' every day," Whistler warned. "Tippin' the scales. Ain't good. Makin' people mad. Not me, course. I could give a crap. But yeh can feel the grumblin'. Anger startin' to simmer. Managers cuttin' the wages left and right; makin' hours longer. I don't like it." Whistler slowed his bowed legs. "See the new owner yet: Mr. 'Arrington?"

"Don't think so."

"Aw, you'd know. Trust me. He's a Yank from heel to collar. Got a new clean suit every day. A real dandy. But got hard eyes, that one. Kind of fella that'll be smilin' while he's hurtin' yeh. Makin' enemies but makin' friends, too. The important ones. Holds parties at the hotel all the time. Got lawyers, doctors, government men linin' up fer drinks an' gamblin'. Even the sheriff. 'Em boys like the ladies, too. Annie's whores used to come t'town every Tuesday. Now they're here three nights a week. Seems everybody wiv a vice is makin' money— the gamers, the whores, the distillers. But us, the good blokes, out here starvin'." He sidestepped a trail of soapy water running from a tent. "Ground gettin' angry. Bubblin'. Don't like it one bit, I tell yeh."

"Always been that way."

"Naw. Not like this. Always been some group or 'nother outta sorts but not like this. Greed is gettin' too big. The big men gettin' bigger; the small men gettin' smaller . . . so small yeh start to not feel like a man anymore—just a big hairless rat crawlin' outta the pit."

Ghan chuckled. "Old age makin' yeh bitter, mate."

Whistler didn't laugh. "Ain't bitter, Ghan. Just seen a lot. Got awake. Near dead in years but finally awake an' seein' things how they is." Whistler's voice turned cold. "This kind of anger, the one that's brewin' from the tents and pits, gives an old man the shivers."

CHAPTER 47

⚜

Winter weakened, rounded a sharp corner and emerged as spring. The new rains came with fury, pounding the iron roof and lashing the windows, tapping and clawing upon the wind. Lightning streaked freely without a tree or a mountain to block its crooked charges, and with each flash Alex's sleeping face grew crisp in feature, the shadows of raindrops spotting his skin. Leonora pulled the quilt to her chin. Thunder rocked the house, shook the foundation. Between spurts, Alex's gin-soaked snoring labored from the pillow. She thought of James and Tom and the stockmen traveling through the Northern Territory with the bullocks. They would be soaked and cold to the bone.

The morning light pushed the rain to the east, brushed the land in brilliance. The red earth darkened to a fiery rust. Leaves were washed of dust, glittered dark green and slick. The sky expanded with endless blue, deep and thick. Cockatoos clung to the trees like trapped clouds.

In the kitchen, Meredith and Clare, the new cook and housemaid, worked the bread, chatted and snickered until Leonora entered. "G'day, Mrs. 'Arrington," greeted Meredith, a pale woman with crooked teeth and the hard, strong hands of a dairymaid. "Whot can I get yeh?"

"Just tea, thank you. But I can make it."

Meredith put her hands to her hips. "Nothin' doin'." She poured the tea and placed it on the table, then tilted her heavy neck to the door. "Got the first egg since the rain. Chooks got it too good. Couple drops of water an' yeh gotta squeeze the egg outta 'em." An iron pan screeched atop the stove. "Mr. 'Arrington want his breakfast now?"

"I'll ask him."

The office door was open. Alex reclined on his chair, his long legs stretched and propped on the desk, crossed at the ankles. He folded his newspaper. "Morning, darling."

Leonora glanced around the office at the shelves of books, the bar crystal and framed photographs—Alex and her uncle in hunting clothes, sporting guns over their shoulders; Alex with an array of Indian dignitaries; a picture of his old stallion with a wreath of flowers around his neck. Not a picture of Alex's wife anywhere. "The cook wants to know if you want breakfast."

"In a bit."

Leonora ran her finger across the desk, etched the lines of the brass desk lamp. "How long until the men return with the cattle?" she ventured.

"About another month." He dropped the newspaper to the floor, pulled his legs off the desk. "Takes a long time to move all those animals." Alex leaned back with his fingers interlaced and smiled with pleasure. "Already have a contract lined up for meat in Britain. Anything left we'll sell for a song down at the mine."

She nodded, moved to the window and spread the curtains. "Looks beautiful out. Do you want to take a walk?"

"Maybe later." Alex opened a drawer, rifled through files, fanning the corners. "I've got to write the church, wire them money."

"Since when do you contribute to the church?"

"Since they're doing us a favor." He dismissed the last comment. "Besides, churches have a lot of pull in these parts. It's good business to keep them happy." Alex rubbed his jaw, looked at her as if surprised she was still there. "Was there anything else?"

"I thought maybe we could go to town for the day. Don't you think it would be nice to get out for a while?"

"Yes, but not today." He pulled out several papers, then swiveled to the typewriter. "Why don't you go exploring? You've hardly been past the house." Alex inserted a sheet into the roller, cranked it to the ink. "I'll tell you what: After I get things settled, we'll take a trip. I'll introduce you to the other wives, have a picnic or a party or something. How would that be?"

"All right. Or maybe I can stay with you in Coolgardie for a few weeks?"

He turned to her, the look on his face akin to panic. "Not a chance."

"Why?"

"A mining town is no place for a lady." He turned back to the typewriter, pressed the round keys—*tap, tap.* "Enjoy your exploration." *Tap, tap, tap.* "Don't get lost." *Tap, tap.*

Leonora crossed the footbridge over the empty stream, now thick as clay from the storm. The station managers' quarters stood not far behind, small and quaint, shaded with a huge blackbutt tree. Sun warmed her face, heated the fabric of her dress. Green parrots squawked and clicked gray, muscled tongues, flapped wings with yellow undersides.

She stepped onto the swept porch, rose to her toes and peeked through the window. A coat hung from a hook on the wall; a slouched hat drooped from a chair back. The room was clean and neat, the dishes stacked on the counter. From her view, she could see part of a bedroom, the bed made with clean linens. It was too private, too intimate, and she hurried back over the bridge.

Leonora continued around the homestead, past the chicken coop filled with brown hens, past the enormous water tower that made her feel cold if she just stepped near it. She walked for miles with the sun and the birds and the sky—felt like her body was still while the world did the moving.

A line of shacks sprung from the cracked earth. The smell of fire, of burnt syrup or molasses, hovered above steel roofs, most of them rusted, some with jagged holes. Leonora approached the first hovel. The door was missing, and in its place a black hole welcomed like a rotten mouth. She stepped closer and peered into the darkness tracing the trodden dirt floor. Two feet with gnarled yellow nails appeared from the recesses and she stumbled back, held her hand against her chest. An old man, white hair stark against his black skin, stood in the opening.

"I'm s-s-sorry," she stammered. "I didn't know anyone lived here."

The man watched her with old, bloodshot eyes. He was tall and thin as bones, dressed oddly in Western clothes that hung from his limbs. "I'm sorry," she repeated, sweat clinging to her hairline.

Leonora saw the people now. A minute ago, there was no one. They were shadows in the light, soft and quiet, blending into the curves of doorways and the edges of tilted eaves. Women sat on stoops, nursing babies or peeling yams into the laps of their simple straight dresses. Even the thinnest of them carried a plumpness of face, with a wide nose and thick hair. Some of them followed her with piercing, waiting eyes; others gave her no more attention than the air. One woman, her belly slightly swollen with pregnancy, smiled secretly at her.

Leonora stopped and smiled back. "Good morning." But the woman continued staring at her, through her as if into a memory, with that strange, secret smile and did not answer back, did not follow her with her eyes as Leonora hurried away from the homes. They didn't want her there. She was nervous, felt ashamed for feeling so.

"G'day," a little voice came from her feet, and someone pulled at her skirt.

"Well, good morning." Leonora bent down, caught her breath as she looked at the child. One eye held no pupil, only milky white that bobbed and danced like a reflected cloud. Her face was odd, distorted with the large angles of the mentally retarded. She wore a woman's faded red skirt cinched around her waist; the ripped hem hung by her ankles. She wore no shirt. Even in the child's ragged state, she was magnificently beautiful, with bronze skin and black silken hair highlighted with threads of pure gold. Her good eye sparkled, smiled as if all it saw were angels; the white eye held the world in a steady, pearly pool.

Leonora reached for the tiny fingers and held them gently. "What's your name?"

"Macaria."

The name, more music than sound, carried on a whisper and tickled her cheek. "Macaria." Leonora sang the notes again, "Macaria. That's the most beautiful name I've ever heard." She released the girl's hand. "I'm Leonora."

"Macaria!" a voice shouted from the shacks. The little girl's face stiffened. She ran off without a second glance.

Leonora squatted in the dirt, ran her finger along the child's footprint. Birds chattered from the trees, cicadas chirped under the sun, but the loneliness of the bush ached. Slowly, she stood, smacked the dust from her skirt.

The walk back seemed longer. The heat burned now. Her shoes pinched her toes. She found a small cluster of spotted gums, eased under the shaded canopy, the ground cool, still damp. It would be a good place for a garden, she thought. She crumbled the dirt in her fingers and the thought grew. Energy flowed back to her limbs. She grabbed a gnarled stick and walked in a square, cut the stick into the ground to mark the perimeter. She put her hands to her hips and looked at the space, could almost see the shoots of beans and tomatoes and cucumbers poking through the ground. She nodded, smiled. It would be her own patch of growth, her own sliver of land—her own.

Two days later, the screaming began.

The screaming filled her dream. First, as a child, standing under a burning tree in the dark, the branches scratching her face, the wind howling in her ear. And then the dream shifted to the orphanage. Flames licked the walls as children tried to escape from the church, the door bolted shut, their cries swirling with the smoke and fire—

Leonora's eyes popped open, her chest heaving, the terror of the dream close to pain. But beyond her thudding heartbeat the air was not silent, and her ears listened, floundered with the muffled sounds. Her breathing stopped and her skin iced. The screaming was still there, unmistakable and horrid. She jolted upright. Alex was not in bed, his boots gone. She grabbed her dress and fumbled with the buttons, clasping them with crooked gaps between. A shriek cut the air. Her throat whimpered as she tried to rush slow fingers.

Leonora bounded down the stairs, tying up her hair as she ran, her feet slipping at the edges, the screaming growing louder as she reached and plowed through the front door. In the blinding sunlight there were police wagons, men and guns. Her head turned, tried to understand the shouting of orders, the pointed and hurried movements, until a pounding—hard and desperate—drew her ears to the barn, dragged her vision. A uniformed man stood before the locked door, a rifle held easily over his folded arm. High-pitched wailing shattered from the cracks of the barn.

Leonora covered her mouth, her mind dizzy. Another man came from the drive dragging a little Aboriginal boy by the arm. The boy screamed at the barn, screamed, *screamed* and fought with the policeman, who gave up on the arm and grabbed him, slung him over his shoulder like a sack of potatoes. And then the sounds congealed— screams that wrenched the gut and hacked it to pieces—howls of women. The nightmare solidified: The police were taking the children.

Leonora sprinted forward with a tearing heart. A priest heard her steps, pivoted like a twisted black pole and smiled. "Ah, good morning; you must be Mrs. Harrington."

"What is this?" she gasped, her voice high with horror.

A woman came up beside him. "We haven't met, yet, Mrs. Harrington. I'm Rebecca Malloy, the Deacon's wife." She stuck out a hand pleasantly. "It's so nice to meet you."

Did they not hear the screaming? She ignored the hand, ignored the introduction. Her body shook. "What's going on?"

"Forgive me." The Deacon fumbled with his hat and held it in his hands. "I assumed your husband had told you."

"Told me what?"

"That we would be coming today to remove the children," the wife interjected sweetly.

"Removing the children?" Leonora's gaze flitted spastically between their faces. "Why?"

The woman clicked her teeth and didn't seem to hear the question. She peered widely at the homestead. "What a lovely home you have."

Leonora held her ears. "*What are you doing here?*"

"We're part of the Aboriginal Protection Board," Mrs. Malloy said, and sighed. Her voice took on the stiffness of authority. "We run the children's mission for this county."

The policeman was back, a flailing, naked baby clutched in his arms. "Perhaps I should explain," Mrs. Malloy began. "Being an American, you wouldn't know about these things." She placed her hand on Leonora's shoulder as if she were a child. "You see, we help the children—the natives and especially the half-breeds—find permanent homes where they can be raised properly, have a chance at a decent upbringing."

"These children already have homes."

"In the rudest sense, yes, but most still live as savages. Our mission gives them exposure to structured society, where they are given proper education, food and clothing. Without our programs, these young children haven't a chance. They're quite neglected."

Leonora stared at them. "They're not neglected! I've seen them myself."

"Mrs. Harrington, the very fact that they are Aborigines is proof that they are neglected." Mrs. Malloy veered Leonora to the house. "Come, I'll explain it all over tea. I must see this lovely home of yours."

Leonora jerked her arm away. "You're not taking these children."

"We are." The woman stiffened. "They're wards of the state. It's the law."

Behind the Malloys, Leonora saw another child plucked into rough arms—Macaria—her angled face frozen in terror, the white eye popping in panic, the view of angels murdered.

"No!" Leonora pushed through the group. "Let her go!" She pried the child from the big hands and hugged her to her breast. Macaria wrapped her legs around her ribs and buried her head under Leonora's hair, shivering uncontrollably.

"Get off my property!" Anger raked and left her blind. Leonora pushed the woman into the chest of the Deacon. "All of you!"

Mrs. Malloy, composed, strode with defiance. "I know this is not easy to watch, Mrs. Harrington." She closed her eyes for a moment as if praying for patience. "But you must remember that the natives don't think as you and I do. They are a simple people. They soon forget that they even had children. I've seen it hundreds of times before. They scream and yell like animals and then they forget."

Deacon Malloy nodded solemnly. "It's true."

Leonora looked at them, one and then the other. "It's inhuman!"

"On the contrary!" The Deacon recoiled. "Savages raising savages, living in squalor without decent clothing or education, is what's inhuman. Taking the children away from their parents is the most charitable thing to do."

"Ah, Deacon and Mrs. Malloy!" came Alex's voice from behind. "I would have been out to meet you earlier, but my ride took longer than I expected." He kissed Mrs. Malloy on the cheek. "You should have come in for breakfast."

A sick, rotten taste filled Leonora's mouth. "You knew about this?"

"Of course." He looked at his wife as an enigma. "I told you the church was doing us a good favor." Alex noticed the child in her arms and scowled in disgust.

The sickness grew and made her weak. Leonora stepped aside and put the child to the ground, held the frozen cheeks between her palms. "Macaria." Leonora's voice quivered as she tried to pull the tone straight. "It's going to be all right. Do you understand?" Leonora tried to catch the child's prancing gaze, held firm to the cheeks. "It's going to be all right, Macaria." She released the face and the child ran under a bush, hid within its scraggy branches.

The group watched Leonora with pity. Alex rolled his eyes. "You have to excuse my wife. She doesn't know the troubles Australia has had with the natives." The Malloys nodded. "What's that pounding?" he asked.

"We had to lock the women in the barn. I hope you don't mind," the Deacon said. "Thought it safer for everyone until the ordeal was over. But we're just about loaded. We'll be out of your hair in a moment."

Leonora's mouth went dry. The window was closing. A policeman locked the back of one of the trucks, pushed a little black head away from the opening. He strode to the driver's seat and waited, his fat red arm slung over the open window. The smell of urine and vomit wafted from the caged door of the truck. The screaming died down— tortured whimpers took its place.

"Alex, may I have a word with you?" Leonora asked desperately.

He winked at the Malloys. "Excuse me for a moment." Alex stepped away and smiled for show, but his voice hissed, "Don't do this, Leonora! The Malloys know everyone this side of Australia. I won't have you causing a scene."

She had one chance, one argument. It had to be right. Leonora took his arm. "Alex, I don't think you've thought this through."

"No?" He folded his arms across his chest. "And why is that, *darling?*"

She swallowed. "How many Aborigines work as stockmen here?"

"Twelve. Why?"

"How much do you pay them?"

"Not much."

"And they're hard workers?"

His eyes narrowed. "I suppose."

Leonora pulled him closer and murmured, "Seems to me that right now the Aborigines are a benefit. As long as they are employed and left alone, they seem harmless enough. But if we take their children away, they'll leave and you'll need to hire all new stockmen, white ones at that." He was digesting her words and she grew bold. "Beyond that, there's no telling how the men will react when they return and find their children gone. I've heard stories, Alex. They may burn the barns, the house. They'll cut the fences. They might even kill the horses." Alex dropped his arms to his sides, his eyes steely.

The door was cracked but not open. She gripped his arm, dug her nails into his shirt. "You do this, Alex, and it's simply too dangerous for me to stay here alone."

He straightened his shoulders and patted her head. "The men would protect you."

"They're out in the paddocks all day; you know that." She squeezed his arm tighter. "I'd have no choice but to come to the mine with you, Alex. I don't mind, really. I can stay in the owner's quarters and we can have dinner together every night." She smiled and caressed his arm, her insides ill. "Might be nice actually."

The door flew open. Alex cleared his throat. "You make some good points." He pinched her chin. "Perhaps you have some of your uncle's logic in you after all."

Her skin cringed with his touch and she smiled wider. Alex passed a look over her shoulder. "The Malloys will be disappointed."

"Just tell them we'll take responsibility for the children. Then give them a large donation and they'll think you the most savvy and generous man around." Leonora linked her arm into his and rested her head on his biceps—hated him.

The Malloys listened to Alex, assented with bent heads, the air pumped out of their worthy cause. The policemen grunted as they unlocked the trucks, let the fruit of their labor escape. Children spilled out and rushed the barn, fled to the bush with tears and jerky movements. A policeman slung his gun to his back and helped the children raise the bolt on the barn. Mothers spilled into the open, blind with sun and grief, fell atop one another and crawled in the dirt for their children. New wails alighted as children clung to necks and hips.

Leonora turned away as she held tight to the sobs, swallowed them as one would a horse pill, one after the other. The horror, the cruelty, of it all nearly knocked her to the ground.

The empty, fetid trucks lumbered away. The Malloys left the station, their greedy pockets thick with cash, to save another round of children at another station, to steal another round of natives from their homes, to rip another round of lives from their mothers' breasts.

Alex came up behind her and kissed the top of her head. And she wished him dead.

CHAPTER 48

❧

Ghan rubbed his shoulder, stiff from lying on hard ground. *Seems age comes to the bones first,* he realized—*thickens the bone marrow and hardens the joints like they're aching for oil. Blood turns to gelatin; skin dries and cracks and spots; hair falls out.* He slid his tongue along his gums. Teeth mostly gone except for a few tombstones lining the bottom. Eyes and ears age, too, making the world wavy and distant. Cold feels colder; heat feels hotter—between the two lie the ache and the weariness.

Ghan fixed his wooden leg, grabbed his lunch—half a loaf of bread and a can of sardines. He left the tent, hobbled with the rest of the ants toward the rising sun and the descending pit. Today was good-bye to the light and down to the dark, back to where he belonged, to the place deep in the basement that hid him from the pretty world upstairs.

With each step, the ground vibrated and sent shock waves up his good leg and rattled his wooden one. Iron cars bumped and shoved along the line; pistons and steel hammers pounded from the smelter. The air choked with oil and ore—the stink of the inner earth fighting against clean oxygen. Ghan passed enormous woodpiles of eucalyptus: dead trees, torn and ravaged, waiting for their turn in the pit or pyre. He looked back at his footprints. The camp was far away now. A great fear crept up his spine, one vertebra at a time.

"Name?"

Ghan was at the dark entrance of the shaft. The checker held pen to clipboard. "Name!" he shouted again.

Ghan wanted to go back. "Ghan."

"Lower in!"

He wanted to turn away from the noise, the smell, the gaping black hole—run to the light, to his tiny canvas tent. But his legs moved forward, stepped into the cold iron skip. Another miner shared the shuttle. The man's skin more green than white, swarthy, probably Romanian. And the green man watched Ghan with black eyes, stared through him, his brows set so low as to be wicked. Ghan turned his head, but the miner's eyes were still on him, shifted to the crippled leg and turned blacker. Ghan knew the look. No miner wanted to be reminded of the dangers that lurked underground.

"Send 'er down!"

The skip lurched in less than an instant, shoved Ghan's stomach to his throat and stretched his lips away from his clenched teeth. They plunged into solid black; the miner inches away from him disappeared with a switch. The skip rattled and bounced and cursed and sped. A thrust of cold, damp air drove over his flesh, followed by the stinking humidity of trapped, heated bodies and lamps. In a matter of seconds, which could have been hours, the skip stopped and they were more than a mile underground.

Miners flowed out of the carts. Ghan settled his insides and pulled himself out last. It would look bad to dawdle. It would be worse to vomit and he swallowed the bile back, gagged. The men who had turned to ants now turned to moths as they walked in a straight line toward the carbide lamps down the shaft. The timber-latticed ceilings, like upside-down railroad tracks, were low and the men stooped as they walked. The sound of picking and digging hid somewhere beyond the halo of light.

The walls, floors and ceilings were thick with oil—moving oil. Ghan's jaws began to shake. He had forgotten about the cockroaches. Hard wings tap-danced across each other as the bugs crawled over every inch of space; a wet crunching emanated under the men's boots. The rats, fat as cats from the roaches, scurried between the men's feet. Only their pale tails showed in the light like giant, flicking earthworms.

A cockroach fell from the ceiling onto Ghan's shoulder, then scurried across his face before he could smack it away. The vomit burned his throat again. The mine was Hell as sure as any existed. His limbs quivered. He didn't know how he had ever done this work before—felt like it had been another life, another man living it.

The men crawled through a hole and emerged in the work zone, the picking now deafening between enclosed walls. The roaches and rats were gone. The lights blinded after the former darkness and couldn't be looked at directly. The foreman directed the miners to their stations and their tools. Then he saw Ghan. "Whoa! Whot the 'ell yeh doin' down here, mate?" The foreman was an old man, spoke with concern, not anger. "Think yer in the wrong place."

Ghan was in the wrong place. He was in Hell. "I can work," Ghan answered.

"Guess they don't care who they send down here anymore." The voice held a long sadness, an apathy to it. He scratched his head with black sooty fingers. "Take the stoop over there. Yeh can sit while yeh pick."

"Don't need to sit," said Ghan gruffly.

The foreman pointed hard at the area. "Yeh'll sit if I tell yeh to sit!" But then his voice softened. "Ain't pity. Sometimes a fella earns a seat. By the looks of it, yeh've put in yer time in the pit, paid yer dues." He handed a pick to another miner just arrived from the skip. "Just take the seat, yeh stubborn bastard."

CHAPTER 49

The house was quiet with trapped, stale heat. Flies were bold and thirsty for sweat; windows needed to stay closed. Leonora folded clothes in the bedroom, spread out the wrinkles, placed the clothing in neat stacks within the bureau. Suddenly, the eaves rattled. The pictures vibrated, the frames smacking lightly against the wall. The floorboards shook under her heels and the iron bed hopped. She gripped the edge of the mattress, her insides throbbing with the noise that seemed loud enough to tumble the house. But then she knew. She ran to the window. A cloud of dirt rose and spread across the distance as thousands of hooves pounded toward the homestead. Leonora held her face, smiled until her eyes watered. They were back.

She left the clothes and hurried down the steps. Clare and Meredith blocked a window each with their figures as they glued their faces to the glass. Meredith turned, her face grim. "Someone's been hurt."

Leonora shimmied between the women and followed their pointed fingers. Two figures limped toward the house. "Boil some water!" Leonora ordered as she ran to the door. "Get clean towels and the medicine case."

Outside, Tom had one arm slung around James's shoulder while his other hand clutched his side, half his shirt soaked in dirt and blood. James held him upright, staggered under the tipping weight. Leonora ran to them, flung Tom's other arm around her neck as they made their way to the verandah, the man's face twisting in pain with each step.

"What happened?" she panted.

"Gored. About a mile out," James said. "Horn stuck him deep. Not sure how far."

They dragged Tom into the house, his teeth gritted against the agony.

"Put him on the couch," Leonora directed.

"Don't put me here." Tom struggled as James set him down. "I'm bleeding."

"I don't give a rat's tail about the couch, Tom. Lie down." Leonora lifted his heavy dust-covered boots onto the spotless sage velvet. Blood flowed freely from his side and dripped down the couch onto the rug.

Carefully, she unbuttoned Tom's shirt, the cotton already hardening with dried blood.

Clare brought the medicine case, a pile of bandages and a hot basin of water before fleeing. Leonora pulled the fabric from the wound. A fresh bubble of blood erupted from the black hole.

Tom felt the gush, looked down, tried to scoot away from it. "Aw, Gawd!"

"It's going to be all right, Tom. It looks worse than it is," she lied. "Lie back. It will slow the bleeding." She met James's worried gaze. "You need to go to Gwalia for a doctor. Take the car. The keys are on the seat." Then, as an afterthought, "Should probably have someone wire Alex and let him know."

James nodded, eyed her gratefully for a moment, then turned to Tom. "Stay put and listen to what she says."

Clare brought a pile of towels, saw the wound and began to cry, "Aw Lord! Aw—"

Leonora shot her a look that made her suck in her lips. "Bring me a bottle of whiskey."

"Sure you should be drinkin' at a time like this?" Tom's grin broke to a tortured grimace.

Leonora turned to the bubbling wound and squared a section of gauze, placed it against the opening. Tom shot up with the pressure. "Please, Tom. You need to stay down. We've got to get the bleeding to slow."

Within seconds, the gauze was soaked and she replaced it with another, twisting Tom into a rail of pain. She brought the whiskey to his lips. "Drink as much as you can."

Tom drank as ordered, his body unclenching slightly.

"This might sting a little." She cleaned the area around the wound with hot water, bit her lip as he writhed. "I'm sorry. I know that hurts."

"Tickles is all," he lied through clenched teeth.

"How'd this happen?"

"My own stupid fault. Damn bull! Agh . . ." He breathed through the pain. "I was tryin' to separate him, put him in the pen. He's in heat."

"Guess you aren't his type," she teased.

He laughed, then grimaced. "Don't do that."

"Sorry."

The bleeding slowed from a stream to a trickle but still soaked every new gauze strip. With the hot water she wiped the blood off his chest and arms, the basin turning bright red with one squeeze of the soft cloth. She pulled out the bandage. "Tom, you'll need to lean up so I can get this bandage around you. I'll go as quick as I can."

He moaned while she wrapped him tightly. "This will hold you until the doctor gets here. You probably have some broken ribs, but overall you got off lucky. Any higher and that horn would have got you in the stomach; any lower, well . . ." She smiled timidly. "Well, just be glad it wasn't. You can still carry on the Shelby name."

"Crikey!" He grinned. "Be a fate worse than death."

She leaned him back onto the pillow, the tight bandages keeping his ribs from shifting. "How'd you learn all this?" he asked. "You a nurse?"

"No. Would have liked to be, though." She held up the whiskey to his lips again. "I volunteered with the Red Cross back in the states when the war broke out. I liked working with the soldiers. Tried to help out the nurses as much as I could."

"James and I were gonna sign up. My brothers went instead. Lucky bastards."

"Don't say that, Tom. This war is awful. People say they've never seen anything like it." Tom's eyes turned soft and she added lightly, "Of course, your brothers are probably faring better than you right now."

Tom grinned. "They'd be giving me a good ribbin' if they saw me. Bunch of foolhardy brutes, those two." A great missing took over his features. "Almost feel sorry for the Turks."

"You have two brothers?" she asked.

"And five sisters."

"Eight children! Your mother deserves a medal."

"She does." Pride etched the lines of his face. "Hell of a lot of mouths to feed. I don't know how Mum does it by herself."

Leonora touched his bandages. "How about some tea? Or soup?"

"Can't drink anything. My stomach's all swirly."

"You did okay with the whiskey," she teased again.

"Never tasted whiskey so smooth." Then he winked. "Alex got good taste."

She took the compliment and smiled, tried to keep his mind off the wound. "Have you and James known each other long?"

"Since we were kids. Like a brother to me." Tom gave a strong nod. "Do anything for that bloke. Gawd knows he's always been there for me." Tom watched her for a long time. "I can see why he likes you so much."

Leonora met his gaze. "Did he tell you about me—about us?"

"Told me before he was even sure himself. I won't tell a soul. Promise."

"I'm glad you know. And I'm glad he's had such a good friend in his life." The blood spread in the seams of the bandage. "Sorry, Tom. Time to change out the dressing again."

"Can't keep your hands off me, eh?"

She laughed and unwrapped the line from his ribs. "So, any ladies in your life?"

"Me? Lots of ladies." He smiled devilishly, then winced as the gauze pulled at his wound. "Too many ladies. That's the problem. Can't just pick one. They're all so damn pretty."

"Don't you want to settle down someday?" She put the soiled dressing on the floor and cleaned the wound with warm water again. "Have a wife and eight kids of your own?"

"Eight! Never. One or two at the most. Who knows, maybe someday I'll get tired of playin' an' let one of the sheilas tie me down."

"How generous of you."

He gave a tight laugh, tried not to spurt out more blood.

"And what about James?" She tried to sound disinterested. "Is he a ladies' man as well?"

"The ladies love James." He rolled his eyes. "Think he's dark and mysterious." Heat grew to her ears, the look not lost on Tom. "But," he said slyly, "James is a hard nut to crack. Like he's always comparin' the poor girl to someone else."

Her fingers slipped and she dropped the bandage. Tom grinned. Quickly, she wrapped him tight and handed him the whiskey bottle. "All right, Casanova. That's enough talking out of you," she scolded gently. "One more sip and then get some rest before the doctor arrives." She stood slowly to leave, gathering the bloodied basin and rust-colored gauze strips in her hands.

"Yes, Mum," he answered drowsily. "Whatever you say."

Four hours passed before James returned with the doctor, a hunched, sturdy little man with red-rimmed eyes. Leonora met them on the verandah and extended a hand. "I'm Leonora Harrington. Thanks so much for coming out."

"Dr. Meade," he greeted quickly. "Know your husband." He shuffled past her, the smell of mothballs wafting from his worn suit. "Where's the patient?"

"On the sofa. He's asleep."

The man entered the house. James turned to her. "Is he all right?"

"I think so," she answered. "Lost a lot of blood, but luckily the horn didn't hit an organ. He'll be laid up for a while."

They sat on the verandah steps, sank into the even, warm air. James leaned his back against the porch post, rubbed one raised knee. "Thanks for helping him."

She smiled. "He's a good man."

"He is." James turned his face to the door. "We owe you a new couch, by the way."

"I don't care about the couch." She stared at her hands. "I don't care about the couch, the mirrors, the rugs or anything in there."

James watched her carefully and she fell into his gaze as if it were a pillow. "You've been riding for nearly two months," she noted, resting her head against the sun-drenched wood. "You must be exhausted."

James smacked the dust off his shin. "Need a long, warm bath. Might soak in the tub for a couple of days straight."

Her mind blinked to him immersed in the tub, his eyes closed in the comfort of the steam, his arms wet. She blinked the image away just as quickly and busied her hands in the folds of her dress. "How do you like the managers' quarters?" she asked.

"All the comforts of home and then some." James shot her a grin. "You should come over for tea one day."

"I'd like that." She laughed. "Maybe I'll make you some curtains."

"Curtains!" he scoffed playfully. "Stockmen'll run me off the ranch."

"All right, all right." She smiled. "No curtains. How about a pie then?"

He grinned broadly, showing the edges of his white, straight teeth. "I like pie."

The silence settled easily this time without a rim of tension. They blinked and breathed lazily among their thoughts.

"How are the horses?" James asked.

"Good. Alex has been watching them like children."

"Anything else happen around here while we were gone?"

For a moment, she wondered if he knew about the Aborigines—wondered if he had been aware, even supportive, of the horror. The very idea hurt like ice pressed into the skin. She swallowed, pushed it away, couldn't think of it. "No," she said softly. "Nothing new."

They grew silent again. James raised his chin toward the cloud of dust coming from the distant road, his brows inching together almost angrily. "Your husband's back."

Sweat dripped down Leonora's nose as she plunged the hoe hard between the lines of vegetables. The plants thrived in the shaded spot. Without rain, the ground dried, but she didn't mind carrying a watering can from the rain barrel. Alex didn't know about the garden; he was gone for full weeks at the mine. When he returned, alcohol hung on his skin like cologne. At times, his face was warm and bright with its effect; at others, cold and dark—either way, unsettling. Often his clothes reeked of women's perfume; lipstick smeared the collars of his white shirts, but for this she only felt relief.

A slow gallop came from the west. Leonora stopped her work,

wiped her hands on her dress and looked up through the trees. A nervous flutter rose in her chest as James rode up through the clearing, strong and graceful, his body lean and shimmering with good health. He pulled up the horse and leaned forward casually. "Thought I saw someone moving over here." Then, with an agile twist, he was off the horse and walking her to the shade. "House garden not big enough?" he asked.

"Haven't gardened in so long." She propped the hoe against a tree. "I've missed it."

"Manual labor suits you." He smiled, then came close, so close his frame blocked out the sun and carried its warmth with his body. He reached over her shoulders and picked up the hat that had fallen against her back, resettled it upon her head. "You're getting sunburned."

She stepped back flustered, fixed her hat. "I should probably get out of the heat." She sat on the cool ground under the shade, shifting her knees to the side.

James followed, leaned his back against the tree near his horse, his body sturdy and tan next to the light bark. "Garden much in America?" he asked.

"No." She peered into the branches. "Let's see—there was piano, French lessons, literature, watercolors and, oh yes, sometimes a little sewing or tea with the old society ladies, but gardening, no."

"Too bad. You're good at it." James squinted from under his hat. "So, what's America like?"

"Hmmm." She thought about this. "It's a beautiful country. The Rocky Mountains, the California coast, the Florida Keys. I lived in Pennsylvania. Pittsburgh. If you don't mind the soot, it's lovely, and so green with rain it looks like Ireland." She turned to him then and asked tenderly, remembering, "Did you ever go?"

"To Ireland? No." He scratched the base of his slick throat. "Never been out of Western Australia."

She nodded, watched him. "What's your family like? The O'Reillys."

"Passed on." His brows knit, the smile lines erased. "It was a while ago."

"I'm sorry."

"The Shelbys took me in." James shoved his hands in his front pockets. "Don't know what I would have done without them."

A slight breeze tickled the hair around their faces, cooled the sweated fabric of their clothing. Leonora wiped her brow with the back of her hand. "Here." James handed her a handkerchief from his shirt pocket. "Can't promise how clean it is." He smirked.

The cloth smelled of soap and hay and earth, manly and rich, and she breathed in its scent with closed eyes and hoped she wouldn't need to give it back. She dabbed her forehead and nose, winced. "My face hurts."

"You've got a good shade of red. Be in some discomfort tonight, I'm afraid."

"I'll be a freckled mess."

"Aw, don't judge the freckle so harshly!" he scolded. "Some men find them quite enchanting."

"Is that so?"

James nodded. He walked over to her and extended a hand. "I better get back and make dinner for the princess. She gets cranky sitting in bed all day."

"Poor Tom." Leonora took his hand, his long fingers gripping her firmly and pulling her to her feet. "I'll stop over later and check on him. Oh, and I'll bring that pie I promised."

Their eyes locked. He slid his fingers from her hand. "Looking forward to it."

The sound of workingmen quieted as it always did before twilight. In its place, the insects took over in a worldly purr; a kookaburra cackled between the ghost gums. Lights shone from the managers' house in the distance, warm and glowing. Tom's dog barked, charged, but once recognition took over the dog whimpered and wagged in apology, escorted Leonora over the footbridge while her heart knocked in her chest and she balanced the pie in her hands.

Tom limped out to the porch and smiled widely. "Hey, gorgeous!" He calmed her instantly. "Hello, Tom. You look all better."

He put his hands up and spun around. "Nearly right as rain, thanks to you. Even rode out with James this mornin'."

She patted his arm. "Just don't push it."

"Felt good." He stretched. "Stung a little but just felt good movin' again." Tom pointed to the pie. "Something sure smells sweet."

She raised the pie self-consciously. "It's cherry."

"My favorite. You're an angel, you know that? Let me go grab James."

"Is he busy?"

Tom grinned. "Just hangin' out with his girlfriend."

"Oh." Leonora grew rigid; her stomach dropped. "I . . . I'll come back later."

"Nothin' doin'. Stay put an' I'll bring him out." Tom jumped up the steps and shouted into the house, "James, put a shirt on an' come out. Somebody wants t'see you. Oh, an' bring Josephina out!" Tom winked at Leonora. "You'll like her."

Leonora swallowed and touched her stomach. She was going to be sick, wanted to crawl under a rock. She turned to leave.

"Hey, Leo," James greeted from the door, slid his shirt over his chest. Her stomach dropped farther and landed in her knees.

James stepped out. "Leaving so soon?" His shirt stayed untucked from his moleskins, his suspenders hanging behind his hips, ruggedly relaxed, the outline of his chest visible through the thin cotton shirt.

She wasn't sure where to set her eyes. "I . . . I didn't mean to interrupt," she floundered. Her face burned and she touched her palm against her cheek.

"Is something wrong?"

She closed her eyes and blindly sat down on the step, feeling such a fool for being there, feeling even more a fool for being upset. James went to the door again. "Wait a minute, all right? There's someone I want you to meet."

Leonora bent forward and tightened her grip around her stomach. She practiced smiling so she wouldn't look a complete mess when she met the woman.

A second later, James stepped out, his coat bundled in his arms, and sat down next to her, so close his biceps rubbed against hers. "Meet Josephina." He opened the coat and a tiny, furry kangaroo head peeked out.

The relief that flooded was audible with exhale and Leonora covered her mouth, laughed between her fingers. "Josephina's a kangaroo."

He eyed her quizzically. "Of course. What'd you think?"

"Thought you had . . . a lady friend."

"Ahhh." He nodded and watched her with humor and raised eyebrows. "No such luck." He turned to the animal and scratched her fondly behind the ears. "Found the little thing out in the bush. Orphaned."

"I like the name." The relief was still so warm and fresh she couldn't stop smiling. James's face was so gentle, the lines strong without a hint of arrogance.

"Thought Joey didn't quite suit her." James held Leonora's gaze, smiled. She reached over and petted the peach fuzz of the kangaroo's nose, her arm grazing James's chest, the heat warming the length of her arm.

It was so comfortable sitting there. So easy. Too easy. She wanted to lean her head against his shoulder, snuggle into it like a blanket. "How long will you keep her?" she asked.

"Until she's eating on her own and grown a bit. Then send her on her way. She wouldn't have made it through the night." His eyes fell over Leonora's face without hurry and she dropped her head. A strand of hair fell to the edge of her nose. James reached over and tucked it behind her ear, leaving a trail of fire across her skin.

A voice called from inside, "Where's my nurse?"

"I guess I should check on the patient," she said with a short laugh.

"Come on in and I'll slice up that pie." She followed him into the small house, the front room smelling like warm bread and fresh-cut wood.

Tom sat up in bed and held his side, his chest bare except for the bandages. "Knew I'd get yeh into my bedroom sooner or later."

James stood directly behind her, reached an arm over her head and held the door frame. "Be good or she'll send Dr. Meade back." His breath tickled the top of her hair. The warmth of his body made her stance uneasy.

"I'll be good." Tom crossed his heart. "Promise."

James tapped her shoulder, his fingertip leaving a spot of heat upon her skin. "Watch him," he warned, then turned for the kitchen.

"He's just jealous." Tom leaned back.

"Heard that!" James shouted.

Tom mouthed again silently, *He's just jealous.*

Leonora sat on the edge of the bed and gingerly unpeeled the bandages. "You're quite terrible, you know that?"

"Och! Not me! You know I'm growin' on you, love. Admit it."

"Yes. You're growing on me," she said straight-faced while unwinding the bandages. "Like mildew." They heard James chuckle from the kitchen. She pulled the bandages from his bruised ribs. A spot of blood appeared under the thinning gauze. "Sure you're not pushing it?"

"I'm orright. Ribs don't hurt as much. Can breathe without screaming."

She reached for a new bandage from her purse. "You're a fast healer."

Tom leveled his eyes, the joking face gone. "Don't know what I would've done without you. I mean that."

"Leave the bulls alone from now on, all right?" She patted his leg, then stood to go. "Stick with the sheilas."

James waited for Leonora on the porch. "You've taken good care of him," she announced as she stepped into the warm night air.

He watched her for a moment, seemed lost in a thought, then cocked his head to the door. "Pie's almost cool. Can I bring you a piece?"

"Should probably get back." She sighed. "Alex comes back soon." She rolled her eyes. "He'll call a search party out for me."

"Too bad." James forced a half smile. "Come on; I'll walk you home."

"It's all right. I can manage."

"Wasn't a question." He went to take her elbow, then stopped. "Almost forgot. Hold on; I have something for you." James turned, took the three steps in one long jump. He returned a moment later holding a jelly jar filled with white flowers. "They're oleanders," he said. "The back paddock's filled with them."

Leonora took the flowers and smelled the blooms, a mix of apricot and lilac. Her throat tightened with the simple, sweet gesture. "They're beautiful." She and James walked toward the big house, quiet. She was aware of the flow and movement of his body with each step.

"How long will Alex be home?" James asked, his jaw stiff.

"Hard to tell. Changes day to day." They grew silent again and did not speak until the bottom of the steps. "Thanks for the flowers," she said, sheepish.

He nodded and began to walk backwards. "Have a good night." And then remembering, "Thanks for the pie, Leo."

Leo. Everything warmed. "Do you know you're the only one who ever called me that?"

He gave her an indulgent wink. "Good."

Alex returned unpleasantly from the start, slamming the door, the house filling with his edge. "Fire in the pit!" he spit. He hung up his coat, his face unshaven and gray, his collar soiled. "Backed us up a full day."

"Was anyone hurt?"

"Two or three. I don't know." He shrugged his shoulders. "Need to go back in a day or two." He plopped down in the wide chair and ran his fingers through his hair, leaving it stuck up at the front. "Just need one night of rest. One night of peace."

She went to the bar and poured him a drink, handed it to him.

He took a long sip, looked up at her briefly. "Have you been running? You're all red."

Leonora touched her face. "Sunburn."

"Didn't you wear a hat, for God's sake?"

"I was gardening and it must have slipped off." She laughed. "I didn't even realize it until it was too late. Hurts, too." She touched her cheek again.

He stared at her, his expression blank. "Gardening?"

She nodded proudly. "Do you want to see it? It's out back behind the house."

He rose from the chair. "You dug in the dirt?" His voice rumbled deep and low and slapped the smile from her lips. "You stood out there in plain sight, digging in the ground, in the full sun like a common field hand?"

She was stunned with the tone, felt a slight chill as he set his eyes upon her.

"Let me see your hands."

"W-w-why?" she stammered. "I—"

He shouted through clenched teeth, "Let me see your hands!"

She held out her hands, visibly shaking. He turned them. "Look at your hands. Look at them! They're hard and red like a man's, the nails broken and dirty!"

She shrank, thought about running for the door, calling for Meredith or Clare.

"This is how you greet me?" Alex screamed. "Dirty hands and sunburned skin?"

"I'm sorry. I . . . I just wanted . . ."

"You just wanted to what? Just wanted to embarrass me in front of the whole station? Imagine what the managers must think! Seeing my wife knuckle deep in dirt, planting vegetables as if I can't provide enough food to feed her!"

"No one saw me, Alex!" she lied. "It's hidden."

He ripped his tie loose from his neck and threw it on the floor. "I was planning to take you to the races this weekend, to meet some of the other wives. You can forget about that now."

"Why?"

"Look at you!" He pushed her to the mirror.

Anger was working its way through the fear. "You're away more days than I can count, Alex. What do you expect me to do all day, twiddle my fingers and wait for you? You've hired a cook and a maid. There's nothing for me to do. How do you suggest I fill up my day?"

"Why don't you do what other women do." He smacked the empty tumbler on the table. "And think about ways to be a better wife."

The blare of the Ford's engine disturbed the horses. Tom pulled them still and continued brushing, irritated by the noise.

"Sure you're up for the work, Tom?" James asked.

"If I stay in bed another day, I'm gonna shoot myself."

James searched the stalls. "Where's Russell?"

"Don't know." Tom winced as he bent down and checked the horse's hoof. "Saw him headed out with a hoe and wheelbarrow. Said he had to tear up some garden in the back."

"What?" James set down the pitchfork. Tom shrugged his shoulders.

Saddling up the brown mare, James set off past the house and the stables. The sound of metal pounding against dirt rose from a familiar spot shaded in the distance. Russell came into view under the trees. The fence to the small garden was torn down and piled in a wheel-barrow, the stalks and vegetables twisted and limp and crushed below the wires.

"Russell," James blasted. "What the hell are you doing?"

The man raised his head dumbly, his lip swollen with tobacco. "Clearin' out the garden."

"Why? Who told you to do this?"

"Mr. 'Arrington." Russell leaned against the hoe, wiped his nose with his thumb. "Says t'make it look like it weren't ever here."

James squared his jaw. "Does his wife know?"

"How should I know?" he spit. "Just doin' whot he told me."

James surveyed the damage, the neat rows hacked, the plants in the wheelbarrow already wilting from the sun. "Tom needs you in the barn," he ordered. "This can wait."

"I ain't messin' wiv the boss." Russell picked the hoe up and smoothed out the lines. "Mr. 'Arrington says finish it, I'm gonna fin-ish it."

"I'll finish it." James grabbed the hoe. "Mr. Harrington can talk to me if he's got an issue."

"Orright, if yeh say so." He shuffled off toward the barn.

James sat on his haunches and put his fingers through the freshly turned ground, let scraps of leaves and flowers run through them. He went to the wheelbarrow and plucked through the leaves, picked what vegetables he could salvage—only a handful of beans and peas, a flaccid carrot. He thought of Leonora's face, the brightness of it as she worked, the smile that curved his lips to match. James scanned the slaughtered plot, a sad pit filling his stomach as he rose and headed for the big house.

James held his hat in his palm as he stepped up to the verandah and knocked on the door. He waited. Knocked again, but no one an-swered. He turned to walk away when he heard the door crack. He hardly recognized the woman standing there so pale and sullen. James cleared his throat. "G'day, Leo." James scratched his temple. "Looks like some rabbits got into your garden, did a number on it." He held out his hat. "Tried to save what I could."

She looked at the contents in the hat and her lips curved into a futile smile. James picked up one of the limp beans and smirked. "A royal feast, eh?"

She gave a short, quiet laugh and the smile broke. But the rest of her face hung with such sadness, he had to turn away. "Why'd he do it?"

Leonora wiped the side of her eye. "I guess he doesn't find freckles enchanting."

James looked at her now, the perfectly dotted nose, the smooth forehead, the lines of her cheekbones as they pointed to her lips. The features tore him. "Is Alex home?" His chest heated. "I'd like a word with him."

"He's not here." Her eyes flickered. "Just let it go, James. It's not important. Just a patch of dirt."

The heat burned now and he looked off into the distance, past the road. "It's not just that, Leo. He shouldn't leave you alone like he does. It's not right."

"Men are always leaving women alone in Australia. Drovers, miners—hardly a job around that doesn't leave a woman."

"This is different. The mine makes enemies, Leo. There's not a person in Western Australia that doesn't know your wealth by now." James shook his head, the worry tightening his lips. "I know it's none of my business, but Alex needs to know. It's not right, not safe, for him to leave you alone."

"It's better when he's gone." Her hand flew to her head. "I didn't mean that. It's just . . . it's just he's got a hard job, a lot of work, and people depending on him. It's better if he's away. It's better that he takes care of his work at the mine."

Leonora opened the door wider and for a minute he thought she was going to reach for his hand. "I appreciate your concern, James. I do. But it's best you just let it go." She worked hard at a smile and a joking tone as she said, "Besides, I have the ladies in the kitchen. I'm quite certain Meredith knows how to wield a frying pan."

"This isn't a joke, Leo."

"I'm a big girl. I can take care of myself, thank you. Besides, I have moves." She squared her shoulders and her eyes sparkled. The color came back to her cheeks.

He crossed his arms, tried not to laugh, the anger fading. "Really? What kinds of moves?"

"Secret moves."

"Please, do show me!"

"If I did, they wouldn't be secret anymore, would they?" she teased.

James exhaled loudly and chuckled, shook his head, worn down. "At least promise me you won't open the door to any strange men?"

"Does that include you?" she asked.

James stepped right in front of her, his face only inches away. "Especially me." He winked. He wanted to kiss her then. The impulse flashed so quickly it startled him and he stepped back unnerved. He dumped the vegetables into a basket on the verandah, put his hat on quickly. He needed space, needed to pull himself straight. "Just be careful," he said without looking back, and stepped quickly from the porch.

"James . . ."

He turned around.

A wave of gratitude choked her for a moment. "Thank you."

CHAPTER 50

The rain hit without warning and lasted for two days and nights, drowned a Slav and an Italian in the pit and shut the work down for the first time since the fire.

The miners huddled under tents. Rain-soaked canvas drooped above their heads and spit out the fires as quickly as they were lit. It was a cold, damp rain, dull and quiet without the fury of lightning. The ground ran brown and muddy between the rows of tents and boots sank. Bedding, packs, matches and food were piled in the corners on warped pieces of metal to keep dry. Men and women stunk of damp clothes that had been dried, then wet, then dried and wet again. The open sewer pipe near the hills overflowed and the fetid sludge slid toward the camp. Old clothes and hemp sacks filled with sand lined the outskirts to keep the muck from entering, but the sludge found every crack and veined intently.

Ghan sat in Whistler's tent on a soaked piece of a flattened cardboard box. They ate quietly, each with a tin of meat and a fork. His was lamb; Whistler ate sardines. Tin dog, they called it. The bread, soaked as a sponge, rotted in the corner.

The rain weakened the spirit. No work yesterday, none today, unlikely any tomorrow. Three days without wages hung on the camp. Even Whistler didn't smile, his face gray and drawn as the clouds. The din of Whistler's fork prongs hit against the bottom of the can as he dug for a final bite. "There's talkin'," he said to his can.

Ghan munched the warm lamb, so tender and overcooked that the texture felt previously chewed. "Whot kind of talkin'?"

"Angry talkin'. Comin' from every side now," Whistler said. "Rain makin' it worse. Nothin' t'do but talk." The old man poked at his food. "Some talkin' strike, some talkin' riot, but everybody talkin' mad. Foreigners hot as piss 'bout those drowned miners. Got a right t'be, too. Managers kept those boys down there too long. Saw the water risin' an' didn't bring 'em up. Can't even bury the bloated bodies 'cause the mud keeps fillin' in the graves."

Ghan cleaned his tin and set it on the ground next to his feet. He looked at Whistler. "Managers want me to spy," he said. "Tell 'em if there's rumblings. Why I got the job. Only reason I got this job." Ghan waited for a reaction.

Whistler finished his last bite, scraped the plate clean and licked both sides of his fork, then grinned widely. "Yeh ain't a rat, Ghan."

Ghan grinned back. "Not a day in m'life."

"Whot yeh gonna do when they start askin'? Even the bosses can feel the water boilin'."

Ghan shrugged. "Stall 'em, I guess. Tell 'em there's complainin', but nothing' organized. Just the normal rantin'."

"Yer in a tough spot, mate. Won't be long 'fore the anger spills over. Somepin's gonna happen that'll knock the pot over. Sure as 'ell it's comin'. Men on every side just waitin' fer somebody t'sneeze an' the pot gonna knock clean over an' burn the 'ell outta people." Whistler stopped, sucked his gums for fish. "The big guys'll blame yeh fer not givin' 'em warnin'. Be happy to take it out on somebody."

The cardboard under Ghan's bottom sank into the mud, but he didn't care. He shrugged again. "I ain't gonna think 'bout it. Take one day at a time. Save my money case I gotta get out. If they catch me, not too much they can do t'me that hasn't been done already."

"Break yer bones," Whistler lamented.

"Like I say, ain't nothin' new. When it's done, go on livin' or go on dyin'."

"Yer fergettin' 'bout the sufferin' in between."

"Didn't ferget." Ghan looked at his big, rough hands. "But I ain't a rat."

Whistler rose stiffly, his joints cracking and sore with rheumatism, all the more rigid with the rain. He dug through a pile and brought out a rusted can, pulled off the top and took out an old sock with a ball at the end. He swung it in the air like a pendulum. "I've been puttin' money away. Little here an' there when I can. Ain't much." Whistler threw the sock at Ghan, who caught it quick. "First sign of trouble, come in here an' take it. Get the 'ell out 'fore they come fer yeh."

Ghan threw the sock back. "Ain't takin' yer money, Whistler."

"Damn right yeh is!" Whistler shot back. "I got family. Got my shitload of girls t'care fer me. Whot yeh got?" He rubbed his stubble. "Look, I ain't long fer this world. My bones so tight feel like they're gonna split in two. Hurts so damn bad to walk an' move my fingers, I come close t'eatin' rat poison just t'make it stop. Only reason I'm still here is my girls. Crush their gawd-ferin' hearts if I killed m'self. Think I'd be burnin' in 'ell, they would."

Whistler squeezed his lips bitterly. "I don't need the money, Ghan. If those sons of bitches hurt yeh, it's gonna hurt me. Hurt me somepin awful inside. Yeh know how those damn girls made me soft like butter! Got enough pain wivout yers."

Whistler stuffed the sock into the can and put the top back on, then buried it in the pile. "If yeh don't need the money, it stays here. But if yer in trouble, gawd damn it, take it!" Whistler shoved a pile of old clothes on top. "Now come on. Let's get outta here an' see if anybody's got a game on."

The old men hunched out of the tent, pulled up their shirt collars over their necks and pulled down their hats against the pelting rain. Cigarette smoke drifted and extinguished from a large tent on the Aussie side. A low hum of voices came from the opening and then a high shout and then the low hum again. Whistler pulled back the flap. The ceiling was high, so they stretched out their backs and dripped. "Boys gotta game on?" Whistler asked.

"Depends," a burly, sunburned man answered. "Got money?"

Whistler jingled the coins in his pocket.

"Orright." The man nodded. "Join in." He scooted his wooden crate over. "Make room for the old-timers!" he ordered. Each rump slid over a spot.

"Whot yeh playin'?" Ghan asked.

"Fly loo." In the middle of the men lay a slab of wood and on top sat six small pyramids of sugar. The men vigorously waved at the flies in the air. "Place yer bets!" the man hollered.

Ghan placed his coin in front of the fourth cone of sugar. The other men followed, each picking a pile, some doubling up. "Bets placed!" the man shouted. "Three, two, one, down!"

The flapping of hands stopped and stilled, every eye watching the buzzing blowflies. A hairy, ugly fly swooped down, circled the sugar while the men held their breath. Then another fly drifted down and without stopping to consider landed on the second mound of sugar and started licking at the granules. Three of the men cheered and clapped while the others grunted. The winners held out hands for the payout. "Flies comin' in like black clouds from the sewage," another man explained. "Don't know whot flies like more, shit or sugar." The men laughed.

"Whistler an' Ghan, right?" the headman asked pleasantly while he divvied up the winnings. They nodded. "Winston. Good t'ave yeh. Yer new, ain't yeh?" he asked Ghan.

"Don't feel like it," Ghan answered while he dug for another coin. "Been workin' the mines most of m'life. One don't seem different from the next."

"Fair dinkum." Winston nodded. "Why yeh boys livin' down wiv 'em stinkin' E-talians? Should be over on our end."

Whistler shot Ghan an *I told yeh so* glance and answered, "Lady down that way feeds us. Damn good cook, too. Only reason. Old farts like us need t'take a hot meal when we can."

Winston frowned with understanding. "Just watch yerself. 'Em people don't wash their hands. Eat same place they shit." Snorts and growls rumbled around the table amid the flapping hands. "Last game! Place bets!"

CHAPTER 51

❧

A steady stream of travelers to the homestead was to be expected: swaggies with the whole of their belongings wrapped in a bag tied to the end of a stick; the prospectors with cut, hard hands and empty pockets; the out-of-work stockmen who hid humiliation under gruff words. Veterans, newly sentimental and crippled, their eyes still distant and shocked with the horror of war, stopped by to track down lost mates. Whoever came, no matter their source, always asked for "a bit of tucker" to fill their thin bodies, most returning on their footsore journey soon after, some taking a quick nap under the coolibah tree.

Food and water were always given—the first law of the bush. And for the most part, the men were honest, polite, hardworking blokes come upon by hard times. Most of the stragglers came from the west and north, heading down to the mines and fields beyond them. Criminals were rare in the Outback, preferring the anonymity and dark streets of the city slums.

Only when the storm ripped inland and flooded the streams and streets to creeks did the travelers pause. For that week and the ones that followed, life outside Wanjarri Downs seemed deserted. But as the water receded and dried and left scars and ruts in its place the travelers picked up again like termites on rotted wood.

But there was a shift. Leonora noticed more and more of the men came from the south now, their faces sallow, eyes more vacant than before the rains. As she loaded them up with lamb pies and peaches and refilled their billies with freshwater she always wanted to ask them where they came from or where they were going, but she never did. Something in their faces did not look interested in conversation, didn't look much interested in anything anymore.

And in all the time she had been at the station, a female traveler never once stopped at the door. A few times, she would see a woman huddled in the back of a wagon or tending to a crying baby, but the woman always stayed to the background, never glancing up at the house or joining her husband on the verandah. So it was with great surprise when, in the highest of the day's heat, Leonora opened the door to a woman holding the hands of two small, scraggly boys.

The woman did not meet her eyes. "Sorry t'bother yeh, miss." Her voice was filled with shame. "Was wonderin' if yeh could spare a bite fer m'boys."

Leonora did not want to prolong the woman's agony and answered a bit too fast, "Of course. Please come in out of the sun."

The boys started forward, but the woman pulled them back. "Won't be a bother. If it's all the same, we'll just take it t'go." The poor boys looked at their feet, their shoes worn to the soles, dirty toes peeking out from the holes.

"Please," Leonora urged. "It's no bother. I'd rather enjoy the company. Besides, we have a fresh stew cooking and it's not quite ready."

The boys looked at their mother hopefully, the hunger clear on their faces. She sighed and gave in. "Just for a bit an' then we'll be on our way. Don't mean to be a bother, miss."

Once inside, the boys stared with open mouths at the space of the room, the high ceilings and the rich furnishings. Their mother cleared her throat to get their attention and gave them a silent order with a nod of her head. The boys quickly took off their hats, sending dead flies and red dust all over the floor. "For crikey's sake, boys!" the mother hissed.

Leonora laughed. "It's all right. My husband leaves a trail of dust around the whole house." She walked to the kitchen doors and called out, "Meredith, how close is the stew?"

"Ready now if yeh like."

"Yes. I'm having guests for lunch." She smiled at the boys, who beamed with their new titles. "I'll need three more bowls and lots of bread and butter."

The four of them sat down at the fresh-linened table, the boys' heads barely above the edge. Their mother looked so uncomfortable that Leonora wondered if it was cruel bringing them in. She knew how Australians felt about handouts, especially the women.

Meredith brought out the dishes of stew, glanced oddly at the faces. The boys tore into the rolls and scooped up the stew before it had a chance to cool. The woman looked at her now, the lines of her face deepened with dust. She could have been anywhere from twenty to fifty years old. "Yer goin' to too much trouble."

"My husband's gone often." Leonora lowered her eyes, spoke honestly. "We don't get many women out here. It can get lonely." The woman's shoulders relaxed, and in less than an instant they shared a common truth that went beyond class or accent.

"Where are you traveling from?" Leonora asked.

"Coolgardie."

"From the mine?"

"Yeah."

"There's been a lot of men coming through here from that direction. Is there another mine hiring up north?"

The woman cocked her head, incredulous. "They're all runnin' from the fever."

Leonora didn't understand. "Fever?"

"Typhoid. All through the camp."

The boys stopped gorging for a moment, their eyes clinging to their mother's face as it hollowed.

"My husband died of it a few days back," she said, her voice curt, numb with anger. "My baby before that." Her knuckles turned white as she gripped her spoon. "Takin' the boys west to Daggar Hills. Husband's family has a small farm."

"That's a long way." Leonora put her napkin to her lips. "How will you get there?"

"Walk."

One of the boys looked down at his shoes and his face fell.

"You'll at least stay the night?" Leonora asked.

"No." The woman looked like she might stand to leave at the mere mention. "We'll be on our way. We've stayed long enough."

"Please, stay. Let the children rest. We have the room. You can leave first thing before the heat." She smiled weakly. "Besides, I sleep better when there's someone else in the house."

As the woman thought about it, she seemed to let her body give in to fatigue. She looked at her tired boys and her eyes softened. "Orright, we'll leave first thing."

After supper, Leonora ran a deep bath for the boys, the rain tower brimming with water from the storm. It gave her a selfish happiness to care for the family, even for just a short time, made her remember the days at the hospital.

The mother tucked the scrubbed boys into the warm covers, smiled for the first time. "They're good lads," she said. "Had it rough. Too rough for their age." The voice rose. "Why I left. Couldn't lose 'em t'the fever." Her eyes moistened. "Just couldn't lose 'em, too."

"What about the doctor at the mine?" Leonora asked. "Wasn't he able to help?"

"Never saw a doctor. We called fer him, as did everyone else, but he was only concerned wiv the top of the gang. My husband was just a digger. Managers only care 'bout whot comes out of the walls, not the hands workin' 'em."

Leonora realized the woman had no idea she and Alex owned the mine; she prayed it stayed that way. "Bath should still be warm," Leonora offered. "Might as well use it before it's drained."

The weariness seemed to overtake the woman. "That would be nice." She gave Leonora a long look. "Yeh've been kind. Too kind. After my wash, I'll just curl up wiv the boys. Won't bother yeh no more."

Guilt waffled over her skin. She had done nothing for this woman. On the contrary, Alex may have made her a widow.

The next morning, the three guests were up early as they had promised, their bellies filled with eggs, bread and bacon. The boys had a new sparkle to them thanks to the rest and food. Leonora wondered sadly how long it would last.

The dray was waiting outside. She had asked James to stock it with feed for the horse and some blankets and canisters of water. Leonora raided the pantry and put in as much food as would keep. In the bottom of a basket she put a few bills, tucked the money far enough down so the woman wouldn't find it until she was too far away to return it.

The woman was mute when she saw the dray and horse waiting, could not have been more stunned if it had been a carriage of gold. She tried to refuse, silently shaking her head, but Leonora stopped her. "The dray hasn't been used in years. The men were going to break it up into firewood. And the horse doesn't have much life left in her, I'm afraid," she lied. "Might not even make it all the way to Daggar Hills. You'd be doing us a favor by taking her."

The woman did not say another word, but her eyes were deep with gratitude as she watched her boys climb onto the blankets under the flatbed's canopy. They left without further words, not even an exchange of names.

Leonora left for the mine soon after the dray pulled out of sight. She knew Alex would be furious, but her fury was greater, a trail of white light speeding over gunpowder, pulsing at the end of each nerve. "Let him be angry!" she hissed under her breath. How dare he let workers, *his* workers, suffer and die, leave children orphaned. How dare he not bring every doctor in Western Australia to help these people. "Let him be angry," she dared. "Just let him try."

In the trunk of the Ford she had as many canisters of freshwater as could fit, a basket of clean rags, several bowls of lemons and oranges and a few vials of opiates. In the passenger seat she packed several canteens of water for herself and some fruit and sandwiches along with a few changes of clothes, not knowing how long she intended to stay. She left Clare a list of house instructions, only mentioning she was going to visit Alex for a few days.

The route needed no map; there was only one road. Every hour or so, a ragged hand-painted sign would point to an offshoot listing the towns east or west. The black car blazed with trapped heat and the following sun. Leonora cracked the window halfway—an even battle between the scourge of dust and stale heat.

Along the way, the smell of soot and fire tinted the air. Rows of scarred and hacked forest dotted the land on either side. Thousands of low-cut stumps spread as far as the eye could bear them—ugly pustules that oozed with hard, weepy sap. And here the maimed land was laid to waste. The birds had gone, the shade nonexistent along the blistered ground. There was a deep grief to this land, almost human in its intensity.

Leonora's hands darkened the steering wheel's brown leather to black with wet palms. She took turns removing one stiff hand at a time from the wheel and stretched out her fingers in an attempt to return circulation to the joints. Blue smoke twirled upward into sight. A sharp acridity hardened the air. She peeked at the hood of the car to make sure the engine wasn't on fire. Then wafts of sewage, subtle at first, grew and swelled like rotten eggs and masked the burning iron. She tucked her nose in her shoulder and coughed into her sleeve. In the radius of the stench the camp came into view: rows of scraggly tents; shacks of canvas and hessian, metal scrap heaps tied into form with green hide and stringy bark.

Leonora slowed the car, stared at the camp through the side window. The lines were quiet. No one seemed sick. Litter was at a minimum. Leonora had pictured the camp akin to a battlefield, strewn with dead bodies and the cries of the sick. But for the smell, the camp was clean, orderly, peaceful. The men were most likely at work, the children in school. Perhaps she had judged too quickly; perhaps a doctor had been sent after all.

Leonora pulled off the road and set the brake, the engine rattling over the silence. She leaned back in her seat, stretched out her numb legs. Smoke wafted from some of the stovepipes jutting from the tent roofs. Occasionally, a person was visible through a window or open door. A thin dog barked from a tied stake. A sudden blockage of wind prickled Leonora's neck. A shadow slid cold across the inside of the car. A man stared at her through the glass, tapped upon the window with a knuckle as if she were asleep. "You lost?" The man sounded Eastern European, but he spoke clearly. He was stocky and small but had full, honest eyes.

Leonora opened the door and stepped out. "I'm looking for the head office," she ventured, not sure what the building was called. "For the mine management."

The man pointed to an empty spot in the distance. "Past the camp. You'll see building on left." He started to shake his head, looked like he wanted to say words that his mouth wouldn't allow. "You go. Not good here. Typhoid." The man said the word almost as a test, not sure if she knew the disease was in the camp.

"I know."

"You nurse?"

"No."

The man looked disappointed. He took off his hat and twisted it in his strong hands. "My baby ill. Don't know if it's the typhoid. My middle one, too." Heavy, unbridled tears wet his cheeks.

Tears in a woman were hard to witness, but to see a man weep so openly cracked into Leonora's heart. "Where do you live?"

He couldn't speak, just breathed hard through his nose as he showed her a building that was half tent and half iron, supported haphazardly with chicken wire.

The man entered the iron part of the structure and Leonora followed. A baby, red and naked, cried from a small wooden bed. A young boy of maybe eight rocked the baby listlessly with his foot. A woman sat on the floor next to him cradling a thin, frail girl in her arms. They all looked at the stranger without interest, stared right through her.

Leonora stooped and picked up the baby in her arms, so light he might have been hollow. His skin burned against her hands. "Please get the water from my trunk and fill up a basin with it," she ordered, fighting hard to steady her voice. As she looked at the baby's bloated belly, she saw the small, flat red rash of typhoid, as unmistakable as the blackness of gangrene. Leonora held the baby against her chest, rocked him softly, looked at the mother who stared at the corner, perhaps looking to a future that held no hope or a past that had once relished it.

The man brought the basin and Leonora submerged the baby into the water up to his neck. He was too weak to complain beyond a dry wail that was getting quieter by the minute. Leonora met the man's eyes and she opened her mouth to speak, but her confidence gave in and she looked at the floor.

"He's dying, isn't he?"

She nodded. His voice cracked. "Is there nothing to do?"

"I can give him something so he'll rest." A tear escaped and fell down her cheek. "He'll go peacefully. I promise." The man nodded and left the house; the wife held the dark corner tight within her focus and did not blink.

Hours passed. Daylight evaporated. Leonora moved from one tent to another, from one bedside to the next. Men and women of various appearances and accents blurred into a nightmarish web of indistinction. Temperaments that raged with anger and helplessness to untethered grief to silent despair called her forth and left her haggard. So many of them—all weak, all thin—some capering with hallucinations, others in obvious pain. But it was the children who made her mind scream, the little lives that had barely begun, who made her want to pull her hair out, even as she worked calmly by their sides, shedding no more tears, offering no signs of the horror that nearly broke her in two. And with each human cry, she shoved her own emotions, her own grief, farther and farther into her stomach.

Leonora brought nothing to this camp. She could offer no more comfort than a fresh, unsickened face who cared enough to be there. She offered clean water and cloths to feverish bodies and opiates to the dying but could not cure any of them. Only God would choose who would live and who would not, who would be the orphans and who would be the widows.

She did not know what time it was when her medicine vials lay empty and her hands were wrinkled and white, poached from the constant dunking in water. All she knew was the camp was deadly quiet and the moon was tall in the sky. No one walked her to the car when she finally left. She couldn't remember a face or a name of anyone she had met.

Her muscles ached as she sat onto the cool leather of the car, but she was wide awake with adrenaline. Leonora gripped the steering wheel but did not put the key in the ignition. For several minutes, she sat there, quietly numb, staring into the silent night. Her hands vibrated on the wheel and the shaking climbed through her arms and down her torso as she broke into violent sobs. All the grief and helplessness she had buried while at the bedsides erupted now. She laid her head on the wheel and pounded the frame with her fists, moaning, until the pain spent itself and made room for what lay immediately below the surface. As the last of the tears dried on her face, the new emotion surged. Anger. Raw and hateful. And a name—Alex. Leonora turned the key in the ignition and the engine, now cool, took with the first try.

With her body weak from fatigue and hunger and helplessness, Leonora sped the car past the sleeping tents to the steel factory and the open pit ringed with lights in the distance, glowing like a chasm to Hell. She parked in front of the neatly bricked manager's wing, barely waiting until the engine idled before storming up the steps and into the empty secretary's office. From outside Alex's door came the smell of cigar smoke and the muffled sounds of men talking, an occasional laugh varying the pitch. It didn't matter Alex wasn't alone—shame on them all.

Without hesitation, Leonora pushed the door open. Fat brown cigars simmered in mid-puff. Tumblers of alcohol raised to lips froze. Alex sat behind his desk, his legs crossed languidly at the ankles. Two men sat in front of him, reclining easily on thick leather wing chairs. And they all stared at her with open mouths and eyes. Had Leonora been an apparition, their faces could not have been more stunned.

Alex recovered first, dropping his legs to the floor and standing like a rod. "What are you doing here?" he spluttered.

She ignored the question, ignored the eyes of the men staring. The anger throbbed her temples, burned her throat. "Why aren't you helping the people in the camp?"

Confusion angled his face toward the floor. "Camp? What camp?" He shook his head. His lower lip hung forward with growing frustration. "What the hell are you talking about?"

"The camp, Alex!" Her voice shattered the quiet. The two men stiffened in their chairs. "The one not five miles from here! The one that houses your precious miners. The one that has typhoid running all through it!"

"That's what this is about?" He put his fists on the edge of the desk and made a short laugh before looking at her with eyes stretched in amazement. His voice started calmly but rose with each word. "You drove all the way out here to tell me about the *fucking camp?*"

Leonora took a step forward, her eyes stinging from lack of sleep. "I just spent the whole day there. People are dying, Alex! There are children too weak to stand, for God's sake. Children who won't make it to the morning!" She glared at the men in the room, her eyes boring into them until they shifted. "Why hasn't a doctor been sent to help them?"

The first man on the right cleared his throat. "I'm Dr. Middleton." His face scrunched with concern, but his voice was smug. "It's unfortunate. We have cases of typhoid here in management as well. Have to keep the miners quarantined." He held out his hands innocently. "I wish there were more I could do, but"—he clicked his teeth—"my hands are full with the men here."

"Yes, I can see that," she said with pointed focus at his drink.

Dr. Middleton straightened in his seat, the smile erased. He addressed Alex: "It's getting late. I should turn in." He nodded stiffly at Leonora but did not meet the eyes that burned into him. "Perhaps we can meet again under more pleasurable circumstances, Mrs. Harrington." The other man rose quickly, followed the doctor out with his tail tucked between his legs.

The door closed. The silence swung like a pounding hammer. Alex did not waver from his place at the desk. His head was low; his fingers tapped the polished wood with a dull beat. Leonora watched the top of his dark hair and hated every strand. "You need to bring a doctor—"

"Not another word," Alex seethed between his teeth. He pulled his head up and stabbed at her with cold, hard eyes. "*Not another word!*"

For once, she was not afraid and her throat was not closed under his stomping tone. Her body flushed with rage as every nerve readied for battle. "You bring in a doctor to care for those people or I will!"

Alex slammed his palm against the desk, clinking the empty tumblers at its edge. "My concern is the mine, Leonora, not a bunch of filthy foreigners who don't have the sense not to shit where they eat! I need every man that is healthy underground and that's where Dr. Middleton's attention needs to be and will stay! In case you haven't noticed, there's a war on. The army needs every ounce of ore we can send out."

A quick, bitter laugh left her lips. "Oh, so you're suddenly a patriot now?" She scoffed, "Says the man who fled the draft!"

Alex rushed at her, grabbed her by the wrists, his lips curled above his teeth. "How dare you, you spoiled little wench!" His hand rose to strike her.

"That's it, Alex! Hit me. That's what cowards do!" she goaded. "How the men will admire you then! Alexander Harrington, who beats women and lets children die like pigs!"

Slowly, with teeth gritted between clenched jaws, Alex lowered his arm and pushed away her wrists. She stood before him unyielding, her voice steady. "You bring in a doctor to work the camp or I'll wire my uncle about what's happening. He would never put a piece of iron, or a pound of gold for that matter, above a human life."

Alex slumped behind his desk, the fight drained. "I'll talk to Dr. Middleton."

"He needs to start tomorrow."

"That's impossible."

"Then I'll stay at the camp until he comes."

Alex studied her as if she had a row of playing cards fanned before her face. He would not call her bluff. "All right. I'll bring a doctor in from Kalgoorlie. Dr. Middleton will work the camp till he comes. But only until the fever is contained."

Leonora breathed for the first time since she left the camp. Her hunched shoulders lowered from her ears. As she did, her feet felt stuck in cement and a wave of light-headedness reminded her that she had not eaten or drunk anything since the morning.

Alex watched her, the coldness strangely gone from his face. "What's happened to you, Leonora?" For a rare instant, his face was open, no arrogance dictating its expression. "What's happened to the shy, quiet woman I used to kiss under the oak trees?" But just as quickly as sincerity had entered, it was gone, the ever-present criticism forcing through any goodness, accusing. "You've changed."

But she hadn't changed, only emerged from hibernation. Australia was her spring and she would never retreat again.

Alex picked up a ledger and opened it, leafed absently through its pages. "You're filthy. There's a bath in the quarters." He picked up a pen and started writing. "I can't talk to you anymore tonight. Get out of my face."

* * *

They left Coolgardie at dawn, without breakfast or tea. Leonora waited in the idling car for nearly thirty minutes, the seat vibrating with the restless engine, while Alex left details with the managers. She stared out the front window, still caked on the edges with dirt and smashed flies, and watched the sun rise above the land and pluck away the shadows. And as the sun rose so did the men and they walked with the pull of the rays over the ridge, one by one emerging out of the dusk, miners drawn to the light, following it, before blasting down into darkness.

Alex returned to the car, slammed the door. His shirt had not been changed from last night and opened to the top of his chest, the collar wide and loose. He smoked and his eyes were red; he had not come to bed. Where and if he had slept she couldn't have cared less.

Alex thrust the car forward, pressing hard on the gas, and sped through the lines of walking miners, sending dust into their backward glances. He kept his head leaned back, cocked to the side, the cigarette chewed and dangling from the side of his mouth, and she hated him.

They drove through the morning traffic of Coolgardie, past the railway lines waiting for activity, the empty gondola cars open and hungry for minerals. They drove past the wood lines, past the miner tents and humpies she had visited the night before. But the misery and suffering did not show in the brightened day, the closed flaps masking the nightmare of the fever. Then, soon, the tents disappeared, the land opened and the sun beat upon the airless car.

Leonora leaned her head against the window, the glass cool against her skin while her back stuck to the seat. She watched the dots of trees rush past, watched the flat red land and the bundles of grass— sharp and silvered stubble bristling an ancient land. Her land.

But she was choking quietly, suffocating in her land and her air. She had seen the weight of typhoid and its ravages, saw the hopelessness that it spread, the despair that it fed. And as her forehead rested against the window glass, she felt her own plague, not of the body but of the spirit. The sickness had set in, had been brewing maybe her whole life.

Dimly, she raised her eyes to the landscape and caught her slight reflection—clear skin and pink cheeks, lips that were not cracked with thirst, a face that was not gaunt with hunger. Within, she breathed with lungs that did not wheeze. And yet the malady was there deep and dull, shrinking her and killing her slowly.

Leave him! The voice rang from her cells. Her eyes widened and she stilled her breath. *Leave him.* The words thumped in her head and in her chest, warmed her stomach with the bouncing words. *I can leave him.* She looked at Alex's profile and her spine grew hard as steel with decision. *I will leave him.*

CHAPTER 52

Ghan's body was tired and aged, so when the bone-numbing fatigue had hit it seemed only an extension of a restless night's sleep or days of poor appetite. Upon his pack Ghan lay shivering, reached for clothes and cardboard and food tins, anything to cover his body and bring some warmth. But the articles only felt heavier and colder and his bones were raw with the chill. Ghan wrapped his arms into himself, his head twitching with spasms. His insides ached as if bruised, all the organs cramped and twisted.

In and out of sleep Ghan flitted, through light and dark. When he woke in darkness, he thought he was in the pit and he called out for light, panicked that they had forgotten him down below the earth and closed up the shaft. The terror of the dark bit at him like fire ants and he wanted to run and thrashed within his tent. Then the light came and broiled the outside of his skin while the inside was still ice. Cold sweat leaked from every pore, soaking his blanket, then freezing him, making him thirst so badly until it was the only thought left in his head—water. Ghan's bag had long been sucked dry, more spilling over his chin than landing in his mouth. His mouth felt swollen and seemed filled with dirty, unplucked cotton that tasted of oil. In the dawn hours Ghan would crawl out and lick the tent for moisture. He would have drunk from a mud puddle or a toilet if one had been near.

The unending thirst brought the shadows to life. Black spots on the tent morphed to spiders, sometimes to rotten flowers with petals dropping from the sky. Ghan would bat at them in his delirium as they turned back to spiders right before they landed on his face.

This was how he was to die, he realized through pinholes of lucidity. *Let it come quick*, was all he asked. *Just make the thirst end. Just make the spiders go away.* And he shook and waited for he did not know how long.

And then the angel came. She entered the flaps of the tent, her face awash in the halo of glow that covered her bent figure—beautiful, pale. The angel put a cool cloth on his head, wiped his face, her eyes chasing away the spiders, the broken roses. She brought heaven to his lips. Cool, wet heaven that she held to his mouth, the water trickling through his swollen throat. His lips never closed and she never stopped refreshing them, pouring and pouring, cup after cup. She squeezed lemon juice into his mouth.

Ghan watched her appear and reappear as his eyelids, as heavy as bricks, slid shut and opened slower and slower. Through his slits, he saw her lantern, saw for a moment the source of the halo. Perhaps she was only half angel; perhaps he was only half-dead. Regardless, she stayed with him for minutes or for months, so hard to tell.

When the morning sun filtered through the holes of the tent he was too weak to move, but he was not dead. Ghan knew in that moment that he had beat death yet again. He couldn't move, was still very sick, but he would live, and this brought even more weariness.

During the day, the fever broke, melted the chill with fire. His body had faded thin and sallow; his pants slid down his hips. He ate—a slice of lemon left from the angel; a few sardines. His body lurched with the sudden tastes, but once the initial shock passed, his stomach growled for more. It wasn't that the strength returned but rather that the weakness unclenched its fist.

The night brought sleep without blankets. He woke hungry. The sound of pots upon predawn fires entered from outside the tent and carried a great heaviness. For he needed to work. Ghan was not well, but he was not dying, and so the pit waited for him, called to him like the gallows to a sentenced man. It was not his time to rest. And the sadness hung because he knew he lived just to breathe and he worked just to eat and it was a hard, sad and tired way to exist.

Ghan stumbled out of the tent to find Whistler. The earth hung tired as his flesh and nothing entered without effort: smoke rose slow, smells were weak and the tents were dirty and still. He didn't know how long he had been sick. But the world still spun and people still moved and life still went on as if he had slept one night.

In his tent, Whistler lay on his bedroll, still asleep. Ghan limped over to wake him, jostled the man's shoulder. But the flesh did not give under his touch, the body hard as stone. A slow melancholy dripped into Ghan's bones as he gently forced the rigid body onto its back. Whistler's face was pale blue, his eyes open and distant, his mouth open and dry, the stiffness of death days old.

Ghan covered the man's inanimate face with the blanket and stood up, bending his neck against the low ceiling. He scanned the tent. The coroner would have it burned. Ghan inched to the back, dug through the pile of food and underwear until he found the can. He plucked the top and took out the tied sock, looked at it hard, squeezed the coins in the bottom and nodded, shoved it into his pocket. He took one more look at the blanket, the outline of his friend, and he found a sliver of consolation. The man's bones wouldn't hurt him now. He'd be warm in Heaven with his wife; or, if Heaven didn't exist, he'd be in the quiet place of death. Either way, Whistler's bones didn't hurt him anymore. His fingers wouldn't twist over rocks; work and rain wouldn't cripple his balled knuckles. After a long, hard life, Whistler could rest. Ghan looked at the body longingly. Fatigue drained him, made the air gray and his body limp.

"Rest easy, mate." Ghan delivered his three-word eulogy and left the tent, limped through the aisles of the Italian shacks and humpies. Mrs. Riccioli stood over her fire, a ragged black shawl wrapped around her shoulders. She saw Ghan and smiled, her eyes still puffy with sleep. "Good a mornin', Ghan. You wanna some coffee?"

Ghan shook his head and said slowly, "Whistler passed on."

"The typhoid." It wasn't a question. The fever was plucking men by the day.

Ghan pulled out the old wool sock and handed it to her. "He wanted this t'go to the widows' fund."

The woman's face fell and a deep frown tipped her mouth as she took the money. "He was a good man."

Ghan nodded and turned away, but she grabbed his arm and said softly, "You a gooda man, too."

CHAPTER 53

Her mind was set, the action clear, as Leonora sat across from Alex at the breakfast table. Her nerves, for once, were stable with decision.

Meredith brought the scones, the jars of jam, refilled their tea, returned to the kitchen. Alex read the newspaper, his ankle resting easily on the knee of his other leg. The slight sipping of tea and the clink of china rose from the table. The grandfather clock in the sitting room clicked and the pendulum swung—*tick, tock, tick, tock*.

"I want a divorce."

Alex looked past the paper blankly. "What did you say?"

"I want a divorce," Leonora repeated, her voice calm and firm.

He continued to stare at her blankly. Neither moved; neither blinked.

Slowly, the corners of Alex's mouth lifted and he chuckled. He looked up at the ceiling and laughed louder as if hearing a good joke. "A divorce?" he chided. He picked the paper back up, shook it straight and chuckled into his cheeks. "A divorce, she says."

"It's not a joke, Alex."

"Yes it is." He laughed. "Quite a good one."

Leonora sat quietly and waited. Her tea rested untouched. She breathed without nerves, slowly in and out so her chest barely rose. And she waited.

Alex's eyes moved up and down the paper, darkening without focus. His lips tightened. "Is this about the blasted camp again?"

"No, it's everything. I'm leaving you, Alex."

His nostrils flared. "You're too stupid to even know what you're saying!" he growled. "Divorce! By God, Leonora, I won't have you throwing around a word you don't even know the meaning of!"

"Alex," she said slowly, her eyes sharp with clarity. "I want a divorce."

"Enough of this nonsense!" He slammed the paper onto the table, sloshing tea over the saucers, any trace of amusement stamped out. "The answer's no!"

"It wasn't a question."

"No?" he mocked. "Well, I have some for you, darling. Where do you plan to go? Back to America? Back to the loving arms of your aunt and uncle? Or, let me guess, you're planning to stay here in Australia, or maybe run off to Paris and get a nice view over the Seine?" He leaned forward, snarled, "I've got news for you, *darling:* you haven't got a penny to your name."

"I'll get a job."

"Huh! There's only one profession that could use you and you're not alive enough under the bedsheets for a repeat customer!"

She pulled all her nerves to fight the anger. "Then I'll write my uncle for the money."

"You will do nothing of the sort!" Alex pounded his fist on the table. "You won't mention a word of this absurdity to anyone, least of all your uncle."

She looked at her hands folded in her lap and a calm rose. For there was nothing Alex could say, nothing he could threaten, that would change her mind. "Why, Alex?" she asked with quiet bewilderment. "Why won't you let me go? I know you aren't faithful. It seems all I do is bring you anger and frustration. I'd think you would be glad for a divorce."

A line of hurt pride or hurt heart tightened across his jaw. "You belong here, Leonora. With me." True pain sagged his features for a moment before they turned fierce again. "Besides, I'm not going to ruin my name or your uncle's by bringing the shame of divorce to it. That's final." He picked up the paper and blocked his face.

"I'm sorry, Alex." Leonora sighed and stood straight from the table. "But my mind is made up. I'm going to meet with an attorney this week and sign the papers. You can have the money from my uncle's estate. I don't want it. I don't want any part of it."

Alex was silent behind the paper and she waited for the next spurt of anger, but after several minutes his voice came out smooth. "So, I was wrong, then? I guess you have thought this through."

"Yes."

He folded the newspaper in half, pressed the crease tight with his fingers, then placed it on the table in a neat rectangle. He stroked the paper gently with his hand. "So, that's it then." He looked up at her. "Your mind's made up. It's over."

Leonora was stunned by the sudden shift. "Yes," she said gently. "It is. I'm sorry, Alex."

"All right." Alex shrugged his shoulders, sighed with defeat. "I'll give you the divorce."

Her mouth fell open and she waited for more, waited for more anger, more insults or struggle. When nothing came, she whispered, "Thank you, Alex."

Leonora moved toward the stairs, the freedom shining ahead like a radiant beacon. Freedom. For the first time in her life, freedom.

"It really is a pity, though," Alex's voice boomed from the table, heavy with concern. "All those poor children."

Leonora stopped in mid-step, her hand cold on the banister.

"It's tough to say who takes it harder," he continued, "the children or their mothers."

Leonora turned. Alex's back was to her, his elbow raised as he sipped his tea.

"Of course, they'll all get over it sooner or later. At least at the orphanage, they'll be with their own kind. Not sure what they'll do with that one with the white eye, though. You know who I mean, don't you? The retarded one? Well, I suppose there are institutions for those types. Poor girl will probably never see the light of day again."

Leonora's chest stung. "What are you talking about, Alex?"

"I'm talking about the Aborigines, of course." Alex spun in his chair, shook his head sadly. "Of course, once you're gone, there is no way they can continue to live here. In fact, I should probably call the Deacon to set up their removal. Better get it done with now."

Leonora's blood turned to ice and her hands went numb, her throat tightening with the noose. Alex continued to ponder, looked at the ceiling. "Once the children are gone, we'll have to disperse the rest of them. The men will be too lost in their grief to work, could even cause trouble. Sheriff will have to bring some extra men in to evict them. Could get ugly. Police don't care for the blacks, you know." His tongue clicked behind his teeth. "I'm sure it would be their pleasure to pluck a few off."

"You can't be that cruel," she croaked.

"Me?" He covered his heart, feigning hurt. "My hands are tied, darling. You're the one choosing this, not me." Alex turned back to his tea. "Such a shame. I don't know how you'll be able to live with the guilt."

Leonora's limbs began to shake and she clutched the banister with a white hand. "I won't let you do it." Her voice rose even as tears burned the corners of her eyes.

He slapped his knee and laughed. "And how do you plan to do that, darling?"

"The m-m-men," she stuttered, "the roustabouts, the managers, will stop it."

Alex reached into his jacket and pulled out the revolver, rubbed the bright silver, peeked with one eye into the barrel. "Doubt they're that stupid."

Leonora remembered the day he pointed that gun at his prized thoroughbred. And she knew, knew down to her marrow, what Alex would do if confronted. The freedom left, disintegrated into the mist of hate and cruelty. "I'll stay," she murmured.

Alex held a mocking hand around his ear. "What's that?"

She swallowed and closed her eyes. "I said, I'll stay."

Alex leaned in, scrunched his forehead. "Still can't hear you."

The tears clawed at her throat and she ate them one at a time, then answered loud and broken, "I said . . . I'll stay."

"I knew you'd come around." He clapped his hands merrily. "Just a lovers' spat then? You really shouldn't take things so seriously, my dear. Throwing around such a nasty word like 'divorce' is in such poor taste—a married woman's tantrum. *Tsk-tsk.*"

Alex stood up and strode triumphantly to her side. He kissed her drawn cheek, his lips curled in a satisfied smirk. "Don't worry, darling. I forgive you."

James worked on the shutter that hung crooked on the back of the barn. A presence disturbed and tilted the air behind him. He turned around, hammer still raised, a nail poking out between his teeth when he saw her. Leonora's face was pale and streaked with tears.

James spit out the nail and lowered the hammer to the ground. "What's wrong, Leo?"

"Take me somewhere," she whimpered. "Anywhere. Please!" she cried just above a whisper. "Just take me away from here."

James watched her face for only a moment, felt the weight of her pain in his chest just for a moment, before he went to the barn and rode out on his horse. He reached a hand down and pulled Leonora up behind him. Her small, soft fingers gripped his hips and burned through his shirt. James kicked the horse and took off past the barn, past the riding ring off to the eastern paddocks. The house disappeared quickly, only the rabbit-proof fence stretched beside them.

A great heat spread through his body. Heat from the sun above, heat from the horse below and then the white heat that burned behind him and shot down his legs as hers lined his, the heat of her breath at his neck. And then there was the red heat of seeing her pain, of wanting to crush whatever had caused it.

They rode in silence for several miles until they entered an area of tall grass that reached to the horse's belly and bent against their feet. Beyond the grass grew the white ghost gums whose tilting bony limbs hung over a large, kidney-shaped pond. James pulled the horse to a stop and Leonora jumped down and walked to the edge of the water, so still it reflected nearly black with shade. She sat on a patch of soft grass, pulled her arms around her knees and stared straight.

James tied the horse, then slowly sat down next to Leonora. He looked past the trees and squinted at the sun filtered between their tiny leaves. A cockatoo shuffled down a limb and then back in a side-step dance. The silence pumped oxygen to the red fire and James clenched his fists under folded arms. "Did he hurt you?"

Leonora bit her lip and shook her head, her eyes glistening with tears. It took her a long while to answer. "No."

James stretched his fingers, let the blood run through the joints again. "Tell me what happened."

Her lips parted, the words of Alex's threat ready to spill to the only ears that would care. But that was the problem. James would care. He would step in, confront Alex. The silver of Alex's gun burned in her memory.

James leaned closer and repeated, "Don't you want to tell me what's wrong, Leo?"

Her chin crumpled. "No." The word was more breath than voice. Then she twisted her body away from him, her spine bent forward like a willow, and sobbed in long, painful waves. Her body wracked as she tried to muffle the cries.

James reached for her before he knew he was going to and pulled her to his chest. The sound of her sadness released and she buried her head under his chin. Her fingers grabbed the seam of his shirt and squeezed it and he held her shoulders tighter. Silken hair rubbed against his neck and he closed his eyes. Her tears wet his shirt, warmed his chest. Each cry ripped into him and he held the shaking shoulders with spread fingers.

Slowly, the sobbing abated and her breathing calmed. Leonora pulled away from him, looked up at his face as if she hadn't seen him before and slid from his arms. Her face was pink with streaked tears and her eyes were wet and shone big and green and reflected the land around them. Leonora rubbed her palms against her cheeks, turned away. "I'm sorry."

Inhaling with effort, she glanced at him. "You must think I'm ridiculous. Crying out here like a child." She made a poor attempt at a smile. "I shouldn't have dragged you away from your work. I'm sorry." Leonora looked at the horse and sniffled. "I'm all right now. The men are probably waiting for you."

His arms were cold without her. And, as if settling in for a long stay, he lay on his side, propped up on an elbow and fiddled with the grass. "As pretty as the stockmen are"—he grinned—"I prefer my present company."

Leonora smiled shyly and her face regained some of its original color. For a moment, their eyes met and a wave of heat crept through his body as her pure and sweet beauty nearly stopped his breath. He turned his gaze to the wide grass. "What happened, Leo?"

A long exhale blew from her mouth and the sadness returned. She shook her head. "Sometimes it feels like there's no . . . I don't know . . . like there's no goodness in the world. Like everyone's gone mad." Her forehead wrinkled and her eyes grew lost. "I keep looking for it. Reach for it. And then it's gone, falls through my fingers." She laughed then. "I'm not making any sense, am I?"

James plucked a blade of grass, rubbed the textured ribbing of the veins. "Yes, you are."

Leonora bent her head down to rest on her folded arms and looked sideways at him, her face open and searching.

"What?" he asked with narrowed eyes.

"Except for you." A sincere amazement held her face. "You've always been good."

An image of Shamus bleeding at his feet sliced through his thoughts. "A lot of time has passed, Leo." His face darkened. "I might not be as good as you give me credit for."

Her hand reached and settled on his, the warmth of her palm spreading to his wrist. James dropped the blade of grass. "If there is one truth in this world," she said strong and clear, "it's that you are a good man."

James stared at the smooth, perfect hand on top of his large one. The shiny, ovaled nails touched his skin gingerly. A small white line ran along her index finger. He tried to focus on it, on anything besides the hot blood pumping under her touch. "How did you get that scar on your finger?" he asked with effort.

She snatched her hand, tucked it into the folds of her arms. Her body rocked.

"I didn't mean to upset you, Leo." James tried to read her face. "It's hardly noticeable. Really. I just never saw it before."

Slowly, she untucked her hand and stared at the scar, traced the outline of it with her nail. Then her fingers floated to her throat, fumbled with the collar, found the first button, played with it for a minute and then unclasped it. Nimbly, her fingers slid to the next button and plucked it open. She stared ahead as she moved down the line.

James swallowed. He watched the skin appear between the open fabric: the pale, pink skin of her neck; the crevice at the base of her throat that glistened lightly; the beginning of a crease that would lead to her breasts. He knew he should turn away, but his attention stuck as he watched her fingers, her skin, helplessly.

Leonora reached inside her dress and pulled out a necklace. She caressed the chain and inched down to the small pendent. Then she pulled it forward and held it out.

He tore his eyes from her skin and picked up the pendent. The gold chain was as thin as thread and led down to a white oval stone. James clicked his teeth. "Hate to disappoint you, but I think your jeweler sold you a bum gem."

Leonora watched his face intently, almost urgently. "Don't you recognize it?"

He turned his focus to the simple rock again and then everything shifted and his whole body softened. "You kept it?" he asked.

She nodded happily, her eyes sparkling. "I never forgot you, James." Then she corrected herself, "How *good* you are."

James returned the chain to her dress. His finger touched the skin below her throat and slid down the warm flesh as he let the chain drop from his hand. Her breathing quickened with the touch and her eyes flitted away.

Leonora picked up the stone and looked at it once more. "After I was adopted," she began, "the Fairfields burned everything I had— my suitcase, my clothes, even my shoes. I didn't have much. But this . . ." She dangled the stone and her face fell with emotion. "This stone meant more to me than anything in the world."

She tucked the necklace into the dress. "As soon as I got the chance, I dug through the hot ashes. The nest and feathers burned up, but I found the stone. That's how I got the scar." Her face was timid. "The jeweler thought I was crazy when I wanted to set it in gold."

They sat quietly together, looking out over the water, their faces comfortable with memories. James stood up. "Wait here. I want to show you something."

He went to the saddlebag of his horse, pulled out a book. He looked at the cover for a moment and then handed it to her.

She tilted her head skeptically. "You're trying to convert me now?"

"Open it."

She opened the worn, dented Bible and stared at the handwriting, cocked her head.

"It's my mother's," he said cautiously. "Her diary."

Leonora's mouth fell open. "That's why you carried it with you all the time. And here I thought you were planning to join the priesthood."

James laughed. Then he stilled and looked at the book sitting easily and naturally in her hands, felt good that she held it. "You're the first person I ever showed it to."

Leonora closed the book, rubbed her hand over the cover tenderly, noticed the charred edges, decided to not ask about the source. She handed it back to him. "Thanks for trusting me."

The sun, now bright pink, waved from the treetops as its descent began. The strong late-afternoon rays reflected off the ghost gums, turning the white bark to a canvas splashed with orange and pink. The water only held light; the leaves and limbs and sky submerged within the painted lines. As the height of the sky turned from orange to pink to lilac, Leonora knew the last moments of her time with James ticked away, the sun pulling her mood back down. Slowly, she turned to James and watched his profile—his brown hair trimmed short and neat around his ear and edged straight at his neck; the long, strong throat and the wide shoulders that curved down to his muscular arms. He turned to meet her gaze.

"I should be getting back," she said quietly.

"You don't have to, Leo," he said just above a whisper, his eyes steady and serious. "Not if you don't want to."

She nodded and stood from the ground, his eyes tracking her movements. "Yes, I do."

James rose and followed her to the horse. Leonora leaned her back against the soft leather of the saddle and placed her head against the mare's neck, enjoying the warmth. James moved closer and patted the horse's nose. The mare nestled affectionately against his palm.

James adjusted the horse's bridle. The space between Leonora's body and his vibrated, throbbed. She gazed at his face while he worked, the lines and features, the way his eyes held everything in them until they were full and deep. He looked at her then and let his hands fall idle by his sides. A silent urgency grew to his face and made her heart leap in her chest. His eyes were taking her in, absorbing every ounce of her, and she couldn't turn away. He looked past her for a moment, gave a measured exhale and slowly leaned toward her.

Leonora's breath caught—pure feeling wiped away any thoughts. In an instant, she leaned in and met his body, raised her face to his. But the thought came too slow, the realization that he was only returning the book to the saddlebag, was too far tucked in the peripheral to compete and it was too late to stop. Leonora placed her lips softly and hungrily against his just as the thought caught up with icy clarity—he wasn't going to kiss her. And his lips were straight and unmoving below hers, stiff and unresponsive.

Her body chilled, mortified, the embarrassment wild and sharp. Leonora's lips opened, fell back from his in horror. Her eyes clamped shut as she pulled back, prayed she'd disappear. "Oh, my God," she choked. She covered her face with her hands. Her stomach and legs weak from shame. "I'm so sorry!" she gasped. "I'm such a fool. I thought . . ."

"Look at me, Leo," he ordered.

"No. No. Oh, God." She shook her head frantically. "You must hate me!"

He grabbed her wrists and pried them from her face. "Look at me, Leo!"

In humble defeat, she unglued her eyelids, hoping to disappear before she saw his face twisted in disgust. But his face held no disgust, only longing. And then he was kissing her. His lips full and alive, warm and pressing.

James released the grip on her wrist and brought his hands to her face, holding her skin with his fingertips and cradling her jaw in his palms. Her skin faded into his skin, her lips absorbed into his lips and the world fell into another place far away from where they stood. She reached her arms around the broad back and slid her hands down the length of his spine. And the breathing grew and the movement of their lips quickened. Falling. *Falling.* She drifted into his body and flowed into the warmth of his curve and her body grew limp, but his strong arm was unyielding around her waist and held her to him, kept her from falling.

Panting replaced breathing. His lips were in her hair, at her neck, in the collar of her dress. And she kissed his eyes and his temples and his cheeks, clutched his hips with clawed fingers. His strong thighs pressed against her and the horse shifted behind her back and moved forward. Leonora stumbled and the kiss broke in two. Through the haze, the outer world sorted its particles, solidified and settled. The land, the sun, the air, rushed in too quickly.

"I should g-g-go," she stammered, disoriented.

James blinked, then nodded. She turned to the only horse, then turned back to James with silent questioning. "Take her," he whispered.

"It's a long walk," she breathed.

"Just take her." James awoke from his stupor, placed his hand on the saddle. "Leo . . ."

Leonora would not look at him but pleaded hoarsely, "I've got to go." His gaze heated her back as she kicked the horse to a gallop.

As the wind whipped across Leonora's skin her mind held on to the look of his face, her fingers could still feel the tight knit fabric of his shirt, her back still burned with the pressure of his arms laced around her body. Nerves mixed with heat and anxiety swirled and burned her stomach. And then the horse ring rose into view and the metal roof of the homestead peeked over the horizon as if only a minute had passed in riding. The windows of the big house were now lit and bright against the twilight.

Leonora rushed to put the horse in the barn, then held the dress above her knees as she bounded up the steps to the verandah and entered the house quietly. Alex's office door was closed, a stream of light leaked from the bottom and she sighed with relief. As she reached the bottom of the staircase she winced at the sound of the door opened from the hall.

"There you are!" Alex leaned against the door, his arms folded at his chest. "I was getting worried. Thought I'd have to send out a search party."

"Why?" she asked coldly. "You know I'm not going anywhere."

"True." He turned back to his office. "Very true. Good night, darling. Sleep well."

Leonora leaned over the steps of the verandah and clipped roses into her basket, cringed at the sound of the horses returning from the hunt. Alex rode up first, a dead kangaroo dragging behind the horse, a trail of blood drying in the matching red dust. Behind him rode Russell, who held the reins of the third horse, its saddle empty. Alex dismounted, looking refreshed and full of spirit. "Ah, nothing like a good hunt to get the blood pumping." He untied the kangaroo legs from the ropes and dropped it to the ground, its lifeless body landing with a dusty thud. "See the size of this boomer! Kicking to the very end."

Leonora turned away in disgust.

"There's something about being out in nature, man against beast." Alex spoke and sniffed at the air, puffed out his chest. "Seeing the bewilderment, the fear, in the animal's eye before," and he mimicked holding a rifle, focusing on the target, then pulling the trigger, "Bang!" He watched her carefully, each flinch of her jaw bringing a great enjoyment to his face.

Leonora turned back to the roses. Alex put one boot on the step below her. He reached into her basket and took a rose, smelled it deeply.

"Where is the black fellow that went with you?" she asked flatly.

Alex looked at the rose in puzzlement, spun it between his fingers. "Black fellow?" He squinted his eyes for the memory. "Black fellow?"

Russell shuffled his feet and laughed, pulled the empty horse closer.

"Oh yes! Allambee. That was his name, wasn't it?"

The roustabout snickered again and shrugged his shoulders.

"Allambee, yes. I remember now. Said his name meant 'quiet resting place.' Odd meaning, isn't it?" Alex asked to the sky. "Anyway, we were out a few miles from here when he just got up and left. Said something about going on a walkabout." He inspected the folds of the rose. "Strange people, those natives. One minute a guide, the next minute walking into the sunset."

Despite the warmth of the afternoon, icy fingers tickled down her neck. "He didn't take his horse," she said.

Alex looked at her as if she were a child. "It's called a walkabout, not a ride-about, my dear." Then he smiled, dropped the rose and crushed it under his heel like a smoldering butt. He turned to Russell. "How many shots did you fire off this morning?"

"Hard t'say," Russell cackled. "Couple at the roo. Few others out t'the bush."

"Should be more careful, Russell," Alex said in mock reprimand. "Never know what could be in the path of a stray bullet. Those Aborigines blend in right with the shadows, especially the children." He gave a slow wink to his wife.

"Clean up the horses, Russell. Wipe up the blood!" Alex ordered. "Abo won't be needing his for a while." The men laughed.

Leonora's stomach fell sickly and her head heated as if it readied for fever.

"Whot yeh want me t'do wiv the roo?" Russell asked.

"Leave it for the dingoes or the buzzards. I don't care."

With effort, Russell dragged the kangaroo to a cart, leaving tiny dots of rust-colored blood against the dirt.

Leonora held her stomach, turned to the house, but Alex grabbed her elbow. His fingers slid down her forearm and squeezed her hand. He stared at her wedding ring, rubbed the surface of it with his thumb, held the diamond up to the light, his expression distant and odd. "My mother's ring," he said softly. "My stepfather tried to sell it after she died, but I stole it. Did you know that?" Leonora didn't move, stilled as the pressure on her fingers increased.

"She would never have left me if it weren't for that man. Wouldn't have sent me away, drowned herself in drink." His eyes shot up to hers, his face taut with warning. "Don't ever leave me, Leonora."

He dropped her hand, the ring tugging at her finger like a boulder. Alex pushed his shoulders back, smoothed out the hair above his ears. "I take it yesterday's conversation has been forgotten?"

She nodded clumsily, just wanted to be away from him, make the icy fingers stop scratching her back. "You were right; I didn't know what I was saying."

"That a girl." He smiled widely and patted her cheek. "Let's hope we never hear that awful word again. Otherwise"—Alex spun on his heel and slung his rifle across his shoulder—"I'll have no choice but to plan another hunting trip."

The shearers arrived with the last of the morning dew. They came carried upon a caravan of haggard-looking utes, three men crammed in the front seat, the rest lounging on the flatbed squatting or hanging legs over the sides, their boots hidden in the pillows of dirt. They came sunburned and strong, the veins raised above the defined muscles of their forearms, their tough voices rich with laughter and the creases around their eyes deep with comradery.

Meredith and Clare neglected their morning duties to scope out the lot, pointed at the faces most handsome, the bodies best sculpted, and scoffed at the ones who weren't so endowed. Leonora joined them at the window and the women hushed their giggles.

"So, these are the shearers," Leonora assessed.

"Just arrived."

"Whew, they're a lot of them."

"Near thirty I'm guessin'. Gonna need more flour." Meredith ticked off the list in her head. "Sugar. Baking powder. Cheese." She rolled up her sleeves as if she were ready to knead bread. "Men work only as hard as their bellies are full."

The men flowed off the trucks. Leonora's mouth opened slightly as James and Tom walked up to meet the men. There were hearty shakes, arms that pointed to the different directions of the land, rubbing of chins, bent backs of laughter, slaps upon shoulders, cigarettes rolled and shared, hats adjusted and hands shoved into trousers.

The women were silent and stilled with the shift and quantity of men in tight trousers. They were rough men and tough men with swaggers and long, tan arms and sharp eyes. The three women exchanged shy glances, then covered giggles with their hands.

Leonora's eyes clung to James's figure and a great heat swarmed her cheeks. She cleared her throat. "Suppose they should be fed straightaway."

"Yeah, good idear." Meredith cleared her throat in equal response. "They're lookin' 'ungry already. Gonna be thirsty for somepin cold."

Clare giggled and covered her mouth. "Me mouth is waterin', too."
Meredith elbowed her, tried to hide her grin. She clapped her
hands. "Orright, off we go."

Leonora hung to the window while the girls pranced to the kitchen, their voices high with excitement and loud enough to filter out
with clarity.

"Gawd, did yeh see the lot of 'em?" Meredith huffed.

"Got m'eye on the tall one wiv the blue tie round his neck," clicked
Clare.

"Naw! Yeh don't want that one!" scoffed Meredith knowingly.
"Dandy bloke. Seen 'em b'fore. All prim an' proper. Kind who prides
himself on restraint. Knew a bloke like that once. Used to slather his
hand wiv lanolin so it's soft when he's touchin' himself."

"Och!" Clare erupted in giggles. "Been wiv a shearer or two an' no
man's got hands like 'em. Got muscles in their fingernails, I tell yeh!
Hands like steel." Clare paused and seemed to reconsider. "Course,
the milkers a fair match wiv their hands."

"Problem wiv the dairymen is they ain't sure they're pleasin' yeh
until they got milk squirtin' outta yer tits!"

Leonora covered her mouth and laughed.

"Ain't that the truth!" cackled Clare. "Swear I was wiv one milker
who wouldn't let go till he heard me mooin'!" Pots rattled against
snorts and snickers. "Still like the one wiv the blue tie."

"Stop droolin' into that dough an' start bakin' it. We got boys
t'feed!"

James led the shearers by horse. The men followed in the trucks
set in low gear. The quarters were new and clean and the men whistled with the new bunks. "How many head yeh say yeh got again?"
asked the head shearer. The man was the oldest of the lot, but his skin
shone with health and his face held the deep lines of years rich with
humor.

"Twenty thousand," James replied.

"Good. Take us 'bout a month at most. Men'll like it 'ere, shame
yeh ain't got more to shear." The man pushed his hat to the back of
his head. "Came direct from the Gillabong Station. Won't work that

piece o' shit place again. Quarters infested wiv fleas. Me an' the boys slept under the stars every night."

"Everything's new. Tools, stalls." James pointed to the shed behind the quarters. "If you find a flea in this place, one of your men brought it in." He slapped the man's shoulder.

The shearer beamed and rubbed his hands, already itching to get started. "And how's the help round here?" the man asked with a sly wink.

James knew what the man was thinking. "Only got a cook and a maid at the big house. I'll let you be the judge of them."

The smell of shorn fleece rode upon the hot breeze, permeated the air until even human skin smelled like wool. The shearers kept out of sight except for the trucks swaying with piled bales that left every morning at sunrise. Little puffs of wool escaped from the wire mesh and floated off into the sky like feathers from a plucked chicken.

Meredith and Clare slunk in late every morning, carried in eggs or brooms to pretend they had been hard at work. But their footprints were still clear in the dirt from their early-morning walk from the shearer quarters, their cheeks still flush with the secrets of their night.

When home from the mine, Alex spent his day at the shearing shed watching the men work. He'd often take his dinner with them and stay late in the evening sharing drinks and helping the men gamble away a day's wages. He'd return to the house well after midnight and climb into the bed smelling of sheep and alcohol and stale smoke. With his weight upon the mattress, Leonora curled to the edge of the bed. He hadn't touched her in months, but the fear was still there that he would. She kept a basket of yarn next to the bed and on top lay the long knitting needles. She would never let him touch her in that way again, never let him take her as a husband takes a wife. She would gladly pay the whores herself to keep him occupied.

Leonora rarely saw James, but he was never beyond her thoughts. He stayed out in the paddocks with the horses or the cattle, left before dawn and returned after dusk. The few times she had seen him at the homestead, they hadn't spoken, but their eyes had held tight until Alex inevitably appeared, breaking their gaze, darkening James's eyes and hardening his face. But James was still here. And that was enough.

In a few weeks, Alex was taking her to Coolgardie for the mine's annual party at the Imperial Hotel. The new dress he ordered from Milan came this morning via post. She would meet the wives of the head managers. She and Alex would stay in the Imperial's only suite. Leonora looked at the knitting basket. She would pack the needles.

This was her life. But as long as James was near—as long as she caused him no harm and she kept the Aborigines safe—this life was enough.

CHAPTER 54

Alexander Harrington leaned against the back wall, his arms folded at his chest. Three men sat at the table, their bodies tilted toward their boss, their eyes alert to his expression. They did not offer Ghan a chair.

"So, fever's contained?" asked Alex under dark, cocky brows.

"Yep." Dr. Middleton pulled at his waistband and flared his nostrils like there was a bad stink in the room. "Burned half the camp. Everything else got scrubbed down with disinfectant. Supervised it myself." The doctor winked at no one in particular.

"What about the sewer?"

The puff went out of the doctor's chest. "Getting to it. Men don't want to touch it." He clicked his teeth and drew out a sigh. "Complain about the fever and then complain about cleaning up the shit that caused it in the first place. Go figure."

Alex turned his black eyes on Ghan. "Men tell me you're doing some listening for us. What's the mood?"

"Sour." Ghan set his gaze on one bastard at a time. "How the 'ell yeh think the mood is?"

The men at the table stiffened, shot furtive glances to Alex, but he only chuckled. The men released their bound shoulders. "You're pretty pissed off, aren't you, Mr. Petroni?"

Whistler's blue, hard face flashed and Ghan fought against the rage brewing inside his limbs. "Yeah, I'm pissed," he said coldly. "Babies dyin'. Mothers too sick t'hold 'em. Men worried 'bout gettin' fired if they don't show up for their shift. Yeah, I'm pissed!" he growled at the doctor. "Doc don't show up till fever workin' its way out. Men complainin' 'bout cleanin' up the sewer, yeh say? Damn right they're complainin'! The mine put that pipe in. Mine's the one that let it crack an' fester. Now yeh askin' the camp men t'clean it up— askin' men who lost their babies 'cause the mine's too bloody cheap to fix the gawddamn pipe." His lip curled and he blinked back the hate that stung his eyes. "So, yeah, I'm pissed."

Alex unfolded his arms and tucked his hands in his pockets, stared at his shoes. The other men clenched lips and twisted them and waited. "Martin," Alex addressed the man at the center. "Send the engineers to the camp and get that pipe fixed. Then clean it up. All of it. No camp men, either. Find some swaggies or black men or Chinamen. I don't care. But you get that mess cleaned up even if you got to use your own hands to do it."

Martin nodded. "Yes, sir."

"All right, that's settled." Alex turned back to Ghan and asked pointedly, "Now tell me, Mr. Petroni, are the men going to strike?"

And there it was. The question. Ghan knew the answer. A strike was coming sure as the sun was going to rise in the bush. Then the scabs would be brought in and the fighting would start. And once the fighting started, it would grow and spread like the fever.

The strike was coming. The hate and the fighting were coming. And here they were, these clean-shaven bastards with warm beds and full bellies asking the question—looking for a heads-up. If they knew about the rumblings, they'd pluck out the men like roo ticks stuck in the skin and scorch them with a tip of a match. They'd round up the Italians, sever them, send half of them packing back to the motherland with barely their shirts and send the other half back to the shaft shivering with gratitude they still got a job and a filthy tent to sleep in. Then they'd rough up a couple of the Aussies, make them a little bloody, beat the rage out of them before they cut their pay. A few weeks later, new Italians come in without a clue and it starts all over again.

Ghan let the steam leave him slowly for effect, the boiler still pumping inside. "Naw. Men ain't talkin' strike."

"Really?" Mr. Harrington cocked his head, incredulous.

"They're pissed. I'm pissed. We're all damn pissed." Ghan slumped his shoulders. "But fever left 'em weak. Mind an' spirit. Men ain't got no will t'fight. Just want t'feed their kids. Even the Aussies seem t'got the wind knocked out of 'em."

The men watched him carefully. "I was sick," Ghan continued. "Never been so bloody sick in m'life. But then I woke up, felt the typhoid leavin' me. Couldn't believe I was still livin'." Now Ghan watched the men. "An' yeh know whot my first thought was when the fever left? Know the first thing that popped in my mind?" The men waited.

"I wanna work. Gotta get up an' go t'work." Ghan shook his head. "Ain't gonna be a strike. Somepin broke wiv that fever. Men just wanna work."

The ugly news traveled quickly through town overnight. Good news pools and ripples, takes its sweet time as it passes from one smile to another. But not the black news. Black news rolls like a tsunami, ripping at ears and sucking anger into its bowels in a greedy swell. And the wave grows and growls and doesn't stop until it has flattened everything in its wake.

By morning, the angry news spread across the miners' camp, reeked between the tents with a gaseous infusion and seeped into the canvas, under the flaps and through the holes of the rusty metal. And the ugly news grew and twisted, the facts pulled apart and added to until the news no longer was a mix of words but had become a life.

The news reached Ghan as news does in a camp, riding upon the lips of a man passing by and added to by shadowy whispers under tent poles.

Fights spilled as freely as whiskey in mining towns. But the news of this fight, Ghan knew, had layers and terrible depths that made an ordinary brawl morph into a war. Two miners, an Italian and an Aussie, threw punches and broke bottles on each other at the Lamb's Eye Pub. Who started it depended on the ethnicity of the man telling the story. But somewhere along the line of the fight, that Aussie got cut straight into his eye to his brain and died. The police came, and before they had the blood sopped up that Italian lay shot in the face along the street. That was the birth. But the details were lost now, unimportant. A new beast had usurped the birth.

Ghan tied the stringy bark tight around the peg leg and wrapped it in loops across his stub. The air was heavy, thick with the hate that had hardly just bloomed with dawn. Saliva wet his mouth and it didn't taste quite right. Outside, men drank black and bitter coffee and their eyes reflected the black bitterness.

Here it is, Ghan spoke in his head, and frowned. The blindness had set in. Men on all sides were growing blind as men do. And these men walked through the rows, knocked shoulders against other men and snarled as dogs and sniffed as dogs do. Forget the strike; this was bigger. They'd call it a strike, use the word that would support and praise their anger and disguise the riot. But this war would have nothing to do with cut pay or scab labor or immigrants or typhoid. This war was because the taste of blood had replaced the craving for sugar on the tongue.

Ghan passed the Italian tents and shacks. Dark eyes watched his movements; speaking lips grew quiet. Green, white and red–striped flags were pulled in and folded ceremoniously. Women set their jaws and shuttled between the blind men. They brushed the ground with brooms, their eyes absent, and they left little crevices in the dirt from sweeping the same spot over and over again. For the women saw what the blind men could not and their faces paled. They saw the change, saw how the anger would turn a husband, a provider, to a growling animal and they, the women, would be left picking up the pieces. And these women felt the anger, too, but theirs was directed at the blind, stupid, *stupid* men.

Ghan cut through the simmering lines to the Aussie side. As it was closer to town, the news had come here first, boiled longer. Voices rose within tents. A ring of men clustered near the camp cook, warmed their thick hands next to the fire. Ghan placed his coins in the open can and took his coffee and eggs to a spot behind the men. He sat on the bare ground, his good leg bent under him, the peg leg sticking out like a broken wing.

Two men came near with their tin plates. They plopped down on the dirt, their shadows edging his own. "Whot yeh bringin'?" one man asked the other, his voice low as distant thunder.

"Knife. You?"

"Fists." The man stretched out his hand over his plate before grabbing the fork. "Like t'feel the bones crunchin' under the knuckles." His face was pockmarked, the holes opening and scrunching with each bite. "Timing couldn't be better, eh? Wiv that manager party at the hotel."

The other man laughed. A piece of egg fell slobbery onto the ground. "Give 'em a party t'remember, eh, Hugh?"

"Bloody hard t'hold back till then. Men want to wait till the party starts, wait till the streets dark. Still, hard t'hold back."

"Shhhh." The slobbery one wiped his mouth. "Careful. Cripple's listenin'."

Ghan shoveled in his eggs without tasting them, tried to keep his face even.

"He ain't gonna say nothin'." Hugh raised his voice. "Ain't that right, peg leg?"

Ghan chewed slowly, kept his eyes straight on the food.

Hugh chuckled. "Told yeh." He rubbed his hand over his scarred skin, his eyes severe. "Heard 'Arrington's gonna be there."

"Heard right. Bringin' that wife of his wiv 'im."

"No shit? Whores gonna miss their favorite customer." The men laughed, snorted again.

"Ain't been wiv a woman so damn long, I'd take half a whore at this point."

"Fair dinkum." Hugh scowled. "Ain't seen my wife for three years. Like t'get my hands on that 'Arrington lady, I tell yeh. Teach her whot a real man feels like."

The other man stuck his fork in the air. "Why don't yeh? Might as well grab some fun while the men gettin' worked over."

"Whoa-a!" Hugh clapped his hands. "Hell, we all deserve a good turn! Get the other blokes fired up just to talk 'bout it. By Gawd, Angus, yeh got somepin there! Pass the lady round so everybody gets a smack."

The food lodged in Ghan's throat. He stopped chewing, stopped moving. His stomach cramped. The air pressed against his body like walls.

"Hey, cripple!" Hugh hollered. "When the last time yeh been wiv a woman?"

Ghan raised his eyes over the plate but did not turn his head. "Go ask yer wife," he spit.

Hugh's face contorted and one lip jutted, but Angus erupted in laughter, slapped his friend on the back. "He's pokin' yeh, mate!"

Hugh's lip settled, curved up; he laughed a little too hard. "No worries, mate. We'll get yeh a turn!"

Angus plowed in a mouthful of eggs and spluttered, "Yeh comin' wiv us tonight, ain't yeh? Kick them E-talians out once an' fer all? Teach 'em managers a little lesson?"

Ghan stayed silent and the men's eyes darkened above their smiles. "Either wiv us or against us, mate," warned Hugh.

Ghan wiped his mouth with the back of his hand, stood to go. "I'll be there."

Torn. Ripped between two parts. Ghan walked. He walked in one direction and then another. He walked toward the sun until it seared his nose and then he walked against it until his back sweated through the shirt. And with the walking came the listening—murmurs and plans, impatient and idle knuckles cracking. If he ratted out the strikers, the Aussies and Italians would beat him; if he kept quiet about the strike, the managers would beat him; if he didn't do anything and some woman got manhandled, he'd beat himself. There was no middle road, no gray. He had to choose one way and then run as fast and far away from the dogs at his heels.

Ghan missed Whistler fiercely. The anger that crowded around the camp made him weak. Whistler had felt it first, tried to warn him. And now it was here and he was in the thick of it. He knew too much.

Ghan cursed that breakfast with grinding teeth. Wished he hadn't heard those men talk, wished he hadn't listened to their poison. He was sick with it now. Thinking about that woman; thinking what they wanted to do to that woman. *The managers be damned. Harrington be damned. At this point, let all the men be damned, white and olive. But not the woman. Not a woman, for God's sake. Man's never got a right to hurt a woman. Didn't matter who this woman was, good or bad, mean or nice, ugly or pretty. A man don't ever touch a woman like that.*

Ghan crawled inside his tent. He lay on his back, stared at the filthy ceiling. Shadows of resting flies dotted the underside of the canvas. He could go to the police. They'd come out with clubs and warnings and stomp through the camp. Men would pout, look dumb. *Ain't no trouble 'ere*, they'd say. But they would wait. The anger would wait and grow. Outcome was still the same, different night, different day.

Ghan let the heat of the trapped air sink into his brain, soften it. He could go to the managers. Tell them the strike was coming. Rat the whole crew out. Ghan shook his head sadly. *But the managers . . . that Harrington . . . they're a cocky crew. They'd go to the police. Or they'd want to fight the miners themselves. They would hold their party. Miners just maggots to them. A rich man with a line of police ain't got no fear of maggots.*

Ghan pulled himself up on his elbow. He put the last of his money in his pocket and climbed out of the tent with an exhale of the inevitable, his decision made.

In town, Ghan crossed to the telegraph office, saw the two men from breakfast stationed in front, watching everyone who passed, listening for loose tongues. Ghan turned back, tried to get his thoughts straight again. Three worn bicycles lined the messenger's office. A lanky boy crouched in the corner between jobs. Take a biker half a day to get to the Harrington place, Ghan guessed. Besides, you couldn't trust those boys, their tongues as loose as their pedaling legs. His eyes moved to an old, roofless ute. A black man slept in the front, his legs hanging out the window, his bare feet covered in dirt. His hat covered his face.

Ghan hurried over to the truck, pounded on the thin metal hood. "This yer truck?"

"Boss's," the young black man said dryly, peeking from his hat. "Boss drunk at the pub."

"Yeh drive this thing?"

"Yeah."

"Want t'earn a few bucks?"

The man dragged his feet in and rested his folded arms on the dashboard.

Ghan continued quickly, "Yeh know Wanjarri Downs?"

"Yeah, know it. Got family there."

"How long it take yeh t'get there?"

"If I speedin'? Three, four hours."

"Need yeh to deliver a message to Mr. 'Arrington. It's urgent."

The man laughed, his white teeth stretching the length of his mouth. "Who gonna listen to an Abo, boss?"

He was right. "Hold up." Ghan dug through a pile of trash rotting near the co-op and found an oily paper bag, ripped off a rectangle. "Yeh got anything to write wiv in there?"

The man searched the floor and pulled up a pencil. Ghan handed him the paper. "Write this down."

The white teeth glistened and he handed the paper back. "Don't write nothin' but an *X*."

Ghan stared at the paper. He put it on the hood and tried to hold the pencil, fumbled it between his fingers, then finally grasped it in his fist. He set the lead down and closed his eyes, tried to remember a word as a picture in his illiterate head. Sweat poured off his nose and spotted the paper. He cursed. He looked down past the station and his eyes settled on the Hotel Imperial and its bold letters vertical on the side. He knew its name. Sounded it out in his head, moved his tongue in his mouth with the sound, rolled each letter. The first was shorter and must be "Hotel."

Ghan flattened the paper and with stuttering wrist copied the word *HOTEL* in big letters on the paper. "Hotel"—the first word he had ever written, no better than a three-year-old. He looked at the heavy print with anger and shame and sadness. He drew a big *X* over the word. It was all he could do. He handed the paper to the Aborigine. "Mr. 'Arrington gets this, yeh hear me?"

"Whot if he don't want it?"

"Then give it to any white man there. Tell him not to let Mr. 'Arrington leave. Orright?"

"Sure, boss." The man smiled and folded the note, put it in his pocket. He held out his hand. Ghan gave him a few bills and the man's eyes grew wide. He started the truck with a roar.

Ghan pounded the hood. "When yeh get back 'ere, don't say a word, got it?"

He smiled his white teeth again. "Who gonna listen to an Abo, eh, boss?"

The car rolled away down the street, the black man's thin body bouncing with each jolt. He watched him go without relief, only resignation. Ghan had done all he could.

Ghan headed for his camp, tried not to look at the rows of tents that would probably be burned by nightfall. He stumbled with throbbing head under his canvas, pulled at the wood post that kept it straight, but then stopped. If he took the tent down, news would run through the camp like sewage that he was packing up. He gritted his teeth. He'd have nothing—no money, no tent. Ghan packed up what he could and stuffed it in his shirt. He left the hovel, looked behind him one last time and scurried toward the trees as fast as his peg could move.

CHAPTER 55

James ran after the shearing truck and waved at the driver to stop. When the truck slowed, he climbed on the rear bumper and pushed in the bales of wool that were sliding out. He retied the rope and jumped back to the ground. "Load nearly toppled out," he said to the driver, then smacked the door. "You're good now." The man tipped his hat and drove off, the load swaying like a dancing rump.

An old ute carried a trail of dust from the other side of the road, turned too fast into the drive, lifting half the wheels off the ground, then settled with an angry bang. The truck parked in front of the house and a lean Aborigine sauntered out, his hat so low that only his chin showed. He climbed the stairs to the big house and knocked on the door. Meredith came to the window, peered out with a grimace and disappeared behind the curtain, closing it tight. The Aborigine waited for several minutes, then laughed, retraced his footprints lazily.

Tom wiped the sweat from his forehead, still panted from loading the bales. "What you think he wants?"

"Maybe a bite." James frowned. "Cook didn't even open the door for the bloke."

The black man went back to the car. "Something I can get for you?" James shouted.

The man flashed him a full set of white teeth. "Lookin' fer Mr. 'Arrington."

"Left this morning."

The man's smile faded. "Too bad. Had a message fer 'im." He reached into his front pocket and pulled out a rumpled piece of brown paper, handed it to James.

The lead had smeared on the oily paper, but he saw the word, saw the pressure of the *X* that had ripped holes. "Who gave this to you?"

"White fella. Told me t'tell Mr. 'Arrington not t'come." The man watched James's face carefully and the black lines lost their silliness. "There's trouble in Coolgardie. Tonight. Everybody steamin'. Everybody lookin' t'fight." His eyes were full then and deep and held James with a steady urgency. He pointed a finger at the paper and shook his head. "Trouble. Gonna get ugly. Men gonna strike. Riot."

James thought of the car that left this morning. Alex had the suitcases. Leonora sat on the passenger side, her head down. He hadn't looked at them further. He couldn't look at them together without feeling sick. The Aborigine was watching him and James balled up the paper, balled up the image of Alex and Leonora.

"You want to rest in the shade for a bit?" James asked. "Can give you some tucker for the ride." He spoke as he would to a white man and the Aborigine relaxed.

"Naw. Gotta get back 'fore the boss wakes up. Drag his arse out 'fore the trouble starts."

James nodded and the man drove away, his body bouncing in the seat of the lurching, burping old truck.

Tom walked over. "What was that all about?"

"Said there's going to be trouble in Coolgardie." James clenched the crumpled paper in his palm, squeezed it until it was small as a pea. "A strike. Came to tell Alex to stay away."

Tom scoffed, "Och. Sounds like a ghost story to me. Somebody tryin' to spook him!" Tom smirked then. "Second thought, serve the cocky bastard right to find a little trouble."

"Leonora's with him." The words sounded like a memory.

"You buyin' it?" Tom paused, didn't get an answer.

"Got a bad feeling about it, Tom. Something in that bloke's eyes. Can't explain it."

"I can." Tom smirked. "You miss your girlfriend." He held his rib with the joke, stretched his arm up to untighten it. "Orright," he conceded. "Won't hurt to check it out. Hell, haven't been to town in months, maybe we can get a good meal out of it."

Tom's lips tired with songless whistling as he and James sped through hours on the straight road to Coolgardie. They passed the hacked forest, the dots of stumps appearing black as holes in the falling twilight. The tires followed the embedded wheel ruts of the road and James fought with the steering to keep the car in steady alignment. He flicked on the headlights, a pale light fighting against the gray and sharpening with approaching night. Tom's bottom slid back on the seat and his back straightened. "You smell that?"

"Something's burning. Look." James pointed. In the gray-blue of falling dark rose the matching thin lines of smoke.

"Christ."

James pressed on the gas and ground the wheels faster. Tom rubbed his forehead. "We got t'think here, James. Orright? We can't just throw ourselves into this thing."

"She's in there, Tom."

"I know." His breath came quick and he moved closer to the edge of the seat. "I know, but we got t'think here or we're gonna get ourselves killed."

The smoke from Coolgardie grew and blossomed in a venomous cloud. From the east another sky illuminated in red with a glowing swell and then the smoke followed, rougher this time as it competed with the flames. "Aw, Christ. This is bad."

The car rose up a ridge, brought the first distant view of a lit Coolgardie. Smoke poured and fought with billowy black limbs to crawl higher and higher into the night. Red flames licked at yellow sparks and the town haloed orange in spots. Tom tried to speak, but his lips moved uselessly. He swallowed, then tried again, "It's all over the place. They don't know which direction they're going."

"Yes, they do." James's voice came hard and deep. "They're circling."

The car churned toward the heated valley. "Remember where the hotel was?" James asked shortly.

"Yeah. To the left of the depot."

"We're going to head out behind the tracks and leave the car, round up by the depot and see if we can get into the hotel."

In town, the smoke joined and thickened. The headlights struggled to cut through the swirling black. The car flew off the main road onto a horse route and clattered blindly to the tracks. The tires hit a steel line of track, pushed over it. They left the car and pulled their shirts up over their noses, ran toward the buildings spotted with fire. Ears throbbed with the shrill bells of the fire trucks. Breaking glass popped to the hard ground. Men shouted; voices echoed.

James and Tom slunk through a long alley perpendicular to the main street. A fire truck stood lifeless, its hose hacked to pieces, the ladder lying in splinters. They pressed backs against a brick wall and waited as a mob of men, a faceless and crawling beast, rushed down the main road toward the hotel. A man broke from the group like a snapped thread, smashed a wood beam studded with nails into the tires of a dead car, beat the ground until the wood snapped. The air reeked of spilled oil and kerosene. James grabbed Tom's shirt and pointed to the far wing of the hotel. "We go in the side window."

One quick breath and then they ran at the hotel, the fourth tier already awash with flames. The back window was smashed and they climbed over the shards of razored glass into the dark and smoky lobby. A few strays of the mob saw the figures and rushed the window, swinging sticks at any moving body. A hit landed to Tom's lower back and left him stumbling. James and two other men caught who they could and sent them flying through the cut window. New pounding erupted from the front doors while men barricaded the entrance.

In a flash, they were spun and separated by the panicked patrons. "Tom!" James shouted, but his voice was lost. A flame shot from the bar and small explosions followed as the bottles of alcohol erupted. In the flash of light, terror streaked faces, women screamed and men barked orders. James scanned the room between the intermittent illumination and searched for her face. And there was Alex—bobbing under the shooting glass, holding collars and shouting into men's ears. James plowed through the people and grabbed his arm. "Alex!"

Alex looked up, bewildered.

"Where's Leo?" James screamed.

Through the chaos, Alex paused, cocked his head, and James wanted to strangle him. "Where's your *wife*, goddammit!"

Alex's face twitched as if slapped, turned tortured. "I can't find her! She wasn't with me when the fire broke out." He grabbed James, frantic as a drowning man. "You've got to find her! So help me, I'll never forgive myself if anything's happened to her!"

"What floor were you on?" *Please don't be the fourth.*

"Second! The whole floor is covered in smoke."

"All right." James scanned the room again, rose up slightly. "Listen, Tom's here, too. Somewhere."

The street erupted with hand-cranked sirens; a gunshot cracked in the distance. Leonora covered her mouth with a wet towel as the black smoke pillowed under the door. She tried to stay calm, tried to think straight above the terror. She didn't understand what was happening. One minute she was dressing for dinner, and the next the whole city turned into a war zone. Adrenaline sped her thoughts, made her muscles tight. She fought the urge to curl in the corner, fought the urge to scream for help. No one would hear her. *Think, Leonora.* She had to keep her mouth closed, keep the smoke from filling her chest. *Think.*

There was too much smoke in the hallway; she'd have to escape through the window. Holding her breath against the rising poison, she pushed at the windowpane. Her hands slipped with the exertion. She tried again, harder, her nails breaking with the strained grip. A panicked sob left her throat, but she swallowed it. She couldn't lose it. She had to think. She had to breathe carefully or she'd choke. Her fingers scanned the windowpane. There were nails in the corner. *No.* The window was nailed shut. She searched the growing and swirling darkness for something to break the window. *Nothing.* She beat against the glass with her fists. *No!* The smoke entered her mouth too quickly and she bent with hacking. She found her dropped towel and breathed into the wet fabric.

A woman screamed. A window smashed above or below or all around, the noise coming from every direction. Leonora coughed into the towel, held her ears against the chaos. Her lungs burned. She could die in this room or take her chances with the smoke in the hallway. She mapped out the exit in her mind, would run until it was clear or she collapsed; either way, she couldn't stay here.

Men's voices rang in the hallway. *Thank God!* They would help her. She was getting dizzy, her gait jagged. They could help her get out. Her eyes stung; her lungs gasped for fresh air. *They'll help me.* She staggered to the door. . . .

Alex peeked above shoulders. "The police are here, thank God." The trapped heat was enormous. Perspiration beaded Alex's face, made it look wet with tears as he yelled at James, "If you find Leonora, take her away. Get her out of here, you hear me!" Another bottle exploded above their heads and they crouched lower. Alex slit his eyes. "Just find her."

James weaved through the bodies until he found the wide stairs, the top ones nearly invisible with smoke. He plowed to the second floor and hid his mouth in his shirt. The smoke burned at his eyes and he choked into the fabric. A large window was still intact in the hallway and the light from the fires cut a sliver of vision through the choking haze.

"Leo!" he hollered above the sirens. James coughed for oxygen and called out again, "Leo!" His voice grew hoarse and raw, the word inaudible now below the coughing. He stumbled across the empty hall, his eyes clouded and watering. He felt along the wall, the smoke slowing him down, his lungs shrinking.

"Leave her!" a voice spit in the darkness. "Police comin'!"

"Ain't goin' till I get whot I came fer!" A rough cough hacked. "Jist need to get 'er fuckin' skirt off. . . ."

A cold hand wrapped around James's heart, squeezed. His hand dropped from his nose. The fire, the smoke, disappeared. Blind, he charged the hall.

"Fuck!" A man fled into the smoke. Another gray face looked up from the floor, startled but fierce, his hand inching up a woman's dress.

James kicked him square under the chin, the thrust of the boot knocking the man flat. Curling to his side, the man tried to rise. James didn't wait, kicked hard into the ribs so the slumped figure rolled into the black. Now the breath came too fast to James's lungs and the smoke filled, left him dizzy and clutching for the wall. A dull dragging sound slid up the hall. James tried to follow the men, but his chest convulsed. He pulled his shirt over his mouth, sank to his knees, slid his hands along the floor until he found the woman's limp leg, his fingertips climbing up her body to her face.

"Leo!" James pulled the wilted body from the space and shook the shoulders. "*Leo!*"

James grabbed her around the waist and slung his arms under her knees, pressed her to his chest. Her head bounced against his shoulder as he carried her blindly down the steps. He coughed fiercely into his shoulder and slid against the railing. Police were shouting, people were screaming and running out the front lobby, but flames licked half the door. James turned away from the crowd and pushed through a black hall to a wooden locked door, beat it with his shoulder until the hinge cracked, then kicked it open.

The new air smacked him in the face. In the alley, James dropped to his knees, leaned his cheek against her mouth, felt no breath. He pressed his lips against hers, breathed from every pore into her lungs, fought against his own coughing until he had to pull back. Her head flopped to the side, hung over his fingertips.

He ripped the top of her dress, slid her necklace out of the way, dropped her head back and arched her spine. His eyes held to the white stone, focused on it as he filled his lungs with fresh oxygen, then pressed his mouth to hers. Years of loss washed over him, each wave a face, a memory. He blew quicker, harder. *No more.* "No more!" he ordered, begged between breaths.

James put his mouth upon her parted lips. "I can't lose you, Leo," he pleaded between exhales. "I can't lose you again."

Leonora's neck craned and her eyes popped open. She choked, her body spasmed with hacking. James grabbed her head against his body and held her shoulders as she coughed and struggled violently for air. When he heard her inhale, he squeezed his cheek into her hair, kissed her head with quivering lips.

Shouts came from the street, woke him from heart-ripping relief. James didn't waste another moment and scooped her up, ran for the tracks.

"James!" Tom rushed from the other end, his face bleeding above the eye. "Aw, Gawd, is she orright?"

"She will be. What happened to you?"

Tom touched his head, looked with amazement at the blood on his fingers. "Guess a piece of glass got me." He wiped his sleeve against the wound carelessly. "I found Alex."

"Me too."

"He told me to grab his car. We'll be right behind you. Just get her out of here."

James lowered Leonora to the backseat, tried to get her to drink water, but she shook her head, unable to speak between hacking. But she was awake, she was breathing, she was alive. He got into the driver's seat and drove over the tracks, his eyes on the mirror—on her.

Hours later, when the night sky was quiet and the stars offered the only light, James pulled the car to the front gate of Wanjarri Downs, got out and opened it, sat back into the seat and drove through. He did not stop to close the gate. They hadn't spoken throughout the journey, only her intermittent and painful dry coughing cut the silence. Now he heard her grab the water, heard her drink it with slow gulps. He pulled over and turned his body, the engine vibrating under the car up through his legs. Leonora's weak eyes met his. They were tired and bloodshot. Her face and dress smudged in soot.

Relief still gripped his throat. "Are you all right?"

She nodded. "Are you?" Her voice was raspy, strained.

"I am now." He took his first full breath. "I'll get you to the house, then grab the doctor."

"No." She clutched the seat. "I don't need a doctor. Really." She stifled a cough and lowered her eyes. "Is Alex all right?"

A pit filled his gut. "Yeah." James turned around, pushed on the gas, stared stonily ahead. "Tom's bringing him back."

As James pulled into the drive, he pounded on the horn. After a minute or two, Meredith came fumbling down from the shearing shed fixing her hair and adjusting her blouse. James opened the back door of the car and slid his arm around Leonora's waist. "I can manage," she said. James ignored her and scooped her body up easily into his arms, met Meredith at the steps wringing her hands.

"Fer Christ sake!" Meredith quivered. "Whot's happened?"

"There was rioting in Coolgardie. They burned the hotel."

"Gawd, no!"

James walked past her. "Make her a cup of hot tea, then run her a bath!" he ordered.

"Right away."

James carried her agilely up the steps. "I can walk, you know," she ventured.

"I know." His jaw was tight, an intensity drawing down the lines of his face.

With his foot James nudged open the bedroom door, and laid her on top of the quilt. He cringed at the space where Alex had slept, where he would sleep. Leonora didn't miss the look. "He's not here, James." He nodded and sat down at the edge of the bed next to her hip.

Meredith clambered up the steps and handed James the tea. "I'll get that bath ready," she said, and hurried back down, stern with purpose.

Leonora sipped the hot tea. Each gulp inflamed, then soothed her throat, the lining still raw from coughing. James watched her face as she stared into the tea, watched the tiny movements of her fingers around the mug. His brows pulled in and his whole face frowned. "Sure you don't need a doctor?" he asked quietly.

"I'm sure." She placed the mug on the nightstand, the ceramic covered in black smudges.

James stared at the door, his gaze reaching far beyond the room. And his silence rattled her, made her pulse speed. She looked down at her filthy dress, the bottom hem ripped and snagged. Then she turned her palms in her lap, the fingernails black with soot and cracked. "I must be a sight," she said softly, retreating into the pillows.

He turned to her. "Is this the life you want, Leo?" James asked, his eyes unwavering, the question gruff and urgent.

Her eyes stung, the smoke long gone. "It doesn't matter what I want," she whispered.

"How can you say that?" His face twisted. "Damn it, Leo, you matter. You matter to me." He straightened his spine like he was going to storm out but then turned, took her chin in his hand and kissed her, hard and firm, kissed her like a dying wish. His lips softened and he drew back slightly. "I thought I was going to lose you."

She grabbed his shirt and pulled him to her mouth. His hand reached into her hair and cradled her scalp as he kissed her and leaned her head farther onto the pillow. She slid her arms around his neck and held him tight against her, let the heat from his body burn through her blood and singe her nerves.

The door slammed from downstairs. "Where is she?" came Alex's desperate voice.

Leonora pulled away from the kiss, the voice icing her skin.

"Upstairs, sir," Meredith answered quickly.

Leonora's eyes leaped to the door. James stared at her lips, lips that weren't his to kiss, and his face was deep with pain. "I can't do this anymore, Leo."

Alex's footsteps rushed on the floorboards downstairs.

She fumbled for his hand. "Do what?"

"This. See you with him." He pushed her hand away. "I can't do it."

Alex plowed through the door. "Thank God you're all right!" He grabbed Leonora and hugged her to his chest. She turned her face away from him with a grimace and searched for James. But he was already gone.

CHAPTER 56

The newly shorn sheep pranced upon the dry land, faster and lighter and scrawnier without the heavy fleece. Their pink skin showed under the fuzz of wool left, the ripples of the shears still patterned in stripes across their sides. The last of the wool left in the morning. The shearers had broken their record for speed, finishing twenty thousand sheep in three weeks. The bales had been solid and heavy, the numbers exceeded. Alex kept good on his promise of bonuses and the men were robust with money, sore muscles, pride and whiskey. They surrounded the pit of fire, ate off of tin plates weighted with steak and mutton. Gravy dripped and spotted the dirt. They passed around the dark liquor until the bottles were clear and empty.

James and Tom sat along their outer ring. Tom yacked it up with the men; James lay on his back, his head resting on clasped hands, and stared at the sky. He couldn't look at Alex. The man curled his stomach.

Since the riots, Alex had stayed home. His lackeys, the managers, came and stayed at the big house, their faces sly with thinking, plotting reprisals and ways to get the workers back on track. The news spread across the Outback as fast as the fire had licked the timber of the old Coolgardie buildings. Two Italians had died in the fighting, one Australian. An Italian boardinghouse, two pubs and countless homes were burned completely to the ground. The Imperial Hotel lost its top tiers, but the main floor still stood in a good, be it hatless, structure. The mine and its buildings weren't touched.

James had not seen Leonora since the fire and he did not look for her. He kept his eyes away from the big house, kept his mind and body strangled with work. But she was in his dreams with soft, waiting lips and skin that slid under his fingertips. And he would wake from the dream and stretch in his bed, flop his arm over his forehead and push the images away. Then he would work—work away the sinking longing.

Alex rose from the ring of men, swaying from side to side. "A toast! To the best bloody shearers in Australia!" Alex raised his bottle into the air, slurring like an arrogant clown. The drunk men cheered and raised their drinks.

"Wait . . . Wait . . . Not yet!" Alex stopped them in mid-sip. "I've thanked them personally but want to do it publicly. James and Tom." He found them with bobbing eyes over the crowd and raised his bottle. "You saved my wife, men." His voice turned somber and firm. "And for that, I will be forever grateful. Cheers!" He thrust the bottle forward and brought it back to his lips. The men drank and hollered and had the sparkle of life in their eyes.

"Well, gentlemen, speaking of my wife"—Alex grinned and winked at the men—"it's time I retire to the bedroom and give her a proper celebration!" He reached for a new bottle and swaggered.

The men broke out in loud hoots and applause. James bolted upright, his mind blank. "Don't you lay a hand on—"

In an instant, Tom had him by the arm, his grip tight against his wrist. The men grew quiet. The flames crackled over dry sticks. Alex turned slowly and put his hand to his ear. "What's that?"

Tom put a gruff arm around James's neck in restraint and shouted out playfully, "You heard him, Alex! Don't lay a hand on that drink or your wife be tryin' to please a limp willy!"

With that, the men hooted even louder. Alex glared at James for an instant, then tilted his head and chuckled. "Duly noted!" Alex dropped the bottle to the ground and held up his empty hands. "Duly noted!" He laughed and swayed toward the house.

James wrenched his body from Tom, thought he might lay a fist into his jaw. But Tom was fierce and grabbed him by the arm again. "She ain't your wife," he whispered hotly. Then Tom released the limb and repeated, "She ain't your wife, mate."

* * *

Leonora lay in the darkness of the bedroom listening to the ebb and flow of laughter drifting in from the field. The men's comradery made the loneliness of the house that much stronger. She tried to pick out the differentiating voices, but they all blended into one crude baritone. She listened for James's voice, tuned her ears to his easy, soft speech, but could hear nothing among the hoots and hollers of drunk men. Her insides shrank and weakened from missing him.

The front door slammed, its loud, swift crack making her body jump in the bed and her heart speed. Alex was back and she knew by the hammering footsteps he was quite drunk. She waited to hear the squeak of his office door and the muffled click of the double mahogany doors. Instead, she heard the dull thudding of his shoes as they walked up the stairs to the bedroom. "Wake up, darling!"

Leonora rolled out of bed and threw herself at the door, locked the bolt tight just as the doorknob rattled. She climbed back into bed and sat with her knees at her chest, scrunched the covers under her chin.

The knob rattled impatiently. "Open the door, Leonora." Alex's voice was even. She didn't make a sound. The door vibrated with a thrust against the knob. His fist pounded on the door. "Wake up and open this door, goddammit!"

Leonora reached for a long knitting needle and tucked it under the covers. The cool metal slid against her leg as her hands shook.

Alex banged his shoulder into the door. *Thud.* She heard him step back and then ram hard against the door, rattling the frame. "*Fuck!*" he screamed in pain. His back slid down the door amid spluttered curses and then it was quiet. Leonora waited, listened as her heartbeat filled the room. She loosened her grip on the needle and brought it with her as she approached the door. There was a sliding sound and then a dull thud as Alex's head hit the floor. She put her ear against the wood. Alex's drawn snoring began and filled the hall. Leonora pressed her cold forehead to the door and closed her eyes.

PART 6

CHAPTER 57

❧

Danny, the postman, handled a fifty-mile mail route. After he traded in his stock horses and wagon for a motorized one, the mail was delivered every week instead of every two or three. Between the normal routes he delivered telegrams. But the gas-filled engine didn't speed the man. Bowlegged as a wishbone and just as stiff, Danny moved unhurried, paid no attention to the impatient nods and quick greetings of his customers desperate for mail and catalogs and news from the outside world. He was a man of few words, but fuller of whistling than a magpie.

Danny tipped his hat to Leonora and whistled through his toothless grin. He rocked sideways on his bowed legs and pulled out an envelope. "Telegram fer Shelby."

"I think he's out with the horses." Leonora took the letter. "I'll bring it out to him."

The November day was intense and pure with dry heat. The temperature reached over one hundred degrees, the hour only half past ten. The dry ground leaped around her steps and dusted the blue dress hem orange. Her heart skipped a beat as James came into view in the riding ring. He was leading the stallion by the bit, calming him with even strokes and pulls of the reins. Tom dismounted from a gray spotted mare and waved. "Hey, Smoky!"

"Hi, Tom." She laughed. James watched her approach, his forehead smoothing before he lowered his gaze.

"You clean up nice." Tom winked. He leaned his arms casually over the wooden fence. "Course, you can even make soot look pretty."

Leonora smiled and handed him the telegram. "This just came for you."

"Whoa-e-e!" Tom took the letter and looked at the address. "From Mum. Boys must be back!" He tore into the envelope, his pupils dancing over the words. But then the dance stopped. Tom's eyes stilled and his lips parted. The paper remained glued to his fingers while his arms fell limp by his sides. The air shifted and grew with the heat and the silence. Leonora's hand inched to her stomach.

James let go of the horse, neared Tom. "What is it?"

Tom raised his head, looked through him without blinking. He closed his mouth.

"Which one?" James's voice was low and soft with knowing.

"Both." Tom's eyes blinked quickly now, his face immobile and puzzled. "The Flu." He shook his head and his upper lip rose in sudden disgust. "They were comin' home." The puzzlement grew. "The Flu. The gawddamn Spanish Flu?"

Tom dropped the telegram and clutched his scalp with his fingers. "They were comin' home," he mumbled.

James stepped another foot forward. "Tom . . ."

But Tom stepped backwards, his hands still holding his head. "They were comin' home!" He shook his head with his fists. "I can't talk. I can't . . ." He stumbled away, stumbled past the barn and kicked up dust as his bent figure ran past the big house.

James stooped and picked up the telegram, rubbed off the dirt and read it. His face was ashen, his jaw like stone.

Leonora covered her mouth as hot, blotted tears fell freely from under her eyelids. "I'm so sorry, James," she whispered. They were his brothers, too.

"We need to go back," James said slowly as he stared at the telegram. "For the funeral." James closed his eyes. "Poor Mrs. Shelby," he hushed.

"I'm coming with you."

His eyes flashed to her face. "No."

She touched his arm gently, then pulled it away. "Tom's mother still has five children and a house to care for, James." Leonora wiped her tears away with her sleeve. "I'll cook and clean, take care of the little ones. Poor woman's deep in grief, James. She'll need the help. Besides that, we can bring the car, leave first thing in the morning."

James watched her with heavy, weak eyes. "It's not a good idea, Leo."

"Why not?"

His gaze flitted to her lips. "You know why."

"I'll stay out of your way, James. I promise," she pleaded, thought of Tom's stricken face. "I just . . . I just want to help."

"Alex will never let you go."

"He won't have a choice."

"No." Alex did not look up from his papers strewn across the desk.

"Tom's mother is going to need the help," Leonora insisted.

"They can bring Meredith or Clare then."

"Alex." Leonora leaned over his desk, made him look at her. "They saved my life. Probably saved yours, too. It's the least we can do. Besides, it's only for a few days. Until the funeral is over."

Alex rifled through his papers, half-listening. "I'm not sending my wife out to the wheat fields like hired help."

The framed picture of Alex standing with his thoroughbreds leaned importantly on his desk. "Aren't you heading to some horse race today?" she asked shortly.

Alex huffed, "Some horse race, she says!" He put down the papers and raised his brows. "It's only the Melbourne Cup, darling."

"Well, I'm coming with you."

He laughed. "Oh no, you're not."

"Look, Alex. I'm not staying here alone. Especially after what happened in Coolgardie. I'm either going to help Mrs. Shelby or coming with you to the race. It's your choice."

Alex tapped his fingers on the desk. With each tap, Leonora knew he was thinking of the Melbourne women, of the parties, of the endless betting, of the freedom from his wife. "All right. Do your charity work."

Tom placed half the luggage in the passenger seat of the Model T; the other bag he placed in the trunk with food from the pantry. Tom turned to Leonora and finally broke his silence. "Mind if I drive?" He rubbed his temple sullenly. "Just can't sit an' think," he explained. "Don't want to think about anything but drivin'."

Leonora handed him the keys and sat in the backseat. James slid in next to her, his face clean shaven and fresh. The light scent of soap mingled with his skin, filled the air between them and made her light-headed. The seat grew warm with his strong body. She felt him against her flesh, felt him without touching him.

The car left the big house in the dust, left the gates behind—one, two, three, four, five. The road stretched in a line that seemed headed toward infinity. The wind blew against Leonora's hair, blew the tiny wisps around her face like the tickle of fingertips. The engine rumbled but had no effect on the quiet of the interior. Each mind ran its own thought or memory or worry or hope and so the car was full with floating, mute chatter. A cluster of emus watched the car pass, their long necks and scrawny haired heads perplexed at the strange, loud beast.

James's arm stretched languidly across the top of the seat, his hand only inches from her head. When the road hit a rocky patch, her hair grazed his fingers, the mere touch resonating down her arms and the backs of her legs. She thought how easy it would be to rest her head against his shoulder, to feel the ridges of his chest beneath her cheek, hear the soothing sound of his breathing as it rose and fell.

The hours zipped by along the route. The sun pressed against her eyelids until they were more at ease closed than open. Between the hum of the car and the push of the midday heat, her eyes fell sleepy and dreams entered softly through the minutes, dreams with kisses and moving hands and pressing bodies. Leonora's lips parted with a deep sigh, the noise waking herself from a sleep she hadn't even known she had fallen into. She blinked, slightly dazed. James was grinning at her, an odd look on his face. "Must have been a good dream," he said. "You've been smiling this whole time."

Leonora blushed to the tips of her ears and turned to the window. The bush scrub thickened, the trees more frequent. Long grass began to spread in golden threads.

"This starts the Wheatbelt." James pointed. "Next is Southern Cross and then we have another few hours till we're home." He leaned forward and placed his arms on the seat top in front. "Want me to take over, Tom?"

Tom shook his head, didn't utter a word.

Another few hours on the road and Tom straightened. His hands moved from the sides of the steering wheel to the top. "Almost there," James told her. "That fence marks Shelby land."

Butterflies woke in Leonora's stomach and she held her hand against the flutter. Maybe she shouldn't have come. She was entering a sliver of James's past, a world that had not been open to her. Perhaps he wanted it that way.

They turned a curve. Dogs rushed from nowhere, sped with tongues flapping between barks. They barreled at the moving car, turned and chased it, nipping at the wheels. Then the squat house rose into view—simple and homey. Red roses climbed the verandah posts and reached for the edge of the steel roof. Five red heads popped up in the window.

Tom parked the car and got out. The dogs whimpered and yelped, jumped to lick his face, clawing his shirt in the process. James and Leonora got out next. The dogs sniffed her curiously and then searched on hind legs for her face.

The screen door on the verandah slammed open and a flood of little girls in red pigtails ran and shouted in different volumes, "They're here! They're here!"

The girls flew at them as the dogs had. Tom crouched down with his arms wide and the girls piled upon him, knocking him on his bottom with hugs. Laughing and dusty, the girls abandoned him and flew to James. In a flash, he scooped up two girls at a time, squeezing and twirling them in his arms.

The screen door slammed again, slower this time. A tall woman, majestic in posture and topped with thickly piled hair, stepped to the drive. James set the girls on the ground. The children quieted and turned their gaze to their feet. The woman's face was strong, but the lines of the lips drooped, her body rigid. She nodded formally at the men. "Tom. James."

Tom rose to his full height and stared at his mother. "Hey, Mum."

Mrs. Shelby nodded—kept nodding. Her lips twitched. Tom went to her then, wrapped his sunburned arms around her shoulders. And in that moment, the woman's frame crumpled against his and he held her. Their faces were hidden. A silence grew to the children and they did not shuffle their feet; the dogs lowered ears and wound in tails.

Son and mother held each other for less than a minute before Mrs. Shelby pulled away and wiped her eyes with the back of her hand. Her face composed and a hint of a smile broke from the white lips. "I'm glad you're here, boys." The woman's gaze turned to Leonora.

"Mum," Tom began. "This is Mrs. Harrington. Leonora."

Leonora brought her belly of swarming wings as she approached the woman. She held out her hand. "Mrs. Shelby, I'm so very sorry for your loss."

The woman did not take the hand and turned away, looked at Tom. "Why's she here?"

Tom cleared his throat. "To help, Mum. Give you a break."

Mrs. Shelby's eyes sparked. "Since when have I needed help? Does it look like I can't take care of my own family?"

A hurt pause filled the space. "That's enough, Mum," Tom said firmly. "She's a fine woman. You know we have the funeral in Perth. Someone's got t'stay with the girls."

Mrs. Shelby dismissed the words, dismissed Leonora with a turn of her back. "Got supper on the stove. You boys probably starvin'." She turned to the children and shouted as she walked to the house, "Come on, girls; clean up! Get the table set. Boys are hungry."

Leonora dropped her head. The butterflies in her stomach died, settled heavy as lead. James came up beside her.

"You were right," she said, nearly mute. "I shouldn't have come."

He placed a finger under her chin and gently raised her face. "I'm glad you did."

She turned away, but he held her shoulders softly. "She'll warm up. I promise." He slid his hands down her arms. "She's sick with grief, Leo."

"I know." She swallowed. "I know."

The family sat around the long rectangular table while Mrs. Shelby made the rounds between kitchen and dining room bringing in steaming bread, stew and buttered beans—all offers of help sternly scoffed.

Two empty seats leaned against the center leaf—a shrine all eyes tried to avoid.

The children stared with open wonder at the new woman at the table. Gracie sat at the edge of her seat, and when her mother returned to the kitchen for more food the girl snuck around the chairs and squeezed between Leonora and James. She pulled at his sleeve and lowered her voice. "Can I ask her somepin, Jamesie?" The twins were nine now but still coveted their pet name for him.

James nodded at the child with a half smile. "She won't bite," he promised.

Gracie turned to Leonora with eyes full of secret curiosity. "Are you a princess?" she whispered.

Leonora bent down with eyes equally curious and whispered back, "No. Are you?" The young girl giggled, her eyes bright and pure.

Leonora looked over Gracie's head to James and grinned. "Jamesie?"

He raised one eyebrow. "Watch it, princess."

Mrs. Shelby came to the table with butter. She looked at James, then at Leonora and then back at James. "Gracie!" Mrs. Shelby scolded. "Get back to your seat!"

A hush fell over the table as forks moved tentatively from plates to mouths. Tom broke the silence, "Gawd, I missed your cookin', Mum!"

"Look half-starved!" she huffed. "Both of you. Aren't they feeding you over there?" Mrs. Shelby cast a hard look at Leonora.

"Just workin' hard, Mum." Tom tried to soothe. "We're eatin' just fine." He wiped his mouth with the linen napkin and leaned back rubbing his stomach. He touched the top of one of the empty seats next to him, stared at the wood for a while and then patted it with his hand as if it were a shoulder. "What time we gotta leave tomorrow?" Tom asked quietly.

"First thing, before daylight," said Mrs. Shelby. "Train leaves at seven."

"Tom," Leonora ventured. "Please use the car. I won't need it."

"Thanks." Tom nodded. "It's a good idea. Save us some time."

"Train is just fine." Mrs. Shelby's cheeks reddened as she stabbed her fork into the meat. "Shelbys never needed charity and don't need it now. A car!" she grunted. "Won't have our family putting on airs."

"That's enough, Mum!" Tom slammed his fist on the table, the girls jumping under his sudden temper. "This ain't like you."

Leonora rose, felt ill. "I'll start cleaning up," she muttered.

"No, you sit!" Tom ordered. "You got no right bein' rude to our guest, Mum. The Harringtons have been good as gold to James an' me. I nearly bled t'death from a bullock's horn an' she fixed me up better than any doc in the county. We got a good job there, Mum. Already paid off the taxes 'cause of it. This ain't like you. An' I don't like talkin' to you like this, Mum. I don't. But you owe this woman an apology."

Leonora wilted, wanted to slink under the table. "It's all right, Tom."

"No, it's not," said Mrs. Shelby weakly. "Tommie's right." She blinked at Leonora as if finally seeing her. "Like I got a thorn in my side that's twistin'. Pain makin' me so mad, I can't think straight." Her fingers fluttered to her cheeks, bounced as if she didn't recognize her own skin. "I just got to bury my boys. You see? Can't think straight. Got that thorn twistin' an' pokin' me." Her voice dropped. "Won't stop till I bury my boys."

Leonora covered her mouth with her napkin and nodded, tried to hold back the tears. She placed the cloth down. "May I help you in the kitchen?" she asked.

The woman took a long breath and stood. "I'd like the help. Thank you."

The Shelby home was just that—a home. Small, cut dashes lined the door frame to the library, marking the many heights of many children over many years; scuffs centered the wood floors from endless walking and running feet; worn, mismatched dishes lined the cupboards. Food, enough for an army, overflowed from the pantry and larder. Laughter and voices and stories papered the walls and the very home; the very depth of the place embraced the body with a sincere warmth. This was where James had spent much of his childhood, and as Leonora let her fingertips caress the patched upholstery and the dusty leather bindings of the books and silken hair of the children she felt a heavy, sweet gratitude that James had known such a life.

In the kitchen, Mrs. Shelby cleared the last of the dishes from the table. James and Tom sat with cups of coffee, looking refreshed and well fed. Mrs. Shelby greeted from the sink without looking back, "Mornin'. There's coffee and eggs if you like." Then the woman turned with a slight smile. "You sleep all right? That bed isn't the best."

"Haven't slept that well in a long, long time," Leonora answered.

"Mum's snorin' didn't keep you up?" Tom teased. "Thought the roof was gonna cave in."

Mrs. Shelby reached over and delivered a slap to his head.

"Ouch!" Tom winced. "Told you not t'beat me in front of company."

Mrs. Shelby shot him a look but couldn't disguise her humor. She turned to James. "Sure the girls aren't gonna be too much for you, son?"

"Sure. Besides, I got the princess here to help me." He winked at Leonora.

"Aren't you going?" she asked him in surprise.

James shook his head, his brows low. Mrs. Shelby saw the expression on his face. "You're family, James. You know that. Got just as much right t'be there as we do."

"I know that," said James with a nod. "Still think it's best if I stay here. I'll check in with the sharecroppers, take care of the animals. Besides, I miss the girls."

Tom and Mrs. Shelby left soon after in the ebbing dawn. "We'll be back tomorrow!" Tom shouted over the engine. "Try an' stay outta trouble till then!"

Leonora and James watched from the verandah as the blue exhaust diffused. "Glad they took the car," noted James. "Mrs. Shelby deserves to ride in style once in her life."

"Fair dinkum." Leonora nodded.

James laughed. "You're sounding more like an Aussie every day, Leo."

She smiled mischievously and rolled up her sleeves. "Enough of this bloody yabber, mate. This 'ouse won't clean itself, eh?" She returned to the kitchen with the warmth of James's grin on her back.

Little eyes lined the edge of the kitchen's door frame and watched her cook. Leonora played their game and pretended she couldn't see them. She scraped the eggs in the cast-iron skillet, the underside golden brown with butter. The bacon and sausage patties spit and left dark spots along the black stove, then hissed with greater fury as she flipped them over. And in this simple work she found Heaven. It didn't matter that it wasn't her food or her pans or her children.

Leonora scooped the food onto the set plates and the children snuck out like rabbits in a freshly tilled garden. She looked up in surprise. "Where did you all come from?"

The little girls bounced to their seats and set upon their food. Elbows and prodding eyes jabbed at Rachael, the oldest and, apparently, the designated speaker. Rachael shushed the children and addressed maturely, "Mrs. Harrington, did Mum an' Tom leave?"

"They did. First thing." She smiled. "And please call me Leonora."

The eyes slithered to their big sister again. "I'm Rachael. The oldest."

"And how old are you, Rachael?"

"Fourteen."

"A woman, then?"

The girl stretched her neck out proudly. "Nearly."

"Well, I'll be counting on your help then, Rachael. We women need to stick together."

A light beamed from the girl's face. "Gracie an' Charlotte," Rachael ordered as her eyes flitted to Leonora for approval, "please keep your elbows off the table when you're eatin'. An' Sarah an' Annie, stop fidgeting!"

James entered the kitchen then, his arms loaded with rough-cut wood, the muscles in his forearms still active and formed from chopping. "Don't think there's a prettier group of ladies in all of Australia than right here," he said. The girls giggled as he stacked the wood near the stove.

James peeked over Leonora's shoulder, his skin smelling of fresh eucalyptus. She nearly dropped the fork in the hot grease. "Want to sit with the girls?" he asked. "I'll clean up."

"No, you go. They've missed you." Leonora looked into the handsome face, let her gaze trail down his neck to the open collar of his shirt. She cleared her throat and turned back to the pan. "Are you hungry?"

"I am. Woke up so early, feels like it's lunchtime already." James sat down with the girls, their faces open in affection.

"James," Rachael asked, "is it true you an' Tom went drovin'?"

"It is." He reached for his fork. "Two hundred thousand head."

The girls stopped eating. "See any snakes?"

"Run into any bushrangers?"

"Abos sneak up on you?"

James finished chewing. "Yes. Yes. And no." He shot Charlotte a look. "Don't listen to those kids at school. Aborigines aren't out to hurt anybody. You know better than that."

"What kind of snakes?"

"Couple of taipans. A gwardar. Nearly stepped on a death adder coming out of my tent one morning."

"They bite you?"

"Wouldn't be here if they had."

"And rangers? Real-life bushrangers?"

James nodded, finished his food and brought the plate up to the sink. "Three of them. Had guns and masks and everything."

"Are you joking?" Leonora asked stiffly.

"Not at all." James pushed up his sleeves and began washing the plate with circular, casual movements. "To be expected."

"What you do?" asked Sarah breathlessly.

"An old trick Tom learned from your dad. Start running around yelling and shouting so much the cattle start stomping in circles. Rangers get scared and confused. Horses get too frightened to control. Crooks end up thinking there's more of us than there are, so they're off."

Crikey, the children mouthed in unison.

"All right, girls." James laughed and clapped his hands to break their trance. "Bring up those dishes and get dressed."

Leonora joined James at the sink, dried the dishes as he washed them. "Was that true about the bushrangers?" she asked.

"Mostly. Except for the end." James chuckled softly as he scrubbed the hot water in the greasy pan. "Tom stripped down naked and started chasing the poor bastards like a lunatic. Probably would have shot him if they hadn't started laughing so hard. Anyway, Tom brought out the bourbon and they all had a good drink."

"Naked?" She laughed.

"Bare-ass naked. All night." James raised his eyebrows. "Nearly left with the bushrangers myself just so I didn't have to look at his white bum. Pale as a full ugly moon, that one."

Leonora pressed her soapy wrist to her mouth and laughed until her side hurt. James bent with his own quiet laughter, then scooted her away from the sink with his hip and scolded her with a grin, "Compose yourself, woman!"

While James met with the neighbors out in the far paddocks, Leonora spent the day indoors with the chores. She made the beds, smoothing out the sheets in careful strokes. She dusted the bookshelves and piano, ran the duster around and over the furniture, the feathered end whipping around like a weasel. She washed the girls' dresses and pressed them with the copper, her face reddening from the steam. And she knew the foolishness of her joy in the work, but it was true joy and she wished silently with each broom stroke and hiss of the iron that this was her life.

Later in the day, she peeled the carrots and turnips and potatoes and watched out the window. James ran in the field with Gracie on his back, the other girls chasing at his heels. Then, when they caught him, he put down the girl and picked up another, ran again. Finally, he lay on his back exhausted even as the girls pulled at his arms and legs to get him moving. Leonora stopped peeling and laughed until tears wet her cheeks. James pretended he was asleep, lulled the girls into a sulking impatience and then jumped up, chased them into a screaming frenzy. And Leonora watched, slowly now, her laughter calmed, her smile even, and once again she wished, with more sadness than before, that this was her life.

That evening, the moon was high. Dinner was over. Little bellies were full again; faces were washed; a few mouths yawned above nightgowns. James lay on the couch, the girls piled on his lap as he read *The Magic Pudding*. One by one, he carried the sleeping children up to bed. When he returned to the kitchen, the house was quiet for the first time. Nature now had the space to enter and the rhythmic drone of crickets and chirr of frogs grew from beyond the screens.

James leaned against the wall and watched Leonora put the clean dishes back on the paper-lined shelves. She turned to him and met his smile. His long, strong body was loose and relaxed and brought her heart throbbing.

"You're really good with them," Leonora told him, her face soft. "You'll make a good father someday."

"Think so?"

"I do."

"I love kids. Want fifty of them," he said shyly.

"Fifty? Guess that explains why you're not married!" she teased.

"Certainly doesn't help," he agreed. James stretched his back against the wall and rubbed his right shoulder absently. His eyes rested on hers and it was too easy to hold the look, as easy and comfortable as breathing.

The heat moved from the stove to her face. "I should probably turn in."

"Not yet. You've been cooped up in here all day." He inched close, took her hand. "You're coming with me, young lady." The touch of his large hand covering and holding hers was stupefying and she followed him without thought or words—only the feeling of his palm against her palm and his fingers interlaced between her fingers and the heat that throbbed up her wrist all the way to her shoulder.

They walked out to the screened verandah and then to the summer night. The warm air wrapped around her skin, felt cool compared to the trapped heat of the house.

Slowly and with prolonged effort, James dropped her hand, but they walked close. Occasionally, their arms would brush. In the balmy air, the crickets and frogs and the strange and shrill call of the curlews grew in volume and engulfed them in a vibration of sound.

Leonora's hand was awkward without his and she stretched out her fingers as if they were numb. "Where was your house?" she asked finally. "The O'Reilly property."

In the blue dark, his features muted with varying expressions and his face was soft with shadows. "About eight miles that way." He pointed with his chin.

"May I see it?"

"No," he answered with stern quickness. "Burned down. Place was hardly a shack." James grew quiet for a moment and glanced at her worried face. "Tess—she was my aunt," he explained softly. "She was a good woman, a great woman, actually. Huge heart. After she died, everything just fell apart. Not many good memories from over that way."

"What was your uncle like?"

"Shamus?" James sighed. "Like I said, not many good memories from over that way."

They crested a tiny hill and James shook off whatever ghost was chasing him. "Close your eyes!" he ordered. She clamped her eyes shut as commanded.

James took her shoulders in his hands. "Now, lie down." Leonora's eyes popped open.

"Trust me."

She closed her eyes again, fidgeting nervously. "What about snakes?"

He laughed. "No snakes, I promise."

He helped her to the ground, cradling her head until it lay cushioned in thick grass. The sounds of the crickets leveled with her ears, seemed to rise from her body. She felt the heat of his length as he lay down, her pulse quickening with the proximity. "Now, open your eyes," he said.

She gripped the grass with her nails, a sudden vertigo rushing over her. The endless night sky seemed to surround from every side. There was no ground to be seen, no edge to the universe as she lay embraced in its enormity—an orb of midnight blue dotted with pinholes of brightness. The infinite magnitude above and around her made her gasp. "It's like I'm floating in space."

"Amazing, isn't it? Makes you feel tiny and large all at the same time." His tone grew gentle. "Seems like the stars are shining extra bright. Like they're showing off for you."

The words melted, nothing completely real anymore. Together they lay side by side, each out of view of the other, their bodies eclipsed by the halo of night. She breathed out in a long sigh and relaxed into the ground. The side of her hand brushed against his—the delicate touch sending an electric charge through her limbs.

Leonora did not move her hand away. With the lightest of touches, James slid his hand closer and placed his hand atop hers. Her breathing stopped as his fingertips whispered over her knuckles and etched the curves of her slender fingers. Her whole body tingled, each minuscule movement amplified through her fingers, then her arm, before radiating through her whole body. She stared at the stars, but her focus did not leave the feeling of his hand across her flesh.

Leonora turned her hand over and their palms pressed hard. She touched the soft and firm spots of his hand, felt the full tenderness of his long fingers as they intertwined. She thought of his hands on the rest of her body—the strong hands, the tender touches, the agility of his body against hers. Her face flushed. If he turned to her now and kissed her, she would give herself to him gratefully. She was tired of fighting.

James turned his head and looked at her profile. His face glowed like porcelain in the moonlight. The stars reflected off his pupils and she drowned in them, the vertigo returning as she fell into the pure pools.

"You're so beautiful," he whispered.

The words swept over her with sadness. He really did think she was beautiful, maybe even loved her, and it hurt like embraced grief. Her longing for him was an almost physical pain and she waited for him to pull her to his body—wanted him to make love to her, here, now, forever. She parted her lips and squeezed his hand—the only signal she had the strength to show.

His breathing quickened and his face shadowed with restraint. He closed his eyes, fought as metal against a magnetic pull and forced his concentration back at the stars. "We should go."

James stood and pulled her to her feet, then let go of her hand. Her mouth opened with disappointment and her stomach sank. He wouldn't meet her gaze as he turned back to the house. "The girls are light sleepers."

James lay on the library couch and slammed the book closed, dropped it with a thud onto the floor. He rubbed his eyes with his palms and flung his arm across his forehead.

She ain't your wife, Tom's voice echoed in his head.

James opened and closed his fist. He tried to recall the sensation of her fingers laced between his and he tried to forget it all at the same time. He didn't know what he was doing. One minute he could stay away from her; the next minute he was reaching for her, touching her. But the wanting never stopped and it pricked him like sharp hunger pains.

Seeing her with the Shelbys made it worse. She was happy. The simple joy glowed from her skin. At the stove, he wanted to wrap his arms around her waist and kiss her neck. At the sink, he wanted to lean her against the counter, lift her around his hips. Wanting her. Waiting. A kiss, an embrace, a caress—mere tastes that only increased the craving.

In a few days, Leonora would be back with Alex, her husband. They would share a bedroom again—share their bodies again. And he would be left with the memory of her rose perfume, the softness of her hands and the reality that she was not his, the reality that he was nothing more than a distraction.

James ran his fingers through his hair, let the brown strands remain tousled and spiked. He thought about her body lying next to his under the stars, remembered her profile as it angled in the moonlight, sending a subtle light down her smooth forehead. He melted into the memory of her slender, perfect nose and the smiling lips. *Those lips!*

At that moment, under the night expanse, he had almost taken her in his arms, almost let his body meld against her body until they became one, almost let the urges swallow him blind. He had wanted to make love to her. There. On hard, cold ground, he wanted to make love to her. Under the black blanket of night, surrounded by the sounds of the night, he wanted to touch her—all of her—and bring their own noise and movement and pleasure to the night and send their own vibrations into the earth.

She ain't your wife.

Leonora was asleep down the hall—three doors down. Three. Only a few walls and a door separated them and he could feel her breathing against his neck, feel her hair across his chest, feel her smile stretch across his skin. A few steps down the hall, a turn of the knob, and he could be in her bedroom. He could pull back the covers and slide in next to her and find her lips, find her hands searching and her body willing. Only three doors down. His legs tingled for movement, slid to the edge of the couch; his back wanted to rise.

She ain't your wife. With a frustrated, audible grunt, James thrashed onto his stomach and wrapped the pillow around the back of his head, clasped his hands in a lock around his ears.

She ain't your wife, mate.

"I know!" James shouted into the sofa, the sound muffled and lost within the cushions.

Upon their return, Tom and Mrs. Shelby shed the raw grief of the previous days and settled into mourning. The weight of the funeral no longer hung on their shoulders. Mrs. Shelby buried her sons; Tom buried his brothers. Life moved forward again, be it slowly and thick with gray.

No one wanted to sit within the confines of the house or walk past the two empty chairs that had been moved to the side of the dining room, so Mrs. Shelby packed a picnic and they all set out beyond the golden wheat to a placid lake nestled at the far end of the property. The day was hot and dry and bright. The ground filled with flowers and butterflies, the sky cloudless and pale blue. James carried Charlotte on his shoulders, her fingers covering his eyes now and then in play, sending him into blind staggers and protests.

Tom walked backwards, the sun against his back. "Where you say the dance is, Mum?"

"Tessler's," Mrs. Shelby answered. "Whole county will be there." Tom turned back and faced the sun, his shoulders slumped.

"Should leave after supper," Mrs. Shelby directed.

"You know I ain't goin', Mum." Tom plodded sullenly. "Wouldn't be right."

"Hell it's not! Nothin' you like more than a good dance!" Mrs. Shelby scolded. "Been workin' too hard, Tommie. You need a break. Be good for you."

"Really?" Tom turned around tentatively. "You wouldn't be sore?"

"Sore? I'd be thankin' the good Lord to have an ounce of peace without your yabberin'!" She wagged a finger at him. "You're goin' to that dance even if I got to drag you there myself!" She pointed at James and Leonora. "You're all goin'. Hear me?"

Tom smiled from one ear to the next, ran at his mother and kissed her hard. Mrs. Shelby wiped her hand across her cheek. "Gawd, hope you're a better kisser than that with the ladies!"

Tom was a different man now—looked at the sun like he saw it. He stepped back and put an easy arm over Leonora's shoulder. "Ever been to a barn dance?"

"Can't say I have." She thought about James and Tom dancing with all the pretty country girls. "But I'll stay back and help with the house. You don't need me tagging along."

"Nonsense," Mrs. Shelby said. Then she leaned into Leonora's ear. "Besides, somebody needs t'look after him. Can see that look in his eye. He's drunk on grog and women already."

"Heard that!" Tom shouted. He poked James in the ribs. "But she ain't lyin'!"

The lake came into full view. Mrs. Shelby laid the blanket onto the thick grass, spread out the food baskets.

"Can we go for a bogey now, Mum?" the girls hollered.

"Long as you stay close to the boys." Mrs. Shelby held up a blanket as the girls changed into their suits. Tom and James stripped off their shirts and socks and boots and piled their clothes on a smooth boulder.

"Coming in for a swim?" James asked Leonora with a grin.

She shook her head, tried to keep her eyes from drowning in his chest and stomach muscles. "I didn't bring a suit."

He winked playfully. "All the more reason." She blushed and threw an apricot at him.

"Last one in is a sheep's arse!" Tom shouted.

"Tommie, watch that mouth!" Mrs. Shelby scolded, but the men were already off toward the water, the girls screaming to catch up.

The two women sat under the shade of the wide, warm pepper tree and gathered their skirts under their legs. They watched the boys play tag with the little girls, feigning leg spasms and slow feet so the girls could knock them to the ground. Then, with a series of big and small splashes, they all plopped into the lake.

"You have a wonderful family, Mrs. Shelby." Leonora stroked a grass blade wistfully.

"Thank you. They're a good bunch," she said with visible pride. "That Tommie'll be the death of me, though." She chuckled. "He don't think much past what's sittin' right in front of him whether it's a beer, a woman or a fist. Just like his father, that one. Always has been." Her eyes twinkled, then grew distant. "Tommie's always seemed like a fleetin' wind."

Leonora plucked the grass stem, twirled it. "How so?"

"He was a sickly child. Wouldn't know it by lookin' at him. Doc said it was general malaise. What a load a crap! That first year, my Tommie nearly died more times than I could count. I nursed him, but I wouldn't hold him, didn't want to get attached. Sounds cold, eh?" The woman grimaced. "But I couldn't do it. Only reason he made it is because his dad never put him down. He strapped little Tommie to his chest an' brought him everywhere, just like a kangaroo with a joey in her pouch." She chuckled then, but her forehead wrinkled. "Still get my heart stuck in my throat when I see Tommie, fearin' something's gonna happen to him." She shook the ghosts away and slapped her knee. "Must be on account of those sickly years. Probably just the guilt I got for not holdin' him. That stuff plays silly tricks on a sentimental woman."

Mrs. Shelby picked at a loose thread on her dress, scanned the lake, the pepper tree and the purple violets hidden in the grass. "I'm sellin' the property," she said suddenly. "Tommie don't know yet." The woman lowered her eyes and her face paled, the skin around her jaw slacked. "Too many ghosts. I still wake up every morning lookin' for my Tom snorin' on the pillow next to me. Man's been dead well over ten years an' I still reach for him. Now the fields are filled with Will an' John. Think I see 'em sometimes, movin' with the wheat. Every time it breaks my heart. Like I'm losin' 'em all over again, a hundred times a day."

"Where will you go?"

"Don't know." Her lips straightened. "Can't stay here, though. I'll break right in two."

Mrs. Shelby inhaled and closed her eyes, her voice hushed and drawn with effort. "My boys are dead. Can't hardly breathe with 'em gone. Like I'm being choked all the time." The woman's chin shook quickly before hardening. "Thought I could handle it. When the boys left for the war, I prepared myself. Had hope but told myself over an' over again, they might not come back. But you can't prepare for death any more than you can prepare your stomach for starvation." Mrs. Shelby touched her red hair, patted it down around her ear. "My boys are gone an' it feels like there's hardly anything in the world that's not movin' in a dream."

Mrs. Shelby looked far into the distance, her pupils moving left and right and back again frantically searching for a world she recognized. She turned to Leonora then, looked over her features gently, the heavy words floating away like the seeds of a dandelion puff. "Look at me yabberin' on." She pulled out the basket and took out a bowl of strawberries. "Help yourself. Not worth waitin' for the rest of 'em. We'll have to drag 'em outta that lake."

Leonora took a piece of fruit, the juices warm and sweet. She watched as James crawled out of the water, his skin slick, his pants slung low on his waist showing the bones of his pelvis. He hollered something out at Tom and then dived over his head. James emerged amid splashing hands and laughter.

"He's a good man." Mrs. Shelby's tone was sober. Leonora knew who she was talking about and chewed the berry slowly.

"He's in love with you, you know. Saw it the first time he looked at you. Never saw him look at anyone like that. Ever."

Leonora's whole body flushed, her throat too frozen to swallow.

"You love him, too." Mrs. Shelby kept her gaze steady on Leonora's face.

Leonora closed her eyes, wanted to cry. The words, now spoken out loud, made them all the more real. Her chest expanded with longing until her ribs hurt.

"This husband of yours," asked Mrs. Shelby, "is he a good man?"

"No." Leonora's voice cracked and she couldn't look at the woman. "No, he's not."

Mrs. Shelby rolled her eyes. "Wouldn't be the first girl to marry a wanker."

Leonora met the woman's kind face and they chuckled shortly. But then Mrs. Shelby stopped. "You plannin' on leaving him?"

The tears began in her throat and she pushed them down. "No."

Mrs. Shelby nodded. "Then you got to let James go."

Leonora squeezed a blade of grass in her fingers until it darkened and ripped.

"That boy's like a son to me." Mrs. Shelby looked off at the swimming hole, her face wrinkled with affection. "He's honest. Good. Weighs everything in his mind. Feels things more than other people. A blessin' and a curse for a man to feel so much." Her face shifted and saddened. "He's had a hard life, Leonora."

Her head shot up and she watched Mrs. Shelby carefully, held on to her words.

"He's had more loss in his young life than any human's got a right to have. After Tess died, O'Reilly took it all out on the boy. Beat that poor child to an ounce of his life."

Leonora covered her mouth in horror. Her ears throbbed with the words. Her throat closed and now the tears fell freely from her eyes, heated a trail down her cheeks.

"I'm only tellin' you this," Mrs. Shelby said kindly and with pity, "because that man don't deserve more pain. If you can't be with him, let him go. It'll hurt him, but won't kill him. If you wait an' lead him on, it very well might. Better to do it now. Let James move on and find happiness, start a family. He'll make a good father, a good husband, someday. But you gotta give him a chance to find his way."

Mrs. Shelby stood and pressed down her skirt. "Know it hurts, Leonora. I can see it in your tears. But if you love him, you got t'stop it now. Poor man's had enough pain to last a lifetime."

The old barn filled with light, its beams blasting through the cracks and knots of the wooden planks. Before they even exited the car, the air vibrated with the hum of voices and laughter, the pulse of ragtime tunes atop male hoots and girlish squeals. The electric charge of the bodies and the music rippled along the patted dirt, drew the young in like moths to a candle flicker.

Ignoring the door handle, Tom hopped out the window of the parked Model T, barely able to contain himself after the stress and grief of the last few days. "A warnin' to you both." He pointed a finger at James and Leonora. "I'm gettin' so snookered t'night, you're gonna have to scrape me off the floor!" And catching the eye of a petite brunette, he added, "Or off of her. Hey, love, wait for me!" Tom was off like a shot, his eyes following every sway of the girl's hips as she sauntered and teased her way into the barn.

Leonora smiled at the bouncing figure. "I'm guessing he'll be true to his word."

"Can count on it," James promised. He put his hands in his pockets and stuck out an elbow for her to link. "Shall we?"

Leonora reminded herself it was just an arm. Shyly, she laced her arm into the waiting one, and the heat came quick and sharp. His biceps rubbed against her forearm, the muscle under his white shirt hard as bone. She tried to bring her focus to the ground, to the air, to the sounds of the barn, but the warmth of his body erased it all.

They headed over the gravel path to the flooded glow of the open doors, her heart picking up the rhythmic blast of music that grew and thumped in her rib cage. The room was alive, flowed and lived and breathed no different than a newly formed organism. The ground trembled under their shoes. The smell of tobacco and burning cigarettes filled the walls and formed a hazy cloud of smoke that hung and drifted near the rafters. A band in the corner took a break, smoking and laughing with one another. The victrola's needle thumped and bounced and tapped as it played "Darktown Strutters' Ball." A strand of sloppily hung lightbulbs dipped and climbed along the corners of the barn. Hay bales, stacked in rows of two, edged the walls, seated the reclining bodies of women with dresses pulled up seductively near their knees while their beaus stroked their calves and ankles and kissed their necks.

Leonora's fingers crept to her throat. The heat was everywhere. The smell of cologne-and-perfume-tainted sweat, of spilled ale and damp hay, of disturbed earth, made her dizzy. Bodies and touches and kisses and wanting, aching, waiting sex whispered from every end of the barn. Leonora dropped her arm from James's bent elbow, turned away from him even as his heavy gaze burned into the side of her face.

Mrs. Shelby's words still haunted—hurt her insides like an open wound. This trip had been a fantasy from the beginning. Tomorrow they would return to Wanjarri Downs; tomorrow she was Mrs. Alexander Harrington again. This—*this* was just a fairy tale, except her pumpkin was an expensive Model T and no glass slippers awaited the arch of her foot. Tomorrow she would be back walking on their broken shards.

But for right now, she was here. Leonora pushed tomorrow away and fell into the beat of trumpets and pianos and the deep, strumming bass. She shoved the heaviness away and tapped her foot to the music, scanned the details of the party. Clusters of young men and women stood in the corners, pointing, eyeing, and flirting with each other from across the room. Young, pretty women swayed in dainty dresses, brightly colored silks and cottons below faces flushed with ale and rouge. Men wearing everything from clean work clothes, to stiff-collared church shirts, to army uniforms chatted with lazy eyes and cigarettes suavely held between lips.

Tom stumbled through the crowd carrying two spilling pints of brown beer, his hair already wet with sweat under his hat. He pushed one at Leonora, sloshing the brew over her fingers, and gave the glass an exuberant clink. "Cheers! To the beginnin' of the end." He gulped down the ale like it was water.

Leonora giggled, flicked her wet fingers and looked at James's empty hands. "Looks like he forgot yours."

"I don't drink," he said flatly.

She blinked once before laughing. "Of course you don't."

He winced, tightened his brows. She reached over and touched his arm. "It wasn't an insult, James," she said softly through her smile. "You just never cease to amaze me."

His face relaxed and he raised an eyebrow. "Be careful with that stuff. Some rogue might try and take advantage of you."

"Thanks for the warning." She sipped the dark beer, felt the warmth of it run down her throat and settle in her stomach, drown out the but-terflies. The ale tasted bitter and awful and she liked it more than anything in the world.

Two women with mirrored smiles stopped short and screamed from the rim of the crowd, "Tommie Shelby!"

Tom turned and whipped off his hat, squeezed a twin sister in each arm, picking them off their feet with a loud, "Wooeee!"

"You're a dog, Tom! Why didn't you tell us you were back?" They stopped suddenly as his reason for being home became clear. "Oh, Tom. I'm so sorry about your brothers," said the slightly taller one, her face genuinely remorseful.

Tom shoved away the sentiment that threatened his mood and

grabbed the girls' hands, pulled them toward the floor until the shorter one turned back and yelled, "James! My God, we didn't see you there. Allison, it's James!" The sisters were charming in their excitement and quite beautiful. Leonora lowered her eyes.

The women ran at James, threw their arms around his neck, nearly knocking him against the wall. "God, we missed you guys. Just not the same without you."

Allison grabbed James's hand. "Come on; I love this song."

"Maybe the next one." James squeezed her hand before letting go of it. "Besides, it looks like Tom wants you both to himself."

The young woman glanced at Leonora and understanding crept through her face. "Pardon me, miss. I didn't see you there. I'm—" But before she could introduce herself, Tom pulled her away into the throng of dancing bodies.

James pointed in their direction and leaned his mouth to Leonora's ear. "Those are the McGinny sisters, Allison and Jessica. Two out of the five." His breath caressed her neck and she found it hard to concentrate on the words.

Leonora thought about the pretty McGinny sisters, thought about Mrs. Shelby's words again, realized her selfishness in coveting James's attention. "Don't you want to dance with them?" she ventured weakly. "They're very pretty."

"I'm not a dancer," James said. And she was shamed by her own relief.

Tom emerged from the crowd, alone. His cheeks were red and flushed, his hair sweated at the tips. His face was so happy, they both had to laugh. Tom smiled and grabbed Leonora's hand. "James might not be man enough t'dance with you, but I am." He pulled the drink from her hand, thrust it clumsily to James. "Sorry, mate!" he teased, and pulled her to the dance floor.

James leaned against the wall and pushed his hand in his front pocket. He watched Tom and Leonora squeeze between the dancers. She wore a pale blue dress. Above the blue, her skin was pale peach, her lips salmon, her cheeks pink—she was a moving, living sunset. He found the air now; near her, he couldn't breathe. It was a constant effort to keep his eyes off her, like they were meant to stare at her face and nothing else. James wafted through actions blindly and helplessly, flowing to her and then forcing himself back, and it made his bones tight, all that pulling back, fighting against every urge in his body.

James put the warm beer on the ground and wiped his wet hand across his trousers. He chuckled as his best friend twirled Leonora in the cramped space. Tom had no rhythm or etiquette for leading. He simply moved himself joyously in any manner his body wanted, taking poor Leonora along on his uncoordinated ride.

Leonora was laughing—laughing so hard James could see tears in her eyes as she tried to keep up with her swinging, spastic partner. He was relieved to find her so happy. Her mood had changed during the picnic earlier in the day. She had turned quiet and distant, her eyes sad. But leave it to Tom Shelby to blow away the clouds.

James watched Leonora, watched her smile, her laughter, her figure, her skin, her golden hair, the curve of her neck, the small waist, the perfect shoulders and the curved back. Tom faded into a haze along with all the others crowded into the space. James only saw Leonora. Even the pulsating music muffled, only the sensation of the beat touching his skin. James stopped smiling. He loved her. It was there now, in his chest and in his blood, in the unwavering certainty that set his jaw and made his muscles tight and his bones thick with knowing. He loved her—all of her. A fight grew now—pumped from the vibrating floor, fueled with the heat of stifled, hot bodies.

Tomorrow she would be back with that bastard. Just the thought of it hardened the lines in his face and straightened his back against the wall. Tomorrow this would go away. He loved her and the fight rose. He had tonight. Only. He would not hide. He could fight or disintegrate with waiting. Decision landed hard and swift. Let tomorrow shine with light or hide with darkness, but tonight he would fight.

James left the wall and strode through the crowd, his body tall and straight with singular purpose. From Tom's swirling, Leonora saw James approaching and raised her eyebrows in a silent, mock cry for rescue. But then she saw the look on his face and stopped smiling, fell idle in Tom's arms. James pushed past Tom and gripped Leonora's waist firmly in his hands. Tom opened his mouth in complaint but then saw James's expression and exited promptly into the moving bodies.

The song shifted to the slow serenade of "Any Time's Kissing

Time." James pressed his palm into the small of Leonora's back and loomed above her, held her eyes so it was impossible for her to look away. Her body trembled under his touch. "Thought you weren't a dancer," she whispered.

"Didn't have the right partner."

James pressed his fingers into her back, the soft silk of her dress unable to slip under his tight grip. He moved his hand up her spine surely and confidently, all restraint now gone. He held her helpless gaze with unwavering intensity, permitted the heat to close in and linger unextinguished. Longing and desire drowned out the other bodies. The voices and music blurred behind the stark beauty that he held in his hands. James tightened his fingers against her back. Her lips opened and gasped with the pressure, her heartbeat clear and fast against his chest.

Leonora did not belong to another man. She was not another man's wife. Not here. Here, at this moment, she was his. Here, at this moment, there was no station to return to, there was no past of loneliness or abuse, there was only her open face and her pink lips inches away.

As the song wound down with the last plaintive notes James stopped moving and held her still against his frame, kept his eyes glued to her wide and urgent pupils. He leaned his face down and whispered in her ear above her neck, "I can make you happy, Leo." James saw the look of fear enter her eyes. "I will *never* hurt you," he promised. "Ever."

He would have kissed her square on the mouth right then and there, fully and without regret, had a drunken woman from the crowd, mistaking him for another man, not snatched him roughly out of Leonora's arms and into the crowd.

In the lapse without him, the air caught in Leonora's throat. Her head dizzied. The burn of his touch still smoldered along her back where his fingers had held her. And that look—the urgency in his eye that nearly crumbled her bones to dust. She couldn't think. She clutched her throat and ran through the crowd to the open barn doors and out into the cool night air. She needed to get away, needed to clear her head.

The sounds of music and laughter wafted, followed her. Leonora looked into the dark sky, sought the fresh air greedily. The stars, millions of them, dotted the blackness. She kept walking past the carriages, past the few cars lining the lot, until the music and the crowd blended to one undulating sound.

Leonora leaned her arms against the split-rail fence, let the slight breeze cool her face as she stared into endless space. It would be so easy to give in. But she sank with the impossibility. It would be so easy to just say yes, to close her eyes, take his hand and leave every other person, memory, behind. But the black children would follow her. Their white eyes, their empty wails for their mothers and fathers ringing in her ears until she screamed. If she left Alex, she destroyed families. If she stayed, she destroyed James.

Leonora rubbed the spot above her nose between her eyebrows. Her stomach fell deeper. She could keep James at the station—hold him hostage with glimmers of hope, shackling him. She could keep her heart still full and beating by knowing he was near. It was enough for her. But James would fade from it slowly, torturously, forsaking his own future and happiness. She thought about Mrs. Shelby's words. The pain he endured in his life. She could not, would not, add any more to it. Her life was of little sacrifice. Knowing what she needed to do brought no comfort; it ripped and clawed at her flesh and made her ill to her toes. Her decision mapped out a lonely, endless future that would leave her more dead than alive.

The stars stretched into diamonds, then distorted and lengthened through the lens of her tears. They flowed savagely down her cheeks and she bit her lip to stop them, but their number grew stubbornly. Deep sobs rattled her whole body and made her hiccup for air. Leonora rested her clenched palms against her lids and let the dark, buried sorrow spill. She loved him, loved him so much that it seemed better to die than to live without him. But there was more to this world than her life. Her happiness had always taken a backseat. This was her curse, her pain.

Footsteps crunched the gravel and she frantically wiped her eyes, tried to stop the flood. James emerged from the shadows. Her stomach was sick and she pressed it with her hand. She was thankful for the lack of light, hoping it hid her red eyes.

"You disappeared," James said cautiously.

"Just needed a little air," she sniffed.

He stepped closer. "Have you been crying?"

She shook her head even as fresh tears spilled. "No."

"I can see that." James gently rubbed a tear away with his thumb. He kept his hand at her face, caressed her cheek with his finger.

Her body was tired, so tired of fighting. She let her cheek sink into his palm. She closed her eyes and placed her hand upon his, wanting only to savor his touch for a moment—a moment that she could store within her memory for a lifetime.

James inched closer to her body, his strong thighs leaning into her hips. He took his fingers from her face and reached for her limp hand, brought it up to his mouth, turning her palm and placing his lips in the smooth center. She leaned against the post for support, her legs completely numb as he brushed his lips over her palm, her wrist, and across her forearm.

Her body burned and her muscles quivered. James placed a hand on her waist and moved closer still until the steel of his belt buckle pressed against the fabric of her dress and blazed and spun her abdomen. He leaned forward and, with the softest of lips, kissed the farthest edge of her cheek right next to her ear.

Drowning. Falling. Sinking. Helpless. The desire crippled her. His lips moved across her cheekbone. She was losing. If he kissed her on the mouth, she would be lost. She would melt into his arms. Clear thinking, any thinking, would evaporate into the night.

If you love him, you got t'stop it now, Mrs. Shelby's words echoed between the kisses. *Poor man's had enough pain to last a lifetime.*

James kissed the middle of her cheek, so close to her lips that it would only take a slight turn of her head for them to meet. *Let him go.*

"I . . . can't do this," Leonora whispered between her tears.

In the darkness James stopped, but his face was close. "You can leave him, Leo," his words hushed with urgency. "*Leave him.*" He gathered her into his arms, his lips poised above hers. "I love you, Leo."

She closed her eyes and swallowed hard, pushed every ounce of love for him down to her stomach. She hardened her face, straightened her neck and forced her wet eyes to ice. Then she brought the new, bitter words up, raised them to her throat like bile and delivered them roughly: "I'm in love with Alex."

His body winced. A thrust of a knife into his ribs, pushed in with her own hand and twisted, would have caused less pain. James dropped his hand from her waist with deadweight. His arm hung loosely at his side. His brows knit above blank eyes. His face clenched with the hard, hard lines of his cheekbones and jaw. James stared at her for only a second, a last second, before he turned silently and walked away.

Leonora did not watch him leave. Her body stood rigid, paralyzed. Only her hand moved—her fingers tightening with white knuckles around the fence post as the pain in her stomach nearly crushed her to the ground.

The next morning, Tom, James and Leonora left the Shelby homestead under the rising, bitter sun. As they drove in the open car, the golden wheat waved in the wrong direction. Back. Back. If only she could go back.

But the sage bush squeezed through the thinning wheat until it did not wave any longer. And this sage bush grew bolder as the red earth grew bolder between the clusters and the stiff, hard grass did not wave but pointed straight into the hard, hot sky. The rabbit-proof fence picked up by the road, blurred outside the moving car until the posts were invisible and only long lines of gray wire pointed the direction home.

Tom slept in the backseat, sprawled and listless with hangover. His boots rested on the window, his ankles crossed; his hat slumped low on his forehead, covered his eyes and nose. At times his body jerked from a dancing dream or a twisted stomach and then went limply back to sleep.

James drove, his narrowed eyes glued to the road. He held the steering wheel with his right hand, rested the elbow of the left on the windowsill. Despite the unrelenting heat, the cold that radiated from him filled the car. Leonora occupied the passenger seat, kept her hands together and interlaced, still as a posed corpse. They had not spoken a word since they said their farewells to the Shelbys—the divide between them as large as if they rode in separate vehicles. In another few hours, the gates of Wanjarri Downs would come into view and then lock, one after another, behind her.

Leonora stared at her fingers fixed on her lap. "How long will you stay?" she whispered.

James did not answer for a long time, kept his gaze straight. "Until I talk to Tom." Then added shortly, "He can stay on if he wants."

"Where will you go?"

He ignored the question, leaned his elbow farther out the window, shifted his body away from her.

She had no right to ask him anything. He would leave soon, maybe by morning. There would never be another kiss, a touch, a look, again. Not even a good-bye. It was over. She wiped a heavy, lone tear. It was over before it had even begun.

CHAPTER 58

The postman did not whistle or nod as he delivered the telegram from Alex. He dropped the note in Leonora's hand and took off to his truck as fast as his wishbone legs could wobble. And in the damp, charged air she could feel the storm coming before she read the words.

Alex was stuck in Coolgardie, delayed by bushfire that had started from lightning and spread through the dry bush. He sent directions to have the homestead protected. But as she read the note, it was not the fire or the storm that translated; it was the relief that Alex would not be returning today, the relief that Tom and James would stay another day.

Leonora had not seen James since returning to Wanjarri Downs. She wasn't even sure if he was still on the property. It was Tom who delivered their resignation with guilt-drawn cheeks and wincing eyes. "You gonna be orright, Leonora?" he had asked.

She nodded.

"We'll stay until Alex gets back," he promised. "Only proper to tell him in person."

She nodded again, bit her lip. Tom stepped forward and hugged her as he would a sister, her chin crinkling against the fabric of his shirt. She pulled away, kept her eyes glued to the wood grain of the front door, stared at anything hard and lifeless just to avoid Tom's soft gaze.

"James'll be orright," he said, reading her mind. "He's a tough bloke."

With the sound of his name, Leonora blinked with wet lashes, bore her focus up to the ceiling and waited until Tom had walked away.

Dawn broke; the darkness remained. There would be no sun today. Pots rattled and echoed from the kitchen. Leonora followed the sounds and found Meredith bent over the lower cabinets pulling out kettles and stockpots and skillets. The woman's face was already red with sweat, her sleeves rolled to her biceps, her elbows wrinkled and puckered from the tight fabric. Meredith dug farther into the recesses of the shelf and bumped her head during the retreat. "Och! Fer the love a . . ." She stood up rubbing her head. "Oh, mornin', Mrs. 'Arrington. Didn't hear yeh come in." The woman gave a significant nod. "Storm comin'."

"Just got word from Alex. There's bushfire near Coolgardie. Roads are all blocked."

Meredith brought the skillet to the stove with a bang. "A big one orright! Things been quiet too long. This storm's plannin' t'make up fer lost time." The woman pulled the stockpot up and placed it on the back burner. "Can't predict these ones, either. Some are real dowsers. Creeks flood over in minutes. Some bring the dry lightnin' wivout a drop of rain. Some bring both. Can't predict. Lightnin' be bad, though. Can feel it on m'skin."

Meredith pulled out a drawer stacked and tangled with ladles, metal spoons and spatulas. "Men are workin' outside. Saw 'em on my way in. They're pullin' out the hoses an' sprayin' down the stables. All yeh can do. Soak the place wet an' pray."

Leonora scanned the burdened stovetop. "Looks like you're planning to feed an army."

"I am!" Meredith bellowed. "Law of the bush, Mrs. 'Arrington. If the bush is burnin', every man in the county be comin' out t'stop it. Station women got t'feed 'em. Take shifts."

The kitchen door opened and Clare staggered in, smiling and sleepy, wearing the same dress as the day before. "Mornin', Mrs. 'Arrington," she said stiffly, the mirth fading. "Storm's comin'." Clare's eyes flitted to Meredith, impatient to chat in private. "Wamme t'close up the house?"

"No, I'll do it," Leonora answered, taking the hint and glad to have a task. "Looks like Meredith is going to need your help."

Leonora walked to the second floor and started closing the shutters. Gray clouds thickened miles and miles across the open, flat land.

Stockmen scurried like ants as they prepped the water towers, dragged rubber hoses and moved hay and dry brush away from the buildings. Then James rode up on horseback, gave instruction to one of the Aborigines. Leonora touched the lace curtains, her insides hollowing, missing him before he was even gone. She pushed the despair away, shoved it down to her corners as a seamstress stuffs a pillow and slammed the shutters closed.

She moved down to the first floor. Russell was on the verandah spraying water at the side of the house. The wave of water smashed against the windows and streaked down the panes as she closed the tall French doors, the room dimming with each click.

"Get yer head outta the clouds, Clare, an' peel 'em potatoes!" Leonora could hear Meredith huffing from the kitchen, "Dense as a stone this mornin'! Whot's got yeh all tickled?"

"Let's jist say it was a good night." Clare snickered. "Good mornin', too."

"Yeah?" Meredith scoffed, unimpressed. "Whot? Yeh ride that swaggie that's been hangin' round?"

Leonora closed the shutters near the kitchen and rolled her eyes at the crude and never-ending gossip. She found no humor in their chatter, no humor in anything.

"Och! To think," Clare retorted hotly. "Spent the night in the managers' quarters."

Leonora froze, her hand flat and still upon the windowpane, her ears focused on every minuscule sound from the kitchen.

Meredith laughed a great bosom-shaking laugh. "Like Tom would 'ave yeh! Save yer lies fer somebody'll believe 'em."

"Ain't a lie!" Clare's disgruntled voice came fast and adamant. "Sides, it weren't Tom that give it t'me. Was James."

Leonora's ears and face burned. She didn't breathe—couldn't breathe.

"That man don't know yer alive, let alone goin' to bed wiv yeh!" spit Meredith.

"Well, he knows I'm alive now, don't he? Took me twice. Nearly left me bowlegged as postman Danny!"

Meredith laughed hard, then softened with affection. "Full of shit is whot yeh is, Clare."

The words punched Leonora in the stomach with swift, blunt force, made her want to vomit. Her body fell limp against the wall, her knees buckling.

"Says he's been wantin' me fer a long time," Clare bragged. "Guess he didn't want t'wait no more. On account he's leavin'."

Leonora buried her face in her hands. Her spine bent and arched forward as her gut cramped. *No, no, no!*

"Hate t'see 'em go," said Meredith. "Good blokes."

"James says he's sick of bein' Mrs. 'Arrington's whippin' boy!" Clare chimed expertly. "Tired of takin' orders from rich folks."

The dull, jagged knife cut through the horror now. The betrayal, hard and cruel, ripped Leonora's heart in two. Her lips stretched over her teeth. A wail scratched up her throat, lodged before it could reach her mouth. It had all been a joke—a cruel, heartless game. Jabbing images bit into her flesh—James kissing Clare's thin, wretched mouth, touching her freckled skin, whispering in her waiting ear, laughing at *her.*

The thoughts weighted her bones. It had all been a lie. The pain turned with a sudden blinding fury. *It had all been a lie.* The tears were coming, but she smashed them away with the anger. Restless hands fumbled for the crystal vase on the table, then hurled it across the room. Shreds of glass shattered into giant prismed chunks just as her heart splintered into a million matching ones. The thrust opened the chasm in her chest and choked sobs rocked her body. She was such a fool! She had fallen for his words. He never loved her—no one ever did.

The closed windows trapped her as in a cage, the image of James with Clare blinding. She wanted to run away. Run away until her legs gave out and her heart stopped beating. She fled the confines of the house, the crushing walls. The wind whipped her hair. She ran to the barn. A stockman was sliding the door closed, his head ducking from blowing dust. She plowed past him, found the black stallion, slick and wide-eyed in the end stall, and pulled at the reins. The man stopped her, pointed in the flashing distance. "No good. Storm's comin'."

But she couldn't see the storm or the wind or the lightning, just the hurt that devoured her insides. She jumped on the horse bareback. The stallion reared, but she held on and with one swift kick pushed him to a full gallop past the riding ring. James and Tom turned the corner, jumped out of the way as she tore past.

Leonora pushed the horse toward the storm, ran for miles under the growing gray sky, chased its entrance. The thick rolling clouds sped in equal speed as she pushed to meet it. She didn't know where she was going, didn't care as long as she was away from that house and Clare's laughter and James's cruelty and the images that beat inside her brain.

Light, intermittent rain began to fall, splattered against her face. Sharp crackles of thunder blasted from the south and made the horse rear again. The lightning was getting closer. The noise snapped with lucidity, cleared her mind. The air's electric charge itched under her skin, raised the hairs along her arms with the static. The nervous horse twitched below her thighs. She scanned the plains, found her bearings and searched for a point of shelter. The closest spot was at a barn in a paddock not far off. Leonora kicked the horse, veered him to the right, the thunder booming overhead.

Rain had soaked her to the skin by the time she reached the paddock. The horse huffed as she dismounted, steam rising like smoke from his nostrils and coat. The rain fell straight down now, pelted her hair. She walked the horse to the barn; the door was open. The new lambs were gone. She tied the horse and went back into the open, squinting at the sky as the rain poured against her face. Shielding her eyes with her hand, she peered across the wet dirt, heard the thunder getting louder, found the lambs huddled with the ewes under a gum tree.

The new lambs walked in circles with plaintive *baas*, disoriented from the thunder. She gathered them near the barn and one by one carried the tiny lambs. Her skirt was covered in red mud and her skin was soaked at every inch, her lungs labored. The ewes stayed frightened under the tiny tree, dug hind legs in stubbornly. Leonora pulled off a branch and whacked one's fleece until it inched forward. She wiped her hair out of her eyes and as she did saw the figure galloping full speed.

Her insides ignited with fresh rage. She grabbed the ewe with full force and dragged her into the barn, then returned for the last one, her limbs trembling. From the gray wet, James jumped off his horse, pulled her toward the barn, the rain pouring off his hat in a steady stream. "Leo!" he called through the downpour, but she didn't answer.

James rushed at her. "What the hell are you doing?" he shouted.

She ignored him, hated him, pushed the ewe on the rump toward the barn. James grabbed the sheep around the belly. "I'll get her!"

Leonora shoved him with all her might, her wet hair flying into her face. "I don't need your help!" she yelled. "Just go away!"

James stared at her stunned, oblivious to the rain. "Leo, what's wrong?"

"I don't need you!" She drove fists into his chest, her voice shaking. "Leave me alone!"

"Stop it!" He grabbed her slick wrists. "What's this about?"

She struggled against his grip, his hands wet and strong. "I heard Clare!" she shouted. "You were with her! I heard it all!"

His face froze. Leonora took the silence as confirmation and with one hard pull jerked from his grip. Her lips stretched. "How could you?" she cried.

"Clare? The maid?" James found his voice equally passionate. "Have you lost your mind, Leo?" He spit with disgust at the rain falling on his mouth. "Do you think I would ever lay a hand on that woman?"

"Don't lie to me, James!" Leonora glared at him, wanted to pound against his ribs. "I heard what she said!"

"She's a damn liar, Leo!" His chest heaved as he pointed into the distance. "Saw her slink out of an Abo shack this morning!"

The rain dripped down her face, curled around her open lips. He was telling the truth. The world pierced with clarity, the noise of the storm suddenly sharp and loud in her ears. Clare had lied. Leonora had heard the woman's gossip and lies a million times before, but it hadn't registered. The thought of James—the thought of him with Clare—had erased all logic. Remorse poked instantly. "I-I-I'm sorry," she stammered.

James's jaw clenched and his lips tightened to a hard line. The anger was fierce in him now. The thunder cracked above their heads, but James didn't flinch. He stepped forward and shouted through the rain, "Why the hell am I defending myself to *you?*" His voice was rough and harsh. "You're the one who's married!"

James stepped another foot forward. "How dare you accuse me, question me on anything!" he yelled. He pointed to the direction of the station, his eyes furious. "Every night you go into that house and share a bed with that bastard when I know . . . I know you should be sharing my bed! Do you know what it does to me when I think about you lying next to him, night after night—thinking about him touching you? Do you have any idea? It eats me alive, Leo! It kills me!" He ran his hand through his hair, pulled at the wet strands. "So, no, I have never been with the likes of Clare, but I'm no saint, Leo. I'm still a man and I want you so bad that . . ." He scowled and stopped, unable to find the words. He stomped closer. "So, you tell me, Leo. Tell me what the hell right you have to ask me anything!"

"Because . . . I love you!" she shouted back, her voice choppy. "I love you."

James grabbed her by the shoulders, kissed her lips feverishly, roughly, endlessly. The rain pelted their hair and ran over lips, the erupting sky invisible and soundless.

James slid his lips from hers, held her face with spread fingers. "Leave him," he pleaded.

Leonora's legs went weak. "I can't," she whispered.

Under heavy, slick eyelashes, James's eyes hardened. He loosened his grip on her shoulders, swallowed with revulsion. "Is it the money?"

"No!" she cried, and grabbed his arms.

James yanked away from her touch. He looked at her lips as if they made him sick. "You're a coward."

She shook her head violently. "No." Her voice choked desperately as she floundered for his hand. "Please don't say that."

James recoiled, stepped back, his face bewildered. "You're a bloody coward."

He hated her. Leonora stood alone under the smashing rain, watched helplessly as he retreated one step at a time. She opened her mouth, her voice washed away, mute.

"Go back to Alex," James ordered with a clear, low voice. His face was ice as he looked at her for the last time. "I don't want you anymore." James turned, walked toward his horse, his body soaked and dark.

Leonora fell to her knees in the mud. He was leaving. Panic, old and hidden, rose to the surface and spread to every cell. Truth hung wet and cold and suffocating—they all left.

She stared at her hands as they sank and stained in red earth. "He'll take the children away!" she yelled above the storm, defeated. James stopped but did not turn around. "The children," she whimpered, hitting her fist weakly into the mud, splashing red dots along her arm.

James turned his head, his brows low, his voice chilled. "What children?"

Don't say it. Stop it now. Let him go. But the loss, the emptiness, grabbed at her heels and clawed her ankles. "The Aborigines!" she cried. "If I leave, Alex will send the children away."

The silence hung like a noose. The voice of caution slinked away. She had said it. There was no retreat—no stopping what she started.

James marched back to her. She sobbed with face down, sick with remorse and infirmity. His boots took shape, paused in front of her knees. He reached down and pulled her gently up by the shoulders to her feet.

"I tried to leave!" she cried without looking at him. "I asked for a divorce. But the mission came for the children and I saw . . . I couldn't let him do it, James." His fingers tightened against her shoulders, kept her from crumpling. "I know . . . *we* know what happens to orphans." She looked up at him then, defended almost soundlessly, "I'm not a coward."

James looked through the gauze of gray, hard rain until he found her eyes. "Why didn't you tell me this before?"

Tears fell harder, mixed with raindrops. She gripped his elbows, shook them without power. "Because you'd confront him. And there's nothing that can be done. Nothing." She lowered her voice and searched his face. "He's a violent man, James." She twisted the soaked fabric of his sleeve. "Promise me you won't do anything."

But James was lost in her eyes, in the beauty of her face. He put his hand around her waist and pulled her body against his. She tried to pull back, needed him to understand. "Promise me, James!" she begged. "Please . . ."

James did not hear her. He wrestled her arms to her sides and covered her words with his lips. And the words, the caution, the hunt for a promise, filtered away with his kiss and she melted into the warmth of his figure and the urgency of his mouth.

The rain fell hard, landed rough and steady upon their skin. It soaked their faces, their hair, their ears, their frantic lips; it soaked the fabric of their clothes until the fabric clung, weighted warm and slack, against their figures. A bolt of lightning cracked the sky, landed so close as to make the wet ground sizzle, its force strong enough to part their lips. James lifted Leonora into his arms in one strong swoop and ran for cover in the barn.

The metal roof pounded as if hammers fell from the clouds instead of water. The new wood walls, still green in spots and smelling of tree sap, trapped the thick humidity between slats. Pressed, damp hay engulfed and sweetened the air along the ground and rose and strengthened as it climbed the eaves. James lowered Leonora to her feet and pushed her against the wall, found her mouth again. Lightning, spastic and frequent, brought light, then dimness, back and forth like a lamp knob turned on and off with indecision. Thunder rode tandem with the white, jagged bolts, did not lag by a beat. The sheep and horses shuffled softly in the straw in a faraway test of sound.

James rolled his head into Leonora's neck, kissed the curves of her throat, tasted the skin slick with fresh rain. *Home.* She clutched his back, her hands too small to touch it all at once. She rubbed her palms along the muscles in his arms, the tight forearms, the hard biceps and shoulders. *Home.* She tugged at his wet shirt, pulled the fabric from his trousers, the buttons tight from rain. Blind with kissing, she fumbled and pulled at them, unclasping some and popping others. He curled his fingers in her hair. *Home.*

Without taking his lips from hers, James shook off his open shirt, letting it fall from his arms onto the ground. Leonora kissed down the ripples of his chest as he pushed her blouse from her shoulders and pressed his mouth along her collarbone. She reached behind her back and unclasped her skirt. James pushed the fabric off her body with hard strokes, and for one moment he paused, looked at the length of her in his arms. And in this pause, they stared at each other, the sound of thunder cutting through the sky, the lightning flashing upon their still faces, illuminating them.

James bent his neck down, kissed her softly and slowly this time, touched her face with his fingertips as if the bones were more fragile than porcelain. She reached to his pants, pulled at the belt. The leather slid against the metal buckle and drew through the loops with the sound of a slow, worn whip. With sure fingers, she undid the steel button below his waist. His body shuddered slightly under her touch. James moved closer, drifted his fingers over her silk slip and touched her breast. Her mouth opened with the touch. He slid his palm over the breast, cradled it in his fingers, then moved up to the tiny straps of the slip and let them fall from her shoulders. The slip draped to the ground under its own weight.

James wrapped her into the folds of his arms, pressed her body against his smooth chest, and lifted her feet off the ground before laying her gently on the clean hay. The storm raged above and around as their limbs and breathing entwined. The steel roof beat and echoed under the pounding; the barn walls vibrated; the ground trembled— the bodies trembled. Rain-soaked skin pressed and quivered below urgent fingers. Lips found the nape of the neck, found the tender nook on the underside of the elbow, found the small indent at the base of the lower back. Fingers etched lines and curved and tightened around the hidden, soft flesh of breasts and buttocks and inner thighs. A slide of hand; an arched body.

The muscles of James's thighs hardened and twitched with restraint, then loosened as Leonora's hips rose willingly—furiously—to meet his. Small muffled cries of pleasure—drawn, high mimics of pain—wafted atop the warm, still air. The lambs bleated plaintively with the strange sounds and writhing bodies and inched closer to the legs of the ewes.

Breathing quickened and labored within the walls and drowned out the pounding of rain. *Home. Home. Home!* The horses stepped nervously as a long cry floated into the thick air. Another cry, low and guttural, followed and then silence.

The barn's air grew sleepy and quiet. The sheep closed eyes and rested chins upon the fleece of their babies. Slow breathing mingled with the rain, with the breathing of sheep and horses, mingled with the slow and lazy smell of hay. Gentle, tender kisses—unhurried and calm this time—lost their need to rush. For time had stopped. The fear, the loneliness, the weakness, washed away. They had a home now. After a lifetime of searching, they were home.

Smooth touches. Caresses over naked skin. Soft whispers exchanged between lips and earlobes. Muffled laughter tangled in hair and at the throat. Kissing. Lips moved across necks and arms and legs and stomachs. Limbs slid and tangled. Stroking. Fingers that would not stay idle inched and played. Searching and touching. Heat and softness; wet and pulsing skin. Crevices. Tender spots. Opening. Waiting. Wanting. And the breathing shifted, came quicker and more urgent once again. And the barn filled again with the sounds of lovemaking below the storm.

Leonora woke to hazy brightness. Late-afternoon sun seeped through the cracks of the barn wood, stretched spears of light across the floor, highlighted the finite crumbs of dust and straw. The rain had stopped. Water dripped gently from the roof and tapped into the rain barrel. The air was rich with wet loam. The ground steamed. Hay bales simmered with internal decomposition.

Leonora's body was weak and relaxed from lovemaking, her bones soft as jelly. Her eyes wandered over James's naked body, his arm still wrapped heavily around her waist like he was afraid she might disappear. His face was calm. She looked upon the features with awe; he had never looked so handsome, so perfect. The old burdens that he carried behind his eyes had faded. His hair was tousled, pointed out in rumpled spurts. Bits of hay threaded through the chestnut strands. She smiled, laughed softly and gently picked out a few bits.

James stirred, stretched out his back and pulled her tight against his chest without opening his eyes. He smiled languidly and whispered into her ear, "I love you, Leo."

She nuzzled against his neck, ran her nails across his side and hip, the skin rising in tiny bumps under her touch. James propped himself on an elbow and touched her face, outlined the curves of it. He moved the wisps of long hair away from her face and tucked them softly behind her ears, etched the thin gold chain of her necklace down to her breasts.

Leonora leaned into him and kissed his forehead, his cheek, the edge of his mouth, before placing her lips against his, parting them with the tip of her tongue. There was no fear in the barn; there was no going back.

Her eyes flitted to the white rays forcing their way between the wood. She sighed and lowered her gaze to her fingers that rested on James's chest. James studied her profile and saw the first lines of worry take shape. He lifted her chin, read her mind. "We'll figure it out, Leo."

"You won't leave?"

"I'll never leave you."

She smiled bravely and nodded, the worry still growing with the sun that hovered too hot and too high. James hugged her in his arms, stroked her hair. Warm tears trickled a line down his neck and he held her tighter. "We'll figure it out." He didn't want to let her go. "I promise."

The stallion whinnied, pulled at his reins. A new thunder pounded, seemed to rise from the very ground, distant but intensifying. The sheep rose with attention; the lambs staggered on bent, wobbly legs at the earth's sudden movement. Leonora sat upright, pulled her clothes to her breast. James jumped to his feet, slipped on his pants. The steady rhythm defined to a horse's gallop. James dropped his shirt over his head, fumbled with buttons as he walked to the door. "Stay here, Leo!" he ordered, all peace gone.

He cracked the door and peered out. "I think it's Tom. Too far away to tell for sure." He glanced at her, the look soft. "Don't come out until I get you, all right?" James tucked in his shirt, closed the barn door behind him.

Tom rode up fast, stopped the horse so quickly that its front legs kicked the sky. "Jesus, James! Been lookin' everywhere for you." He shimmied off the horse, his pupils darting. "Is Leonora with you?"

James gave a short nod, hardened his face.

"Christ." He spit. Tom grabbed his arm, his speech firm and clear. "Listen, James. Alex has the whole bloody station out lookin' for her. I tried to get a head start, but they're close behind. You gotta get out of here. Now."

James sped to the barn. Leonora was already dressed. "I heard," she said.

James grabbed the horses. "Come on; we've got to get out of here."

"I can't leave, James. Besides, we can't take the chance of being seen together. You go."

"I'm not leaving you."

Tom opened the barn door, his eyes wild. "James, you need to get outta here! You got a five-minute lead at the most."

"Go, James!" Leonora begged. "Please."

James looked at one and then the other. With gritted teeth, he mounted his horse.

"Stay toward the eastern paddocks," directed Tom.

James turned to Leonora, opened his mouth to speak.

"Go!" Tom yelled.

With one final look, James snapped his mouth shut and spurred the horse.

Tom watched the trail of upturned dirt, rubbed his forehead, the fear complete in his features. "I'll wait until he's out of sight and then I'll send the signal that I found you."

Tom left the barn. A shot fired, the gun cracking echoes over the plain. Two more followed. Leonora flinched with each blast, squeezed her eyelids and held her ears.

The sound of horses, maybe four or five, clamored toward the barn. Her muscles tensed. Alex shouldn't be back. Her legs went limp. Maybe he knew. Blood drained from her face and left her fingertips cold. The horses were near. Men's voices rose and fell above the hooves. Leonora walked through the doors, the sun blinding.

Tom stepped next to her protectively, shielding her with the rifle. "Tell him you got caught in the storm and stayed here to ride it out," he hushed. "Orright?"

She nodded just as the rush of men and horses ground to a halt. Tom shouted to the group with forced ease, "She's orright! Just a little scared from the storm."

Alex got off his horse and walked toward her, his gait stringent. She tried to read his eyes, his mood, but they gave nothing away. "I've been looking everywhere for you," he said. "Had every man out on the search."

"I'm sorry. I got stuck in the storm," she answered with caution.

"Fell asleep in the barn." She reached out a hand and rested it on his arm. Her wrist shook. "I'm sorry I worried you."

Alex looked at her shaking hand, seemed to assess the movements, then drew his focus to her face. He was unusually quiet, darkly calm.

She hid the faltering hand behind her back, swallowed hard. "How did you make it through the storm so fast?"

He was quiet for a long moment. His eyes lowered. "Something's happened, Leonora. It's your aunt," he spoke softly. "She passed away."

Her eyes dried, the frantic blinking stopped.

"I'm sorry." Alex dropped his voice, his chin. "Just got word last night. I wanted to wait and tell you in person."

Her thoughts blurred. She couldn't place where she was or what she felt. A haze of disbelief clouded. There was no sadness, no relief—only numb, stilted incomprehension. She pivoted slowly, turned to the barn like a figurine in a music box, wondered if she was dreaming. She had been in James's arms. Now she stood before Alex. Now her aunt was dead. And the haze thickened and closed her throat.

"I've already made arrangements for us to go back to America," announced Alex.

She snapped her head up. "America?"

"For the funeral, Leonora."

"Of course." Her mind swirled. She didn't know what the words meant.

"The steamer leaves Friday from Fremantle. We need to leave first thing tomorrow."

Tomorrow. Tomorrow! The word rang in her temples.

"We're lucky." He nodded. "With the war, the ships are limited."

Leonora stopped listening. She was leaving tomorrow. Leaving James. Tears welled in her eyes.

"Your aunt was a good woman," Alex offered with rare compassion. "She'll be missed."

CHAPTER 59

Sixty seconds in a minute.

The sun beat relentlessly upon James's back as he busied his hands with the already-tight wire fences, with the polishing of the already-gleaming saddles, with the endless chores that he completed and restarted.

Sixty seconds in a minute. James counted each one. Over and over again, he counted—each endless second a tiny wave pushing the steam liner, his heart, across the Pacific. And each second, he knew, Alex was with her.

Sixty minutes in an hour.

The minutes of the day were torturous, but the minutes of the night were inhuman with infinity. The minutes of the night reminded him that Alex would share her bed. The minutes wondered if Alex would touch her. The minutes grew malicious and promised that Leonora would forget him, forget what had happened in the barn, forget that they were meant to be together.

Twenty-four hours in a day.

Twenty-four hours of held breath. Twenty-four hours of waiting. Twenty-four hours of ripped insides missing her.

Seven days in a week.

Four weeks in a month.

One month of agony and Leonora would still not be on America's soil.

Two months.

The telegram was brief and did not list a sender.

I love you.

The letters were bold against the open space of the paper. James read the three simple words again. *I love you.* He could live through the seconds and the minutes and the hours and the days and the weeks and the months until Leonora returned to him. *I love you.* And it was enough.

CHAPTER 60

❧

Owen Fairfield was a ghost as he dragged the heavy chains of grief. The white suit sagged from his limbs; his potbelly drooped over his belt like a deflated balloon. The skin of his cheeks and jaw clung to the bones beneath and the white hairs of his beard stuck out prickly and sharp, the softness gone. The once sparkling, alert and wise eyes stared to distant points, their focus inward to memories that flowed and brought absent smiles to his lips and, an instant later, hanging frowns and a quivering chin.

In turn, Alex swelled. He met with lawyers and accountants, arranged the details of the funeral and burial. He supervised the steel mills. His ear was red from overseas calls, his voice steady and intent as he kicked Owen's worn loafers from the business with his own Italian calf ones. The Great War was over. Shipping lines opened and flowed like unclogged veins, the blood seeming to pump straight into Alex's arteries. And between the tasks of business, Alex hovered around his father-in-law and catered to his needs, stayed closed to the Fairfield ghost in case the folly of philanthropic inclination might cloud the man's slow, grief-stricken mind.

On the day of the funeral, they were escorted by police motorcade. The church bell swung wide and deafening. The cathedral could not hold the crowds that flowed to its wide wood and wrought-iron doors and so the people lined the steps and carried into the street. The casket was closed, the embalmers having to hold the body until Leonora and Alex arrived. The sermon was long, with devout words espousing the goodness and generosity of a rare soul, of the wide arms of the Lord that awaited Eleanor Fairfield in Heaven. And Leonora listened to the words as one listens to the hammering of nails onto brittle wood and eventually found grief—the grief of a cold and unloving childhood bestowed by this praised woman.

It was a few days later on a cold December day, an ashen day without the comfort of snow, when she escorted her uncle to the cemetery. They walked between silent rows of granite stone, their footsteps crunching the frozen grass. Leonora buried her chin into the wool coat, thrust gloved hands deeper into pockets. Her uncle walked with open, unbuttoned overcoat and did not seem to notice the cold. They did not speak.

The Fairfield headstone towered in height and girth above the others. Even in death, the woman had a way of minimizing those around her.

"I'm not long for this world, Leonora," Owen reflected.

She took his elbow. "Please don't talk like that."

"I'm not being morose, dear." He tried to smile but failed. "Quite the opposite." His Adam's apple rose in his thin throat as he swallowed. "I miss my wife."

He stared at the grave for quite a while before stretching out his neck. He gave a quick rise to his chin and then nodded as if the stone had conversed. Then he turned to Leonora; the alertness, though not as sharp, had returned. "Sit down, Leonora," he instructed. "I have some things to tell you."

The chill from the frostbitten ground inched up her boots. She followed her uncle to a limestone bench and sat upon the ice-cold slab, waited. Owen reached into his coat and pulled out a brown envelope and handed it to her. The back was not sealed and she raised the flap, unfolded the parchment paper inside. Leonora passed her eyes over the words, the legal jargon and raised seals. "I don't understand," she said.

"It's a deed," he explained. "For a thousand acres in New South Wales. It's yours. Eleanor wanted you to have it." Owen looked down at his hands. "Alex doesn't know anything about the property."

Leonora looked over the document again. A name that she did not recognize inked bold and black. "Who is Elizabeth Granby?" she asked.

Her uncle paled. "The property was originally set aside for her. When

Eleanor was"—his voice faltered—"was dying, she asked that the deed be transferred to your name." The man sighed deeply and added, "Granby was Eleanor's maiden name."

A great tiredness washed over her body with the riddles. Leonora looked at the name again, rubbed the tight spot between her eyebrows. But then she remembered. "Elizabeth Granby is her sister, isn't she? The one that died in the hospital in Sydney."

Her uncle shook his head then—long, low, wide swings like the church bell that had chimed at the funeral. "There was no sister, Leonora." He clasped his eyes shut. "Elizabeth Granby was her daughter."

The cold disappeared; sweat beaded under her wool coat. "What?"

He brought his hands to his face and bent forward, sobbed into his fingertips. Leonora was helpless as he crumbled under grief, too shocked to offer comfort, too confused to do anything but stare at the side of his face.

With a final, waning cry, Owen pulled out a handkerchief and wiped his nose and his eyes. "I met Eleanor when she was sixteen. I was in my early twenties," he began, his voice raspy. "I had just graduated from Stanford University and was traveling through California before I started my first geology assignment." The tears dried, left white streaks across his cheeks. "Along the way, I stopped at an inn to stay the night. I can't even remember what the name of the town was. Isn't that funny?" he said, mystified. "That's where I met your aunt. She was changing the bedsheets in my room. She was the maid."

Leonora did not hear correctly. The grief had left him senile. Eleanor Fairfield had never been a maid.

Owen read her mind. A small grin curved his lips. "Doesn't seem possible, does it? But it's true. And I fell in love with her that very moment." The grin grew and he chuckled. "Eleanor didn't want anything to do with me. Can't say I blame her. I was eight years her senior. But I was relentless. I stayed at that inn for a week trying to woo her. Even postponed my new job."

The half smile faded and he rubbed his slack jaw. "On the day that I finally gave up and had my bags to leave, she grabbed me by the hand and took me to the tiny basement room where she lived." He paused. "That's when she introduced me to her daughter.

"When Eleanor was thirteen, her father passed away. They weren't a wealthy family but had lived comfortably, were well respected in their community. The local priest performed the rites and stayed with the Granbys for a time after the funeral." Owen's cheek shook violently. His voice became shrill. "That man, *that priest,* raped her."

Leonora's eyes burned; hot tears dripped down her cheeks, ran down her neck.

"Eleanor became pregnant, and when she told her mother the woman called her a whore, said her lies would ruin them. *That bastard* and her mother sent her away. They put that child, pregnant and without a nickel, on a train to California to fend for herself." Owen's lips were hard and white. "Eleanor got a job as a maid, delivered that baby by herself, hid her from the world and cared for her as best she could." His eyes flickered to Leonora and he said quietly, "The baby . . . Elizabeth . . . was severely disabled, both mentally and physically."

His mouth opened for more air before he continued, "I married Eleanor Granby a week later. And I promised that woman that I would take care of her and keep her demons away. I promised her that I would never, *never* let anyone hurt her again." The deep breath of air now left his lungs. "And I kept my promise.

"Over time, over the first years," he went on, "I acquired money quickly. We traveled. Once I bought the steel mills, we decided to settle in Pittsburgh. It was then that she sent the child away." Owen shook his head. "Eleanor lived in constant fear of someone finding out about the child. Lived in terror that her past would be realized and put on display. Part of her always thought I would leave her—that she would be alone again, on her own, poverty-stricken. She sent Elizabeth to the farthest civilized spot she could find—Sydney, Australia." He nodded with conviction. "It was a good place—a good hospital. We paid the nurses and doctors very well. They took care of that little girl better than we ever could." A long pause stretched. "But a piece of Eleanor froze when she sent that child away; a part of her died the day she put her child on that ship. She found herself talking out loud to people about Australia, made up a story about her sister and niece to cover up the sentiment that teared her eyes. Then, Elizabeth died." Owen stared up at the gray, soot-filled sky. "Eleanor was devastated. Wouldn't speak a word about it, not even to me. She was just a shell, her eyes blank all the time. I didn't think the light would ever come back to my Eleanor. But it did." He turned to Leonora. "The day she met you."

Leonora dropped her head into her hands, held her ears, shuddered to her toes.

"She loved you, Leonora," he said, his voice drawn and plaintive.

She pressed her ears with her fists.

"She *loved* you." Owen gripped her knee, his gaunt features begging. "Listen to me, Leonora. You didn't know her before. I did. I saw her change with you. I saw the way her face softened. I saw the glint in her eye when she dreamed of you happy and secure, with babies and wealth. I saw the way she secretly kissed your photograph every night before she fell asleep. She loved you, Leonora, and a part of her thawed, *healed*, when you came into our life."

"How can you say that?" she snapped, and pulled her hands away from her face. "*You* know how she treated me! All I did was try to please her. I made myself sick trying to please her! Don't you remember? I never had any friends; I studied every day; I never spoke out of turn. And all she did was push me away, ridicule me." The pain clouded every thought, came through every fiber like a physcial pain. She choked on her sobs, couldn't breathe with the pain. "I was a child. *A child!* All I did was try to get her to love me and what did I get in return . . . 'I'll leave you, Leonora. I'll leave you!' And every time she said it, a part of me died and turned numb until I hoped—I *prayed*—she would carry out her promise."

Owen covered his eyes, nodded painfully. "Yes, I know," he agreed ruefully. "She was cruel to you—heartless at times. I suppose I should have done more to stop it."

I suppose! her mind screamed. *I suppose!*

"But Eleanor thought she was protecting you." Her uncle looked far away, as if he was trying to explain it to himself. "When she met you at the orphanage, when she saw that priest's affection for you, all her old memories flooded back—the terror, the helplessness . . . the rape."

"Father McIntyre was a good man!" Leonora screamed, horrified. "He cared for me more than almost anyone in my whole life."

"I know." He raised a hand in a sign to stop. "I know. But Eleanor didn't trust priests. What I'm trying to say is that she tried to rescue you. She sent those tutors to protect you." Owen rubbed his forehead. "It all came down to fear, Leonora. There was no logic with her actions, just pure, raw fear. Every time she threatened you, she thought she was protecting you. That was how she knew how to love." He put his hand on her shoulder and looked into her wet eyes. "This is why she wanted you to marry Alex. I think Eleanor knew she was sick for a long time. She wanted someone to take care of you, to protect you in case she wasn't around. But even after you married Alex, the old fear came back. Even marital securities can falter. And that's why she wanted you to have this property. She wanted you to have something that was yours—something that no one could take away."

Leonora's stomach swirled with nausea. "I can't think straight," she cried.

"I know." The ghost reappeared as the grief and remorse and demons wrapped their arms around the old man. "I'm sorry, Leonora." His eyes drooped. "I can't change the past. But I hope you might find a sliver of solace in what I've told you." He rose, dragged his feet to the car.

The cold entered again. Her legs and fingertips were frozen and trembling. The tears numbed her face. Leonora turned her head and looked at the gravestone. *Eleanor G. Fairfield*. She stared at the block writing, at the hard, gray granite, and she thought about the woman. And she could see it now—the fear behind the pupils. She saw it for what it was, for what it had been—the ferocity of a mother pushing a child from a speeding bullet.

CHAPTER 61

Three months after the Ford had disappeared in a predawn haze and taken Leonora from Wanjarri Downs, the Ford returned.

The January day was one of the hottest on record. The flies were fierce, swarming in black tornadoes around any breathing, warm body. Tom watched the car approach dustily from the road, smacked at the fat, hairy flies; James remained still and absent to everything but the moving car that finally parked with a dead rattle. James walked briskly, forced himself not to run. Tom grabbed at his shirt, but James ripped his arm away. Alex stepped out first, looking bright and satisfied. A dark pit spread in James's gut. *So help me if he touched her . . .*

Tom jogged up and greeted Alex before James had a chance to lay his hard eyes on the man's face. "*America, America!*" Tom crooned. "*God shines his grace on thee!*"

Alex laughed. "Shed," he corrected. "God *shed* his grace on thee." Alex gave Tom a hearty handshake and slapped him on the back.

"Lucky I got 'America' right! Geography isn't my specialty," Tom joked even as his eyes watched James from the corners. Subtly, he turned Alex away from the car. "James'll grab your bags. So, how was the trip?"

Leonora opened the car door and stepped out. His breath caught at the sight of her—of her pink lips, the smooth skin, the silken hair. She was here. And the torturous ticking of eternal seconds finally stopped— just stopped. His lips tingled to kiss her. Each nerve ending waited to touch her skin. He stepped toward her, but she shook her head. *Not now,* she mouthed.

He glanced at Tom, saw Alex's back was turned. Keeping his eyes glued to Leonora's face, he reached over her shoulder for the suitcase on the backseat. He brushed his lips against her cheek. The smell of her perfume wafted from her neck. He leaned into her hips and touched her waist. James pulled the suitcase out and stepped back.

"Come on, Leonora!" Alex hollered from Tom's side. "I'm starving."

Leonora couldn't shake the seasickness from the rough ocean waters that had bullied the steam liner; she couldn't shake the carsickness that had left her green over the endless straight roads. Sleep did little to revive her fatigue. Each day, she retired before evening had set and rose long after morning had begun. And she knew. She knew with heartbreaking joy and cold terror that it was not the journey that left her bones weak as jelly and her stomach retching.

She sat across from Alex at the table. He perused the newspaper without focus, rambled on and on about metals and labor and dollars. Her head was heavy and her forehead beaded with sweat. The monotonous words churned her stomach like a bad smell. Bile came quickly to her throat. She covered her mouth and gagged.

Alex inched down the newspaper and grimaced. "What's wrong with you?"

"I don't feel well. . . ." Her stomach twisted again and she jolted for the toilet, knocking her hip into the table corner and clinking the teacups in the process.

After a few minutes, Leonora returned, her face white, hands shaking. A plate of scrambled eggs sat on the table, curled her stomach with fresh vigor. She covered the eggs with a napkin and pushed them away. Meredith refilled her tea.

"Feeling better?" Alex asked, his mouth half-full of food.

"Yes," she lied.

Meredith set the teapot on the table. "Guess congratulations are in order, eh?"

Leonora's stomach plummeted to her legs like a cut anchor.

Alex stopped chewing. "Congratulations for what?"

"Fer the baby of course! My mum had twelve children. Know a pregnant woman when I see one!" She winked at Leonora and left the room.

Crouching dread stretched like a waking cat. Leonora touched her belly protectively.

Alex's fork hung suspended in his fingers. His eyebrows spread and his forehead softened. "Is that true?" he whispered.

"I-I don't know," she stammered.

In a strange, choppy dream, Alex neared, knelt before her, clutched her hands, his eyes glistening.

Her insides retreated with his joy. It was crumbling. James. The child. It was all turning to dust under Alex's fingers.

"A baby?" Alex's face bloomed with wonder. His lips stretched over his teeth. "We're going to have a baby?"

Leonora stared at her hands, limp and dead in his grip. And she waited—waited as the sentenced wait for the slice of the guillotine. It would all register within his skull. There was no use lying. She would be showing soon. And so she waited, felt it all dissolve—for Alex only needed to calculate the days and weeks and months—a baby could have been conceived and born within their abstinence. Her body chilled, shivered uncontrollably. Tears pushed behind her eyes. And she waited.

His hands tensed. The waiting stopped. He knew. Leonora raised her eyes in surrender, met his black pupils. The tenderness, the joy, was hacked to shreds—only ice and hate and black ugliness remained. "Whose is it?" he growled.

"I . . . I don't know."

Alex squeezed her hands, dug nails into her skin. *"Whose is it?"*

Leonora whimpered and tried to pull her hands away. The nails dug farther, cut through the skin. *"I don't know!"*

Alex dropped her hands and slapped her square across the face, the force snapping her head to her shoulder. Leonora clutched the burning cheek, tasted the blood that trickled out the corner of her mouth. "Please, Alex!" she begged.

But he was blind. He seized her by the shoulders and shook her as a dog shakes a rabbit. "Tell me who it was or so help me . . . !"

"He was from the hospital!" Leonora screamed with a desperate attempt to end it. Her mind scrambled for a name. "Dr. Edwards!"

Alex released his hands like her skin was acid.

"It was after the funeral . . . ," she hurried, "when you were at the mill." Her mind sped with the lie. "I'm sorry, Alex."

For a moment, he stood perfectly still. But then his black eyes flitted, back and forth like the insane. He twisted his neck, his lips wet. "Dr. Edwards died in the war."

Leonora screamed in terror. She backed up, shielded her stomach. Alex lurched and grabbed her by the hair, tossed her against the wall, sending a mirror crashing to the floor.

Meredith ran in from the kitchen. "Whot's wrong? I heard—"

Alex grabbed Leonora by the throat. "*You lying whore!*"

"Get yer bloody 'ands off her!" Meredith shouted as she tried to pry his fingers from Leonora's neck. With his left hand, Alex smashed his palm into the woman's face, sent her flying. Meredith scrambled for the front door, crawling on her hands and knees.

James led the stallion around the riding ring. A noise, high-pitched and indistinguishable, caught his ear, raised the hairs along his arms. The sound drew in from its echo, sharpened to screaming. James jumped over the split-rail fence.

"Help!" Meredith's large frame circled in front of the house. "Somebody help! Help!" She saw James. "Mrs. 'Arrington!" she screamed. "He's tryin' t'kill her!"

James charged the house, his mind blank, every muscle, every nerve, a live, twitching wire. He plowed through the front door, heard Alex's curses from the next room, heard a head thumping against the wall.

"No!" James pounced on Alex, grabbed his shirt and threw him to the floor. Leonora slid down the wall. "Leo!" James grabbed her limp neck in his hands, frantically kissed her forehead. "Leo, can you hear me?"

"You!" Alex spit, pushed up to his knees. "*It was you!*"

James turned just as Alex's fist barreled into his shoulder. But the white rage blocked out the blow and James balled his hand, punched Alex square in the jaw. Alex fell, but James grabbed him by the shirt collar, pummeled him again and again until his fist slipped on blood and Alex's body flopped in his grip. James saw the blood then, looked at his raw, red-stained knuckles, dropped him with quick release. Alex lay hunched and crumpled as a rag.

James pulled his gaze from his bloodied hands and slid down to Leonora's side. He rubbed her hair, tried to rouse her. Her mouth was bloodied, her cheek purple and swollen.

"That fuckin' bastard!" Tom stood in the doorway, his eyes bouncing from Alex's body to Leonora's and then back again.

"Get the doctor!" James ordered. "Better get the sheriff, too."

Leonora moved her head, opened her eyes and looked at James, let her gaze drip over his features as if she couldn't quite see them. James kissed her eyelids. "Thank God." He kissed her hair. He pressed his forehead against hers. "Thank God you're all right."

Leonora touched her cheek gingerly, then pulled her hand away from the pain. She saw Alex's body and her mouth dropped. "Is he . . ."

"No." James seethed for a different answer. "He's not dead." James stroked her hair. "What happened, Leo?"

She touched her belly. "I'm pregnant."

James's jaw dropped. Adrenaline flooded under his skin.

"It's yours. Ours, James." She squeezed his hand. "Ever since that day in the paddocks, that first day you kissed me, I never let him touch me again. I swear it, James."

It wouldn't have mattered. But the relief was still there, warm and full. James put his hand against her unmarked cheek and kissed the bridge of her nose. He moved his hand down and placed it against her belly. He smiled, closed his lips in amazement.

James turned to Alex and his eyes turned hard again. "We're getting out of here."

"But James—" she started, but he cut her off.

"I don't care, Leo." His face grew fierce. "I only care about you right now." James looked down at his bleeding knuckles. "Tom went to get the sheriff and the doctor. Then we go."

Suddenly, Leonora bent forward and grabbed her stomach, her face distorting in agony. "What's wrong?" James wound her into his arms. "Leo?"

She gasped soundlessly. James took her elbow and helped her up, scooped her gently into his arms. "You need to lie down, Leo."

The usual warmth of her body was fading, her face pale. An old image of Tess flashed, left him unnerved. James pulled Leonora closer to his chest, carried her up the stairs. Her eyes were down, the focus directed at her stomach. James lowered her to the bed and she faced the wall, curled away from him, brought her knees to her chest and held them with her arms.

James swallowed, reached out a hand to rub her shoulder, then pulled it back. "I'll bring you some tea," he said, the offer hesitant. Leonora did not move, did not answer, her gaze vacant.

James nodded at the curved spine and turned away, rubbed his eyes with his palms and pulled at the front of his hair. His limbs were heavy and sluggish as he left her, walked down the steps to the dining room. Alex's body remained broken and clumped on the floor.

James stopped with his boot against Alex's back. The man's face was crusted with blood, the nostrils blocked and black. The white shirt was ripped and stained with rust-colored fingerprints. James knelt down slowly, his knee hovering over Alex's purpling, bruised face. "I should kill you."

A stream of light filtered from the window. The sharp gleam of metal picked up the yellow light and highlighted the revolver hanging inside Alex's jacket. James reached for the gun, rubbed the cool, smooth steel with his fingers, his reflection blurry and distorted in the cylinder's curve. A painful vibrancy itched under his skin. His palm wrapped around the sculpted handle, his index finger found the arch of the trigger. James stood to his full height. He pointed the gun at Alex. The gun grew into his hand and up his arm, turned his flesh into one cold, silver extension. Then, without a bend of his elbow, James lowered his arm, let it drop straight by his side. The gun dangled loosely from his finger and he didn't look at it again. James turned from Alex, entered the kitchen and dropped the gun into the garbage.

James scraped the teakettle harshly across the stove burners and set it under the faucet. His brows pulled at the skin of his forehead, tried to drag it past his eyes. The water splashed into the bottom of the hollow kettle, the sound dull as it filled. He smacked the faucet off and dropped the kettle to the stove. Beads of blood formed across his knuckles as the thin, newly formed scabs broke open again. He lit the pilot light, stared at the blue flames as they licked the bottom of the black iron.

James opened the icebox and shoveled some shavings into a bowl. He slammed the door closed and thrust his cut fist into the hard ice. It numbed the raw pain. His fingers throbbed, matched his pulse beat for beat. James glanced at the garbage, saw the gun resting upon broken eggshells and coffee grinds and wilted lettuce. James stuck out a long leg and kicked the garbage can into the pantry. He slammed the door closed and pounded his fist back into the ice.

The teakettle hissed. Boiling water spluttered out of the spout of the overfilled pot and fell upon the flames, turning them white and yellow as they flickered. The kettle blew its whistle, shrieked with sudden impatience. James snapped off the flame. A shadow elongated and took shape above his own. A shift of air passed across his back. His head cracked. James fell hard to his knees. The teakettle exhaled with a waning wail. The smack crashed across his lower back. His head bounced and landed hard on the floor.

Leonora's throat ached as she swallowed, the pain waking her. She didn't know she had fallen asleep. James hadn't returned with the tea. She bent into her abdomen, the pain grating and cramped. At intervals, the pain grew with steady steps and cut like razors, every organ twisted like a wrung towel. Then everything loosened, returned to grating and cramping again. She was sweating, her body tired with the straining waves of pain. She didn't want James to see her like this. She tried to straighten her body, but her knees wouldn't leave her chest. Her head was fuzzy. She was thirsty. The clock on the wall ticked loudly, each second noisy and magnified within the quiet room.

Leonora closed her eyes. With the lack of sight, her ears heard more and listened. There was another sound—a muffled one behind the rhythmic swing of the clock's pendulum. She opened her eyes and tried to focus on the dull drumming. It was coming from outside. She cursed the clock to quiet. There it was again—a shout or a horse or a yell. Her flesh iced. There was anger in the noise. A distant laugh. A voice. *Alex.*

Leonora shot out of bed. Vertigo seized and she grabbed the bedpost for support. A knife ripped at her stomach; her mouth gasped for air. She forced her legs to move against the agony. At the stairs, she hugged the banister with two hands. Something warm trickled down her inner thighs. A cry left her lips.

The steady beats from outside grew louder. She tore her thoughts from her body and propelled herself through the rooms, through the open front door. The sun flashed in her eyes as she stumbled to the verandah. The sounds stopped. Her eyes focused. *"No!"*

Alex stood at the drive; standing before him were Beecher and Russell. Between them, a man stood hunched over, his arms pinned behind his back. The two roustabouts saw Leonora, their faces suddenly shamed and contrite. They let go of the body and it dropped with a lifeless thud into the dust. Alex stepped back, wiped his bleeding nose and looked with pleasure at his red, raw hand. He bowed to Leonora and waved a hand out toward the slumped body. "Your prince!" Alex laughed between labored breaths. Beecher and Russell backed away.

Leonora screamed. She tried to move, but her insides cramped in roped knots.

The smugness washed from Alex's face and his jaw fell slack. "You're bleeding."

Leonora looked down at the growing circle of blood. The world was made of blood. Blood. James. Pain. Blood! Claws ripped. She doubled over and collapsed upon the steps.

A horn blasted from the road, grew louder and more urgent as the two vehicles sped closer, the honking quick and high as a goose searching for its young. Beecher and Russell ran off. A police truck drove in first and Tom jumped out before the wheels slowed. "You fuckin' bastard!" Tom dived at Alex. The men fell to the ground with fists buried and jabbing at any skin or bone within reach.

Two men bolted from the police car and worked to pry Tom off. As they held him, Alex recovered, landed a hard blow to the side of Tom's face. The sheriff grabbed Alex hard by the shirt. "That's enough!" he ordered. Alex jerked away from the hold and wiped his mouth with the back of his hand, his chest heaving and his lips twisted.

Tom struggled as the deputy fiercely screwed his elbow up to his shoulder blades. "Let me go, you fuckin' . . . !" he hissed under his breaking arm, and slammed his head back into the deputy's face.

The officer dropped Tom's wrist and clutched his nose with his hand before reaching for his gun, his round face red and crazed. "So help me, I'll kill yeh!"

The sheriff smacked the gun. "Enough, I said! Jesus Christ, Murphy!" The sheriff peered at the ring of angry men. "Everybody just settle fer a fuckin' minute!" he shouted. "Somebody wanna tell me what the hell's goin' on?"

Tom knelt down next to James and turned his body over, the face motionless and caked with blood. The sheriff looked hard at Alex. "What's this all about, Alex?"

Alex rubbed his jaw and grinned. "Son of a bitch broke into my safe."

Tom stepped forward menacingly. "You lyin' bastard!"

"Check his pockets!" Alex ordered. "Go on. See for yourself."

The sheriff knelt next to James, pulled out the wad of bills from the hip pocket. From the other he pulled out a gold watch, read the inscription on the back.

Tom's eyes danced wildly. "He fuckin' planted it!" Tom lunged at Alex's smirking face again, but the deputy held him tight by the elbows. "Can't you see what he's doin'?" he yelled.

The next car stopped with a screech. Meredith ran out the passenger side, her dress hunched up around her knees. Dr. Meade ran after her in a stilted gait while he held his hat to his head and his medical bag in his fist. He leaned over James, checked his pulse.

Meredith squeaked, her heavy figure staring agape at the big house. All eyes shifted to her focus. "Mrs. 'Arrington!"

Leonora felt the hands upon her skin, felt someone pry her fingers from her abdomen. She opened her eyes, saw the scared faces around her converge and distort as if she were looking through a glass bowl. She followed their gaze to her dried, red hands and the saturated dress beneath them. Her mouth fell open, her throat closed. She met Meredith's sorrow-filled eyes and the woman turned her face away. And then the world took shape, the lens of her vision widened. She saw past the doctor to the drive, saw Alex and the police and Tom. She saw James still unconscious. "James!" she tried to scream, made a weak, incomprehensible wail.

Dr. Meade pushed her down. "Be still, Mrs. Harrington!" He held her arm with one hand and dug in his bag with the other. "Hold her," he directed Meredith.

Leonora fought to free herself. "Tom!" she shrieked. "*Tom!*"

Tom broke from the deputy and pushed past Meredith. His face turned white with the sight of blood. Leonora scratched for his arm. "James?" she cried.

"He'll be orright." Tom squeezed her hand.

Something pricked her arm. She turned and stared at the needle. "No!" she shouted, struggled from the doctor's grip.

The doctor pulled out another syringe and aimed it in the air. "You need to rest!"

"My baby!"

"Ain't no baby!"

The needle stabbed again. Her arm turned to lead, the heaviness spreading up her shoulder. She pulled weakly at Tom, who was fading by the second. "Don't leave James alone with those men!" she begged, her words slurring. "Don't leave him!"

Tom nodded rapidly, his eyes wet. He turned to Meredith. "I'll stay wiv 'er!" she growled as rough as a guard dog. "Mr. 'Arrington won't touch 'er."

Tom was leaving. Meredith faded. The doctor and his needles disappeared. Through slit lids she searched the darkness for James's body. Her mouth opened and closed like a fish set upon dry land before the world went black.

Sharp, steady points jabbed his lung. His head bounced against the back of the seat. *Thump. Thump. Thump.* James moaned. He tried to open his eyes, but only one allowed a slit of vision.

"You orright, mate?" Tom asked quietly, his voice deep and low.

James bent forward and hot pokers burned his insides. He gasped with the thrust of pain and leaned back. "*Christ!*"

"Your ribs?" Tom asked.

James nodded, winced with even the smallest movement. He opened his eye a crack again. Tom sat next to him. Two men sat in the front seat. He could only see the backs of their heads and the sweaty, unshaven necks. "Where are we going?" James asked dryly.

"Police station," Tom answered.

"Police? What's going on—" James stopped. The pain blasted away. "Leo!" He jolted upright, hit his head against the car ceiling. "Where's Leo?"

The deputy watched him through the mirror as he drove. The sheriff turned around with a slung arm. "Sit down, James!" the sheriff ordered.

"Where is she?" James yelled. Tom wouldn't look at him.

"She lost the baby," Tom whispered.

The pain came back bright and flashing and had nothing to do with his bruises. "Is she all right?" James choked.

Tom looked at him now and nodded. "The doc's with her. Meredith, too."

Alex. James grabbed the sheriff's shoulder. "You got to go back!"

"Settle yerself!" the sheriff warned.

The deputy reached for his gun, his eyes black and mean in the mirror. "Put that thing away, Murphy!" The sheriff pushed the man's arm away. "Christ, yer trigger-happy t'day."

The sheriff turned his body around to face James. He was a strong, lean sunburned man, his eyes steady. "This didn't have anything t'do with the money, did it?" he asked.

"What money?"

"Alex planted money in your pocket," Tom seethed. "Said you stole it."

"What?" His mind blurred like the trees speeding outside the car. "When?"

"After they beat the crap outta you."

The car was quiet. The sheriff nodded, pursed his lips. "Any fool can see this is about the woman. If yeh was messin' wiv his wife, Alex got every right beatin' yeh."

"Fuck right!" growled the deputy.

The sheriff glared at the officer. "Got somepin yeh want t'say, Murphy?" The man sank down into the seat, his eyes glowering. "Well?" The sheriff rolled his eyes at Tom and James and pointed his thumb back at the driver. "Fuckin' new guys," he joked. "Get all hopped up wiv the badge." The deputy slunk farther, held the steering wheel with white knuckles.

The sheriff folded his arms on the top of the seat. "Ain't none of my business whot goes on between a man an' a woman," he told James. "If yeh break the law, then it's my business."

James leaned into a cracked rib. "Alex had her by the throat."

"Ain't none of my business, like I said. Ain't yers, either. Men an' women got t'settle things between 'em." He inspected a fingernail, then shrugged. "Don't care fer that rough business, beatin' on a woman. But sometimes it happens."

James and Tom shot matching daggers. The man chuckled. "I know whot yer thinkin'. Yeh think Alex got me in his palm, don't yeh? See why yeh'd think so. Cops in Coolgardie on his payroll, sure as 'ell is hot. I know Alex well. Think he's a bloody prick. I know yeh didn't steal that money, but I had t'get yeh outta there 'fore he killed yeh both."

Tom's shoulders relaxed. The sheriff grinned. "We'll take yeh to Gwalia to the station. Get yeh fixed up, James, bind up those ribs. We'll get this mess settled. No worries." He smiled. "Yer good boys."

"I got t'piss," said Murphy, squirming in his seat.

"Pull over there," the sheriff said, pointing.

Low, rocky hills lined both sides. Mulga roots veined across the boulders and wrapped like fingers into the cracks. A few ancient eucalyptus trees stretched to the sky. Crows, so black that their feathers gleamed indigo against the sun's glare, dotted the limbs and turned their heads with the fluttering leaves. The air was still now, hot and dusty. The flies buzzed around the open windows, whizzed in and out. The deputy left the car, his head down, and walked slowly to the edges of stones. The sheriff craned his neck, looked at the sky from the open part of the roof. "Long day, eh?" he sighed. "Where yeh boys from?"

"Wheatbelt," Tom answered, rubbing his leg in tired strokes. "Outside Southern Cross."

The sheriff turned around with interest. "Yeah? Murphy's wife is from there. Sweet girl. Jist had a baby, too." He smiled as he searched his memory. "Abby? No, Ashley!"

Tom stiffened. The spots of crows stretched wings and leaped from the tree limbs into the air in a cackling frenzy. The sky exploded with sound; the air cracked in two. The three men froze in the enormous split second, stared straight and motionless. The sheriff's head dropped forward—the back of his scalp gone.

The next shot bit James in the shoulder, sent him tumbling against the side, the door opening with the thrust of the weight. James spilled out to the ground.

"James!" Tom crawled out and grabbed him, tried to drag him to the back of the car, dodged his head from another whizzing bullet.

The gun's thunder echoed, ricocheted between the hills of rocks and moved forward steadily. Murphy's footsteps were slow and methodical, his arm outstretched, his lip curled above his top teeth. "She told me it was you!" he screamed.

Tom stood up, opened his legs to shield his friend.

"She told me whot you did to her! Told me how you paid her to keep quiet!"

Tom stepped forward. "It ain't what you think." He raised his hands into the air.

Murphy's arm shook. *"I saw that baby and I knew!"*

"No—"

"Told me how yeh forced yerself on her! On my fuckin' wife!"

Tom's arms dropped to his sides. His fingers stretched and fell limp. He stopped arguing. He looked back at James for less than a moment, his eyes clear to the future, clear with his truth, clear with waiting and surrender. "Under God, I swear I never—"

The shots came swift, deafening:

One—two—three—four.

Tom's body collapsed at James's feet, his eyes empty as glass, the pupils still. *"Tom!"* James screamed. In a white fury, he was on his feet, charged at Murphy's figure. The gun turned idly toward him. The black circle of the barrel smoked. The shots smashed the silence of the bush and ripped through his skin.

The sofa was firm under Leonora's back. A pillow propped her neck. She could not feel her body. Her eyelids rose and fell like cooking clams. Upon her eyes' opening, a line of the dark room took shape before disappearing under heavy eyelashes. A lazy light glowed from a table lamp, the edges of the hazy orb ubiquitous. There were no thoughts—only numb, visceral images and sounds and textures that accented the distance.

Dull footsteps traveled across the wood floor. *Step. Step. Step.* The movement ceased in front of the sofa. With a great pull, her eyelids cracked. A body blocked the light from the lamp. The pants were dark. A man's hand fanned a square piece of paper above her face, sending short wisps of breeze along her nose. The hand stopped and released the card. The paper fluttered, danced on the air and landed upon her hip.

"Your boyfriend's dead." The words floated on the air as the paper had done, turned and trailed behind Alex's retreating footsteps.

CHAPTER 62

Ghan jammed his body against the rock face and slid down to the ground. Sand and dust crumbled from the stone and sprinkled down his collar. His mouth dried with held breath. His lips trembled. Gunshots still rang against his eardrum.

Another shot broke the still air. Ghan grabbed his knees and rolled into a ball. More shots fired, each one jerking his body as if the bullets landed in his back. Then silence. Ghan's ears strained against the drumming, soundless noise that kept tempo with his throbbing veins. An engine started, drove away. And still Ghan listened, kept crouched below the rocks. He didn't want to look up—didn't want to see what had happened.

Ghan settled his insides, unclasped his knees. He closed his eyes, stretched his body up past the rocks, sucked in air and then opened his eyes. A sick wave rippled down his body. Three bodies lay flopped and crooked across the ground—a bloody massacre.

Ghan peered down each end of the road and licked his cracked lips. *Man might come back*, he reminded himself. His gaze became more frantic. *Might be a bunch of men.* Ghan limped out to the open, his crippled body exposed in the wide terrain. He hurried across the dirt road, his peg leg leaving circles in the soft dirt.

Sweat drenched his back, made his beard itch. He stepped up to the bodies. The first one was facedown, the back of his head open and raw, his clothes dark red down to the backs of his legs. The sickness thrust upward too quickly and Ghan vomited onto his boot. He bent over and gagged. He turned away, but the smell of blood hung to the heat, cooked under the sun.

The flies began to gather and swarm. They flocked to the wound of the open skull. The crows flapped from above, their black shadows elongating across the bodies and the ground. The bile churned again. These men would be picked apart within the hour. The flies would start it, then the crows and the buzzards. Dingoes would smell the death and come running—growl and tear them apart.

They needed to be buried. The fact poked Ghan with wizened fingers. *No way*, Ghan argued with himself. He was too old to bury one of these men, let alone all of them. Ghan stared at the sun. He'd die trying to dig the graves in this heat—four bodies instead of three. The crows watched him, wobbled sideways up and down the branch in wait. More flies came. *Can't let a man get picked away, though. Not right.* Ghan could feel the burden of the shovel in his empty hands. *They're already dead!* his mind shouted. Skin and bone were going to fall away whether buried or not. *Not worth the sweat.*

Ghan slapped a fly, cursed the crows, then stomped to his tent for the shovel.

CHAPTER 63

Maybe she died first.

Maybe she had always been dead.

Perhaps the world had always been black, inside and out.

Perhaps she had died with the child who had only begun to warm within her, the child who had never known a breath of air or her kisses or his father; perhaps she had died as a child, in that desert, and life had been a slow dream waiting for the final nail held in this moment.

It was morning, but there was no light. Leonora could see through the window, the sun high above the trees—an odd, bright ball that did not belong in a world of darkness. Meredith, hunched and quiet, lifted the cold, untouched tea from the tray and replaced it with a new steaming cup, wiped a wayward splash with a napkin. But a dead body does not see things quickly and Leonora watched the woman and the activity absently.

"Is it true?" Leonora heard her own raspy, dead voice—the question lifeless as a corpse.

Meredith did not turn around. Her head dropped and nodded weightily.

The monstrous black swirled. The hollowness spread to every dead limb. "Where's Tom?" asked the dead, dry lips.

The woman turned slowly now, her forehead wrinkled. "Don't you know?"

Leonora moved her chin up, the muscles in her neck weak with sedative. "Know what?"

Meredith's chin dented under the bulk of her frown. "Tom's dead, too."

Leonora's eyelids blinked—over and over and over again. Meredith left. And still Leonora blinked with blind sight. From far away, through the mass of closing eyes, she heard her heart beat. She waited for it to stop—waited for the deadness to reach the pulsing muscle and silence it.

Blink. Blink. Blink.

Wait. Wait. Wait.

The strange ball of glaring sun moved along the fingers of the trees and slid to the back of the house. Rectangular shadows expanded along the floor in front of the French doors. Meredith returned and brought new tea. A bowl of soup steamed and then chilled on the tray.

A long, lean shadow passed the sofa, turned and passed it again, back and forth, over and over between her blinking. Finally, the pacing stopped. "I didn't do this, Leonora." Alex stared at her with a drained face, his words hollow and distant, only grazing a dying sense of hearing. "Say something, goddammit!" he shouted.

Death was cold and black. Numb. The air moved slowly in and out of her lungs—two dead shells—each respiration strange and dull and foreign. And still she waited for the air to stop. And still she listened at the stubborn pulse ticking in her chest. The pain in her pelvis was detached—just there, sitting on a distant shelf with the obstinate heart and intrepid lungs.

"I can't take it." Alex pulled at his hair, cried out, "Look at me!"

Her dead eyes scrolled upward, set and hung on his. Alex stumbled backwards and clawed at his hair, began to pace back and forth again with long strides, unable to escape the dead, heavy eyes that followed him. Alex stopped at the window, forced an inhale. He clasped his hands behind his back. "I need you to know that I didn't do this." His voice calmed. "Part of me wishes I had. Part of me wishes I had been the one pulling the trigger." He turned to her. "But I had no part in it. I swear it."

The sound of truth—pure, unfiltered truth—stabbed at the numbness. That strange organ began to beat faster and saliva wet her dry mouth. *No!* The word screamed in her mind, awakening it from its quiet. The life, the air, the pulse, was moving in the wrong direction, moving away from death. She pulled at the numbness, at the frayed ties. She could taste the pain that was hiding in the corners, waiting for her, and tinged her nerves with terror.

Alex walked toward her, his face blank of ego or anger, his jaw and eyes raw and honest. He knelt and took her dead hands in his. "I didn't do this. And I can't live with that hatred in your eyes." His voice crumbled. "The men attacked the sheriff, Leonora. Killed him in cold blood when they tried to escape. The deputy had no other choice but to shoot them." He squeezed her hands. "Your precious James did this. Not me."

The name crushed her pelvis in a hard, tight fist and she cried out. The pain was breaking. Alex grabbed her elbows and his lips quivered. "It doesn't have to be this way. Don't you see? We can start over, Leonora. Now that you know the truth about him, we can start over. No one knows what happened except for us. No one knows."

The words swirled in her stomach, made her sick with grief. She covered her mouth with her hand, wanted to retch. Alex took her hand away and held her face. "I blame myself for this. I should have never brought you to Australia. It changed you."

His words spun around her temples, twisting her mind like a toy top.

"You didn't know what you were doing. I left you alone too often. I see that now. You've always been like a child. You needed guidance and I wasn't here to give it to you."

Alex jiggled her arms as if she had fallen asleep. She looked at his face blindly, searched the distorted features for something that made sense and didn't make her ill.

"I forgive you, Leonora," he said happily. "I forgive you. Don't you see? It wasn't your fault. You didn't know what you were doing." His eyes lit. "We'll move away. Go back to America. Move to California. I'll watch you better now, darling. I promise."

She watched as he formed each word with his lips, watched as the mouth moved with sound. She watched as his white teeth showed with some words and were hidden with others. His tongue was pink in his mouth. The hairs of his mustache traced each curve of his lips.

"You understand now. Don't you?" he prodded.

"Yes." Her voice was dead.

His mouth curved with pleasure. "You see I won't ever let you go again?"

"Yes." The sound of her voice echoed in her ears from a long tunnel.

He squeezed her tighter. "We'll start a new life."

She swallowed and croaked on the words "a new life."

Alex hugged her rigid body. He showered kisses on her forehead and cheeks and stiff lips. "It's all going to be better now. You'll see." He propped up a pillow behind her head.

The pain waited until he left. The cuts frayed and beaded blood. She clutched her stomach. The grief rolled over her now, clawed and tore with each wave, one on top of the other. Her mouth ovaled to a howl and her body shuddered under rupturing despair. James was gone. Dead. The thought wracked her tendons and wailed in the creases of her brain until there were no thoughts or feelings beyond the entity of pain.

Weeks or months passed. Leonora fell dully into the folds of grief as a pebble falls into the murky dark of a bottomless lake. She did not try to fight the pain any longer, for it was part of her now, part of her skin and blood and organs.

Alex watched her always. She could not move from one room to the next without him asking where she was going. He was hiring a new manager to run the Coolgardie mine. He was making plans to divide and sell Wanjarri Downs. And Leonora knew, even in her grief, she would not leave Australia, even if it meant she had to be buried under its soil.

"Where are you going?" called Alex from his office.

"To take a walk," she answered hoarsely.

"Good." Alex tucked his nose back into his papers. "Fresh air will do you good."

The sun mauled her sight; the dry heat engulfed and stuck to the skin. Her limbs felt the pull of the managers' quarters, but she pulled back, forced her head toward the west. But it didn't matter; James was everywhere and the missing pressed into her temples and her gut and her shoulders. Dust climbed up her ankles. Bull dust, they called it, she remembered weakly. Leonora kicked it idly. She was blind to direction, put one foot in front of the other. *Step. Step. Step.*

The sun burned the back of her bent neck. Her breathing was shallow. *Step. Step. Step.* The dust lessened; the ground grew more compact and cracked, reddened. *Step. Step. Step.* Sweat inched down her nose, soaked the collar of her dress. Her chest thickened with awakened grief. Her footsteps quickened. *Step. Step. Step.* Sobs broke with the energy. She ran. Her lungs fired with fast, searing air. Tears fell and dried before they reached her neck and still she ran. *Step, step, step.* She stopped. Shade covered her head. A wail left her lips. She grabbed at her hair and curled into the grief. Her knees gave up. She fell at the base of the lone tree, scraped her cheek against the warm bark and twisted her legs around the roots. *Sinking. Sinking. Sinking.*

Her body chilled. She had been here before. The same tree, a different tree—it was all the same. The memory left her cold. Old terror wrapped fingers around her shoulders. Leonora looked up through wet tears and she was a child again. Her eyes searched the barren land for a figure. Her body shook. It was the same. The panic, the swirling sick, the gaping loss. *The same.*

Her hands convulsed as she brought them from her lap to the air. She stared at the shaking, thin fingers, stared at the wavering palms. A jolt. And then something shifted. It was not the same. Her hands were not those of a child. Her fingers spread and stilled. *I'm still here.* The thought entered like a rush of fresh, pure oxygen. *I'm still here.* Her rib cage expanded; the hot bush air filtered into her lungs and flooded the rims. *I'm still here.* And it all came quickly now. The catalog of images fanned under the shade of the moving tree limbs. Left to die in the desert. Thrown from the sea. Raised to wilt under soot-filled skies. Scorned in marriage. A torn love. A baby's loss. *But I'm still here.* And at that moment, in the still of the silent bush, Leonora was not her grief or her pain or her loss. She simply was.

The answers came. As loud as if they had been words, the answers thumped in her chest and screamed in her mind and breathed in her lungs and cushioned her heart. The answers came now. And they were so easy. For so long they had been out of reach, and here they were sitting before her as clear as if they had been written in the red ground.

She could leave now. She would tell the Aborigines. She had land to offer. They would not take it; this she knew. To present them a deed for land was like having them sign a contract for air. But she would tell them. They could choose to stay or to leave. But she would not stay. No more. The rest of the land she would give to Tom's mother. She remembered the woman's prophecy—Tom, a fleeting wind.

Leonora rose to her feet and grew again. Grief had not left, but she was not the grief; she was the one who carried it. She would sell her jewelry. She would take what money was rightfully hers and she would leave. Even penniless, she would leave.

Leonora walked, clutched her grief like a handbag but did not fall into it. The Aboriginal camp glared in the distance, the metal roofs pearly and white under the sun's unstoppable rays. She swallowed. For she saw the sun now, saw the blue that surrounded. The gray was leaving.

A group of Aborigine women washed clothes in a rusty tub between the shacks. They watched Leonora approach and this time they did not turn away. Their dark pupils were calm and the whites of their eyes held her. For they saw the lines of her loss, the grief-drooped lids, and they knew this look. Perhaps knew this look better than anyone else on the planet.

Children bounced on the outskirts, played fetch with a thin, rib-lined puppy. The men were gone out in the paddocks or in the fields or with the horses. The women turned back to their wash and Leonora did not know how to begin, her mouth and thoughts failing. A tall, thin black woman reached to a slung wire and hung a wet dress upon the line. She turned, revealing a pregnant belly. Leonora stared at the swollen stomach, watched as the woman tenderly touched the curves of it. Absently, Leonora's hand came up and rested upon her own flat abdomen.

The pregnant woman neared, tall and black as night. Her head blocked out the sun. She picked up Leonora's hands, her palms hard and rough, and placed them on her bulging stomach. Tears fell again but not of grief. Under Leonora's fingers throbbed life—rich and hot and full. There was no jealousy. This was a gift, the woman's gift to her, and she let the wonder of the budding life flow into her veins and replenish what had been lost.

Leonora whispered, "Thank you."

The woman nodded and mouthed one word . . . only one: *Life*.

Leonora took the word, let the vibration of its sound shudder through her body. *Life*.

Late in the evening, four days later, the front door hammered. Leonora bolted upright in bed. The pounding grew louder and more urgent. Alex moaned, then silenced with attention. He shot out of bed and grabbed his revolver from his pants. "Stay here!" he ordered.

Leonora dismissed the warning and followed. The whole house rattled under the knocking. Alex peered out the window. "What the hell!" In a rage, he flung open the door and screamed at the wide-eyed Aborigine, "What's the meaning of—"

The man ignored Alex and stretched his neck at Leonora. "The baby!" he screamed. "Baby not comin'!"

Alex turned to Leonora. "I told you to stay upstairs."

"What's going on?" Leonora pushed past Alex to the man at the door. "What baby?"

Alex growled and shoved the dark man in the chest. "Get out of here!"

"The baby!" the man cried, his focus still tied to Leonora. "Alkira pushin', but baby won't come!"

Leonora looked at her hands, remembered the pregnant Aboriginal woman, could still feel the pulse of the baby underneath her fingertips. "Stay there!" she ordered. "I'm coming."

She ran for the stairs to change when Alex grabbed her. "You're not going out there."

Leonora ripped her arm away. "The woman needs help, Alex."

"I don't give a shit!"

Leonora spit with hatred, "Do you really want the blood of another child on your hands?"

Alex glanced at her pelvis, stepped back with the memory. "Go!" He waved his hands in the air as if it were rotten. "What the fuck do I care."

* * *

Leonora brought her medical bag and fumbled with her dress buttons as she chased after the black man, nearly invisible in the dark night. The moon was new, the sky a thick blanket of onyx. There was no break of color from ground to sky, only a line of stars pointed to the edge of land. The air was cool. The curlews were loud, their wails suffocating the ears and night. The Aborigine moved agilely on silent feet. Her breath came choppy and strained; her feet fumbled and slipped over stones and dry, sharp grass as she tried to keep up.

They neared the camp and she stopped. The shacks were still and without sound. Wide, empty shadows clung between the corrugated iron shanties. The air was heavy with absence; the very particles of the night did not fit. Something was off. There were no fires, no lamps lit in the windows. Her flesh shivered. Her feet inched backwards.

The man stopped and turned around, waved her forward. Leonora forced her body against the dread. It was too quiet. The cool air did not carry any scent, and with the lack the air cooled further beyond temperature. She was breathing quickly; her hands clutched the medical bag to her chest. She swallowed through her tight throat and walked slower but ever forward into the rows of sleeping iron boxes.

The man entered the largest shack, a long, rectangular tin can with sawed holes for windows, the edges warped and rusted. Leonora entered the dark room. The pounded-dirt floor sloped unevenly. She couldn't see past the man beside her. "Where is she?" Her voice cracked.

"In 'ere." The man put a firm hand on the small of Leonora's back. Her already-tense nerves jumped at the touch and he let go, waved her ahead to another door.

The shadows of the corners shifted. There was breathing beyond her own. The man threw open the door. She stepped back, the urge to get away sudden and fierce. Someone moved behind her back and with a hard thrust pushed her to the black room. Leonora stumbled blindly and turned around. The door slammed. Leonora spread her palms over the closed door, tried to find the edge, tried to find the handle. "What are you doing?" she screamed.

The door locked. The hairs along her forehead and behind her

neck and along her arms and legs stood straight. She found the handle, a twisted wire wrapped around more metal. She rattled the knob,
tried to move it back and forth. She shook her whole arm trying to
force it open. The terror moved down her back and filled the darkness. She pounded the door with her fist. "Let me out of here!" she
screamed. "Somebody, help! Let me out!"

"Leo."

She froze. Her fist hung in the air. Her heart raced until it nearly
broke through her ribs. Her pulse thundered in her ears and eclipsed
every other natural one. Then, beyond the throb of blood, bedsprings
creaked.

"It's all right, Leo," the air whispered.

Her body trembled. Her lips stretched across her teeth. Her fist
faltered and opened; her fingers twitched with spasms. A deep, long
wail left her throat.

"Please don't cry."

It was a ghost. His ghost. His voice. Leonora tried to hold on to the
sound. Knew it would fade, knew it *was* fading. She shook her head
and cried out, "Don't do this to me!"

The sound would disappear again. She would lose him all over
again. Her forehead fell to the door and pressed against it. She shook
her head into her sobs. "Please don't do this to me!"

"Turn around, Leo."

"No!" she wailed. If she turned around, the voice would go away;
the ghost would disappear.

"Please." The voice was rising, thick with pleading. "Just turn
around, Leo."

Her body twisted in the dark with defeat. Her feet flopped over
each other as they stumbled to the back of the room. She shouldn't
have moved. The voice would be gone now. The hole would rip open
again, bleed and grow, and this time it would never leave, never
scar—just sit open and raw for eternity. But her feet still moved. Her
knees bent without bones. Then something touched her arm. Her
breath caught. Fingertips etched down her arm and found her hand,
squeezed it tight.

Her legs gave out with the touch. Leonora crumpled to the floor.
She felt the cold metal bed frame against her cheek. The hand pulled

her up. Lips brushed her forehead, kissed her eyelids. A mouth opened and sighed against her jaw.

Leonora shook her head and cried and the lips kissed the tears. Her hands reached up to skin. *To skin.* Her nails bit into the long, smooth back. Her head rolled into the warmth—*the warmth* of his neck. Her fingers danced over his face. *His face.* Her fingertips quaked against the lines of the set jaw, the hot skin, the long, sloped nose, the drawn eyebrows, the creased forehead, the silken threads of his hair. It couldn't be and was all at the same time. A cry left her throat.

"Shhhh," James hushed her, and wrapped an arm around her waist, pulled her to his chest. "I know," he whispered into her neck, the pain in his tone matching hers. "I'm here, Leo. I'm here." His fingers curled in her hair, held her head against him. "I told you I'd never leave you."

She tried to speak, but there were no words. She tried to kiss the lips that brushed against her cheekbones, but her lips were still frozen with the freshness of the grief and the new sheer, jolting disbelief. Her mouth opened and gasped, "I . . . I thought you—" The cry broke again before she could say the word.

"I know." One kiss did not stop before another began, his lips inching along her face. "It's all going to be all right now."

The weeks, the months, of dying without him filtered in and laid their knives deep across her stomach. "Why didn't you tell me you were alive?"

His kiss slowed and stopped; his lips hovered above hers. "I almost wasn't." James pressed his forehead against hers. "I didn't want you to know until I was sure."

"Sure of what?"

"That I was going to make it."

She gripped his shoulders. A small, constrained sound left his throat and his body winced sharply. Leonora pulled back. "You're hurt!" she gasped.

"I'm all right." He was quiet for a moment. "The worst is over."

In the dark, she touched him gingerly down his arms, his chest, around the bandages that covered so much of him. She reached for his face and fell into his chest, tucked her head under his chin. "How?" she whispered through her tears.

"I don't know," he answered. "Someone found me. Brought me here."

She found his lips, the warmth of his mouth. James gripped the back of her neck and held her to him. "I never stopped thinking of you, Leo," he hushed between the drawn kiss. "Never." With his bandaged arm, he touched her stomach lightly with his fingers.

The baby. The memory attacked and twisted. He didn't know. She pulled away with horror and shame.

"What is it, Leo?" James reached for her retreating hand, pulled it back tightly.

"The baby . . ." she choked. New, hot tears spread down her face, dropped onto his wrist.

"I know." James slid his hip along the thin mattress to near her, the effort bringing constrained winces of pain. James kissed her neck and swallowed his own tears. "I know about the baby, Leo." His voice was nearly silent. "Tom told me."

A heavy quiet dropped and settled with the utterance of the name. *Tom.*

Leonora was glad she could not see James's face and the anguish and bitterness that would sculpt his features. But she was more relieved that he could not see her face and the shame and mortification that froze it. The silence between them grew as the name still echoed. Tom's death was her fault.

Her hands stretched upon her face and she cried deeply into the creases of her palms. "I'm so sorry, James," she choked haltingly.

"No, Leo." James pulled himself up, grunted against his wounds and kissed her hands, her fingernails. His strong arm wrapped around her back, the biceps firm and unwavering against her bent spine. "This had nothing to do with you . . . with us. Nothing." James touched her hair, tucked it behind her ear, kissed each strand that fell between his fingers. "Trust me, Leo."

Leonora fell into his arms and sobbed, but his body was calm and loose. "It's over, Leo. The pain. The loss. It ends now." He kissed her forehead and she felt his lips smile softly against her skin. "Now we start a new life. Together." He kissed her. "Like we were always meant to."

CHAPTER 64

This ain't your doin', son.

Mrs. Shelby's words had stayed with James on that day of Tom's death and in the weeks that followed, whispered and flowed through the holes of his consciousness.

This ain't your doin', son.

His mother died upon his birth. Tess had faded with his growth. Shamus died with hate. And then Tom. Their faces had flashed as the bullets entered.

This ain't your doin', son.

Somewhere between the stretched and thoughtless black, the words entered the pores of his skin. Somewhere between the stilted and weary lucidity, the concept seeped into his veins and moved steadily through his blood. And when the fever shook his body and the blackness nearly flooded and won, the knowing took root and gripped his bones like muscle. It wasn't his doing. None of it.

There were always whispers. Even after the Aborigines changed his dressings and left the herbed tea and bathed his body and then left the room, the space was crowded with the whispers. His mother held his head, kissed his sweated brow. Tess held his hand, her soft, tiny fingers strong against his. Shamus was there, too. The anger gone, the sparkle of Ireland in his eyes as he told him to hold on. His father held his hand with a firm and silent grip. Father McIntyre never left his side, strong and good and proud. And they shared a message for him, told him he was not an orphan but, instead, the son of many.

And then there was Tom—his friend, his brother—there with him always. He would sit casually at the end of the bed, easy and cool and smiling. And when the darkness came too quickly, Tom punched him in the arm and brought James back. These were the bodies that willed him. These were the whispers that vibrated in his ears along that fine line of life and death. The Aborigines healed his wounds, but the spirits healed the scars.

James pressed the bandages wrapped around his ribs. The pain was manageable now. In a month, he could leave. He closed his eyes and thought of Leo. The softness of her skin and kisses and hair washed over him. It was awful not telling her that he was here. It was awful that they had to trick her into the meeting. But it was the only way. No one could know he was here. Soon they would leave.

James relaxed into the thin, lopsided mattress. He closed his eyes. A vision of the sea rose behind his lids and he remembered those days beside his friend, their legs hanging fearlessly above the sea, the sun warming their bodies and the hope that surrounded them.

The hope had returned. They were going home.

CHAPTER 65

❧

Alexander Harrington stretched under the thin sheet and spread his legs. Stale whiskey soured his mouth. His tongue was dry as cotton. He let out a long, waking sigh and flexed his toes. He was hard. With one hand, he sleepily stroked the long shaft. Leonora should be ready for him now, her body healed. It had been too long. He flopped to his side and reached for her hip, but his hand fell flat to the bed. Blindly, he patted the empty space, grunted and turned onto his back.

Suppose I should be glad she's up, he reconciled. *At least she's not moping around the house like a fucking ghost anymore.* Almost a month had passed since she lost the death look. Her cheeks had grown color again; her figure curved with healthy skin instead of bones. She was gorgeous again, almost painfully beautiful, and he wanted her again. Besides, he was tired of the whores, tired of their fake moans and cheap perfume. Alex turned to his side and pulled Leonora's pillow to his face, sucked in the gentle rose scent.

All she needed was time. The shit was behind them now. Leonora's tantrums were over and she was subdued. California would be a new start. Australia had been a curse.

California. They'd get an estate along the coast—raise thoroughbreds in a place that didn't burn the horses' skin. Alex grinned and stretched his arms above his head. Owen Fairfield's days were numbered. Man was half-dead already with grief. They'd have more money than they could spend in five lifetimes. Alex stroked his penis, but the arousal had fallen away. He needed to piss.

Downstairs, he took his tea black and fanned the newspaper on the table. Meredith placed oranges and scones and butter down stiffly. "Where's Leonora?" he asked without looking up.

"Don't know," she answered curtly.

He cocked his head. "Well, did she have breakfast?"

She glowered and crossed her arms over her bosom. "No."

He dismissed her with a derisive snort. It would feel good firing that bitch.

After breakfast, Alex went to his office, pulled out the Monterey property listings. His eyes flickered over the acreage, the profiles of the land. Alex glanced over the edges of the papers and scanned his desk. Something was out of place, felt odd. He searched the walls. The pictures were all there staring back at him. His desk was in order. He twisted his neck to the bookshelves lined neat and polished. The crystal decanters in the bar were nearly full. The safe was still—

Alex bolted from his chair. The safe door was unlocked and swayed easily with the touch of his hand. His blood boiled. His eyes bulged from their sockets. Half the money was gone. Gone! As if someone had taken a hatchet and cut the box in two—on one side the bills reached nearly to the top; the other side was only blank, gaping, empty steel. They were robbed. His hands balled into fists, the nails cut into his palms.

His eyes blinked violently as a new thought entered. *No.* The air in his lungs steamed from his nostrils, hot and slow. *She would never.*

Alex tore from his office, ran upstairs taking three steps in each bound. He flew into the bedroom and pulled out the top drawer of Leonora's bureau. Empty. He pulled the next one open. Empty. His teeth clattered with the stone fury pressing at his jaw. He ripped open drawer after drawer after drawer. Empty. Empty. Empty! Alex whipped open the closet doors, the hard wood banging sharply against the wall. Empty.

"Noooooo!" he howled, and picked up the table lamp, hurled it across the room to where it smashed into a shower of glass.

Alex ran and slid down the stairs. Clare waited at the bottom, her eyes wide with fear. "Where is she?" he screamed. Clare trembled mutely and stepped away from him. He grabbed her by the shoulders and shook her until her neck bobbed. "*Where is she?*"

"I don't know!" she cried, her voice undulating under Alex's jerking.

Alex pushed her away and she crawled on scattered limbs for the kitchen. In a blind rush, Alex was in his office, found the revolver, cocked it and barreled outside. The Model T was gone. *That bitch!* His body twitched. He pointed the gun in every direction and then stopped with sudden focus and clear intent.

Alex ran. His boots pounded against the hard ground. *Thump. Thump. Thump.* Sweat dripped down his face and stung his eyes. His neck was wet and slick. His breathing was loud—panting, grunting, spitting breathing. His head felt swollen and dizzy under the beating sun. The fiery air entered his nostrils too quickly and burned his throat. "I'll teach you!" he screamed into the quiet bushland.

The Aborigine camp rose from the barren earth. The flies greeted in swarms, flocked at his eyes and nose and mouth. He ran past the rusted, bent homes. He twisted on his feet, spun his outstretched arm at every building. His mouth watered for death; his eyes searched for any movement to strike. But there was no movement—no shadows— no life to take away.

Alex stilled. Clouds of black flies flew unmolested in and out of the abandoned doors and windows. His one eye twitched. The bewildered tic moved to his other eye and then to his jaw and then to his chin. The anger erupted through his hands. He pointed at the buildings and shot wildly. He screamed with each shot, screamed as each bullet clanged against dull metal, screamed as the bullets puffed into the dust, screamed as the shots ricocheted between the buildings and reverberated in the unmoving, listless air.

A spark of fire bit his foot. "*Fuck!*" The gun fell from his hand. Alex rolled on the ground clutching his shot foot. The bullet had gone straight through his boot and blood poured from the hole at the sole.

Alex writhed with the pain, rocked on his hips. He cried—hard, choked, childlike sobs. "Look what you've done, Leonora!" he screamed, his leg burning as if it were surrounded with red coals. "You did this!"

EPILOGUE

Two Years Later

CHAPTER 66

The torn canvas flapped tiredly from the two gnarled posts. A thin slice of shade formed a gray line down the center of Ghan's body. The hot sun found the holes in the tarp and compounded their focus on bits of his skin. His mouth was open to assist the fading lungs. Dried saliva caked the corners of his mouth. The flies clung to these spots and walked upon the slits of his eyes. There was no strength left to bat them. Ghan was dying.

The next labored breath hurt his chest. The weakness in his lungs spread to his muscles like a yawn in a listless crowd. Ghan's slow eyes stared at the dirty fabric hanging low above his head. Shadows of passing clouds moved along the threads, played hide and seek with the ball of sun. The smell of dust had fallen away, his nose chapped and raw and senseless. Sounds drifted away with the scents. The world was void now—just sun and shadows and waning breath.

Ghan's body drifted and dragged toward death, but thoughts were still alive, would kick fighting until the very last beat of his heart. He never thought it would end this way—quiet and slow, without violence. The pain of death was not like the pain of life had been. This pain was a caress, a rocking in a mother's arm. Still, he never thought he would be an old man, never thought he would greet death—always expected to be beat or blown or broken into it.

Ghan's neck arched. His body gasped for more air. The rest between breaths had been too much for the lungs and they did not want to wake. But they did. And another breath came jilted and prolonged.

Death still waited lazily in the wings. Ghan's body relaxed back into the dirt.

He missed the camels. The thought came upon him too quickly, brought its own ache. The camels had been with him on the hardest of days. And they were gone now. He never got to say good-bye or to make sure they were being cared for and he missed them. A heaviness seeped into his body and pushed his limbs and flesh farther into the ground. His fragile heart began to pound. Panic rose suddenly. *I don't want to die.* His cold hands began to shake. *I don't want to die!* The shaking tracked up his arms and went down his legs. His feet flapped. The flies scurried but hovered stubbornly above the spastic body.

A worthless man. Ghan's eyes were dry and crusted, but the tears came. They were light tears and the fluid stung the corners of his lids. A worthless life for a worthless, horrid man. His mouth opened wider and a raspy cry left his lips. He had brought nothing to this world— only ugliness. The immediate wretchedness seized the breathing parts of him. The terror pinched and begged him to run and hide from the death and the loneliness and the ugliness, but his body could not move. He was trapped in a closing shell, could only listen to the fear pounding on the outside. Things were fighting and things were dying in him all at the same time. And he was alone. Scared to die. Scared to die alone.

But a new voice answered, came from the same body, from a place buried much deeper than the loneliness. *You are not alone!* It was clear. The words screamed loudly but without fear or urgency. Ghan stilled— his mouth agape—and listened to the thudding, soundless words.

The tears came again. His mouth twisted. He nodded into the words. The air was fading and the darkness was coming. A child touched his hand. He could feel the heat of it on his dying flesh. The eyes of the little one engulfed him. She had found him beautiful. And now more fingers touched him, held him in death and cradled him. Suddenly, there was not just a child but a million open, sweet children and a million tender touches and a million answering calls that he was beautiful. *You have never been alone!* they all cried.

Ghan's body trembled now without fear. They surrounded him and hugged him from all cells and he rested into their folds and let their light and warmth love him, *love him!* And in that instant there was no abuse, no pain, no loneliness, no violence. There never was.

The last breath hardly moved in his lungs. The trembling stopped. His fingers uncurled. His body sank limply, evenly, into the earth. His mouth hung open. His lids slid down. The thoughts stopped. The heart beat once more and stilled.

CHAPTER 67

Sadness wrapped around her instantly, came from nowhere and was suddenly everywhere. Leonora brought her hand to her mouth, shook her head against the sudden flow of tears. A soft breeze slid past her hair like the brush of an angel and the tears fell faster.

There was a gentle tug to her skirt. "Why yeh cryin', Mum?" came the soft little voice.

Leonora looked down at the little boy and smiled through her tears. She knelt and took his hands, wiped her eyes against her sleeve. "I don't know," she answered. The sadness began to fade, blew away like clouds over the sea. She laughed softly. "I don't know."

The little boy still stared with worried eyes. Leonora glanced down at his polio-ravaged legs held upright by steel braces. The orphanage had all but given up on the poor child. Leonora grabbed him to her chest and hugged him.

James walked into the kitchen, his back bent under the weight of a little girl clutching his neck. "I can't breathe," he choked dramatically. The little girl erupted in giggles, her blind eyes bobbing with amusement. He plopped her down next to her brother.

"Mum's been cryin'," Nathan alerted with adult significance.

James shot her a look. "You all right, Leo?"

Leonora laughed at her own silliness. "Just a little sentimental today, I guess."

James watched her carefully and then nodded. He moved behind the children and clapped his hands. "Kids want to sleep at the Shelbys' tonight." He winked at her slyly. "Feel like having the house to ourselves?"

"Please, Mum!" the children begged in chorus. "Pleasssse?"

Ever since Mrs. Shelby and the girls moved into the guesthouse, Leonora and James had to fight for custody of their own children. The Shelbys had kept busy catering to the Aborigine children for the first few months, but then the Aborigines moved on—left in the night without a sound.

"All right," she consented. "But first thing tomorrow morning, you're both mine!" She grabbed them in her arms and covered their squirming, giggling faces with kisses.

"Nathan," James ordered, "help your sister get her things and then we'll head out." The little boy grabbed his sister's hand and retreated happily to the bedroom.

James put a hand on Leonora's waist and kissed her neck. "You ready to adopt more?"

"Only another twenty." She faded sleepily into his mouth.

"Well, tonight, it's just the two of us. And you're all mine," he said sternly in her ear.

"Yes, sir." She kissed his warm cheek. His body was full of heat and strength and still left her heart beating too quickly.

Behind them, the setting sun turned the sky to purple, seemed to widen the length of the world. A pink and orange line highlighted the edge around the tremendous gum trees and turned the waist-high grass to emerald. And between their kisses, the sea breezes blew in from the jagged New South Wales coast and captured every strand in an endless, moving zephyr—their whispers singing one endless word—*home*.

Please turn the page
for an exciting Q & A
with Harmony Verna!

This novel takes the reader deep into the beauty and harshness of Australia's Outback, yet is it true that you've never been there?

That's right; I've never been to Australia. People find that hard to believe, but it's true. For as long as I can remember, I've had a near obsession with this country . . . the land, the people, the history. I remember when I was eight years old I got a map of Australia and hung it above my bed. I would run my fingers over the elevations and the strange city names, but my attention always stopped at a tiny town called Leonora. It's hard to explain what effect this place had on me. I would simply start to cry, like a deep longing for a place I knew nothing about. I was just a child, so I never understood why or where those feelings were coming from. Only later did I realize I was homesick.

Are you saying you were in Australia in a past life?

Yes. And I know that must sound a bit out there, but it's my truth. As I got older, I started to have distinct memories, visions of Australia. They always started the same way, at that time of lucid sleep. I would see a flash of white light and then one image . . . a cemetery, a name, a face, a fence post. The image was almost always in black and white like a photograph. It would only last for a second and then I would wake up, my heart racing, and I would *know* that it was part of a past-life experience.

So, is the novel autobiographical or purely fiction?
The story and characters are absolutely fictional. I did a tremendous amount of research into the history and landscape of the country. But the feelings around Australia, the emotions and oneness to the environment, were quite real for me. Writing the book was like going home.

You infuse a number of different accents within the character dialogue. How did you get the language to flow in such a manner?
I started off listening to recordings of people with different dialects, but found it was hard to translate those subtle speech nuances to the written word. So I started to read Australian poetry and eventually picked up on the general cadence. After a while, the characters would just chat away in my ear and I was able to get their words down while conveying a proper accent.

With so many colorful characters in the novel, do you have a favorite?
Ghan is my favorite. When I first started writing the novel, Ghan was not going to be a main character. He was going to find Leonora and get her to safety and that's it. But I couldn't get this man out of my head. Ghan is so special to me because here is this man who has "an ugly face to match an ugly life," the roughest and loneliest existence, and yet at his core he is full of goodness and kindness. All he sees is his scars, without ever seeing his true light. I often think most of humanity suffers in the same way. We tend to focus only on our ugly parts, our scars and flaws, instead of our beauty and light.

Now that the book is published, do you plan to make a trip to Australia?
I don't know. My whole life I dreamed about visiting Australia, but after finishing the book the need is gone. Perhaps one day I'll get there, but if I don't I'm fine with that. All I know is that as I was writing I was there.

DAUGHTER OF AUSTRALIA

Harmony Verna

ABOUT THIS GUIDE

The suggested questions are included to enhance
your group's reading of Harmony Verna's
Daughter of Australia!

DISCUSSION QUESTIONS

1. The novel begins with the heart-wrenching scene of a father abandoning his daughter in the harsh Australian Outback. What would drive a parent to leave his child? Do you believe the father's intent was for her to perish? As she was found in an area of only "saltbush an' dust," where do you think they traveled from?

2. Ghan, the crippled mine worker, has had a lonely existence of scars and hardship. Yet, through his actions, we are exposed to both the rough and tender sides of the man. Do you find him a vulnerable character and, if so, why? Do you believe people are born with innate traits of compassion or is this an acquired emotion? If you met Ghan in real life, would you be afraid of him?

3. When the injured child is brought to Mirabelle's boarding-house, she is surrounded by strangers and does not speak, exists within the house as a ghost. But when she saw Ghan again, she touched his hand and "looked at him as if she thought him beautiful." Do you think she was simply grateful for Ghan saving her life or do her feelings go deeper? Do you think she sees something in him below the scars and distorted features? Do you think she would have wanted to remain at the boarding-house if given the choice?

4. Upon the cliffs of the orphanage James and Leonora develop an unlikely friendship and an unbreakable bond. Why do you think they were so drawn to each other? What did each gain from the other?

5. James chooses to leave the orphanage, the only home he has ever known, in order to live with his Irish relatives, the O'Reillys. The land and work are hard and James grows up in poverty. Did James make the right decision in leaving the or-

phanage? Do you think Father McIntyre would have committed suicide if James had not left?

6. Leonora's life with the Fairfields is filled with abundant wealth and loneliness, her childhood spent under the threat of being abandoned yet again. Her only taste of freedom comes from working with the wounded soldiers at the hospital. Could Leonora have done anything to change her lot? Could she have run away or acted out? Once a legal adult, did she have any real power?

7. By marrying Alex, Leonora can finally escape the confines of the Fairfields' grip, even if it means she must live with a man she does not love. Did Leonora have any other choice but to marry Alex? With so little love in her own life, would it be difficult for her to know true love or what it would feel like?

8. After James's aunt passes away, he is left to face the wrath of Shamus until the Shelbys fold him into their home as if he had always belonged there. Why didn't James ever retaliate against Shamus's beatings? Would James have survived if the Shelbys hadn't rescued him?

9. When Leonora returns to Australia to her new home at Wanjarri Downs, she is reborn in a sense—"She was Australia. Its air was her air, its cells her own." Given that her early years in Australia were not favorable, why does she feel such a longing for the country?

10. James and Leonora finally reunite at Wanjarri Downs, but the first meetings are uncomfortable and tense. Do you think the attraction was instant? How had they both changed since the orphanage? Whose upbringing had been more difficult?

11. When Leonora and Alex return to Pittsburgh for her aunt's funeral, she learns the truth about Eleanor Fairfield's past. Does this explain why Eleanor treated Leonora the way she did? Do

you believe Eleanor truly loved Leonora? Is this enough reason for Leonora to forgive her aunt for her traumatic upbringing?

12. When Alex learns of Leonora's pregnancy and her affair with James, a series of violent events unfold, leaving Leonora in grief over the loss of her child and the apparent death of her true love, James. Why does Leonora still stay at Wanjarri Downs? Does she believe Alex murdered James? How did these events "awaken" her?

13. When James heals from his wounds and struggles against death, he realizes that he is not an orphan but "the son of many." Do you think this is true? Do you think this realization finally heals his emotional wounds? Was it necessary for him to go through the violence and near-death experience in order to heal the scars of his past?

14. As Ghan approaches death, he is gripped with fear and grief until a soft inner voice and angelic image of a little girl guide him gently to his end. Why do you think Ghan's and Leonora's paths continued to cross? Do you believe the connection was coincidence or spiritual? Was Ghan her guardian angel?

15. James and Leonora are finally home. They have adopted children of their own and built the life together that they had always dreamed of. Does it make all their hardships worth it? Do you have examples in your own life where the darkest of days brought the brightest future?

GREAT BOOKS, GREAT SAVINGS!

When You Visit Our Website:
www.kensingtonbooks.com
You Can Save Money Off The Retail Price Of Any Book You Purchase!

- **All Your Favorite Kensington Authors**
- **New Releases & Timeless Classics**
- **Overnight Shipping Available**
- **eBooks Available For Many Titles**
- **All Major Credit Cards Accepted**

Visit Us Today To Start Saving!
www.kensingtonbooks.com

All Orders Are Subject To Availability.
Shipping and Handling Charges Apply.
Offers and Prices Subject To Change Without Notice.